I0687676

# Blue Water Dead

*a novel*

Stephen M. Goodrum

Copyright © 2012 Stephen M. Goodrum
All rights reserved.
ISBN: 0615627552
ISBN-13: 978-0-615-62755-7

## WHAT PEOPLE ARE SAYING

*Goodrum's debut is noteworthy for the ease with which its characters interact and for its crisp, back-and-forth dialogue,* which manages to be clever while moving the story along. The residents of Detroit come from believable molds, magnified for a slightly larger-than-life tale. The novel reflects a high attention to detail, especially as it concerns Detroit, a city that becomes as much of a character as its main characters. It also makes fitting use of its thematic elements of pop music and Motown, with a story structure that mimics their spirit, keeping things fun and simple with an occasional twist. A crime novel that's exciting despite its unhurried pace. ~~ **Krikus Reviews**

***** **Blue Water Dead by Stephen M. Goodrum**
*You're gonna think you've got this book all figured out right away, but you have no idea what's coming. I love this book. It's not normally my type of read, but WOW, I'd so read this one again. The characters are lovable and could easily fill the real jobs they hold in the book. It was also scary to think something of this magnitude could happen. This is one for the TBR pile! I recommend this book and this author.*
~~ Melanie Carrico,
http://www.goodreads.com/review/show/390815024

**great read!** *thoroughly enjoyed...has it all...intrigue, suspense, colorful characters and lots of interesting and fun facts....be careful...i made the mistake of reading the end at bedtime...could not stop reading....hard to function the next day with lack of sleep!...waiting for a sequel.* ~~ beaG, Indiana

**A MUST READ FOR ANYONE WHO HAS BEEN TO MICHIGAN!** *This was a GREAT read! I would recommend it to anyone who lives in, lived in, or just visited Michigan! The author went in to great detail and made me feel like I was THERE! Could place myself in the locations! Storyline was excellent! Loved it!* ~~ Jan Lincourt, South Carolina

**New suspense novel lives up to name.** *From the first page, this novel takes the reader on a suspenseful journey into international intrigue - it is a page-turner from start to finish. This is a work by an author who not only knows Detroit but more importantly, human nature.* ~~ Kathleen Frame, Instructor-Communication Arts, Schoolcraft College

**Blue Water Dead** *takes the reader on a refreshing journey, featuring the author's vast expertise on a multitude of subjects. Unlike other novels that tend to focus upon a one particular topic at a time (ie: religion, politics, etc.), the author very confidently and capably demonstrates mastery of a variety of things and interweaves them effortlessly, into a compelling destination. True twists (not just the clichéd reference in a typical review) highlight this book. The author's descriptions are dynamic and compelling, as are what clearly is a working knowledge of behind the scenes points of view into city, federal and international operations. A trip well worth taking!* ~~ D. Renaud, Grosse Pointe, MI

**Take My Word For It This Is One Book You Will Want To Add To Your Collection!** *I Blue Water Dead encompasses everything from the really great Adventures, to some sweet Romance, to terrific Humor, and then even sweet sorrow as well! This story unfolds in such a way that it takes you in right from the very first page. The characters in the book really come to life throughout their different wonderful experiences in the Beautiful State of Michigan Mr. Stephen Goodrum really portrays this story in such a way that it left you wanting even more. Now I cannot wait for the Sequel to Blue Water Dead!* ~~ Nicki H. Lincoln Park, MI

## DEDICATION

To the two strong women who shaped my life: my wife, Donna Lesher Goodrum, and my mother, Mary Hardesty Goodrum.

And to the man who taught me hard work and commitment to the community with dedication and humor: my father, T. Ernie Goodrum.

# CONTENTS

Stephen M. Goodrum

## Preface

*Enjoy the simple pleasures of Michigan's Sunrise Coast – you'll find an open invitation to the good life. Spend the whole day exploring stunning turquoise blue waters and charming small towns... where getting back to the water is Pure Michigan. --* *Pure Michigan* radio ad: Michigan.org

# Prologue

Labor Day 2005

It was Alberto Martinez's last day. He quietly slipped out of his retirement party while his co-workers continued to celebrate his thirty-five years with Michigan's U.S. Customs and Border Patrol.

Hired right out of the army, military police in Vietnam, Alberto had worked his way up the Border Patrol food chain until landing a shift supervisor position on the Blue Water Bridge in Port Huron. He thought it ironic that his long awaited retirement began today.

His boss, Frederick Williams, the Station Operations Supervisor, had told him that he could leave early today. His lunch hour, normally from ten to eleven, had turned into two hours, as his six a.m. morning crew alternated coming and going to say their goodbyes on their time away from the Port of Entry gates. Despite his boss's suggestion, he stayed his full shift until two. He was old school. A full day's work for a full day's pay.

He hated Williams, one of those political appointees taking the position he had worked over thirty years to reach. It had all changed when the new Director for the Great Lakes Border of Homeland Security took over three years ago. They had probably known each other in the past. He figured the Great Lakes Director owed his boss a favor. Outsiders.

Alberto's consolation prize was the morning shift supervisor position in Port Huron, a seventy mile drive north from his home in Southwest Detroit. Thanks a lot. He rented a room in a boarding house in town during his work week just to cut down on gas and the wear and tear on his car, not to mention all the time spent on the road.

Port Huron was a pass through town for travelers going to Canada or straight east to Niagara Falls and New York. Living here twenty days out of the month, Albert had found the other side: a beach and fishing spot for summer and a *fifteen minute town* to the residents.

Alberto didn't trust Williams. He was never there when you needed him, like when you made a bust for contraband or illegal aliens. He always gave some story about how he had other important matters to deal with that didn't concern shift supervisors. Then, items started missing from the holding warehouse: watches, DVD players, even money. Williams had either changed the inventory manifest or said he needed evidence for prosecution, even though it was all photographed and labeled for the court. Alberto was glad to be out from under such an asshole.

At two o'clock, he turned in his ring of keys, along with his nine millimeter gun and holster to Billy Larouso, the afternoon shift supervisor. Billy gave him a bear hug and wished him well.

Alberto stepped out of the building and stood still, taking one last look toward the twin bridges that crossed the shimmering waters of the St. Clair River. The brilliant blue and turquoise of Lake Huron flowed south down the shipping channel of the river to Lake St. Clair, then down the Detroit River to Lake Erie. The largest gathering of fresh water lakes in the world bordered Michigan and Canada and passed through this port of entry, hence its name, the Blue Water Bridge. He would come back. He had found a small cottage on the lake that he and his wife would enjoy in retirement.

He turned around and walked away from the booths, past the truck inspection garage and then to the freight warehouse where suspicious or illegal items were tagged and stored for authorized removal. He thought he'd have one last look around and verify his inventory before heading out. He wanted no one to say that some important item was missing on his watch.

The security guard buzzed him in and gave Alberto a farewell salute as his head bobbed up and down to some loud beat plugged into his ears. Kids. Somebody could steal us blind and this guy wouldn't even know it. Some kind of security.

Alberto picked up the inventory printout and began one last walk-thru, checking everything from unregistered boats, to cars that hid illegals, to pallets of marijuana and FDA watch list prescription drugs hidden in semis. As he made his way to the back of the warehouse, he saw daylight coming through one of the garage doors. He turned the corner of a ten foot high stack of electronics to find an older model Chevy pickup truck. The tailgate was down and a tarp covered pallet sat in the bed. The sound of the backup warning beeps of a forklift was moving toward him, so he ducked back behind the wall of electronics and waited. When the forklift pulled up and the hydraulics lowered a second pallet into the truck, he came around to see who it was. He reached for his holster and found it missing, forgetting he'd just turned it in minutes ago. What a memory.

The steel arms slipped out from under the pallet and the forklift turned to ride away when the driver looked right at Alberto. Surprise came across both men's faces.

Alberto only saw the blur of a hand as he felt a sharp pain at his throat. He suddenly couldn't breathe and his legs when out from under him. He pulled at his throat trying to dislodge whatever was holding his windpipe, his lungs on fire for air. He blacked out and his head hit the concrete floor. His last thought was for his wife and children.

## Part I  THE BAIT

*Rivers course through my dreams, rivers cold and fast, rivers well-known and rivers nameless, rivers that seem like ribbons of blue water twisting through wide valleys, narrow rivers folded in layers of darkening shadow.* -- Harry Middleton *Rivers of Memory*

Chapter 1

Monday Evening

"Al, get the cameras and get over here right now. I've got the batteries charged, the bikes mounted and the van gassed up."

"What's up?"

"Just get over here and I'll explain." The phone clicked off.

"Shit!" Al Majors said. He was the first born of fraternal twins, and he hated it when his brother called like this. All in a hurry and no explanation. Why did he have to take orders from his *younger* brother, Cane, the crew cut nerd of the two, and definitely bossier? "Sonofabitch."

Al pulled open the tech closet, pulled back his long red hair into a ponytail and surveyed the collection. Which camera did he need? Cane said bring the cameras, plural.

"All right smartass, I'll bring 'em all."

The two of them talked like this all the time, even when the other one wasn't present. They didn't have to be. Cane would hear it all in his head and answer him out loud when he got there. He could already hear it now.

He grabbed the Canon, or as Cane called it, the big one, *Buddha*, the *Mini Me*, their first, small and cheap Digira 8 that fit in the palm of your hand, and the *Micro*, the secret one on the end of a wire that could broadcast two hundred yards. He slipped them in the foam slots in his back pack and headed out.

"Is that what you meant?" He heard Cane say, "Yeah."

He jumped in his 95 Mustang and peeled out up Grand River toward the suburbs. 'I'm movin' on up," is what Cane called it. 'Movin' out' is what Al called it. Cane lived in a basement apartment in Farmington, about five miles outside of Detroit. He liked it because his neighbors were quiet: retired blue collar workers who had moved to the "burbs" soon after the Detroit riots, part of the white flight that followed. Perfect for his computer nerd brother.

Al pulled into the parking lot and squealed to a stop next to Cane's van. He was in the driver's seat and the motor was running. Cane waved him over. Al grabbed his bag and hopped in the front seat.

"Got it all?" Cane asked.

"Yeah, let's go. Then you can explain what the hell all the hurry is about."

Cane spun out of his parking spot, sped to the street and laid rubber, barely making the yellow light and curbing it as he flew down Grand River.

"What the hell are you doin? You gone crazy or something?" Al asked.

"I'm headin to Telegraph, then to 75 south to Gibralter."

"No, I mean, what the hell are *we* doin? And why the hell are you askin for a speeding ticket along the way?"

"We're on a mission." Cane started.

"From God?" asked Al. "Now we're the *Blues Brothers*?"

"No. We're on a mission from our boss. Dave called and said we had an opportunity to make five- hundred bucks if we high-tail it down to the Lake Erie Metro Park and scope out a dude supposedly cheatin on his wife. He wants us down there when they're down there, which is supposed to be at sundown."

"How romantic. Sunset on the lake, except it's on the wrong side of the lake, dumbass," Al said. "And you know what else, man? This is a side of the wedding *bizz*-ness I don't like."

"It isn't part of the wedding *bizz*-ness. It's private dick *bizz*-ness. We're going to catch a cheatin husband with his dick hanging out in an Escalade. Here's the plate number and here's his picture. For five- hundred, split in half, it's worth a speeding ticket."

"As long as it doesn't make us late, *Dawg*. If you get pulled over, they're going to take you downtown, and we'll be really late. Then, *you*, and notice I said *you*, will be out not only the five-hundred, but *you'll* owe several hundred."

"Shit, you're right."

"Wow. That's a switch. I'm actually right this time," Al said. "See, I'm getting more mature every day."

"Yeah, right," Cane said, pulling onto Telegraph Road.

"Did you bring all the equipment? All the cameras?"

"Yes, doubting twin, and all the mikes too."

"Cool. I knew you'd come through."

"See, more mature" Al replied. "If we're goin to Erie Park, why the bikes?"

"Cause there can't be any sign of the van. And, well, uh, I didn't get a new Metro Park sticker for this year and I don't have the twenty bucks. That's why all the rush. I need the money, and two-fifty will cure my current tech crisis. We'll park at a High School about a mile away and bike into the park. You need the money too, right? Got a hot date for the weekend?"

"Of course!" Al said.

"Of course," Cane echoed.

"How about you big dog, got anything goin on?" Al asked.

"Not exactly."

"That means no, nothing, nada, nuh uh," Al said with a chuckle. "I could hook you up with my neighbors.

"You mean those Vietnam*ese* sisters?"

"I think they're hot, and they're not *easee*. Like I said, you could actually get a date for a change, thanks to your dear older brother."

"Like a hunk of burnin love? More like napalm, Al. Ready to burn your ass."

"Kiss mine, Cane."

Cane turned on the radio loud, punching channels until he got Kid Rock singing *Picture* with Sheryl Crow. They looked at each other. *Appropriate.* They didn't talk again until they pulled into the empty high school parking lot.

"We're goin to the picnic area and checking out the parking lot near the water," Cane said. He jumped out of the driver's seat and went around back to take down their trail bikes. Al opened up the side door and pulled out their back packs, divvying up the video and audio equipment. They checked their phones, put in their ear pieces, put on their helmets and peddled through the entrance to the park, waving to the girl in the booth.

Al took off and started racing into the park. Cane eventually passed him and headed to the end of the road with a parking lot near a picnic area facing Lake Erie. They sped past parents and kids leaving after the last day of sun and fun before school started the next day, and then couples, old and young, walking down to the water's edge waiting for the moon to rise over the lake. They biked to a parking lot at the end of the trail and raced each other around the perimeter. They did wheelies back out of the lot and went back up the road.

Al yelled over to Cane. "Didn't see any Escalade, *Dawg.* Sure we got the right park?"

"Let's try the other side of the park." Cane answered.

"If I remember right, that's the boat launch. Why there?"

"Don't know. Let's go see."

They biked past the park entrance and took the winding road past the nature center to the boat launch. The wide trailer lot was empty except for one Escalade. They circled the lot, did their circus act wheelies again and stopped by the trees.

"That's the car," Cane said.

"Looked like a guy in the driver's seat on the phone. Guess this would be the lonelier spot. No boats. No Trailers, " Al said.

See a woman?" Cane asked.

"Might have seen some long hair low in the passenger seat. Maybe she's *doin* him while he's on the phone. Nice call."

"OK. Give me *Buddha*", said Cane, "and I'll go back and take video of the lake. You take *Micro* and see if you can stick it to their rear window."

Al gave him a *what the hell* look. "How you want me to go unnoticed while I stick it on the window?"

"I don't know. Zip around the car and skid off your bike. Act like you're hurt and walkin it off, then stick it. Bleed a little if you can."

"For three-hundred?" Al asked.

"Two-fifty a piece."

"Not if I'm the one gonna bleed."

"We'll see," said Cane.

"Which means *you'll see*, which means to me, *no see*."

"Hey, I'm the guy they're goin to watch through the windshield," said Cane. "And I'll pan over toward them as you're going around and falling off your bike. I'll keep the camera going while I walk up to you to see if you're okay. You get up, brush yourself off and I'll head back to the docks and that way they'll watch me instead of you. We're both taking the same risk, but I'll get a shot of the girl in the front. With your antics, she'll probably come up for air. Okay?"

"Good plan," said Al with a note of sarcasm. "It might even work."

~~~

Al watched Cane take off for the parking lot. He got out the *Micro* camera with the wireless microphone and put a piece of bubble gum in his mouth. Sugar and Spit, best stickum in the bizz.

Cane rode into the parking lot, stopped at the docks, took off his helmet and got off the bike. He pulled out the camera and began to video the water, panning from the houses on the other side of the channel and then out toward Lake Erie. Al came speeding around from the back of the lot, getting up to twenty miles per hour as he got near the Escalade. He leaned into a turn and went into a controlled slide, skidding to a stop in front of the car. He screamed for the full effect. Cane turned around, still rolling, and jogged over. The woman's head popped up and the driver got out and ran around to the front to see what happened. He had his pants on and zipped up.

Cane reached him first, "You alright, Dude?"

"I, I think so." He had scraped his wrist and it was bleeding. *I should get more for this stunt.*

"Hey, you're bleeding," the woman said as she joined the driver.

Cane turned the camera toward her without looking in the viewfinder, making it look like he wasn't recording. He turned back to the driver. "Good thing he didn't slide into your sweet ride, man."

"Yeah, really. You gonna be alright?"

"I think I'm alright. Nothin broken. I just need to check my bike." Al picked up his bicycle and started rolling it by the side of the car and then around it. Without stopping, he pulled out the wireless camera, spit out the big wad of bubble gum, stuck it on the back and slapped it on the rear window.

"It works okay," he said as he came back around to the front of the SUV. He jumped back on the bike and took off.

"Take it easier next time, Dude, or you'll be in traction," Cane yelled for the benefit of the couple. He turned back to the couple. "He's a crazy-ass. Have a nice day." Cane lowered the camera and walked back to his bike, got on, peddled off the lot, out of view of the couple. Al biked over and met him.

"Have a nice day? *Dawg*, what a line."

"Shut up, Al. I've done some serious filming here on the beautiful shores of Lake Erie. Good enough for *The Discovery Channel*, if you know what I mean. I've got a good shot of the man and one of the woman as they were standing together lookin at you. How's the wireless set up?"

"Stuck to the window with a whole pack of bubble gum. It ain't goin nowhere. I'll head back to the van. By the way, how are we goin to get *Micro* off when we're done?"

"You mean, how are *you* going to get it off after she gets him off?" Cane asked, thrusting his hips with his fist by his crotch.

"Come on, Man. We can't leave that camera on the back of their car, and we sure as hell can't have them see us grab it. How we going to pull it off?"

"By distraction. I'll be the distraction, Dog, you'll be the retriever. Woof, woof."

"What you goin to do, hike up your riding shorts?"

"No, I'm going to drop my shorts. Actually, I'm going to drop the bike in the middle of the road and make it look like I'm hurt, put a little ketchup on the knee and leg. They'll stop long enough to ask if I'm alright, and for you to come out from the bushes and grab the camera."

"You've got ketchup? Want some of my real blood?" Al asked, holding up his wrist. "Good plan, again," he added.

"Yeah. No, and right," Cane answered. "I'm going to sneak back on foot through the trees and get a shot of the two of them in the car."

"And I'll call you when I've got a picture," Al said.

~~~

Cane moved his bike into some shrubs by the nature center and hiked back along the tree line on the road so he could get a shot of the Escalade and not attract attention. He set up a short tripod, attached the camera and changed to a zoom lens. "In place with camera rolling."

"Roger that," Al answered. "I'm back at the van and we're recording from inside the Caddy with only silhouettes. Let me know if you see anything better."

"Will do."

Al listened more than watched since the sun had gone down and the Escalade was dark. He only heard idle conversation. No heavy breathing or clothes rustling. Then, he heard the doors open and shut. "Cane, you see anything?" Al asked.

"They got out of the vehicle and they're walking down to the dock."

"Great. We won't be able to see or hear them. So much for the five hundred."

"Al, we got them together, right? That ought to be worth something... wait."

"What?"

"There's a boat approaching. It's scanning the shore line with a search light. *Shee-it!*"

"What?" Al asked. Silence. "Cane?"

"I've got the shot," Cane said. Then more silence.

"What the hell is going on?" Al called back.

"I'm moving," Cane answered. "You have the camera feed?"

"Yeah. What's goin on, Cane?"

"Just keep the video and sound up and running. I'm on my bike and moving."

"Great. I can't see anything," Al said.

"You will," Cane answered. "They're heading back from the dock with a guy from the boat who's pulling a hand-truck with two pallets. Is the remote working?"

"Yeah, like I told you," Al said. "Not much light to see...wait. They're opening the side doors and the dome lights came on. Good picture. Now they're opening the back doors. Can't see in the car, but it looks like they're sliding one, now a second pallet into the back."

"Good. You've got the shot," Cane said. "The man with the pallet jack is heading back to the boat. Now the boat is moving out and turning to the lake. It's a …"

"It's a what?"

I'm going down the road back toward the nature center. When they drive out, I'll fall down in the middle of the road at the bike path so they have to stop. Head back this way and be ready to grab the wireless off the back of the SUV."

"Okay. They shut the doors," Al said. "Uh, oh."

"What?" Cane asked.

"I've got no picture. Shit! I think they found the wireless. I'm heading your way."

After some phone calls, the Escalade started up and headed out of the parking lot. When Cane could see the headlights coming around the last curve toward him, he slid off his bike and lay down in the middle of the road. The Escalade slowed down and stopped when they spotted him. He got up and rubbed his knee. The driver rolled down his window and stuck his head out.

"You alright?"

Cane limped toward the car, acting like he was walking off an injury. The man and woman were looking at him as he spotted Al come out of the bushes behind the SUV. Cane walked to the driver's side, tripped over his feet and caught himself on the side view mirror. Al peeked around and shook his head and dodged back into the bushes.

"Oh, sorry," Cane said. "I think I'm okay. I'll get my bike and get out of your way."

The driver suddenly swung open the door and knocked Cane to the ground. "You're not going anywhere, punk."

Cane tried to get up and get away, but his bike shoe clips kept slipping on the black top. The man grabbed his arm and lifted him off the ground. "What do you think you're doing out here, first shooting us with your camera, and then sticking this on our rear window." The man pulled out the *Micro* camera.

"Let me go, you sonofabitch," Cane yelled.

The woman appeared from around the front of the car pointing a black gun at Cane. "Get his backpack," she told the man. Turning back toward Cane, "If you run, I'll shoot."

Cane was shoved face down on the ground and he felt the camera pack being yanked backward, bending his arms behind him. He yelled out in pain. Simultaneously, the woman with the gun crashed to the ground, the front tire of Al's bike hitting her full speed in the head as he did a wheelie. When Cane felt the man's grip loosen, he pushed up from the ground, flinging himself backward and knocking the man off balance. He turned quickly and kicked him the crotch. As the man doubled over, Cane ran, picked up his bike and took off.

Cane looked back for Al. "Go! Go!" he yelled, but Al was nowhere in sight. A few seconds later, he heard a gunshot. He slammed on his brakes and screamed, "Al! Al?"

Al whizzed by him. *"Mother-fuck!"*

Cane stood on his pedals, took off and caught up with Al in a few minutes. Pointing to the trees, Cane yelled, "We gotta hide. They'll be on top of us in a minute."

"I don't think so," Al yelled back. "Before I wheelied the woman, I punched their back tire with my handy dandy screw driver. They ain't goin nowhere, fast."

"Cool. And what the hell, man?" Cane growled. "That bitch tried to shoot us."

"No shit. This must be serious."

~~~

"So, what's with those pallets? And a boat?" Al asked as they loaded their bikes and back packs in the van.

"Shut up and let's get the hell out of here." Cane said.

"All right. All right!"

Al jumped in the van as Cane started the engine. They drove out of the school parking lot and headed north. The dashboard lights cast a blue glow on the frown on Al's face "What about the boat?" he asked.

"Ever had a gun pointed at your head?" Cane asked. "It scared the shit out of me. Well, almost. They wanted the camera bad, Man. Probably because of that boat."

"Again, what about the boat?" Al asked.

Cane looked over at Al, and then looked back to the road. "Coast Guard."

"Coast Guard?"

"Yeah. We're in over our heads now."

Neither one said anything on the way back to Cane's place. They didn't know what to think, or say anything about what had just happened. When they got to Cane's apartment, he took the bikes and Al grabbed the equipment and headed to his computer room.

Cane had converted the second bedroom of his apartment into a high tech room. Al called it the *nerd* cave. It had a Dell with all the usual programming, except for the professional version of a video editor that David Miller of Miller Studios had given him

Al took the memory stick from the wireless receiver and put it in a USB slot. Cane came in and sat down next to him and they both watched in silence.

Al looked at Cane. "Who are those guys?"

Cane stared ahead, thinking.

"We need to make a phone call," Al said.

"Let's think about this first," Cane answered.

"Why?" All asked. "We've got to call Dave…"

"Not so fast," Cane said, shaking his head. "Listen, Dave sends us out to spy on a guy for supposedly cheating on his wife, but they end up taking two pallets from a Coast Guard boat. Then, when I stopped them, they had the camera and came after me. Then when we get away, they shoot at us."

"Dave was right about the guy, but wrong about why."

Al answered, "Or, he knew something about it and bribed you into getting us to go down there and get video."

"Right. So, do we call Dave or someone else?" asked Cane.

"Someone else."

Chapter 2

Tuesday Morning

Reginald Vincent *Vince* Hardesty drove through the historical gated entrance of St. Vincent's at the corner of Grand River Ave and Indian Street near the infamous Eight Mile border of Detroit. The circular drive took you around the back side to the front door. There in the middle of the circle stood St. Vincent DePaul, carved in white stone, hands out, reaching toward a needy world. Vince liked old St. Vincent, called him his patron saint, not just because he shared his name, but because of his own attempt at trying out the saint's work.

He pulled into the staff lot and locked his ex-cop car 2000 Chevy Impala. The body had some rust like most Michigan cars, but he'd had a new V8 engine installed, one of his few requirements when he'd bought it.

He quickly walked up the front steps and recalled his first time through the front door. He looked up and saw the words of St. Vincent engraved on the stone archway:

*"It is our duty to prefer the service of the poor to everything else and to offer such service as quickly as possible. Charity is certainly greater than any rule."*

He preferred service to rules, so he had said "yes" to a Sister who was the director of St. Vincent's outreach program. He met the good Sisters when a car accident had laid him up for a week at Providence Hospital, the other mission of the Daughters of Charity. He told her that he hadn't known nuns did outreach work. She answered, "We're not nuns, we don't live in a cloister, and we don't stand around posing for holy pictures."

She said they were looking for a few good men to work in a program mentoring young fathers. Vince thought he might qualify since he had coached young men for over ten years, just not about parenting. More about life and death. And that fit these young men as well. They had a new life to care for and their young age and lack of education and employable skills was killing them, not to mention many of the neighborhoods where they lived. He eventually said yes, but only on a volunteer basis. He didn't need the money. St. Vincent did.

When visitors came to the program, Vince explained that even though he was named after the French priest, and people often said he had the demeanor of a priest, whatever that meant, he would say, "I'm not a *Father*, a priest like my long dead friend, but a father to be sure. First, a father to an unborn son who had died, and now a *father* to hundreds of young men from the Detroit Metro area who are new dads, though not necessarily by intention. At least that wasn't their goal," he would explain to skeptical visitors, "but it was the result."

Vince often went into Detroit to meet young fathers. When he knocked on the door, the number one question from the young men was, "Are you with the po-leece?" Well, what did a strong, lean, thirty-six year old white guy look like in the hood? And so much for that priestly demeanor. Probably his years in special ops shown through in neighborhoods known for violence. He never carried a weapon on the job, that was frowned upon by the good Sisters, but he could handle himself without a weapon. He was a black belt in *Krav Maga*, a combination of martial arts developed by the Israeli *Mossad*. He used it on many occasions to *subdue combatants*. That demeanor made him look like a cop carrying.

The mentoring program received most of its referrals from the Teen Mother's Program. Half of them said that they didn't know who the father was or that he was not involved. Vince discovered that half of them were lying to protect their "baby daddy" from being hauled into court and slapped with an unpayable child support order to the state. The other half said they would let the father know, and they never did, much for the same reasons. Eventually, they had to convince the female social workers not to ask, *Is the father involved*? He was involved. They were to ask, "Who is the father and where is he?"

Most of the young men didn't really trust agencies, either because they were run by women, or they had heard the stories of sting operations by Friend of the Court: "Congratulations, you have won a brand new projection television. Pick up your prize at the Joe Louis Arena on Saturday. Be there!"

Vince might not have been the same skin color of most of the young fathers, but he was a guy, and he knew how to relate to young men. He'd done it for years as a military trainer. And just as he had gone into battle with young men under fire, the young fathers he worked with were under fire as well.

In the world of teen parents, Friend of the Court and the State Office of Child Support, young fathers were often considered public enemy number one. Even though the goal of these agencies is to support children, teen dads often described their experience with these agencies using their acronyms: "They *FOC* you and *SOC* you with a child support you can't pay." Not exactly terms of endearment. Then to add insult to injury, even the attorney general had gotten in on the act. You could see his billboards up and down the interstate with a picture of the back of a young man in hand cuffs. It read: "We don't handle dead beats with kid gloves." It propagated the popular message that all *dead beat* dads were criminals, when in reality, most were just *dead broke* dads. But the attorney general was preparing to run for the governor's seat, and there's nothing like free advertising.

In recent years, both agencies had become more *father-friendly*. A decade of academic literature on the importance of fathers being involved in their children's lives, even if they were non-custodial, had begun to change the culture of child support. The agencies and courts joined fatherhood coalitions and presented at annual conferences to inform young men of the assistance they could offer in supporting their children. But old reputations die hard. The old stories of sting operations and stake outs to arrest fathers persisted.

Vince stopped at the office manager window. Juanita Alvarez, a spry seventy year old, slid open the window and said, "Hello my dear Vincent," and gave him the mail. Juanita was a retired office clerk who needed full time work after her husband died of cancer some fifteen years before. She was one of that rare breed that came in early and worked well into the evening, never reporting her overtime. She had adopted the young moms and fathers and their children of St. Vincent's as her own.

"And Vincent, you need to update your case files by the end of the week."

"Yes, Ma'am." Vincent Hardesty, late on the paper work again. She handed him a phone message. "Oh. I almost forgot," she said. "It came in at *seven* this morning."

He looked at the message and saw that it was from the Major brothers. And if they called that early, it *was* something major. Neither one of the twins would normally be up before noon.

He told Juanita thanks and she buzzed him in. By the time he got upstairs to make the phone call, he heard car doors slam and looked out his second floor window to see Al and Cane running in from the parking lot. He put on some coffee and waited for the call from Juanita.

The phone buzzed. "The twins are here," she said.

"Send them up."

He could hear them running up the wooden steps and waited for them to burst through his office door. Al and Cane Major. A couple of twenty-two year olds he had taken under his wing soon after he arrived. Al, the taller and long haired one, was referred to the program by a Providence nurse. His daughter was born two years ago. His twin brother, Cane, shorter, neater, and more organized, had come with him. The twins had never met their father, an army vet killed in Nicaragua, and their mother had died just last year. His paternal urgings had taken over.

"Vince, Vince. You've got to help us, man," Al said winded.

"Yeah, we don't know what to do," Cane added.

"Hold on you guys," Vince said. "Take a seat. Have a cup of coffee. Sit down and breathe for a minute."

"But, Faa-ther, we..."

"Stop! Breathe." Vince poured them coffee, sat in his brown leather office chair, toasted the twins and took a leisurely sip. The twins sat down and followed suit.

"Mmmm, the good stuff, the *Big-B* I see," Al said.

"Okay, guys, what happened, and did anybody get hurt or arrested?" asked Vince.

"No, Father, but almost" Al began. "We saw something really strange last night and then we got shot at. We knew you'd be the best guy to help us figure it out."

"So, no one was actually shot and no one we know has been arrested. Is that right?" asked Vince, knowing Al's propensity for exaggeration.

"No, Vince," Cane said. "But almost. Dave gave us a private-dick job to video a guy and his girlfriend because his wife thought he was cheatin on her. Dave sent us down to Lake Erie Metro Park, and sure enough, we found him with a woman."

"Sounds pretty straightforward, so far. But I can't say I'm happy about hearing Dave sending you guys out on a snoop job."

"Does that make us *Snoop Dawgs*?" Al asked. He loved it that their parents had named them after the summer constellation Canis Major, commonly called the Dog Star. So they were cool with calling each other *Dawg* like their black brothers in the program. The brothers also called each other *Cuz,* short for cousin. The brothers called the twins *Cauz,* short for Caucasians. Who said blacks and whites couldn't get along in Detroit?

"Al? Cut it."

"Sorry Cane, tell Father the rest."

"Like I was saying, we found the guy with this girl and we set up our equipment to get a recording of their hook up when we saw something way worse than we expected."

Not being able to contain himself, Al got up out of his chair and began pacing to get into it when Cane jumped up and shushed him with a whispered "Shut the fuck up and sit down."

Looking back at Vince, Cane whispered the rest of the story, finishing with writing down on a piece of scrap paper, *Coast Guard.*

"They really took a shot at you?" Vince asked.

"Yeah, after I knocked that bi... uh, woman, on her ass."

Vince sat quiet for a long minute looking back and forth at the twins. "Remind me to have a word with Dave and..."

Cane interrupted, "We don't think Dave had any idea what this was really about, and now we have a video of something shady going down with," he lowered his voice to a whisper, "the Coast Guard."

"Could we be heroes or something?" Al asked.

"Or something," Vince said, giving Al a look so serious it stopped him from saying anything else. Vince looked over at Cane and saw that he had become very quiet.

"Okay, this is what you're going to do," said Vince, all business. "You've got the file, right?"

"Yeah, right here on this memory stick," Cane said. He paused, thinking he should tell Vince that the couple got the wireless camera, but Vince interrupted.

"Good. Give me the boat drop. Give the first part with the guy and the gal to Dave. Tell him the couple was there and you got some video of them in the Escalade. Skip the part about the boat. I'll call a couple of friends and call you back when I figure out what to do. Now run back out of here like you did when you came in so Juanita won't ask you any questions. Go home, or go cycling, or whatever else you normally do. Okay?"

"Okay," they said in unison.

"Thanks," they said as they ran out the door, down the steps, and past Juanita. She called out "boys," but they were out the door before she could say anything.

Vince returned to his desk, sat back in his chair and closed his eyes. He cleared his mind and said a prayer.

Ten minutes later, the phone buzzed.

"Vincent, I have a call for you," said Juanita.

"Alright. Thanks."

"Hello?"

"Vince, this is Dave."

"That didn't take long."

"Yeah, the twins called me and said they had talked to you about a job they did for me last night. They said I should call you right away. Is everything all right?"

"Dave, that's not the kind of videography I was thinking of when I sent them your way. And you know their mother's gone, and I'm their only," he hesitated, thought *parent*, then said, "guy to look after them."

"Yes, Father."

"Stop calling me that."

"Yes, Father. Anyway, the twins said they were bringing me a video of last night's job."

Vince filled him in only on the part he wanted him to know, the first video file from Cane's camera.

"They felt very uncomfortable about the whole thing and they just wanted to talk. And I'm just saying they shouldn't have to do anything they're not comfortable doing."

"Okay, right. I'll be sure to ask them about their feelings next time. Come on, Vince. You know how they are. They keep bugging me to give them more work and they love being private-dicks, and they make more money doing that than they do taping weddings, christenings, and confirmations."

"Keep 'em safe, Dave," said Vince.

"Of course. Hey, they're good at it, man. No one suspects a couple of boys of being snoops."

"*Snoop Dawgs*," corrected Vince.

"What?" asked Dave.

"Nothing," Vince answered.

"I just wanted to reassure you that I wouldn't do anything that would put them in jeopardy," Dave said.

"Knowingly," Vince replied.

"Right. Nothing to be concerned about, Vince."

"Right."

*How many times have I heard politicians say those very words?*

Chapter 3

Tuesday Noon

Pat *Sandy* Sandelen took a walk up Baubien Street from the Renaissance Center on the Detroit River, now the new General Motors International Headquarters, to the aging, dirty stone building of the Detroit Police Department. Even though it was a hot, steamy day, he wanted to check his wire taps on a Mafia informant at the Eastside Precinct, and he wanted to look into the eyes of the detective that was checking it. When he arrived, as usual, the unit pretty much ignored him, either from jealousy for his current *cushy* position, or out of bad blood from some past unsolved case that *he* had closed. When he asked about the taps, he was told there was nothing new. *Same ol' shit.*

He had needed a break from the non-stop committee meetings on the security to be put in place for the upcoming Super Bowl in February. His six foot five, linebacker frame needed a walk after sitting all morning. He needed something to spice up the day. Consulting on security wasn't all it was cracked up to be. After being a Detroit street cop, then detective with Drug Enforcement, making busts no matter who it was, earning him a snub from the then DPD chief, and now DP liaison with Homeland Security, sitting around on your ass hearing the drone of GM suits was mind numbing. If this was the way they built cars, it was no wonder the Japanese were beating them at their own game.

On his way back to his temporary office at GM, he stopped at a restaurant in the Atheneum Hotel for a spicy barbecue lunch. Greektown, the home of Greek restaurants, bars and Trapper's Alley, a collection of take out, art, clothes and T-Shirt vendors, was now the home of one of the three casinos in town.

It was part of the entertainment circle that surrounded Detroit's business district.

Detroit, a French settlement, was built on a street template modeled after Paris, with avenues radiating out from rectangles, a wheel hub-and-spoke design that Washington D.C. duplicated. The hub is located a few blocks north of the Detroit River at a park called Campus Martius. This is the *point of origin* for the city's coordinate system of streets. The inner hub contains the business district with buildings named Cadillac, Guardian, GM, Ford and Compuware. The next circle houses the bars, restaurants and the casino-hotels with the names of Greektown, MGM and Motor City; theaters called Century, Fox, Fisher, Gem, and State; and ballparks Comerica, Joe Louis and Ford Field. Like the progress of civilization, after business and recreation comes the educational and cultural layer: Wayne State University, the museums: DIA, Historical, Science, and African-American History; and the teaching medical hospitals of The Henry Ford and The DMC, Detroit Medical Center. What follows are pockets of old mansions and then the directional grid of old stable neighborhoods and overly documented boarded-up and vacant blocks of middle class housing.

Sitting back at his desk on the tenth floor of the Ren-Cen overlooking the Detroit River, he felt his cell phone vibrate on his belt. He saw that he had missed a call from Vincent Hardesty and he'd left a voicemail. *Please be something other than another meeting.* He dialed his voicemail.

"Hey, it's Vince. I need your help with a couple of my guys. Give me a call."

Thank God. Vince never called unless something crazy was going on or he had some box seat Tigers tickets. He called him back.

"Hey Vince, got tickets?"

"Sure Sandy. Can we meet? I got somethin' for you, personal."

"Sure Vince. When?"

"How 'bout now?" asked Vince.

"Give me an hour," Sandy said. *Hot damn, I hope this is somethin' good.* "See you at the usual place?"

"Yep. One hour." Vince rung off.

Sandy rubbed his hands together, glad to have a diversion from consulting with the suits. Hopefully, it would get him back to where he loved to be, in the middle of an investigation.

~~~

Pat Sandelen paused the video file from the Major twins. He looked up over his laptop through his condo's glass wall and saw the Detroit skyline. Beyond the Ren-Cen's silhouette he could see the Ambassador Bridge crossing the river to Canada. The Department of Homeland Security, DHS, patrolled the international border with crews from the Coast Guard marine and air base. He had been the Police Department's representative at the first meeting of the DHS in Detroit when then director Tom Ridge came to town bringing sixteen million dollars with him.

He remembered the first collaborative meeting of all the local agencies. After an hour of bullshit, they all realized that the DHS Feds would essentially take over any suspicious activity near the border. Now even the FBI would know what it felt like when an outside government agency came in and took over your investigation. He felt sorry for them, but not much. What goes around... blah, blah, blah. In the end, it felt like another layer of red tape with guys in dark suits and sunglasses adding to the already cumbersome administration. To a policeman used to making quick decisions on the street, it was a massive waste of manpower and time. And with another layer of admin came the decision makers who were one more step removed from the real foot soldier. The possibility of a Coasty, or DHS agent, making an illegal drop was evidently possible. So who are these guys and what are they up to? And who could help him find out? As he looked back down at the black ribbon of the Detroit River, a smile came across his creased mahogany skin. He knew just the officer.

They had met at that meeting when Ridge and the Homeland circus had come to town. They kind of hit it off last year when they both agreed to disagree with one of the DHS's local directors on the security needed on the waterfront for the upcoming Super Bowl. Here was a brash Coast Guard heelo pilot who had flown a Black Hawk for the Army. Having a pretty face and a fit body didn't hurt. Lt. G. V. Sanchez could fly her helicopter anywhere and anyway you needed.

She was one of the first female officers to be decorated from the war. She took a bullet and risked her life flying rescue missions for wounded soldiers during the opening phases of Operation Iraqi Freedom. Returning to the states in May of 2003, she resigned from the Army and signed up for the Coast Guard. At her request, she was transferred to the Detroit Guard Air Base just as Homeland was expanding operations in the area.

She had said that having two HH65 Dolphin helicopters hovering over the river for several hours while people were checked in and scanned at Ford Field was, as she said, "a big ass waste of time and fuel." That didn't sit well with the Homeland brass. She said they needed the helicopters for rescue, not Detroit River babysitting. If there was an incident, they could be there in five minutes. The brass didn't agree then, but later Sandelen heard that the Army Reserve would station troop trucks on Jefferson near the river walk, Coast Guard divers would be placing heat sensors in the river, and the Dolphins would be on call.

After the meeting, Sandy and Graciela Venusuela *Venus* Sanchez had talked in the hall. Finding out that they were both war vets, they started having coffee together after DHS conference meetings. She liked Sandy's street wise experience and he liked her common sense, solution minded outlook.

Venus had grown up in Southwest Detroit where Blacks and Latinos didn't necessarily get along. While her older brothers and sister were having babies, she decided to join the Army right after high school. Her dad had been a Border Patrol officer for his entire career after the army. She loved the water, living near Lake Erie where her dad took her fishing every weekend. But she also wanted to fly. Hovering over land, and now water, seemed the best fit.

Sandy went to his laptop address list, found her number under "Tamale," the nickname the corpsmen had given her, and dialed.

"Hey Sandman."

"Hey Venus, *que pasa*?"

"*Recupero*!"

"From what?"

"Nada."

"Cat fight?"

"*Muchacho!*" Hicho o' chucha!" She paused. "He cheated on me, and I shoulda known better than to date an *A-ganger*."

"Did you say *gangbanger*?"

"No, *A-ganger*. One of the auxiliary crew. They operate and maintain our boat's auxiliary equipment, like air conditioning, distilling units, air compressors, shit like that."

"Not a Coasty, huh?"

"I'm not dating no more Guardies. No way, *Jose*!"

"Okay, Venus. You always share your personals with people who call?"

"You're more than people, *Amigo*, you know that."

"Thanks, cause I need a friend for a big favor, *por favor*."

"And sorry, I just had to let you know. When I found out about the boyfriend's activities over the past month, I went over to his place today and broke it off."

"Ouch."

"Ooh, not that, but I wish I had. No, I mean I just broke up with him, and kicked his ass in the process. I made sure it was loud enough for everyone in his building to hear, maybe even his new girlfriend. So, *que'pasa*, Sandy? What is your favor?"

"I got somethin' I want you to see."

"Like what."

"A video file."

"Video? Does it have Antonio Banderas in it? I could use a little Banderas right now."

"Sorry, no Antonio. I've got it on my laptop. It's spooky."

Venus understood. The word *spooky* meant it had to do with Homeland. "Gotcha. I'm not working today or the rest of the week after pulling forty hours over Labor Day weekend.

"Can you come over to my place, say this afternoon?" asked Sandy.

"Sure. I'll give your neighbors something to talk about."

A smile came across Sandy's face. He could see it now. Venus strutting across the lobby looking good. They had more of a father-daughter relationship, but when people saw them together they didn't necessarily think that, especially when Venus got out of uniform and dressed up. And boy, could she dress up. A Spanish Mona Lisa. Oh, how the locals will talk. "You gonna increase my stud rating with the residents?"

"You know that's what I do. Anything to help you with your girlfriends."

"Hey, girlfriends... Hello?" She'd hung up. Always had to have the last word. She might not have the last word on this visit. He was going to put her on the spot. Once she saw the video, he knew she would not let it go until she found out exactly what was going on. She was loyal to the Guard, but she'd been in the military long enough and seen enough to know that not everyone who wore a uniform honored what it stood for. She would leave the meeting pissed, but proud to know he'd trusted her enough to call her rather than the brass.

~~~

Sandy opened the laptop, clicked on the desktop icon labeled *CG-drop*. He stepped back from his desk and invited Venus to sit down. He took a deep breath and sighed, knowing what was coming. Part of him hated what he was about to do to her: put a frown on that pretty face and a doubt in her heart about her beloved Coast Guard.

She looked up at him and winked, sensing his reluctance to show her what she was about to see, and reminding him of the little scene she'd given his neighbors. He'd almost forgotten how good looking she was out of uniform. She was a sight seldom seen in the Lafayette Towers. Short-shorts accented with three-inch-high heels, adding to her five-foot-six inch curvy frame, long brown hair flowing midway down her back, a bright red Mexican top with lipstick to match, and calling for him in Spanish.

"Practicin' on me, Venus?"

"Who's *practicin*. It's the Latino me. Upgrading your reputation at the *The Towers*."

"Thanks."

He looked over her shoulder as the video started. The car, the couple, the Lake. Then the camera zoomed in as the couple went to the shore's edge to a Coast Guard skiff.

She gasped. "What the *hell*?"

Two black tarp covered pallets were handed over from the guardsman to the couple. The boat's spotlight lit up the shoreline, and the skiff captain's face could be seen, but barely.

Sandy reached over and stopped the video. Venus looked up at Sandy with a tight-lipped smile.

"You got a drink?" she asked.

"Sure. Beer or stronger?"

"Corona?"

"You got it." He handed her the beer.

"You know Sandy, I've never really trusted those bastards. Homeland comes in and starts running everything and everyone, some of them contracted through private security units, former guards, Special Forces, you know? They..." She stopped abruptly. She looked into Sandy's eyes and her mouth went tight.

"Why *me*?"

He knew it would come down to this. "Because you have Integrity."

"Bullshit"

"No. Bulldog"

"Screw you."

"You won't let it go 'til we know."

"You're the devil."

"And you're an angel."

"Is that what the neighbor's think? No. Just like they think I'm doing you, you want me to put out."

"I know no one who can do it better."

Venus put her hand on her chest. "Is this any way to treat a friend, a girl who's vulnerable?"

"Oh, please. You don't look so, uh, vulnerable in that outfit," Sandy said as he bounced his eyebrows.

"Shut up."

"Think about it. We need someone inside."

Venus was silent. Sandy could see the wheels turning. He had her. She got up from her chair, grabbed the beer, turned on her heels and walked across the room, chugging the Corona. She took a final look over her shoulder. "I'm in!"

She turned back and walked up to the laptop. "Damn it, print me that frame with the Guardy's face on it."

"Yes, Ma'am. Right away."

Sandy sat down at the laptop, backed up the video, found the frame and made a print. He gave Venus the picture. "I'll give you a call when we meet up with my partner and the videographers. It'll be at Vince's. Dress, uh, appropriately."

"Vince's? What's that, an Italian Restaurant?"

"No. He's a friend of mine, my partner in crime."

She opened the door. "Call me." She slammed the door and yelled something in Spanish. She was back in the act, imitating a lover's spat. He could barely contain his laughter.

Chapter 4

Tuesday Evening

Pat Sandelen pulled around St. Vincent's circular drive thinking about all the different directions the video file could take them. It was obvious it wasn't about a tryst. More than likely, it was about smuggling something worth money across the border for profit, like drugs, either illegal or prescription, or guns. He knew the street value in Detroit for either was a thousand percent or better. This was one of those times that he was glad he knew Vincent, both for the mystery that got his blood moving, and for the camaraderie.

Sandy found Vince through a trainer at the FBI Academy at Quantico when he attended investigative training on the Mafia and white collar crime. The trainer mentioned to Sandy that there was a retired Navy SEAL that had moved back to Detroit to run a family business. Several years later, while Sandy was attending the Detroit welcoming event for the new head of Homeland Security, and he couldn't sit any more, he got up and walked to the back of the auditorium and stood next to what he thought was a clean cut contract security type. Sandy extended his hand and introduced himself, and the suit leaned in and whispered, "Vincent Hardesty."

Sandy stepped back and did a double take. "You're Vincent Hardesty? Special Forces, right?"

Vince put his finger to his lips. Like the trainer had said, he didn't look like the superhero type, more like an athletic business exec in a tailored suit. "I've heard about you from an instructor at Quantico," Sandy said.

Vincent shook his head and said, "Not here."

Sandy invited him to his place for beer. Since that day, they had become good friends, trusting each other to cover their backs: Sandy with anything that might involve DHS, Vince for incidents dealing with the DPD.

~~~

Sandy stopped at the receptionist's window. Juanita said, "Good evening, Mr. Sandelen." She never forgot a face or a name. She buzzed him through and he went upstairs to Vince's office. They grabbed hands and then hugged without a word. They had become as close as brothers. As they released, Sandy looked into Vince's eyes and said, "What the hell you got us into now?"

"Oh, you know, the usual *unusual*." Vince smiled. They heard a car screech to a halt in the parking lot. Out the window they could see the twins bound out of their van and run up the front steps.

Juanita waved them through. As they burst through Vince's office door, they said "Hey Father" in unison, giving him the St. Vincent handshake, smiling and slapping him on the arm. Vince introduced them to Investigator Sandelen and their expressions changed to serious. He was a big and tall intimidating black man with a badge.

"I want you guys to tell Detective Sandelen everything you saw and heard yesterday. Especially anything that isn't on the video. He's already seen your file and I'll let him ask the questions."

The boys gulped and said "Okay, Father." They looked back at Sandy. He smiled at them. Instead of its intended effect at friendliness, it looked more like the smile of a defensive back about to tackle the opposing ball carrier.

Sandy had them take him through the entire evening from beginning to end. When they wanted to rush to the end and the gunshot, his questions would bring them back to the details about the couple in the van and the Coast Guard skiff. When they finished, Sandy gave Vince a look.

Sandy pulled out his card and gave it to Cane. "Call me if you think of anything else. And I mean any- thing, okay?"

"Yes, Sir," Cane answered.

"What about Miller?" Sandy asked Vince.

"Dave said that the guy's wife thought he'd been going out a lot at night and wanted him followed. She overheard a conversation he had with a woman named Janet. She had picked up the other phone and heard that her husband was picking up this Janet and they were going to meet someone at the Lake Erie Metro Park. The wife called Dave to try to see if he could catch him in whatever was going on."

The twins nodded. "That's how we got to the park," Cane said.

Juanita buzzed Vince's phone. He picked up and said "Okay, thanks."

While Cane continued to explain to Sandy how Dave had them do private eye work, Al noticed that Vince had left the room and gone downstairs to meet whoever was at the door. Several minutes later he walked back in the room with a woman wearing a navy blue baseball cap with the Tigers old English *D* on it. She had black silky hair pulled back in a ponytail bouncing out of the back of her cap down to her shoulders. She wore a concealing windbreaker with what looked like some kind of insignia and a patch with three green stripes below it. What he noticed more was that she had on the tightest jeans he'd ever seen. He looked back up and saw her staring at him with big brown accusing eyes. She had a straight definitive nose and red tight lips that said she had caught him in the act. He gave her an embarrassed smile and she looked back to Vince with what he thought was a smirk on her face.

Al looked back at the group and realized Vince was introducing her to everyone. Her name was Venus something and then heard, "Homeland Security, Coast Guard." He looked down and thought he'd made a fool of himself checking out the ass of a sailor. But she wasn't quite dressed like any sailor he'd ever seen. Then he heard his name and said "What?" before he realized that he was being introduced. He looked at his brother who was shaking his head and rolling his eyes at him.

"Who are *these* guys, exactly?"

He heard his brother say that they were the guys who had recorded the video in the park and had seen the couple in the SUV pick up two crates from some kind of boat with Coast Guard painted on the side.

"Coast Guard skiff" she corrected him. "We do all the patrols with *Defender* boats and *Dolphin* rescue helicopters along the Detroit River and the Great Lakes," she said.

"Oh."

"*Swishers*," Vince said with a grin.

Venus gave Vince the stink eye. "Tryin to get on my good side, *Gringo*?"

"What did you say?" asked Cane. Always the curious one.

"*Swishers*: Shallow Water Sailors, the Coast Guard," Vince answered.

"And what kind of sailor are you, Mr. Hardesty?" Venus asked, looking around his office for clues. She spotted a picture of Vince with two other officers in tan fatigues.

"The kind in deep waters," he answered. "I'm in the Reserve."

"Venus looked back at Vince. "Reserves for what?" she asked.

"Uh, Navy," he said.

"Great! But *we're* the only navy in the country that can arrest and convict, *sailor*," she said, shaking her head with a smile on her face.

"Points for you, Guardy," Vince replied, and then he got down to business. He had the twins review everything they had seen Monday night. He asked Sandy and Venus to start thinking about what they thought was going on. While they talked, Vince kept watching Venus. She was a few inches shorter than him, spoke with a slight Mexican accent and talked with her hands. Her silk black pony tail bobbed up and down with agreement and her body seemed to sway when she disagreed, which was not at all disagreeable. In fact, she was mesmerizing. He noticed both boys were staring at her, too. They gave him a glance and wiggled their eyebrows. He nodded. He thought the same. He realized he was thinking like the twenty year olds.

Venus said she had given the picture of the guardsman on the skiff to a friend of hers who worked at Coast Guard headquarters. Maybe they would get a lead on the guardsman and whatever was in the drop.

When the meeting broke up, Vince asked everyone to meet again tomorrow evening at his house. When they heard "198 Boston Boulevard," Venus and Sandy said, "Oooooh." The twins said, "What?" Sandy said, "You'll see. Learn some Dee-troit history."

As Vince escorted everyone out the front door, Al told him that Cane was taking him down to the Friend of the Court for a DNA test, hopefully proving that he was the father of his three year old daughter. Vince wished him luck, though, that had little to do with it. The deed was done. He noticed Venus stopping Sandy and talking to him excitedly. Sandy motioned him over.

"Vince. I think you need to hear this."

"What can this *re-zervist* do to help?" Venus asked.

"Maybe more than you think, Venus," Sandy said.

"What's up?" Vince asked.

"After I dropped off the picture to my friend, Angela, I got a call from a friend of the family. One of my Dad's best friends did not make it home yesterday."

"Sounds like a missing person's report, Sandy," Vince said.

"Listen to the rest, Vince," countered Sandy. "I think you'll be interested in this. Go ahead Venus."

"His name is Alberto Martinez and Monday was his last day on the job. He retired after thirty-five years and he was due back home in Dearborn yesterday afternoon. He kept an apartment in Port Huron during his work week, and yesterday he was supposed to rent a U-Haul trailer, load up and be back in Dearborn by evening. He never showed up. His daughter, a one of my best friends, called him several times and got nothing. She drove up to Port Huron Monday night only to find all of his stuff in the apartment, his car parked out front, no trailer and no dad.

"She couldn't get a hold of his boss. She called one of his work friends and he said her dad had left work at the end of his shift after a long going away party. He saw him leave at two o'clock and heard that he went through a warehouse on his way to his car, but that was it."

"Okay. So what would all of this have to do with me?" Vince asked.

"I don't think it has anything to do with you, *Mister* Hardesty," Venus said with a scowl.

"Tell Vince where your friend's father worked," said Sandy.

"Border Patrol. He was a Port of Entry shift supervisor."

"*Oh*," said Vince.

"Oh, is right," Sandy said.

"So, does *Oh* mean you can help?" asked Venus.

Sandy Answered, "Yes."

Vince answered. "Yes, it does."

## Chapter 5

### Wednesday Morning

Al and Cane headed down Grand River Avenue to downtown. You could tell when you crossed into Detroit. Not because there was a sign that said *welcome*, but because you felt like you weren't. Sometimes you got the feeling that not much of anything was welcomed, especially from the suburbs, if you could call Redford a suburb. What stood out was how much was missing. Block after block of empty lots, missing storefronts and houses. There was a scattering of churches and liquor stores, both offering some kind of spirit to fill in the gaps between the haves and the have-nots.

Eventually you could see a lone tall cylindrical glass building with its side towers: the Renaissance Center. Built to start a renewal in the almost abandoned downtown years ago, the actual renaissance started only recently, adding renovated theaters, new sports arenas, casinos, and restaurants in anticipation of Super Bowl Forty. Detroit got the nod when the Ford family agreed to build a new indoor stadium downtown, taking the Lions out of the Pontiac Silverdome. Coincidentally, they named it *Ford Field*.

Closing in on the wheel of downtown, Cane drove by the old Michigan Theater, a gutted opera house turned into an ornate parking garage. Seeing it gave Al a small smile in the midst of his nerves, remembering the last time he and Cane ventured down here. They were locked in all night on the second floor of the garage, enduring take after take of a diverse crowd dancing in a music video. Eminem and his crew were belting out *Lose Yourself*. Everyone guessed it was the title song of the yet untitled movie he was filming *in the 313*. After what seemed like a long all-nighter, they got to meet their hero: a white guy from one of Detroit's older suburbs who made it in rap music, and like Al, a young dad in the middle of *baby mama drama*.

They came around the Grand River curve and turned right on Griswold past the downtown DOT bus exchange. Al jumped out of the van and went through the tall brass rimmed doors of the Penobscot Building. His appointment was for eleven a.m. and it was already quarter till. Cane said he would drive around and be back in an hour. The current high price for gas was cheaper than parking in the city.

Just inside the door was a closet-sized snack shop with a small cardboard sign that read *gun drop*. Al figured the Family Court didn't want matters settled with violence in its own building. He asked a guard where he should go for Friend of the Court. He was told to take the stairs on the other side of the double glass doors across the lobby. A guard would direct him to the basement for a security check.

As he headed to the stairs, another guard called to him and asked him what floor he needed. Al glanced back and for a split second froze. He quickly looked away and kept moving toward the stairs. "Second floor," he yelled, continuing to walk away from the guard.

"Downstairs. They'll put you on the elevator," she said.

He quickly got through the glass doors and to the stairway, hoping that his hoody had hidden his face. He glanced back at the female guard and confirmed that it was her. He hoped she hadn't recognized him.

Half way down the stairs, the line had stopped. He looked back up the steps hoping the guard hadn't come after him. So far, so good. From below he could hear commands for the line to separate men and women. When he reached the bottom, he saw why it went so slow. The line down the stairs became two lines along two long tables and a metal detector in front of two separate elevators. The guards ordered everything emptied from pockets, taking off shoes, checking purses, checking IDs and patting down everyone. Al now understood the *gun drop* in the snack store.

As he moved down the line into the basement floor for inspection, he again looked back up the stairway to see if the guard had come to get a better look. He didn't see her, but one of the guards received a phone call and started searching faces. The same guard took an extra minute to look at his driver's license while he was being searched.

Once through the line, he and six other men were crammed into a small, musty elevator to go up to the second floor. Everyone stood silent until somebody in back said, "Just like jail." Everyone gave a nervous laugh that subsided back into silence. The elevator was so slow it seemed like they were going up twice as many floors. At this point, he just hoped there wouldn't be a power failure like they had a few years ago. He had heard of people stuck in elevators and not found for a couple of days. He looked around and saw others might be thinking the same thing.

The doors finally opened and everyone gave a sigh of relief and walked out like they knew where they were going. For Al, it was confusion. What was once a large two-story lobby of marble and brass was now a labyrinth of cubicles with a wall of windows. He wondered past several before spotting a guard at a desk waving him over. He broke out in a sweat.

"What do you need, son?" said the man with a deep baritone voice.

Al swallowed and cleared his throat and said, "a DNA test." It came out in a high pitch.

"Go to window three. Tell them you're here for the DNA and they'll send you back when it's your turn."

He said thanks and headed over to the window. He was then sent through a door at the end that led down a long corridor made of the back side of cubicles and what was the original row of marble counters. He looked up the side and saw a gold and white ceiling that looked as if it belonged in a ballroom.

Reaching the door with the DNA sign, he walked into a small seating area with a receptionist at a small grey desk. She asked him to sign in and take a seat in one of the plastic chairs. He wanted to ask where the baby and her mother were, but he suspected they were in a different room. No fights or screaming matches would be allowed in the hallowed halls of the FOC. Wait until you were back in the neighborhood. After sitting there for a half hour, his hope of seeing his daughter today, even just for a minute, faded away.

He was called into an inner room by a nurse. When he sat down, she gave him a form to read, and told him to print his name, address and social security number, his baby's name and then sign at the bottom of the page. She then asked him to open wide. She took a long Q-tip and rubbed it against the inside of his cheek. She put it into a long plastic tube, pulled off the label and attached it to the container. She thanked him and showed him the door.

He went back out into the waiting room and asked if he needed to stay. He was told no. That was it. He felt embarrassed. His anticipation had turned into a huge let down. It was so uneventful, all he wanted to do was get out of the building as fast as he could. He skipped the slow elevator, found the stairway and ran down the steps two at a time. He felt like he was twelve again, running from the law. He ran pass the guard station and out the front door, hoping Cane was idling out front. Not there. Al started pacing back and forth along the corner of the building. Everyone on the street seemed to be walking briskly to a business meeting. Some had frightened looks, others serious. No one seemed to smile. It was either lawyers, accountants, engineers or litigants.

The van pulled up a few minutes later. Al jumped in and looked back at the glass doors. The female Metro Guard was staring at them with a phone to her ear.

Cane took off with a start. "An Escalade just pulled up behind us."

"What Escalade?" Al Asked.

"*The* Escalade," Cane answered as he sped around the corner through a yellow light. The Escalade ran the red and drove up behind them. They made the next light and sped down Congress Street and took the ramp to the Lodge Freeway. The Escalade ran up and hit them, bouncing the van.

"Son of a bitch," Al yelled as he fought to get his seat belt on. Cane kept the van under control as they merged onto the freeway. He hit the gas. The Escalade pulled up right on their tail.

"I think these guys are serious," Cane said.

"The guard in the Penobscot was the woman from the park. She must of called the guy."

"No fucking shit!" Cane said. He pushed the accelerator to the floor.

"What we gonna do?" All asked.

The Escalade sped up around them and pulled alongside.

"The dude's got a gun, man," Al said.

Cane looked out his window and saw the driver pointing the gun at him, waving him to pull over. Cane looked ahead and saw that the car in front of him was taking the next exit and he would be able to pull ahead. He punched the pedal and the old van leapt ahead. The Escalade driver swerved around the car blocking his way and was back to tailgating. The van reached ninety miles an hour and started vibrating.

The Escalade pulled up around and beside them again, this time swerving right into the van. The van lurched toward the right shoulder wall of the below ground level section of the freeway. The Escalade hit the van again and Cane lost control just long enough to veer up onto the shoulder and clip the wall with the right front tire. *Bang!* The tire blew.

"Sonofabitch," Cane yelled. He fought the steering wheel as it pulled to the right, causing the side of the van to crash against the concrete with a loud metal screech, slowing them down.

"Shit!" Al screamed, leaning away from the passenger door as it repeatedly hit and scraped against the wall. "Stop, man. Stop! You're gonna kill me here."

"Shut the fuck up," Cane yelled back, taking his foot off the gas. "Just shut up!" The van slowed and came to a sudden stop.

The Escalade pulled in front of them and stopped. The Metro Guard jumped out and ran back toward them. Cane reached down under his seat trying to pull out a crow bar when the guard reached his door and yanked it open. He grabbed Cane and pushed the barrel of a gun in his gut.

"You guys are coming with me."

"Run for it, Al," Cane yelled.

"I can't. The door's jammed."

"This way," the guard yelled. "Now!"

Al crawled across the middle console as the guard watched with the gun visibly pointed at Cane. Al got out of the van, and a Detroit Police cruiser pulled up behind them squawking his siren. The guard hid his gun as the officer stepped out of his car.

Al leaned toward Cane. "I've never been so glad to see the cops in my whole life."

"Thanks for stopping, Officer," the guard said. "I was just stopping to see if these boys were alright. It looked like they were going too fast and lost control."

"Please step back and get into your vehicle, Sir," the officer said. The guard turned and did as he was told. Al gave a sigh of relief.

"I can explain, Sir," Cane said.

"Get back in your vehicle, both of you. Then I want license and registration."

"Yes Sir. That guy clipped us and ...."

The policeman put his hand up. "Shut up! License and registration."

Al crawled back across the console and Cane got in and pulled out his billfold, slid out his license and flipped down the visor and grabbed the registration. He hesitated for a second, but then opened up his billfold again and took out Detective Sandelen's card. He handed all three to the officer.

The policeman looked at the license, the registration, and then Sandy's card. "What's the detective's card for? Trying to get out of a reckless driving ticket?"

"No, Sir," Cane answered. "Just please give officer Sandelen a call, please. This involves more than just hitting the wall."

They looked up as they heard a roar. The Escalade took off.

"What the hell?" the officer said.

"I'm telling you officer. This is about more than meets the eye."

"You're not *telling* me anything, Son." The officer turned away and walked back to his car.

"Great, Cane. Piss off the *po-leece*," Al said shaking his head.

Cane turned to face Al. "Shut up!"

"Maybe that's what *you* should of done."

Cane just gave him a look and they waited in silence.

Ten minutes later, the officer came back and handed Cane his license and registration. "Detective Sandelen will be here in a few minutes."

"Thank you, officer," Cane said.

"Thank God," Al added..

An unmarked police car pulled up and parked in front of the van. Pat Sandelen got out of the car, walked up to the officer, told him to call the Detroit PD wrecker service and have them put the van in impound. He turned to the van and opened the driver's side door.

"Thanks for coming, Mr. Sandelen," Cane said.

"You guys get out of the van and get in the back seat of my car."

Cane saw the serious look on his face and got out of the van without a word. Al slid across the console, the driver's seat and stepped out.

"That Metro Guard chased us down and slammed us into the wall."

"Get in the car," Sandy said.

~~~

"Did you catch them?"

"Caught 'em on the Lodge. Pushed them into the wall. And..."

"Great! Where are you holding them?"

"Not."

"What?"

"A cop pulled up and ordered me back to the car. While he was carding the boys, I took off before the officer could look at my license."

"Shit," she said.

"Sorry."

"Well, at least the cops didn't get your name."

"Yeah. At this point, that would have been the worst case scenario."

"But, we've got the name of the bastard who hit me with the bike. I want that little fucker."

"I want 'em both."

~~~

Young fathers were filing out of an agency transport van and into St. Vincent's for a lunch meeting when Al and Cane ran past them through the front door. The inside door was open for the group, so the twins also ran past Juanita without their usual "hello" and up the stairs. Vince heard the running and looked in the hall to see them heading his way. He motioned them into his office and told them to wait there. Then he saw Sandy following behind them. He told the director he was meeting with a young dad and would join the group later.

"What's up?" Vince asked Sandy.

"The twins were run into the wall on the Lodge. Al said it was because a Metro Guard at the Penobscot recognized him from the Lake Erie Park."

"Great," Vince said.

Vince walked into his office and saw a scared look on Al and Cane's face. "Tell me what happened," Vince asked.

They both started talking at the same time. Something from Al about a guard, a female guard at the Friend of the Court, and Cane started talking about getting hit by a car and how nothing good could come from their spying on a couple in the park. Vince put his hands up and silenced them both.

"Al, you first."

"Vince, I went downtown to do my DNA test. As I was walking toward the elevators, a guard called out asking where I needed to go. I looked over and quickly turned away. I kept on walking because it was the woman from the park. I'm not sure if she got a good look at me, but I answered that I was there for Friend of the Court and she yelled out to go down the stairs. I waved an okay without looking back, but just as I was going down stairs, I shot a quick glance back and she was staring at me. She was just picking up her phone to call somebody."

Cane jumped in. "That lady saw you, man, and she called her partner to let him know she recognized you. Then she probably called downstairs to have someone check your ID while you were getting searched."

"Yeah. One of the guards was checking me out and taking an extra minute to look over my Driver's license. And then to top it off, I had to wait for Cane outside the front doors when he picked me up. When I got in the van, the woman guard was staring at me through the glass doors."

Cane jumped in. "The Escalade from the park pulled up behind us and followed us to the Lodge. We were going ninety trying to lose him, but the driver pushed us into the wall, waving a gun at us. He tried to pull me out of the van. It was the guy from the park."

"This has gone to a whole new level," Sandy said. "They're goin to track down Al and then Cane, where they live and where they work."

"Hold on," Vince said. "The twins have done nothing illegal, but apparently this couple has, and they believe they've been compromised, and..."

Cane interrupted, "I think they knew something was up with that act Al put on with his bike. Besides, they *were* doing something wrong, and after dark and in a Metro Park where they thought they wouldn't be seen. Then here we come with a video camera. They didn't look very lovey-dovey before we arrived, and they weren't very happy when they saw Al and me. It looked like they were caught in something illicit. I've seen that look before."

Vince didn't like hearing either that Al was recognized or that Cane had seen that *look* before. It confirmed that they had done more than a few stake-outs for Dave. Now the female half from the drop had gotten Al's name and address, and the male half had committed a hit and run in broad daylight. He didn't like where this was headed.

# Chapter 6

Wednesday Noon

"Get Seaman Roberts," Coast Guard Lieutenant Commander Clay Starke called from his office to his assistant. He watched her go around her desk to the base public address system and grab the mic to announce Jason Roberts' name. It was always a pleasure to watch Angela walk in any direction, whether she was in uniform or not.

Angela Weaver, Coast Guard Petty Officer, First Class, took a quick look back as she went around the desk. She caught the commander's stare at her back side, let out a sigh and kept walking without showing her disgust. Not that she minded certain men admiring her backside, but her boss was another matter.

She keyed the microphone and called in Roberts. She went back to her desk and got back to work, looking busy. Venus had given her the assignment of finding the guardsman in the picture.

A few minutes later, Jason Roberts walked through the door and right up to Angela's desk. "I understand the commander wants to see me?"

"Yes, Honey. Hold on." Angela picked up her phone and called Starke.

"Yes, Sir," she answered into the phone. "I'll be going to lunch, Sir. Thank you, Sir."

"You can go in now." She gave Roberts a smile so he would look at her a few seconds more and she could check out his face. A look in the eyes with a smile always got a man to look a little longer, even if their boss was calling. When he went into the commander's office, she double checked the picture just to be sure. It was Roberts.

Angela was tempted to call Venus right away, but she had warned her not to make any phone calls in the office. They would only speak with each other face to face at their usual place. And since it was five minutes till lunch, and Starke would take a while with Roberts, she grabbed her purse and headed out the door.

Jason Roberts walked into the commander's office and Starke waved for him to shut the door.

'Take a chair Roberts."

"Yes, Sir."

"You'll be on duty all next week," the commander said as he pointed to a small white erasable board he brought out from under his desk. Knowing Homeland, Starke knew his office was bugged. As he continued talking about roster duties, he asked his real questions on the white board. *Drop delivered?*

Roberts answered, "Yes, Sir."

Starke cleared the dry erasable board and wrote *crew settled in?* as he asked "How's the new place?"

Roberts nodded his head as he answered, "It's been great, Sir."

Roberts had been transferred to the Detroit station in June by Starke. Roberts had served under him in Desert Storm, defending the oil ports in Basra. Then they were reunited at Homeland Security Training at Quantico two years ago.

Starke had Roberts and his crew in New Orleans for the rescue operations after hurricane Katrina. Roberts had rescued three brothers from a rooftop near the West End Boulevard after the 17th Street Canal levee gave way. They were Palestinians. When Roberts told Starke about them, he smiled. He told Roberts to follow up on them and have them moved to Dearborn. He had them housed in a three bedroom upstairs flat where Roberts and a roommate lived downstairs. It was the perfect set up. Nothing like being in the right place at the right time.

~~~

Matek Hakam woke up in his new upstairs flat just off Hubbard Street in Dearborn. He could hardly believe he and his two brothers' good fortune.

Thanks to a Coast Guard officer in Detroit, they were living in a newly remodeled three bedroom apartment with a large living and dining room. It came with a new stove, refrigerator, garbage disposal, washer and dryer. Unbelievably, they were now living in a city with the largest Arab population in the United States. He was thankful for their blessings from Allah. It made last week seem almost like a forgotten nightmare.

He and his brothers had been rescued out of the devastation of New Orleans from hurricane Katrina. They made it out alive because they made it to the third story attic from their second floor flat. When the 17th Street levee broke, it was just a matter of minutes before the water rose to their second story windows. They scrambled up into the attic and then onto the roof and watched the horrifying spectacle around them. After two days and nights of huddling together on the roof, a Coast Guard boat arrived and took them to safety. Now a week later, they were recovering in a new upstairs apartment where there were no hurricanes.

Over the last couple of days, the officer updated their green cards with immigration, signed them up with welfare and food stamps, and had one of his guardsmen check in on them every day. Yesterday, Mat, as the guardsman liked to call him, and his brothers, Musa and Malik, were given bus cards and a map of the Smart Bus and Detroit DOT routes. It was good to get out.

Musa, his middle brother, ever the skeptic, thought it was all too good to be true. Maybe this apartment was just the officer's way of keeping an eye on them. They were Muslims after all. Malik, the youngest, just wanted to meet Arab women, and here they dressed so provocatively, showing legs and arms and sometimes more. He was the happiest to be in Dearborn. Mat wanted a good job and to make enough money to pay for their apartment and buy a new car, preferably a Ford. Here, he saw them everywhere.

Mat got up and looked out the front window. He saw the guardsman drive into the driveway of the two-story duplex, get out of his car and look up to the second story window. Mat stepped back and wondered if Musa was correct. Just then, his two brothers got up and walked up behind him.

Roberts came through the door and yelled out, *"Honey, I'm home!"*

A short wiry black guy with a goatee came down the hallway waving one hand back and forth and raising the other to his lips to say *shut up.*

"What's up Paul?" Roberts asked.

Paul Peters was now waving both hands in front of him and pointing up to the ceiling. Jason finally got the message. The guys upstairs were talking and Peters had them on the recorder.

Roberts still couldn't believe he was living with this guy. Peters was born in Lebanon, his father Jordanian and his mother French. It wasn't just that he was dark skinned. As a jock, Roberts had never gotten this close to such a nerd. Peters was meek and geek all the way, never saying much, never doing much, but glued to his laptop or some new electronic toy that military types wanted him to test out.

Little did their upstairs neighbors know what Peters was seeing and hearing. And his total unobtrusiveness was to his advantage. Any number of times this guy could be in the field doing surveillance with a wire or a video feed and no one noticed him. The crew called him the *Invisible Man.* One of the other Detroit guardsmen said the title fit in more ways than one, but Roberts wasn't that into literature.

In a loud whisper, Jason asked, "What'ya got?"

Peters motioned him to the back bedroom turned office, his domain. It contained a couch, the most modernistic office chair Jason had ever seen and two walls of electronics. Once through the door Peters pointed to a fifty-inch HDTV flat screen with all the bells and whistles that Peters had excitedly rattled off when he brought it home. It didn't make much sense to Roberts then, but now Jason could see why Peters had been geeked by it. They were seeing right into the living room of the guys upstairs like they were sitting in the room with them. It was so clear that they could see all the way through the living room and into the kitchen and read the digital clock on the microwave.

"Holy shit," Jason said.

"That's right. And check this out." Peters picked up the remote and turned up the sound. No matter where anyone was sitting or moving around, every word could be heard clearly, even though most of it was in Arabic. To Jason it was like a TV show needing subtitles. With his background, Peters spoke fluent Arabic, Hebrew, and French. He didn't need translation.

"How'd you do that?"

"The tall wizardry of Paul. I bring every one up short."

Jason looked at Peters and smiled. Starke was going to love this. And he understood why this guy got into electronics, and why Starke brought him to the United States after the Iraqi war.

"These dumb ass *muthafuckers* are not far off the boat," said Peters.

~~~

Angela waited until she got into her GMC Envoy before getting on her cell phone and calling Venus.

"Venus? Found him. Now don't say anything. Just meet me at *The Spot*."

"Will do. See you in twenty."

Growing up on the East Side of Detroit off Jefferson on Marquette, Angela Weaver could walk down the street and see Belle Isle, the Detroit Yacht Club and beyond that, Lake St. Clair. The then famous mayor of Detroit, Coleman A. Young, lived nearby in the historic Joseph Barry subdivision that looked like Grosse Pointe on the Detroit River. She lived on the other side of the water works plant in the Marina District in a shot-gun two story brick house that her dad was constantly fixing with duct tape and bailing wire. Walking around Belle Isle gave her a spectacular view of not only what locals consider the *Other Great Lake*, but also the beautiful Canadian side of the river, as well the international ships and the shiny boats and yachts that came through the channel. It became her escape and eventually her dream. One day she would sail away.

In high school she discovered that the way a poor black girl could get a boat, sail away and see the world was with the Coast Guard. They had a station right on the island and they motored up and down the Detroit River and from Lake St. Clair to Lake Erie all day long. That dream had kept her in school, kept her grades up, and kept her from getting pregnant.

*The Spot* meant the old house where Angela grew up. After her parents died five years ago in a car accident, the result of a police chase on Jefferson Avenue, she bought out her brothers and sisters for a few thousand dollars and set about restoring it. She was still working on it and didn't yet live there, but it became a meeting place to a select few friends like Venus.

When she pulled into the driveway, she saw Venus wave from her Jeep. How Venus had beaten her there was a miracle, so like the spitfire chopper pilot. Angela waved her into the driveway so that her Jeep wasn't left on the street. They quickly hugged and went into the house without saying a word.

Angela shut the door behind them, took Venus's hand and led her to the kitchen. Venus started to say something, but Angela held her finger to her lips and shushed her. She went over to the counter and turned on the radio to WJLB. Rap music blared from the speakers. She then flipped on a switch marked *vent* next to the light switch above the sink. She waved Venus to the kitchen table, put her chair next to hers and sat down.

"We can talk now," Angela said.

Pointing to the radio, Venus asked, "Why the music?"

"It's an old trick. I used it whenever I didn't want the family listenin in on me and my friends."

"But no one's here but us girls."

Angela nodded her head toward river. "Don't you work for DHS?"

"Yes, but they're not listening to us."

"You bet they aren't. Besides the radio, that little switch I turned on is more than a vent. I have this room rigged with an electrical interference system. The walls are lined with a wire grid that gives off radio waves that cancels all electronic devices."

"You can't be serious. Aren't you being a little paranoid?" Venus asked.

"Really? You know better than that. They can listen to anybody, anywhere, anytime. Besides, the FBI's probably got ears on the Mayor's mansion on the other side of the water works as we speak. So, I take all precautions. Plus, there's somethin I haven't told you about me, and I didn't think you needed to know until now."

"Oooh. A secret."

"Yeah. I worked with the intelligence service while stationed in Iraq. I have a knack for languages. In high school I was in the honor society and we had a student exchange program with other schools in the area. I chose Dearborn and got to know a Mid-Eastern family and learned Arabic. So, when my commander saw me speaking to the locals in Iraq, they drafted me to monitor radio and phone communications.

Believe me, they can listen from down the street or," pointing upward, "satellites away."

"Holy shit," Venus said.

"Yeah, holy somethin, and somethin's goin on. Why else would you have me lookin at a grainy picture of a Coasty movin crates off a skiff? And now that I've ID'd him, you can tell me what's goin on. Spies, traitors, terrorists?" Angela pointed a long finger at Venus. "Spill the beans, *Sister.*"

"We don't know. A Detroit Police detective who's the police liaison with Homeland gave me this picture and said to find him."

"Oh! Oh! Oh! It's *we* and *detective* and *police* and *Homeland* is it? This is some serious shit you've stepped in, Honey. Now you've got me in the middle of it too."

"I'm so sorry, Angela. I didn't mean..." Angela quickly cut her off.

"Shush! Let me just say thank *you.* And I'm goin to *stay* right in the middle of *it.* I'm back, in black."

"AC/DC, 1980."

"What?"

"You know, music trivia," Venus answered.

"Right," Angela said. "The Coasty in the picture is Jason Roberts. I'll keep tabs on him and anybody else you want. This is goin to be fun."

Venus shook her head. "I don't want you to get into any trouble at work. I don't want you to become a suspect of anything that might...."

Angela suddenly stood up nearly knocking over her chair and stated pacing. "Don't worry about those dumbass Coasties. They think I'm just a stupid curvy black bitch that can only do office work. I put on that act and sway my ass around so they keep thinkin that too. They don't know about my intelligence clearance, so they'll never suspect me of nothin. They transferred me to the Dee-*troit* office so they could have someone here from the home team, somebody who knows the neighborhood. Besides, I wanted to be back home to care for my parents." She threw her arms out wide, "Hell, I am the neighborhood, and I love it. I've got everything now. I escaped the hood, saw the world and came back home with some money and pride. Made my mama and daddy proud," she said, pointing her hands upward.

Venus stood up and wrapped her arms around Angela. Angela brought her arms down and held Venus. "Don't worry 'bout me," she said. "I'm the right person, in the right place, at the right time."

Angela sat Venus back down and scooted her chair closer. "So, besides the detective, who else knows about this?"

Venus looked away. "A guy named Vincent who works at a Church, he's Navy Reserve, and two young men who attend there."

"A minister? Now we've got the church and God in this too? Lord Almighty, we're beyond Homeland now. We've got heaven and hell in the mix. But, wait a minute. I've got one more question. The two young men, are they cute?"

"They're too young for you, Angela."

"I'm a fit Guardy-*woman*, hee-lo girl."

"Yeah, you're sailing an office desk with a telephone at the helm," Venus corrected.

"I walk and sway around in there; always on the move," Angela said pointing at Venus.

"You've got moves, all right," Venus said nodding. "But I think you'll be more interested in the detective. More your type."

"Black, huh?"

"And good looking. A friend of mine and more your age."

"Hey. Maybe I want to get my groove back."

"Whatever," Venus said, rolling her eyes.

"What's his name?"

"Sandy. Pat Sandelen."

"Will you introduce me?"

"How about tonight? We're meeting at this guy Vincent's house in Detroit. 918 Boston Boulevard."

"Are you kiddin me?"

"No kidding. I don't how he got that place, working at a church. How about I'll pick you up."

"And *take me to the mansion*," Angela sang.

"Don't you mean, *Take me to the river*? Al Green, 1974."

"Whatever."

Chapter 7

Wednesday Afternoon

Vince picked up the phone on the first ring. Juanita said it was Detective Sandelen.

"Yea Sandy."

"Venus called. She found our guardsman. It's a skiff captain named Jason Roberts. He's stationed at the Coast Guard on Mount Elliott. He currently lives in a first floor flat in Dearborn. Venus said he served with Commander Clay Starke in the Iraqi invasion and they worked together in the Katrina rescue in N'Orleans. Venus flew rescue and said that Starke coordinated the Coast Guard's mission.

"Roberts got any record?"

"Record's clean. I checked."

"Is Starke involved?"

"No way of knowin' at this point. Venus said she has a friend in the Commander's office. She's the one who found Roberts. Matched with the picture when he was called in to speak with Starke just at lunchtime."

Vince paused, then asked, "Can we trust this friend of Venus?"

"If Venus says she's okay, she's okay. She works for Starke and she's a Coasty too. Calls Motown her hometown. She's been cleared by the Guard and Homeland."

Vince thought a minute. "So has Roberts."

"Point taken. Either Roberts is out on his own smugglin' something illegal, or for all we know, it's some kind of undercover job. Does Miller know about the drop?" asked Sandy.

"No. I had the boys give him the first video file of the couple in the SUV. I have the wireless camera video and Cane's second video shot of the skiff. Did you get to run the SUV's license?" asked Vince.

"Yep. Belongs to a private security company called Metro Guard where both are employed. So, now we've not only got an agency of Homeland Security, we've got a local private security company, and the only way we know about any of this is because of a suspicious wife?"

"Sounds crazy. But, remember, we got crazier," Vince answered. "First, they shot at the twins, and now a hit and run."

"You've got to get them boys out of town 'til this thing cools down," Sandy said, knowing that Vince had another house or two where he could keep the boys out of harm's way. "Vince, we either got real lucky and found some slick money-makin' operation, or we've sniffed out some covert operation with national and local security that could make us and everyone else very unlucky. As the FBI would say, *inter-fering with national security, obstructing justice,* or some other kind of bullshit."

"Right, Sandy. Got to keep our head down. You know anybody at Metro Guard?"

"Yeah, I know a guy. And I'll keep snoopin' around, but Vince, the minute this looks legit, I blow the whistle. I don't need no blowback."

"Got it. You check in with your guy at Metro and I'll see you tonight."

~~~

Vince hopped off the I-96 Jeffries to the Davison, turning onto Linwood, past Central High School to Boston Blvd. He saluted his neighborhood security detail, the security detail he had beefed up for The Boston-Edison Historic District.

The District is bordered by Boston Boulevard on the north, Edison Avenue on the south, Woodward Avenue on the east and Linwood on the west. Early residents of Boston-Edison included Henry Ford, James Couzens, Sebastian Kresge, and Joe Louis. It contained over nine hundred homes and most were constructed between 1905 and 1925, ranging in size from modest two-story brick houses to impressive mansions. Today it is a multi-racial, multi-ethnic neighborhood with people from diverse occupations and professions. Vincent loved it.

His address was well known among the elite circles of Detroit: 918 Boston - the Motown Mansion. Berry Gordy had left it empty twenty years ago when he moved Motown to L.A. A local attorney bought it in 2001 and restored it over the next two years. Vince picked it up for a cool 1.5 million and then had it renovated to fit his needs, adding the latest in state of the art security: infrared, heat and motion detectors, cameras, on call and mobile security by Metro Guard.

The Mansion has a black walnut paneled living room, a marble-columned grand ballroom, seven dining areas, four bedrooms, each with their own fireplace and bath, a private gymnasium, a wine cellar, a billiards room and a two lane bowling alley. Vince converted one of the bedroom suites into a separate apartment on the second floor for his housekeeper, Maria Alvarez, installing an elevator for her that opened into the kitchen, *her kitchen*.

Vince converted the first floor carved quarter-sawn oak library and parlor into offices for the company that made it all possible: an oil import company, his oil import company. It was named with a derivative of his actual first name, Reginald: *Regent International Petroleum,* or *RIP,* as he liked to call it. It produced enough money for him to be an undercover watchman on the country's porous northern border and to volunteer his time at St. Vincent's.

The company was set up by his father-in-law, a Kuwait oil sheik, first in gratitude and then in sympathy. In gratitude for saving him and his family's lives from retreating Iraqi Republican Guardsman during Desert Storm. He was assigned as Director of

Security for the sheik and Kuwait's rulers. He eventually married the Shiek's daughter and lived in the family's seaside compound while training the Kuwait Special Forces. In sympathy when Saddam Hussein's revenge unit returned and his wife and their unborn son were caught in the crossfire, as well as two of his young Special Forces soldiers. He lived in the desert for a year afterward, mourning the loss of his family. He moved to the SEAL team's Little Creek Naval Amphibious Base, Virginia Beach, Virginia, to train recruits. He joined the reserves and moved to Detroit in 2002.

He hired Detroit natives who were graduates of Wayne State to maintain the company and paid them handsomely. Some had even bought houses in the Boston Historic district to be close to work, that is, as long as *Mister Man* installed comparable security systems in their homes. Others lived in the University district lofts and had him install the same security for them as well. He checked on his staff daily; if not in person, by secure phone, and presided as CEO at the monthly business meetings, or for any crisis that might arrive.

There was a pool house across the driveway that faced Boston with an Olympic size indoor pool and an outdoor screened-in patio. An unattached five car garage with a three bedroom apartment above it sat directly behind the mansion. All of the buildings were connected through a series of underground tunnels, as well as to the back of the property, where there once stood a livery.

He pulled the Impala into the drive, hit the garage door opener and drove into the middle bay next to his brand new all-black '05 Shelby Cobra Mustang GT. In the next bay sat his classic '62 Corvette that he drove every August in the Woodward Dream Cruise. When friends saw his vehicle hat trick they asked him why he always drove the Impala. His answer: "It's a Chevy in the Motor City, a regular old car in a rusty old town," not to mention it had a V-8 corvette engine. The other two were for special occasions, like fast driving or showing off. Whenever he heard the commercial, "Gee, I could have had a V-8!" he smiled. He had three.

He walked up the drive to the back door, activating the interior and exterior motion detectors for the garage, deactivating the one for the house. He had purchased the cars and the house with cash when he moved to Detroit, his father-in-law encouraging him to do something with his money. He also upgraded his dad's Pentwater cottage on Lake Michigan into a five bedroom house.

Living in a city with a burglary rate two and half times the national average, his final line of security and what he considered the best alarm system known to man, greeted him at the door. A brown and black German Shepherd named Greta. As he liked to say, "A German name for a German dame. Greta Hardesty!"

He told Sandy that he was looking for a good watch dog for his new house. Sandy found a year old Shepherd that had failed bomb squad training. Vince gave her a home and put her through security training. Over the past couple years she had become the early warning system before intruders stepped on the property. She couldn't detect gun powder or bomb residue, the reason she had failed training, which was just as well with the arsenal he had stored in a vault in the cellar, a cache of every weapon he had ever fired in the military. He believed in his dad's solution to everything: *Always keep handy what you know how to use.*

Greta could smell and hear somebody on the front sidewalk or on the other side of the fence before the electronic security devices could engage. All in all, the Motown Mansion was the safest house on the block, the safest house in the country, well, next to his boss's house.

He petted Greta vigorously in the mud room and then entered the kitchen. It was all white, hence the need for a mud room, with marble top counters and the latest appliances. Maria called it *a dream come true* and she had strictly forbidden him from attempting to cook in *her kitchen*. He was only allowed to make coffee and use the microwave. He'd only burnt the popcorn a couple of times.

He walked to the vaulted living room and sat down. He laid his head back and looked up at the carved wood ceiling. The house was big and beautiful, and lonely. The RIP staff in the house and the young dads at St. Vincent's had filled part of his life, especially Al and Cane, but there was still a deep, dark hole in his heart that his wife Rachel and their unborn child had once filled. His father-in-law had told him to look for a new wife, but his CIA's SAD, Special Activities Division, operations made that very difficult, if not impossible. He'd pretty much given up finding the next *right* woman, but the words he learned in the desert gave him hope.

*"Why am I discouraged? Why is my heart so sad? I will put my hope in God!"*

Over the years, the deep crushing pain of grief had turned into a literal heart ache. His military discipline, along with professional counseling, had served him well in moving on, as well as moving back to his home state and serving in the way he knew best.

*What will be the next chapter in my life? Only God knows.*

~~~

Commander Clay Starke sat at the head of the table in the first floor flat of Roberts and Peters in Dearborn. The meeting was planned to be a Wednesday afternoon Tigers party, so everyone came in wearing the old English *D* hats or jerseys. Peters thought it was lame because the team was under five hundred and most fans had given up on the playoffs, but they had the game on anyway with sound up to cover their conversation. He thought the Arabs upstairs were out anyway, so he really didn't think it was necessary. What the hell, undercover is undercover.

Richard Daniels and Janet Schmidt sat together. Both were more than a little nervous about the possibility of having been caught on video. Across from them sat the bean counter, looking uncomfortable in a jersey and cap. Next to him sat the Border Patrol officer, who in contrast to the couple, was as calm as a corpse. At the opposite end of the table from Starke was the man no one knew and Starke had never introduced. The group called him *Mr. Stranger*. He always wore a business suit and never smiled. They assumed he was the real leader, probably the military higher up who had spear headed the oil for cash embezzlement in Basra.

"Let's get started," Starke said. "Since last week, we've put our Arabs in the flat upstairs. Roberts picked up the package and made the drop to Dick and Janet at the Lake Erie Metro Park. Problem is we believe the drop from Roberts was caught on video by two young men who were contracted to spy on them by Dick's wife. Janet spotted one of the young men at the Penobscot Building. What did you find out?"

"The boy is Alpha Canis Major," Janet answered. "He came through the Penobscot building to Friend of the Court for DNA testing. He lives in Redford and he works for Miller Studios, a photography and videography business."

Paul Peters spoke up. "Miller specializes in weddings, bar mitzvahs, birthdays, and, as we *now* know, private dick work. Alpha also has a twin brother, Cane Noris Major, who also works for Miller. Here are their pictures. Recognize them?"

Janet and Dick looked at the pictures. "That's our bicycle boys from the park."

"How did you get these?" Janet asked.

"The techies don't share," replied Peters with a smile on his face.

"Janet, do you think that he recognized you?" asked Starke

"Definitely, yes. When he walked by me at the Penobscot, I inquired where he needed to go. He looked at me and then quickly turned away and kept walking as he answered." She said nothing about Daniel's car chase and subsequent hit-and-run.

"Okay. Let's assume he did," said Starke. "That means, ladies and gentlemen, we have a possible breach in the operation. As you know, we are down to five days and counting. No one outside of this room knows about the operation, and now we have two boys who have not only seen our drop, but possibly have it on video. We have to get to them to get any evidence that might incriminate us. The question today is how."

Daniels spoke up. "We follow those guys, pick them up and give them the national security speech. They turn over the video and then we keep them in a safe place."

"What if they've shown it to someone else?" Janet asked.

Stark answered. "We simply ask them. We visit Miller's studio, give him the national security speech and threaten him with shutting down his business for conspiracy. He gives up the twins and we do a search of their places until we find the video."

He looked around the table for a reaction, and then to *the Stranger*. The man nodded.

"The wireless micro camera recorded remotely. Someone else has a copy." the calm man said.

"We'll burn that bridge when we get to it," answered Starke. "Peters will locate them and Dick and Janet will pick them up. Once you have them, take them to Homeland on Jefferson for interrogation. I'll take care of the questioning. We've got the perfect deception and we're not going to let a couple of amateurs screw it up." Starke looked at Peters. "After questioning, we bring them back here for safe keeping until the mission is complete. Clear?"

"Got it," Peters said, nodding reluctantly. He hated personal contact with detainees and everyone knew it.

The Port of Entry officer spoke up. "I have what we need for the transfer. My, uh, *partner* has been most cooperative. Just part of his appreciation for all I've gotten for him over the years, and that's not to mention the handsome reward he's going to get when we're done. Peters? You can install the pallet screens. The trucks are ready."

"Good," Starke said. "Now, I don't need to remind any of you that we only have five days to go." He paused. "This mission has been in the works for months. So, we've got to find and apprehend those *Major* pain-in-the-ass twins. With them and their video out of the way, we'll not only pull off our operation, we'll actually be heroes. Any questions?"

No one spoke. The *stranger* in the suit nodded, stood up and left.

"That's it," said Starke.

Everyone got up and headed for the beer and snacks. There would be a lot of drinking and final preparations for the rest of the afternoon.

Chapter 8


Wednesday Evening

Vince and Greta welcomed Sandy out on the back patio of the pool house that sat across the drive from the mansion. The ribs were grilled to perfection and wrapped in aluminum foil to tenderize, the sweet smell of the southern style barbecue wafting through the air. Vince was grilling the hamburgers on the other side of the grill, the smoke floating up through the colored party lamps.

"Sandy, grab me another beer out of the cooler and one for yourself if you want."

"Thanks," he said, putting his hand into a large chest full of ice and pulled out a bottle with an orange label. "Ooh wee. *Bell's* brew from *Kal-mazoo?*"

"Nothing better than an ice cold one on a hot night," Vince answered.

"Speakin' of hot nights, I got a call this afternoon. Remember that meetin' I told you about last month?"

Vince stood up straight. "Yeah?"

"It's tonight."

"Short notice."

"As always."

"What time?" Vince asked.

"One in the a.m."

"Location?"

"Belle Isle Boat House."

"The abandoned marina?"

"Yep, that's the one." Sandy said. They heard a car door slam. Sandy looked toward the street and saw the twins get out of a yellow cab. Greta began a low warning growl. "Well, lookee who's here."

Al and Cane walked down the driveway with their eyes as round as saucers staring at the mansion and then the pool house. Cane stopped suddenly, grabbing Al's arm. A large brown and black German Shepherd stood before them, head down, teeth bared.

"Greta! *Cool*."

The dog sat, looked up and raised a paw.

Vince walked over to Sandy and said, "We'll talk later." He waved the twins over. "Hey guys!"

"Your dog, Vince?'

"Yep."

"She bite?"

"Yep, but I've called her off. Her name's Greta. She's cool with you. Shake her hand."

They did, carefully

This *your* place, Father?" Al asked.

"Yep. Come on over here, guys. The big house is off limits."

"Okay," they said in unison as they walked to the patio. Cane walked up to the grill. "Smells good, I'll take two." He looked over at Al who was fishing through a cooler. "Want a brew, *Bro*?"

"Stop. I'll take a pop," Cane answered.

Al picked out a bottle and cocked his arm back. "Go long, then turn and *Fay*-go."

The bottle arced through the air. Cane trotted into the yard, caught it, twisted off the top and foam squirted all over Cane's shirt.

"There you go, Bro," Al said with a laugh

"Thanks for the Red Pop cologne," Cane said.

"You're welcome," Al said. "I understand some girls are coming over, right Father?"

"Ladies are coming over, gentlemen. Just remember, it's a meeting and you need to be on your best behavior," Vince said.

"Yeah," said Cane.

"And the ladies are a little too old for you guys anyways," Sandy chimed in.

"That's all right. We like cougars, right, Al?"

"Speak for yourself, *Dawg*," said Al.

Just then Venus and Angela drove in the driveway. Greta gave her signal again and Vince called her off. "Make nice with the ladies." Greta wagged her tail.

Venus parked her Sahara Jeep and was greeted by Greta with a paw up for a shake. Angela greeted her as well. The twins mouths dropped open and o's eyes lit up.

"Wella, wella, wella," exclaimed Sandy. "Now it looks like a party. Welcome ladies. And you fellas can put your tongues back in your mouths."

Venus and Angela giggled and posed like teenagers. "Like, what-*e*-ver," they said, and broke up laughing.

Angela gave Venus a look.

"Oh, hey Sandy, this is my girlfriend, Angela Weaver, a desk Coasty at the Guard."

Angela held out her hand, "*Thanks,* Venus. I'm a real Guardsman, Sir, First Class Petty Officer, and I'm *sooo* glad to make your acquaintance. Venus has told me all about you. And, yes, I'd be glad to come by your place and give your neighbors a thrill. Would this dress be all right?" Angela turned around to give a complete view.

An embarrassed grin broke out on Sandy's face. He took her hand, shook it, then put it above her head and gave her a twirl. "Yes, yes my dear. Hell, you could come in your sailor outfit for all I care."

Angela moved in closer and gave Sandy a peck on the cheek. He put his hand on his cheek and then to his lips. He looked over at Vince and said, "Well, son, you do know how to make it a party."

Vince had been busy with the grill and hadn't really paid attention to the give and take between the girls and Sandy. He finally looked up and gave the girls his best smile. "Welcome. I think everything's ready. Why don't you guys grab some drinks, get your plates and sit down while I get the ribs off the grill. I wanted to keep this looking like a party, just in case."

*Just in case*, thought Venus, looking at Vince with a frown. *Is this guy serious, or too serious?*

Sandy saw the look on Venus's face when he went over to the cooler to get a drink with Angela. He turned up the music and walked over to Venus. "It's all right. Just takin precautions. We know Al got made downtown by the couple who were at the drop. You know how Homeland can be. We'll talk later."

Vince flipped the burgers on a plate, grabbed the ribs from the grill and put them on the table. He grabbed a bottle of champagne and poured everyone a drink. He stood at the head of the table and raised his glass. "To the Nine-One-Eight Boston party. Welcome to my home."

Sandy raised his glass and said, "Here! Here!" Everyone clinked glasses together across the table and took a drink.

"Dig in," Vince commanded.

"Got any chips?" Al asked.

"Better believe it," Vince answered. "*Better Made.*"

"Only Dee-troit 'n Michigan for our *Mista'* Hardesty," Sandy added. He leaned toward Vince and said, "Party, huh?"

"Yeah, you know. Conspiracy, Homeland, the Guard, we've got all the players."

Sandy rolled his eyes, shook his head and smiled as he pulled some meat off a rib and sank his teeth into the best of Detroit, southern style. He looked around the table and saw Al and Cane trying to be cool around the ladies. Venus winked at him when he caught her glancing down the table toward Vince, but Vince was too busy to notice.

"How about those Tigers?" Vince asked.

Everyone looked at him with a scowl and groaned.

"I'm waiting for Hockey," Cane answered. "You girls like hockey?"

"Football, baby," replied Angela. "Go Lions!" Another groan emanated from the table.

"*Futbol, Gringo,*" Venus said with a smile. "The real football, or as you Americans call it, soccer. Next year my country should at least beat Japan."

"Roundball's my game," Vince said. "And the Pistons are my team, the 2004 NBA Champions! They made the finals this past year. See, I was born a Hoosier."

"A what?" asked Venus.

"Hoosier. I'm from Indiana where basketball is king. I was born in Gary, but my dad moved us up to Scottville, Michigan when I started junior high. He took a teaching job there to get us away from the steel mills. He taught me the beauty of basketball."

"Wait. What is a *Hooz-yer*?"

Sandy could see a light in Venus' eyes as she was questioning Vince.

"It's just something people are called from Indiana. It was probably an American Indian word that meant something derogative about settlers."

"Huh. Yes, we Mexican Americans have some names for you white boys as well."

Now Vince was smiling. "Like what?"

"You're a nice man, *Muchacho*, and throwing us a party," Venus said with a big smile. "So, I will not say anything nasty about you and your two friends here, even though you have sucked us into some kind of, how did you say, *par-tay*?"

Vince swallowed and said, "Yes, but right now we'll just stick to the par-tee. But back to your favorite names for me and my kind."

Venus's face flushed as she looked into Vince's eyes. "Well, there's always *The Man*, and *Gringo*, and..."

"Oh, come on Vee, tell him the good ones," Angela said as she winked at Sandy. "You know, like, and this is with translation, instead of *Gringo*, *Grinnin-to-go*, and instead of *The Man*, *Under-the-covers-Man*."

"Angela, you're embarrassing me," Venus said, looking back at Vince.

"That would be a first," Sandy said. "Venus embarrassed. It's usually the other way round," nodding back at Angela as he said it.

Vince felt his face flush. "Is it hot out here, or is it just me?'

"Oh, it's warming up, Mr. Hardesty. It's warming up," Angela answered.

Al and Cane were watching all of this, their heads swiveling back and forth like watching a tennis match.

"Am I missing something?" Cane asked.

"Yeah, honey. You're missing somethin all right," Angela said. "We'll find you boys some nice girls, or as you like to say, *hook you up*."

Cane answered, "Oh, Al's already hooked-up, more like jacked-up. Got an ex with his baby and now his ex won't let him see her. Paying the dime, but can't get no time."

"I'm so sorry, Honey." Angela said shaking her head. "I know there are women out here lookin to get pregnant and get out the house. Is she black or white?"

"White like me," Al said.

Angela broke into a laugh. "White like me, that's cute. I'm sorry for your baby mama drama. How old is she, Hon?"

"She's three and she's the one that's cute. Got my red hair. I miss her."

"Oooh. A little girl. When's the last time you got to see her, Honey?"

"About three months ago, in court. Now my ex says she ain't mine. So, I had to go downtown to get a DNA test. That's when I saw that lady, the one with the guy at the metro park. The one on the video."

"And she's with Metro Guard just like the guy," Sandy said.

"The plot does thicken, doesn't it?" Venus said.

"We'll talk about this after we eat," Vince interrupted. "How about the Super Bowl coming to Detroit? Think the Lions will ever get there?"

Everyone groaned again.

"This is probably the only way we'll get to a Super Bowl," Sandy said. "The Ford's build a field, *and they will come.* Or more like, *we will go.* Anyone who's police, Coast Guard, Metro Guard or *federales* will get to go downtown and literally surround the place, and never *see* a down."

"Well, get *down!*" Angela said.

"*Backstreet Boys,* 1996," Venus commented.

"Oh, no," Angela said.

"Yeah, we'll be in the back streets, alright" Sandy said.

"No. That's not what she meant," Angela answered. "She meant the singin group, *Backstreet Boys.* They recorded *Get Down.* She's a music trivia junkie."

"Really?" Vince asked with a smile.

"*Si, Gringo.*" Venus smiled back.

"That's my girl," Angela said.

"*My Girl,*" Vince sang. Sandy joined in: *My girl, my girl.*"

"The Temptations, 1964," Vince interjected.

"Not you too?" Angela asked Vince.

"Yea, yeah, yeah," Vince answered.

"*She Loves You,*" The Beatles, 1963. First major recording to be heard in the United States," Venus stated.

"Oh, great!" Angela said. "Please stop."

"*Stop, in the name of love,*" Venus responded. "The Supremes, 1962. The most successful of the Motown acts, and America's most successful vocal group.

"Who as the *Primettes*, were the sister act to the *Primes*, later known as *The Temptations*." Vince added.

"Ooh. You do know your Motown history."

"Helps to be in the *house*."

"Hey, excuse me. What's for dessert?" Cane asked.

"Thank you," Angela interrupted.

"Stroh's with Sanders," Vince answered.

"Beer with chicken?" Al asked.

"No silly," Angela answered. "Ice cream with fudge topping. This is Dee-*droit*. Don't know much about its history?"

"*Don't know much bi-o-logy,*" Venus sang.

"Sam Cook, 1958," Vince said with a chuckle.

"Good one," Venus said.

"Really?" Angela asked. "Can we get back to dessert?"

"Yes sir," Sandy interjected. "Again, with Vincent, everything is Motown or *Pure Michigan*"

"*Your trip begins with Michigan dot org.*" Vince added. "And *your* trip begins tomorrow."

"We're going on a trip?" the twins asked in unison.

"Yes. I think we need to get you two out of town for a while. We'll talk after dessert."

"Cool!" they replied.

~~~

After desert, the group retired to the basement of the pool house. It had a lounge area that ran the length of the Olympic pool and opened up on the back patio. On the lower level it had a two lane bowling alley and a billiards room that Vince converted into an office with walls covered in book shelves.

"No one will be able to hear us in here. I've got an electronic eavesdropping deterrent in the walls."

"Woo hoo," Angela said. "Big time security. I noticed the motion detectors on the property. What are you, a spook?"

"Not really. Just Navy reserve with security issues. Served during Desert Storm."

"Uh huh. Venus and me served in Iraqi Freedom," said Angela. "I did boat duty, she's a *chopper dropper.*"

"Army search and rescue," chimed in Venus. "Flew a Black Hawk then. Fly a Dolphin HH65 now."

"Cane and me was Boys Scouts," Al said. "Does that count?"

Everyone smiled. "More like girl scouts. Scouting girls don't count," Angela countered.

Vince interrupted the give and take. "Okay, let's review what we have so far."

Sandy started. "We've got one covert drop from a Coast Guard, Homeland Security skiff. We know the guardsman's name, Lieutenant Jason Roberts. He served with Commander Clay Starke in Iraqi Freedom."

"Next, we have a couple in an Escalade at Lake Erie Park picking up the drop," continued Vince. "The gentleman is Richard Daniels. Works for Metro Guard at one of the Federal Buildings downtown. This we know from David Miller, the twin's boss, who sent them to the park. And now, thanks again to Al, we know that the *other* woman also works for Metro Guard at the Penobscot Building."

"You boys been busy," Angela interrupted. "We now know how good you twin spooks are."

"You're welcome," said Al, looking proud of their work.

Cane looked at Al and mouthed *shut the fuck up.*

"Busier than you know, Sister," Sandy said. "The dude tried to abduct 'em. When they left Friend of the Court, the Escalade followed and ran them into the wall on the Lodge. Cop cruiser got there just in time."

"That's a miracle. So, both of you will stay here tonight," Vince stated.

"Great," Cane said. "Now we gotta be on lock down, just like the good ol' days, huh Al? Where is this place, Vince?"

"Did you see my garage out back when you drove in?"

"Yep," Cane said.

"It has a three bedroom apartment on the second floor. It has more security than a bank, but you won't be on lock down. You can go in the yard, over here to the pool house, just not in the mansion. Staying here means you'll be safe at night. During the day, we want you to be in contact with me or Sandy on a regular basis. I'll give both of you a secure cell phone that can't be traced."

"Isn't this kind of overkill?" asked Cane.

Sandy looked both of them in the eye. "We have personnel from Homeland Security and two guards, one federal and the other with the court. They're after you, and don't mind shooting at you or crashing you in broad daylight. We don't know if it's legal or illegal. They recognized you as the guys who saw the drop and got video. They now know who both of you are, where you live, and probably everything you've ever done. So, no, we don't think we're overreacting."

"Great," said Cane. "There goes my love life."

"You got a love life, Honey?" asked Angela. "You got internet in that garage, Vince?"

"Wireless throughout the property, with encryption, of course."

"See, Honey, you still got your love life."

"Very funny," Cane shot back.

"What about you, Al?" asked Venus, looking at him with concern.

"My daughter is all the love life I want right now. At least she's not in the middle of this."

Vince shot Sandy a look.

"Yeah, right," Cane said. "He'll try to pick up anything with cleavage."

It was Al's turn to mouth *shut the fuck up.*

"And how about you Vince?" asked Angela. "Got a love life?"

"Uh, yeah sure. I've got Greta."

"I mean a *girlfriend*, not a *bitch*," Angela responded.

"No. No other bitches right now."

Angela elbowed Venus. She slapped Angela's arm away, but smiled at Vince as she did it.

"What about the trip?" Al asked.

"I'll tell you about it on the way to the apartment."

~~~

After the meeting, Vince led Al and Cane to the five car garage down the driveway and around the backside of the mansion. On the way, Vince held Cane back and told him he would have to keep an eye on his more impulsive brother. Cane rolled his eyes and said, "Wish me luck."

Once upstairs, Cane ran to the living room where Al already had the surround sound stereo blasting. One wall contained a home theater and entertainment center, equipped with Projection T.V and six large reclining chairs with cup holders. Off to the side sat an authentic theater popcorn machine and a kitchen with a double door refrigerator stocked with drinks. The twins yelled with excitement.

Vince showed them their bedrooms which also had their own TV with sound systems and X-Box video games. They both thought they had died and gone to electronic heaven. They whooped and bounced up and down on their beds as if they were ten years old again.

Vince reminded them that they were guests here and the purpose for staying at his place was to keep them safe and out of sight, at least for tonight. He would be sending them to the west side of the state on Lake Michigan. They cheered.
~~~

He reminded them that they were to only use the secure phones he gave them and not use their regular cell phones. Later he wished he had confiscated them.

Chapter 9


Wednesday Late Night

Vince and Sandy said goodnight to Venus and Angela. They headed back to the secure room to talk about tonight's meeting.

"So, this about the *Partnership Capo*?" Vince asked.

"More about the dirty eastside cop who's been dealin' with the *Capo's* nephew. The boss has been straight and legit since servin' time, and he doesn't want some young punk to send him back by association. So, he's meetin' me at the Boat Club to tell me what he knows."

"How can I help?

"With a little insurance. I don't want the punk or the cop to show up and ruin our little chat. Since you were a SEAL, I thought you could swim 'neath the McArthur Bridge and hide out behind one of those concrete supports. You'd have a clear shot from there."

"I can do one better than that," Vince answered.

"How's that?" Sandy asked.

"Let's head to the house and I'll show you."

"Hot damn! To the arsenal," Sandy said, rubbing his hands together. "Before we go, I've got somethin' to say about the twins."

"Shoot," Vince said.

"How appropriate. Anyway, I don't think we should let the twins out of our sight. You can keep an eye on them at St. Vincent's, but if we let them loose to work with Miller, or anywhere, we're throwin' 'em to the wolves."

"Right, Sandy. I've already thought of that, and I've got a couple of friends to take them out of town. But if we keep them totally out of their normal weekend work, it will leave Miller in the lurch and look suspicious to whoever is behind all of this. For now, it should look like the twins suspect nothing about what they saw."

"Yeah, I suppose so. But let's call Miller and let him know what's goin' on. Have the guys work the weekend, but that's all. Maybe one of us can get invited to the wedding, or go as an assistant and keep close to the twins."

"One of us, meaning me, Sandy?"

"Well, cops look like cops wherever we go. Plus, I'm the liaison to Homeland. One of these guys is goin' to recognize me. You're the only unknown in this party. Besides, I know you know how to do recognizance." He waited for Vince's response.

"All right. I'll see where they're working this weekend. We'll figure out how to assist from there."

"You don't look much like an assistant. You look more like a one dee-termined dude who'll knock the lights out of anybody getting' close to those guys," Sandy said.

"I've done undercover work, Sandy. I can look less intimidating when I want to."

"Okay, Stallone."

"More like Sylvester," Vince with a wink.

"Well, I do need you to be the sly *cat* tonight."

'Yeah, let's go to the house and get ready."

"One more thing, Vince. Thanks for introducin me to Angela."

"I think you'll have to thank Venus for that," Vince said.

"And, speakin of Venus, *you're* welcome."

"For what?" Vince asked.

"Really?" Sandy said.

Vince gave his best *I-have-no-idea* look and raised up his hands in resignation. "What?"

"The Navy SEAL of the kiddie pool. Come on. Let's get into the deep water you're more used to."

~~~

Sandy had been told by an FBI Academy instructor how deep and the kind of water Vince had been at home in during the Iraq war. He had gone out for beers with the instructors, and in the course of the evening, after trading war stories, Sandy asked if there was anyone besides police or FBI who had gone through the academy living in the Detroit area. He was looking for someone to bounce ideas off of, or do undercover work, without raising inter-agency suspicions. The trainer told him there were other officers and agents he could hook up with but Sandy wasn't satisfied. He wanted somebody off the books.

After six more beers for the instructor, and six half beers for him, pouring out the other half whenever he picked up the next round, the trainer got to an actual war story about a now undercover guy who *"retired"* and recently moved to the Detroit area. He said he would never forget him.

*Hardesty was a part of what he called the Freelance Unit of the CIA Special Activities Division. If they were called in, you were FUC'd up. They were the crème de la crème of Special Forces, recruited from the Navy's SEAL team and the Army's Delta Force.*

*We were doing a pre-invasion insertion into Kuwait before Desert Storm. I was the radio operator from intelligence, my partner, the computer geek, and this guy Hardesty and his Arabic speaking friend Bashnir, who he called Bashem, or something like that. We did a HALO. You know what that is? It's a High Altitude, Low Opening parachute drop from thirty-five thousand feet. Make you think you were earning a halo, man. Anyway, we dropped right down into Kuwait City. At night.*

*We boarded a domestic Delta Airlines DC-10. "Delta, Huh?' I asked Hardesty. "Isn't that the name of one of your Special Forces...?"*

"Ironic, isn't it," he answered with a smirk. "I'm former SEAL; Bashnir's Delta Force."

He said they sat in the front half of the plane, which looked like any other passenger jet, for the eight hour flight to Heathrow. They disembarked and ate breakfast while the plane refueled for the next leg to the Ben Gurion Airport in Tel-Aviv. Once there, the jet taxied from the runway straight into one of the military hangars. They were briefed on the operation while the Delta plane emblems were removed and replaced with Saudi Arabian Airlines. Afterwards, the crew took a siesta and ate dinner.

They re-boarded the plane, only this time through the rear door. The back half of the plane was empty of passenger seats; replaced by wall seats with tall oxygen tanks strapped next to each one, and the HALO equipment that each mission member needed: sport glider parachute, altimeter, automatic parachute activation device, oxygen mask and tank, helmet, night vision goggles, insulated gloves and free-fall boots. As well, each member was issued a Special Forces survival pack: field camouflage suits, tactical knife, a silenced .22 caliber pistol and the modified 5.56mm M4 carbine rifle. The M4 is a shorter and lighter version of the M16 assault rifle with sound suppressors and a single shot grenade launcher attached underneath.

*What was normally a two hour flight from Israel to Kuwait, took five hours, heading south over Saudi Arabia to Dubai and then back north over the Persian Gulf to Kuwait. Two hours from the target, Hardesty gets up from his seat and gives a demonstration like a stewardess.*

*"Ladies and gentlemen, please fasten your seat belts and put on your oxygen mask, like so. Hook the hose to your wall tank and begin breathing pure oxygen. Do not at any time unseal the mask from your face. If you do, you will experience what divers call the bends. For them, it results from rising to the surface too fast and causing nitrogen bubbles to build up to fatal*

levels in the bloodstream. For you, HALO divers, it prevents nitrogen build up in the blood when free falling from thirty-five thousand feet at two hundred fifty feet per second, one hundred seventy miles per hour. Not to worry, it's just like jumping out of a jet with no parachute. Our destination is the U. S. Embassy, and let me tell you, somebody's gonna get hurt, before this is through..."

"Oh, hell no!" Bashnir yelled. "Not more fucking song lyrics. Quick, somebody know this song? Next, he'll start singing it. If he does, we're all gonna hurt tonight."

"Heartache Tonight, the Eagles!" I called out.

"Thank God. Good job," Bashnir said to me. "You just saved us a delay in mission. Hardesty here is obsessed with anything Michigan and anything music." He looked up at Vince. "What? Oh, go ahead, give us the details."

"'Lyrics, Detroit's Glen Frey and Bob Seger, along with some guy named Don Henley, 1979." Everyone chuckled, then Hardesty finished with, "Have a nice remainder of your flight."

Me and my friend looked at each other and just shook our heads. How can this guy be so relaxed? We quickly put on our masks, bowed our heads and prayed. When we looked up, Hardesty gave us a thumbs-up. Nothing like a stand-up operator. But, I totally trusted the guy.

I'd been told we were in good hands with Hardesty. He was supposed to be one of the best. Before I met him, I expected some tall, muscle bound, crew cut, unshaven, foul mouthed warrior. What I met was a lean, five-ten, clean cut, wavy haired athlete built like a swimmer. He was relaxed, friendly and seemed like a straight arrow. Before the night was through, I knew he was a real life warrior, as sneaky and brave as they come.

Well, once we were near Kuwait, the DC-10 pilot called back to Hardesty. "Fifteen minutes to deployment." Hardesty closed and sealed the airtight interior door in the wall that separated the front and back sections of the plane. He called back to the pilot to depressurize the rear compartment at altitude, leaving the front compartment pressurized. He instructed everyone to open the valve on their backpack oh-two tank and unhook their masks from the plane's oxygen bottles and attach to their own. He showed me and my friend how to slip on a balaclava mask that covered the head and face with three holes, one for the mouth and two for the eyes, protecting us from the forty degree below tropospheric temperature where we would soon be diving.

We put on our helmets, strapped on goggles and stood in line. Hardesty checked everyone's chute and gear several times, and then strapped on our M-4 Carbines. The pilot called out, "five minutes to deployment." We stood and steadied ourselves with handles on the sides of the plane, lining up near the modified back door as the DC-10 decreased speed. The pilot called out "one hundred and seventy-five knots," two hundred miles per hour. When Hardesty saw that the cabin pressure indicator read altitude, he pulled the lever to hydraulically open the enlarged back door. Immediately a blast of incredibly cold air rushed into the cabin. It was a shock, to say the least. I could tell Hardesty was laughing at me as the freezing air rushed into the rear cabin. This causes the jet to slow to less than a hundred fifty knots, a hundred seventy miles per hour. The pilot called out, "Thirty seconds and counting."

Hardesty takes one last look at us and yells, "Follow me." I give him a shrug, not sure what he meant. So, Hardesty bends over and shows me a cross painted on his helmet. I nod, too nervous to do anything else. He signals with two fingers to his eyes and then to his helmet. I nod again and give Hardesty the OK sign. Hardesty turns to the door and jumps. I feel a push and before I know what's happening, I'm suddenly flying past the jet, or, I should say, the jet is flying past me.

*The earth comes into view and I see a cluster of pin lights in the middle of darkness. It looks like a night picture from a satellite. Then I spot the cross on Hardesty's helmet glowing in the dark. Weird. I follow it as we free fall for two entire minutes, the pin lights growing into buildings and street lights. You know how long that feels when the ground is rushing up at you? For-fucking-ever. We're going about a hundred twenty miles an hour, man, before we pull the cord. And when we finally do, it feels like somebody just grabbed you by the ass with a rocket.*

*Immediately Hardesty starts gliding in circles because he's located the target. A minute later we land right on the roof of the American Embassy. I'm thinking,* Fuck, this guy's good. More like, this guy's nuts. *Hardesty flips down his night vision goggles and motions me and my friend to do the same. He opens a door and we're running down an interior stairway. We meet Hussein's Republican Guards, and pop-pop, he hits them with his Carbine and takes them out left and right.*

*Down we go till we're in the basement. He pulls out a floor plan, runs down a hall, shoots off the lock, opens the door and there's the local embassy staff. Hardesty announces, "The Calvary has arrived," whips off his goggles and gives me a big grin. He pats me on the shoulder and says, "Good job. Get your radio up and running. Our work here is not yet done. It has only just begun."*

*All I could say between gulps of air was, "Don't fucking ever do that to me again."*

~~~

Sandy was meeting with one of the *Detroit Partnership* bosses, the local Costa Nostra out of Grosse Pointe Park. Even though the *Partnership* was into legitimate businesses, the meeting was about one of the *Capo's* nephews who had gone back to the old ways: smuggling drugs, illegals for prostitution and the extortion of those participating. Sandy was called in because the *Nuovo Partnership,* as the young crime boss liked to call himself, had recruited a mole inside the Detroit Police Department's North Eastern District. He wasn't sure if the meeting was truly about catching the *Nuovo,* or due to tough economic times, if the *Capo* was back to his old ways and using the cousin as cover.

Sandy was to come alone, no police and no escort, meeting the old boss on Belle Isle at the docks of the Detroit Boat Club, an abandoned rowing club since the 90's. The location guaranteed that no one followed him either by car or by boat without being seen.

Vince would cover him from atop a building across the river on Jefferson Avenue just east of the bridge to Belle Isle. Sandy asked how he could cover him at that distance. Vince answered that it was only a half a mile shot. Sandy was skeptical, so Vince pulled out his M40 bolt-action sniper rifle with silencer. He assured Sandy that he had been an expert shot from the time his Dad had taken him hunting to becoming a decorated sniper. He was a *natural.*

The meeting was held in the middle of the night with the bridge, the park and the river illuminated in the silver light of a full moon. All the better to see unwanted police backup. It was so bright, Vince could see Sandy drive over the bridge, up to the boat club, park and walk to the docks without his night vision goggles. Two men emerged from the clubhouse, one pushing a wheelchair containing the elderly *Capo*. Vince had no problem sighting them in, their silhouettes outlined against the fading white paint of the abandoned building. If necessary, it would be a turkey shoot.

Sandy was ordered to strip down to his underwear so he could be checked for weapons or a wire. Once done and cleared, the old man in the wheel chair shrugged his shoulders and said, "What can I tell you? Old habits die hard."

"I understand. Thanks for meeting. I know you've gone legit since you got out, but I hear talk about traffic on the Eastside. I'm closing in on a cop I think is in partnership with one of your relatives."

"I've heard talk, too," the *Capo* said. "And I don't like what I hear. You know I've educated all my sons and daughters, and they're doing well in their chosen professions. But, there always seems to be a black sheep in the flock. Uh, no pun intended." The *Capo* chuckled.

Sandy smiled, his white teeth gleaming in the moon light. "None taken."

The *Capo* continued. "I've heard of smuggling across the border," he nodded toward Canada, "using our trucks. Our fleet is doing well, so I don't want no suspicions. That means, besides the cop, I think we have border patrol involved."

"I've heard 'bout that too," Sandy said.

Just then, they heard someone grunt and fall from the Boat House second floor balcony and crash to the deck below. The body guards quickly turned around, pulling out guns. They saw the dead body and turned back to Sandy, pointing their guns at him.

"Don't," Sandy said.

One of the guards screamed as the gun flew out of his hand.

"What the fuck?" the *Capo* said.

"Put the gun down," Sandy told the other bodyguard. "I've got a sniper across the river."

The guard complied.

"Why don't you go see our dead guy."

The *Capo* nodded. The guard walked back toward the boat house, rolled him over and pulled out an I.D. "It's the cop."

"Sorry, Sir," Sandy said to the old man. "I've got a friend on a building off Jefferson watchin' us. I thought either your nephew or the cop might show up."

"I guess you were right." The *Capo* nodded toward Jefferson. "Some kind of shot."

"You have no idea."

Vince had seen a flash of moonlight on metal from the upper balcony through his scope. He flipped down the night vision goggles and spotted a rifle aimed at Sandy. Vince squeezed off a round with only the muffled sound of the silencer. The man dropped from the balcony and fell to the deck below. When the guards aimed at Sandy, he took a shot at one of the guns. When it flew out of his hand, everyone stopped.

When the conversation was over, he saw Sandy put his clothes back on and shake hands with the *Capo*. Vince smiled. *Another great night on the town.*

Chapter 10

Thursday Morning

Vince roused the boys out of bed and led them into the apartment kitchen. "Get your stuff. You're going on a little trip."

"Oh Faa-ther. It's too early," moaned both boys.

"You guys are going out of town, but I think you're going to like it."

"How's that?" they asked in unison.

"You like the beach?"

"Yeah!" they said in unison.

"You taking us?" Cane asked.

"No. Some good friends of mine are taking you, in a Jeep."

"Cool," they cheered.

Vince's phone buzzed. "Then get your stuff. My friends are here. You're leaving in ten minutes. Meet me down in the garage."

Vince walked out and saw a black four-door Sahara Jeep Wrangler with the driver's blond ponytail hair bobbing up and down as she got out and walked toward him.

"My dear Vincent." A petite woman with the bounce of a Cheerleader ran up to him.

"Hi Debra." They embraced and she gave him a quick kiss on the cheek. "How've you been, Vince?" she asked.

"Great. And thanks for the help."

"You know we're always happy to work for you, Vince, especially if it involves a beach." A brunette came around to the front and asked, "We can have one half of the house, right?"

"Hi Diane. Absolutely."

"Hello Vin-cent." Diane said in a melodic southern accent as she gave Vince a tender hug. "You're lookin good, big guy." She looked into his eyes. "But still alone. Wait. Is that a glimmer of..."

Vincent interrupted her. "Like I said on the phone, these guys need to be out of town for a while. They don't know either of you, and they don't know about you."

"And we won't tell, 'til later, that is," Diane said with a devilish grin.

"Story of our lives," Debra said.

"I'm sure they'll hit on both of you and decide between the two of them who's going to make it with whom," said Vince.

"This'll be fun," said Debra.

"The boys will be down when they finish packing their stuff."

Just then the twins ran downstairs and out to the driveway. They cheered when they saw a black Jeep, and their jaws dropped open when they saw the two women. Cane found his tongue first.

"Well, Hi. I'm Cane. What's your name?"

"Di-anne. Nice to meet ya, Cane."

Al went around to the driver's side and barely got out "Hi." It's hard to talk with your tongue hanging out.

"Hi, I'm Debra. Throw your stuff in back and get in."

"Yes Ma'am."

"No, I'm Debra, that's Diane."

"Yeah, uh, right. Okay, let's get goin."

Cane looked at Vince. "You didn't say your friends were *girls*, man. Girlfriends?" he asked.

"Yep." *You'll find out soon enough what that means.*

"I wish we could take our bikes. We need to keep training for a race we're ridin in next month."

"Just get going. I've got bikes where you're going. Call me when you get there."

"Right. You're the best, man," Cane added.

When the twins hopped in the back seat of the Jeep, Debra revved the engine and pealed out down the driveway.

~~~

Five hours later, Debra pulled off State Highway 31 to Lakeshore Drive just north of Pentwater on Lake Michigan. They pulled up to a drive with a wrought iron security gate. The gate opened after she called the code on her cell phone. They drove down a long paved driveway about a quarter mile to a sprawling two story house. Behind the house, they could see the crystal blue waters of Lake Michigan.

"Wows" emitted from the guys in the back seat as the ladies in front sighed. They pulled up to a central atrium that divided the house into two complete sections. Debra announced that the guys get the right side and the gals get the left. They would meet in a half hour on the back deck for lunch.

As the twins walked through the front door, they entered a great room the length of the house with a sitting area and a fireplace on one side and an opaque window screen the width of the room on the other. Cane found a panel on the side wall with a switch labeled *west window*. He flipped it up and the screen slid open revealing a panoramic view of Lake Michigan. More wows. They saw the beach, looked at each other and said, "Let's go!"

They looked through a side door and saw a bedroom with two single beds. They ran in, threw their bags on the beds and rustled through them to find their swim trunks. They quickly changed and ran back through the great room and kitchen to a door wall that opened onto the back deck. The deck covered the entire length of both sides of the divided house. They raced down the stairs to the sugar sand beach and into the September warm waters of the lake.

~~~

After Debra, Diane and the twins had left for Pentwater, Vince showered, shaved and dressed in a black business suit. He ate breakfast in the kitchen with Maria. He told her he would be gone most of the day up in Port Huron. He didn't say why. She knew better than to ask. He had told her when she moved in that it would be better if she didn't know all of his activities. That way she had deniability if ever questioned. When she had questioned him as to why, he had shown her his Homeland Security badge and ID. She was content not to know.

He went to the garage, dialed a code on his phone, and the far left bay door opened revealing a new Ford Shelby Cobra GT Mustang. A smile formed on his lips as he started the 450-plus-horsepower, supercharged, six-speed engine. When he had seen pictures of the concept car shown for the first time at the New York City Auto Show in March, he had ordered and paid for one with a metallic black exterior and all black leather interior. To make it totally black, he had all of the silver chrome replaced with polished black chrome, including the Cobra icon taken off and replaced with a black pony poised on the wide front black grill.

He held the ponies under the hood in check until he was out of the city on east I-94. He flipped on his Cobra XRS fifteen radar/laser detector. It had the longest range with the best possible advance warning for even the fastest of the instant-on radar guns. *A Cobra for a Cobra. One to go fast, the other to get away with it. Nice!*

"Giddy-up!" he said and gunned it. His body was pushed back against the seat and the feeling of a plane take off rushed through him. The car had been appropriately named after the WWII P-51 Mustang fighter plane. He hit a hundred and twenty in a manner of seconds. As cars and scenery flew by, an involuntary smile came over his face. "Yee-ha!"

Once he was cruising through traffic at a safe eighty miles per hour, he called Debra in Pentwater. She was sitting out on the deck overlooking Lake Michigan, saying the boys were doing great, and still trying to hit on her and Diane. So far, the boys didn't suspect anything and she and Diane were sticking with the *don't ask/don't tell* method they used in the military. She said they planned on taking his Humvee H1 down to the Dunes after lunch. He cautioned her about staying close to the twins and letting him know of anything or anyone suspicious. He told her about the concerns he had with the Metro Guard and how they might try to find them.

"Pay for everything the boys want, and don't let them pay with their own debit cards." Vince said. Debra assured him they could handle it.

Debra and Diane were former military MP's and now owned a successful private security company, thanks to Vince. Two good looking women were the best security you could get. With a blonde and a brunette around you, no one suspected they were bodyguards. They usually looked more like escorts. Yet, they could outsmart any man with the element of surprise, knew every kind of hand to hand combat move and were crack shots with any weapon.

They had left the military when someone did ask and did tell. They were lovers and they weren't going to deny who they were. Vince had worked with them on some undercover security details with Secretary of State Rice just after 9/11. They were both professionals and highly disciplined, but, when another Army security detail didn't get the high profile job, they did their own investigation and caught Debra and Diane coming out of a gay bar holding hands. They were reported and they were discharged, but thanks to the Secretary, with honors. Vince found out about it, called them and set them up in their own security business in Detroit, making himself their number one customer.

Vince passed the Selfridge Air Force Base exit at M-59, or Hall Road, as it was known to the locals, about twenty-five miles north of downtown Detroit. The Air National Guard Base was home to the Coast Guard Air Station. He thought of Venus and decided to give her a call and let her know where he was headed. She sounded surprised when she answered and Vince got a funny feeling in his gut. She sounded pleased that he had called, and then realized he had a big grin on his face.

"Well, Hi Vincent. It's so nice to hear from you, calling a girl back after having her out to your house."

*She made it sound like we slept together, a not unpleasant thought.*

*Where did that come from?*

Vince paused for a minute, speechless. "Uh, oh sure. I just thought I'd let you know I'm headed up to Port Huron to check on your missing friend, the Border Patrol Officer."

There was a pause. "Thank you, Vincent," she said. "I'm going to his home in Southwest Detroit this afternoon to visit his family. Our families are good friends."

He could tell the smile had gone out of her voice. "That's nice of you, Venus. Hopefully I can find out something up at the Bridge."

"Thank you again, Vincent," Venus said.

Vince cleared his throat. "Could you have your friend Angela keep a close eye on Starke and Roberts, as well as anyone else who calls them?"

Her voice perked up a little. "Sure, Vincent. Anything we can do to help." Another pause, and then in a more sultry tone, "How are those two cute and horny twins of yours?"

Vince got a dry mouth and a tightness in his chest. He licked his lips and said, "They're out of town, on a beach somewhere, ogling a couple of girls I sent along."

"Well, aren't you the *casamentero*. That's very sweet of you."

"Thanks, I guess. Uh, anyway, Sandy and I think the guys might be followed."

"Are they safe?"

"The two girls I mentioned are actually military trained body guards. They'll keep them safe, until the weekend anyway."

Vince had an idea. "The boys are supposed to be back at work with David Miller for a wedding this Saturday. So, I was wondering, if you were free Saturday evening, could you help me keep an eye on them?" *Feeling like a teenager asking a girl out on a first date.*

"Are you inviting me to be your date for a wedding *Mi amigo*? You are such a *romántico*." Her voice gave away a little chuckle.

"Well, what I mean is, that, well, we'll need both you and Angela, along with Sandy, to act like guests for a wedding so we'll be able to watch the twins without looking suspicious."

"What time is this wedding? I work on Saturday from eight to four."

"The wedding is at six. I could pick you up at your apartment at five."

"That works," said Venus. "I look forward to this, Vincent. But could I ask you a question?"

"Uh, sure." *Now I'm starting to sound like a teenager.*

"Why don't you just keep them out of town? Then we could just go to the wedding for fun?" Venus giggled.

"What? No, no. The twins need to be there so that we don't tip off Starke and whoever he has following them. We want them to keep thinking that the guys only got a video of the couple in their Escalade."

"Of Course, Vincent. *Es una broma, quizá.*"

"What did you say?" he asked, getting more uncomfortable, feeling sweat form under his arms and on his brow.

"Just kidding, *mi amigo*. I'm a fun girl, Vincent, and we'll have fun even if we are watching out for those bad boys."

"Well, we're not sure about that. I just don't want the twins in the middle of anything dealing with Homeland."

"Understandable, Vincent. I am so much looking forward to our date."

"Uh, yeah, sure. Anyway, thanks for volunteering."

"Do we need to get together to plan how we're going to be inconspicuous?"

*Venus, inconspicuous? With her looks and vivacious personality, I don't think so.*

"Uh, yeah. Sandy and I will meet you and Angela. Uh, how about tonight?"

"Great! Where and what time are we meeting?"

"How's the Detroit Beer Company down on Broadway across from the Opera House, say 6:00 p.m.?"

"Ooh. They have great nachos, *Muchachos,* to go with their homebrew. And we can practice our *amorosa* so we are ready for the wedding, *si*?

"*Si.* I mean, yes. We'll plan our act for the wedding." He began to imagine her in a low cut evening dress... *cut that out.*

"Till then, Vincent. I'll call Angela and tell her to be there."

"And remember, have her keep watching Starke and Roberts."

"Anyone talking with them, yes, I haven't forgotten."

"Okay, thanks, Venus."

"*Adios.*"

"Goodbye." Vince hung up and realized he was sweating. He cranked up the air. *What is it about this woman that makes me so nervous?*

He called Sandy and told him he was driving up to Port Huron to check out the missing Border Patrol Officer. He talked about meeting later downtown and about attending the wedding on the weekend to look out for Al and Cane. "Venus thought going as couples would be a good cover."

"Oh, really," said Sandy. "Well, I think it's a great idea too," thinking that he and Angela would make a fine looking couple. "Who's idea was it to go as couples?"

"It was my idea," said Vince. "Why? Would going on a date with Venus be a problem, or you with Angela?"

"No. No problem Vince. You just sound a little defensive about it, that's all. I like the idea of goin' on a *date*, as you put it, with Angela."

Vince swallowed and said, "Oh, okay Sandy. See you tonight."

"You bet. And Vince?"

"Yeah, Sandy."

"Watch your backside, okay? Don't be distracted thinkin' about Venus's back-side."

"Got it, Sandy," Vince said as he rung off. He was still sweating.

~~~

Venus called Angela on her cell phone at the Coast Guard office. After Angela walked out of the building, Venus told her about Vince's call. "He wants you to be on the lookout for anyone who's having conversations with Roberts and Starke. On the brighter side, we're having a meeting tonight to catch up with one another and make plans for the wedding on Saturday."

Once at the railing by the river, Angela spoke in a whisper. "We're goin to have us a good time while *servin* and *protectin*, aren't we Venus. I'll be lookin good next to that Sandman. How 'bout you, Venus? Gettin all lovey-dovey with Mr. Hardesty will be good for you too. Yep, you'll make a fine lookin couple."

"I think Vincent got embarrassed on the phone. I was playing him a little, told him it was nice to hear from him and I was looking forward to our date, the wedding date."

"Venus! I think you're puttin the moves on Vincent for real now. You are, aren't you?"

"He's cute, he's smart, he's good to people, and, of course, he has a great ass."

"You're hoping he'll be good for your great ass."

"We'll see. When I was kidding him about taking me on a date to a wedding, implying a serious date, he got a little flustered and reminded me that we were protecting the twins. So, I don't know how *close* we'll get."

"Venus, I have one suggestion. Tone it down a notch. Your Latin blood can come off a little strong for an older white guy. Give him a little space so he doesn't feel like you're smothering him.

"*Smothering him*, hmm, that could be fun. Okay, back to business."

"I thought we were talkin 'bout *bizz-ness*?"

"You know what I mean, your commander and the seaman."

"That sounds suggestive," Angela said with a chuckle

"Now who needs to tone it down? Have any unusual meetings or calls been going on with Starke and Roberts?"

"They've met in the office, but that's normal. Then they've left together for what Starke called a *Homeland meeting*, also not out of the ordinary. But there is something I looked into and maybe Sandy or Vince can make something out of it."

"What's that?"

"I was looking through some invoices and found that Starke has rented a two flat house in Dearborn. Roberts and another guy are living in the downstairs flat, and three guys they helped rescue in New Orleans are living upstairs."

"That sounds noble," Venus said with a hint of sarcasm.

"Oh, he got federal rescue money for the house, and only half of it is for the three men upstairs."

"Okay, skimming half for two guys who probably pay rent to him. He makes some spending money."

"That's not all. The three upstairs?"

"Yeah?"

"They're A-rabs, *Sista*."

"Okay. So, you *pro-filing*?"

"No, Venus. I haven't told you the best part."

"What's that?"

"There's also an invoice for fifty thousand dollars in surveillance and technical equipment for the house. I know because I've used it myself some years ago. That's company issue stuff."

"So, you're telling me that Starke rescues these guys, gets them an apartment where two of his men are living, and they're spying on them with government sanctioned equipment?"

"May-*bee*, bay-*bee*."

"Bring that up when we meet with Vince and Sandy tonight."

"Shouldn't I call that Sandman and tell him now?" asked Angela.

"No, not yet. Keep snooping and see if you can find out anything else."

"Well, I think I need to talk to Sandy anyway. I should call him."

"No! Angela, wait. You'll get to see him later tonight and you might have more to impress him with."

"Oh. I see. Impress him. Trust me. I was plannin on doing *that* anyway."

"So who's making moves now, my Angel?" asked Venus

"Angel. Hell, I'm going to be the *Devil with the blue dress, blue dress, blue dress. Devil with the blue dress on.*"

"Mitch Ryder and the Detroit Wheels, 1967."

"More music trivia, as usual. Back to the subject. I'm sure you'll be dressed for success at our little beer fest," Angela said.

"Who me? I'll just have on my little red dress," Venus said.

"Yeah, I'm sure you will, my little La-tin *la nov-eea*."

"*Sea lo que sea, mi ángel caído.*"

"What you call me?" asked Angela, but Venus had hung up.

Chapter 11

Thursday Mid-Morning

Melissa Miller greeted the handsome couple as they walked through the front door of Miller's Studio. "Can I help you?"

"Yes, we would like to speak with David Miller," Dick Daniels answered.

Melissa picked up the phone and called the back office. David Miller came through the lobby door and around the counter to greet the well heeled couple. David noticed first the serious eyes. He always noticed people's faces and eyes to see how he would photograph them. From the first meeting to the actual session, he would instinctively know how and where he would pose them. He would photograph this couple in a modern office setting.

The couple was impeccably dressed in business attire. The gentleman had a new haircut and had been closely shaven in a barbershop. The woman had natural make up as if done by a professional with a subtle shade of red lipstick. They would pose perfectly in the new Ernst and Young green glass office building on Campus Martius in downtown Detroit. They said as much when they introduced themselves. They were naming places like Compuware, The Ren Cen, and the Guardian Building.

He invited them to his portfolio room to review photographs of professionals in some of the same locations. He heard the gentleman close the door behind them when he was reaching for the Detroit album. He turned around to see the woman holding out a badge with *Metro Guard/Homeland Security* on the top of the I.D.

"Mr. Miller, my name is Janet Schmidt, and this is Richard Daniels. We're here to ask you a few questions about a video taken by two young men in your employ who were apparently spying on us in Lake Erie Park on Monday evening."

The gentleman sat down next to her and held out his I.D. as well.

"Richard Daniels?" Dave asked.

"Yes. Sound familiar? My wife is Lisa Daniels. She had you follow me."

"Right," said Dave. "Lisa Daniels. She hired me."

"We're sorry for the deception when we came in," Daniels said, "but this situation is of such a sensitive nature that we can't have anyone else hearing our conversation, and..."

The woman cut him off. "An incident occurred while one of your young videographers was recording the two of us." She took a notebook from her purse, looked at it, and faced him. "We know them to be Alpha Majors and Canis Majors. This happened this past Monday evening, Labor Day, September 5th. We need to review and secure the video clip."

"Look, my two young men were just doing surveillance of a possible tryst and you two are the suspects. You're the man and woman in the video."

"That is correct. We are part of an undercover operation involving national security. We need to see the video and take it with us. Have you made any copies of the file?"

"Undercover operation, really?" asked Dave.

"Yes, pertaining to national security," Daniels said.

"No. I've made no copies. I'll go get it. I've got it in the photo storage room."

"We'll go with you."

Dave led them back to the rear photography vault. He sorted through his files catalogued by date and pulled out the chip with the video. "You should know that I called your wife and told her that you were with a woman in the park."

"Yes, I've talked to her about it. My supervisor has talked to her as well and she understands that it was work related. She won't be calling you again."

*The way this couple looks*, Dave thought, *the two are sleeping together. The wife is usually right.*

Daniels took the chip. "I'd like to see it."

"Sure." Dave slipped it into a laptop on his desk. A video of the lake and then a scan of the parking lot with a Cadillac Escalade parked by the docks came into view. The camera zoomed in on the man in the driver's seat and a clear picture of Daniels appeared. Slowly the camera panned over to the passenger side, showing the head of what is clearly a woman. Suddenly the camera moved and a boy on a bicycle flew around the lot and then slid into a fall. The camera bobbed up and down moving toward the Escalade and the woman came into view.

"That's it?"

"That's it. He was pretending to video the lake and then panned back to your vehicle, zoomed in and got your picture, and then a shot through the windshield of your partner," nodding toward Schmidt. "When his brother came around to distract you with his fall, he got both of you together. As you remember, he put the camera down and helped his brother get up."

"Saw that. But sometime later, after dark, I saw the boy with the camera lying in the road, having fallen off his bike. Why was he still there?"

"You don't know these guys. Once they've done their job, they goof around on their bikes racing each other. They think they're going to ride on a professional bicycle team someday. Anyway, the next day they brought the camera in and this is what I got."

"Nothing else?"

"Nothing else," Dave answered honestly.

"Then, what's this?" Daniels asked as he pulled out a micro wireless camera from his jacket pocket.

"I don't know," Dave said. "I've never seen it before."

"We took it off our vehicle's rear window in the park."

Dave stared at the device and said nothing.

"We'll know who owns this later today. Better hope it's not yours. Must be your boys are sneakier than you thought."

"The only video I have is what I gave you."

Daniels eyed the man, but couldn't see any tell of a lie, but he'd have Peters check out the video chip to see if it had been edited. He knew this was too important of an operation to have a screw up at this point.

Daniels pulled out a business card. "Have the Major twins call this number at DHS and make an appointment for questioning."

"I'll tell them," Dave said.

"Tell them we've got their spy camera and we require the video."

"I will."

"Thank you, Mr. Miller, for your time," the woman said sarcastically. "We won't be returning this file since it now serves no purpose in your, uh, undercover work. And maybe you ought to leave young men out of your investigations and stick to weddings."

"You'll probably be getting a call from a supervisor at Homeland," Daniels said. "Be sure your private investigator's license is up to date."

"Yes, Sir. I will."

Chapter 12

Thursday Afternoon

Vince down-shifted the Shelby and took the I-94 Business/East Gratiot exit into Marysville. He decided to start with the Border Patrol Station Headquarters; get an authorized pass for all of the installations at the Blue Water Port of Entry. He hoped the station director could fill him in on Venus's best friend's dad's last day and if he had any theories on what might have happened. His cell phone buzzed as he turned on East Huron. The screen read Dave Miller.

"Hi Dave."

"Hi Vince. I'm using the phone you gave me. So this is secure, right?"

"Yes, Dave. They can't trace it. Where are you?"

"I'm in the back office."

"Go outside near the street. Your office is probably bugged."

"Oh, shit. I didn't think of that. Okay, I'm heading outside." Dave walked to the front of his office building on the always busy Southfield Road and got back on line.

"Vince?"

"Still here."

"The couple came here just like you said. They came in looking like professional models interested in having shots done in Detroit. But once they got me in my office, they pulled out some Homeland badges and questioned me about the boys and their video. They told me they were on an undercover operation, *national security* and all that."

"Did they ask for the file?"

"Yep. They asked me if that's all I had."

"And?"

"That's all I had. So, I gave it to them. Don't worry, Vince. I didn't give anything away about the other video. I've got a good poker face. Remember, I work with bridezillas every week. I know how to smile and be neutral in the face of unrealistic expectations."

"Good, Dave. I appreciate your discretion. Thanks for calling. I've gotta go." Vince said as he pulled onto Willis Street.

"Wait. There's one more thing. They had a micro wireless camera they claimed the twins stuck on the back window of their Escalade. It's not mine. So, I'm not sure if they're telling the truth or not. They want the twins and the missing video. They finished by telling me that a Homeland supervisor would be in touch, and that I better have my private investigator's license in order."

"You do, don't you?" Vince asked, skipping the part about the missing video file.

"Always."

"Let me know when the supervisor comes around."

"Will do. What about the micro camera..."

"Thanks, Dave. I'll call you back." Vince hung up and pulled into the Border Patrol Station headquarters and parked.

*Damn, they know about the other video file.*

Vince called Sandy and filled him in on Dave's visit from the couple and their suspicions. It was interesting that the two Metro Guard employees had Homeland badges. Sandy's guess was that they were actually Homeland posing as Metro Guard employees. But Vince wondered then why the lady was stationed at the Penobscot building when Al went through for the DNA test. Sandy said he would look into it.

After hanging up, Vince sat very still and relaxed, putting his mind in a state of meditation. Ever since meeting a Rabbi in the Kuwait desert, he would put himself, as the teacher said, *in the hand of God and wait.* It had served him well in the past, and now it needed to serve him in the present. His friends asked how he kept so calm and collected in the middle of difficult, if not life threatening, situations. His answer: meditation.

Some said that he was simply getting in touch with his subconscious, or he had a high level of intuition. Early on, he thought that might be true, and on the subjective side, there was some truth to that. But as time went on and he looked back on his meetings with the Rabbi, he knew differently. He believed his spirit was being led by *the* Spirit.

*First question: did the twins stumble on an undercover operation, or did they catch a Metro Guard couple connected to the Coast Guard smuggling something illegal?*

*Second question: does this couple and their partners see the boys as innocent employees of a video and private investigative agency and simply caught the couple together as the suspecting wife believed? And does the video file they've taken from Dave satisfy their curiosity?*

He let go of the questions and waited in silence.

*The video has not calmed their curiosity, and proof of a second video has only increased it. The boys are still being sought. The Metro Guard couple and a Guardsmen are part of an undercover operation, whether sanctioned or not, and they have Homeland security passes.*

The hair on the back of his neck stood up. *Why make the drop at a Metro Park and not at the Coast Guard base?*

*Above all else, keep the twins safe.* He broke out in a sweat. *I will not let two young men in my charge be apprehended, held hostage, or be killed. That will never happen again.*

~~~

Vince entered the reception area, pulled out his Homeland badge with a big smile for the cute young female receptionist. He read her name plate and said, "Hello, Patricia Posey, I would like to see the Station Director."

She returned his smile, blushed and read his I.D. "Sure, Mr. Vincent Hardesty." She picked up the phone and said that a Homeland official was here to see Director Williams. The receptionist invited Vince to have a seat when a well-built fortyish Border Patrol officer walked up to him and extended his hand.

"Good afternoon, I'm Director Frederick Williams, what can I do for you today?"

Vince shook the man's hand, pulled out his Homeland badge and returned the introduction. "Good to meet you sir, I'm Reginald Hardesty, Inspector for the Secretary of the Department of Homeland Security, Washington. I'm here to inquire into the disappearance of Supervisor Alberto Martinez." Vince saw a blink and a tightening of the director's mouth. His antenna went up.

Williams looked down and shook his head. "It's a very sad situation." He looked up into Vince's eyes. "A man on his last day of work with his whole retirement in front of him disappearing into the blue. I'm not sure how much light we can shine on your inquiry, Mr. Hardesty."

"Can we go to your office?" Vince asked.

"Sure. Right this way." He led him through a door to the side of the receptionist station. Vince looked over to Patricia as he went around the counter and gave her another smile. He knew that the receptionist usually knew more than the officers were willing to share. He would talk to her later.

The director motioned for Vince to take a seat on the other side of his desk as he sat down. "The last time I saw Supervisor Martinez was just after lunch on Labor Day. I wished him luck and told him he could check out after lunch. I came back here to the station headquarters and took care of some paperwork for some confiscated contraband. You know how it is. Lots of red tape to go through." Williams nodded at Vince with a smile.

*Trying to make us partners in Homeland bureaucracy,* thought Vincent. *Looked more like a used car salesman trying to be my friend.*

"So, you didn't see him when he left the Port of Entry complex?" Vince asked.

"That's right."

"Who might have seen him leaving?" Vince asked.

"Maybe one of his officers, or maybe the afternoon Shift Supervisor, Larouso. I understand Martinez turned in his badge and gun to him just before he left. Would you like to talk with him?"

"Yes, I would, Director. Thank You."

Williams picked up the phone and dialed. He arranged for Vince to meet with the supervisor when he came on shift at two o'clock.

"Anything else I can do for you, Mr. Hardesty?"

"I'll be heading up to the Blue Water Bridge. So, yes, just one thing." Vince said.

"Sure. What is it?"

"I'd like an all Port of Entry pass," Vince said.

"Sure thing. I'll have my receptionist make you one. She'll have to take your picture and laminate it, you understand. Might take a few minutes."

"That'll be fine, Sir," Vince said.

The director got up and escorted Vince through his office back to the receptionist station. "Ms. Posey, could you please make an all Blue Water Port of Entry pass for Mr. Hardesty?"

With a polite smile, she said, "Yes, Sir. Right away, Sir." She turned to Vince and gave him a bigger smile. She looked forward to spending a little time with this nice, handsome man. Vince smiled back. He would get his ten minutes with Ms. Posey and check on the director's schedule for Labor Day.

Williams said, "Well, nice to meet you Mr. Hardesty. I'm headed to the Detroit Station for a directors meeting at four. I'll leave you in the capable hands of Ms. Posey, or as we like to call her, *Pat*. She'll help you with anything else you need."

"Thank you, Sir," Vince said as they shook hands. Williams headed out the door and into a government issue Ford Taurus.

As Vince turned back to *Pat*, she said, "Right this way, Mr. Hardesty."

She had Vince stand in front of a blue wall and took his picture. As they waited for the picture to print and laminate, Vince leaned over the receptionist's counter and asked her personal questions about how long she had worked for Williams and if she lived in the area.

She said, "I live in downtown Port Huron in a high rise apartment. It has a great view of the river and Lake Huron. If you're going to be around, maybe I could show you just how good the view is."

"Thank you for the offer. I'd like to take a rain check on that, maybe when I'm here on personal time. By the way, could I see the official schedule for Labor Day? Like to familiarize myself with Martinez's last day, and whoever he was in contact with."

She smiled and said, "I'd be more than willing to share anything you might need, Mr. Hardesty."

*I bet you would. I guess I can still turn on the charm.*

She returned with the computerized schedule of all of the Port of Entry staff. He saw that Martinez checked out from the Blue Water Bridge at two, and after further study, noted that Director Williams had checked out of the Port's warehouse at the same time.

He looked up at Pat and smiled. "When did Director Williams return here to the Station on Labor Day?"

Patricia frowned. She looked at her computer, clicked some keys and said, "I'm not sure. I wasn't here. I had the long weekend off. But give me a minute and I'll look it up."

Vince gave her his hundred watt smile and said, "That would be great. Thanks."

She smiled back and searched through the data on the screen. "It looks like he came into the office at eleven and then left at noon. He apparently did not return to the office."

"Those were the only entries on September fifth?" Vince asked.

"Yes. Those were the only entries. Looks like the Director came in for an hour and then left. I think he officially had the day off."

"Okay, great. Thanks," Vince said.

*Why did you lie to me, Williams?*

Just then a clerk brought Vince his Blue Water Port of Entry pass. He stood up, took the pass, thanked the clerk and put it over his head. Pat stood up, walked around the counter, and with a grin, came face to face with him. She straightened out the lanyard and centered the pass on his shirt, patting it against his chest, slipping a piece of paper into his jacket pocket.

"There. That's better. Well, it was nice meeting you, Mr. Hardesty, can I call you Reggie?" Pat asked looking seductively into his eyes.

Vince backed up a step. "Uh, yeah, sure. And nice to meet you too, Ms. Posey, uh Pat." He took her hand from his chest and shook it in a business-like manner.

"Remember my offer, Reggie. Just give me a call when you're back in town."

"Will do," Vince said, turning on the smile.

Vince got back into the Mustang, started it up, pulled out of the parking space, and looked back at the Station. He saw Pat Posey and her clerk watching out the window. They gave him a little wave. He sighed and peeled out of the lot. When he checked the piece of paper that Pat had put in his pocket, it had a phone number written on it.

~~~

Vince met the afternoon shift supervisor, Billy Larouso, at the administration building of the Blue Water Bridge Port of Entry. The officer said that Martinez handed in his badge and gun at his normal check out time at two.

"Alberto walked toward the warehouse," he said, pointing west. "The stairway to the employee parking lot is just north of the warehouse."

"Were you the last one to see him leave that day?" Vince asked.

"I think so." Billy answered. "I didn't follow him out to his car, though I would have liked to. My shift had just started and we had a line of traffic returning from Canada for the long weekend. I had to check in with all of my entry booths to be sure they were all manned and the electronic devices were all working."

"I understand," Vince said. "Thanks for your help. Here's my card. Call me if you remember anything else."

"I will, Mr. Hardesty."

Vince started to walk away when Larouso called back. "You might want to talk to the freight warehouse guard. Alberto had a habit of checking the inventory roster after every shift. He was a real stickler for keeping track of anything confiscated on his watch. Not sure if he did it on his last day, though."

"I'll do that. Thanks Mr. Larouso," Vince said.

Vince took the long walk to the warehouse and stopped at the guard office. A young guy in a uniform sat at a small desk with a laptop opened and earplugs in his ears, bobbing his head up and down to a music video on the screen. Vince had to knock loudly on the door frame for the guard to look up and stop the music.

*A bomb could go off at the bridge and this guy wouldn't even know it. Some kind of Homeland Security.*

Vince showed the guard his Port of Entry pass and his Homeland badge. "Were you on duty on Labor Day?" Vince asked, looking at the Metro Guard name tag clipped to his dark blue shirt, "Bruce?"

The guard pushed the laptop closed. "Uh. Yes, Sir."

"Do you have a record of everyone who came to the warehouse that day?"

"Yes, Sir," Bruce answered. He sat down, re-opened the lap top, stopped the music video and brought up a screen that displayed the activity log. He scrolled down and found September fifth and turned the screen around for Vince to see.

Vince looked through the list and found Alberto Martinez's name logged in at two ten p.m. Then he found what he was looking for. Frederick Williams entered the warehouse at one thirty p.m. and exited at two thirty p.m., along with Alberto.

Pointing at the screen, Vince asked, "Did you see Martinez and Williams leave together?"

"Well, no, not really. The director brought the clipboard back that Officer Martinez had taken to check inventory. He said that Martinez headed to the parking lot and the director brought it back as a favor."

"What was the director doing in the warehouse?" Vince asked.

"He said he was picking up some items he needed in court on Tuesday."

"What items were those?" Vince asked.

"Uh, let me look, Sir." The young man flipped the screen around and clicked on a new screen, scrolled down and clicked on an entry. "It was two pallets, Sir."

"*Two* pallets?" asked Vince.

"Yes, Sir."

"What of?"

"It just says electronics, Sir. Could be most anything."

"Was that all?"

"Yes, Sir. That was all, Sir."

"Okay, thanks, Bruce. I'll let you get back to work," Vince said as he handed him his card. "If you think of anything else, please call me, anytime."

"Yes, Sir. I will, Sir."

*Metro Guard at a Border Patrol warehouse? Coincidence? No such thing. And Director Williams, lie to me once, shame on you. Lie to me twice, I'm coming for you.*

Chapter 13

Thursday Night

Vince took Woodward past the Fox Theater and Comerica Park to John R Street and the parking lot on the corner at Broadway. He paid the attendant for two spots and tipped him to "take extra care of the Pony."

Thursday was not quite as busy as the weekend at the Detroit Beer Company, so Vince got a table upstairs at the front window. He ordered a couple of brick oven pizzas and told the waitress he was expecting three more.

Sandy came in first. They took a few minutes to collect their thoughts and review the day's events. Sandy cautioned Vince again about what he found out about the Port Huron Station Director.

Vince spotted Angela and Venus getting out of a cab, standing on the sidewalk and looking up at the restaurant sign. They were pretty hard to miss in short skirts and low cut tops. Vince swallowed and went downstairs to meet them.

"*Buenas noches, el señor Hardesty,*" Venus said as she shook his hand then kissed him on the cheek, her breasts brushing against his arm and chest.

Vince swallowed and small beads of sweat broke out on his upper lip. *Dear God.* "Hello. Sorry we called this meeting on such short notice."

"Think nothin of it, Vincent. You know us girls just want to have fun," Angela said with a smile and a shake of her shoulders.

Venus broke in. "Cyndi Lauper, *She's So Unusual...*"

"1983," said Vince, with Angela looking at both of them like they were crazy.

"Music trivia," Venus said with a wink at Vince.

"Always, "Angela said.

Vince led them upstairs to their table. Sandy greeted Venus with a hand shake and then took Angela's hand and twirled her around "You make the home team proud, my Angela."

"Why thank you, kind Sir," Angela said with a curtsy.

They sat down and Angela spoke first. "So, what's up, gentlemen?"

Vince cleared his throat and answered. "This morning, our Metro Guard couple made a visit to David Miller of Miller Studios and Private Investigations, the twin's boss. They pulled out Homeland badges and said the video clip the boys took of them is now an issue of national security and promptly confiscated the file."

"Holy shit, Sherlock," Angela exclaimed in a whisper.

"Exactly," Vince said. "And even more, they've asked Dave to inform the twins to call a number at DHS and make an appointment for questioning." He pulled out a card with *Homeland Security, Metro Guard of South East Michigan* embossed on the top and passed it around. "Anyone recognize this number?"

"Holy double shit!" exclaimed Angela in a whisper, "That's Commander Starke's private office number. That sonofabitch."

"Good to know," Vince said.

"Good thing you sent the twins out of town," Sandy said. "And with bodyguards."

"I see you stay ahead of the curve, *Amigo,*" Venus said with a smile.

Vince smiled back. "Thank You."

Sandy cleared his throat and said, "What's most inter-*resting*, boys and girls, is that this video is not the one of the drop, and that's why they want to catch and question the twins."

"And even more interesting," Vince said, "is that they've said it's a matter of," Vince made quote signs with his fingers, "*national security*. But the drop is at a metro park, not a sanctioned Homeland station."

"Coming from the Detroit River and off a Coast Guard skiff is what we Coasties like to call *freeken-fishy*," added Venus.

"It's more like, pardon the French, *fucked up*," Sandy said.

"Angela, can you get the log of that skiff from Monday night?" Vince asked.

"Yes I can, and I will," Angela replied.

"Good," Vince said just as the pizzas arrived.

After twenty minutes of eating and raving about the food and beer, Venus asked Vince about his trip to Port Huron.

"I met the station director, a Frederick Williams, at headquarters in Marysville. He said the last time he saw Alberto was at the farewell party. He said that he told Alberto that he could leave after lunch and didn't need to stay for his entire shift.

"When I went to the Blue Water Bridge, I met the afternoon shift supervisor, Billy Larouso. He said that Alberto turned in his badge and gun and then walked toward the freight warehouse on his way to the employee parking lot. He mentioned that Alberto made a habit of checking the warehouse inventory to be sure all of the confiscated items taken on his shift were accounted for.

"I went to the warehouse and met a young guard who said he saw Alberto on Monday shortly after two o'clock. He said that Alberto did take the inventory printout and went around the warehouse checking out the latest confiscated items." Vince paused and looked over at Sandy. "No one on the Bridge or at the Station has seen him since."

Vince looked at Venus and saw that tears were running down her cheeks. He handed her a napkin and she dabbed at her eyes.

"I'm sorry, everyone. This is very upsetting. I was just over to the family's house this afternoon. They are worried sick. It is so unlike Alberto to be gone and not contact his wife or one of his kids. They said the Port Huron police have found nothing. Two of his sons drove up to his place and found his car parked in front and nothing disturbed in the apartment. It's like he never came back. And now I'm afraid they think he will never come back. His boys believe there is foul play and he's injured or dead. His wife and his daughter, one of my best friends, are holding out that Alberto went on some kind of binge and he'll show up for his retirement party on Saturday. I hope she's right, but I think his sons are closer to the truth.

Vince looked over at Sandy and he gave Vince a slight shake of the head that said *don't*.

"I'm not done looking into this, Venus. I promise you I will keep looking until we find Alberto."

Venus dabbed her eyes one last time and blew her nose. "Sorry," she said. She looked at Vince with a frown and said, "How did you get into the Port of Entry so easily to question everyone?"

Vince pulled out his Homeland badge. "I have one too," he said.

"What kind of reservist did you say you were?" she asked.

"Navy," he answered.

"That's all?" she asked with the tone of 'I don't believe you.'

*Don't ask any more questions, sweetheart. How can I change the subject?* He looked at Sandy for help.

Sandy caught the look. "Vince, tell us about the wedding on Saturday."

"Right. Saturday," Vince answered. "Everyone's free for Saturday evening, right?" Vince looked at Venus. She nodded, going with the new subject. Sandy and Angela nodded as well.

"The twins have work on Saturday evening for a wedding at the Royal Park Hotel in Rochester. David Miller spoke with the event coordinator and put us at a table of our own for the wedding reception. We will be two couples acting like we're part of the bridal guests and we'll keep an eye on the boys the entire time they're there. I'll take the twins at four o'clock for the pre-wedding pictures after my body guards drive them back from the west side of the state. I'm going to join Dave's wife, Melissa, as an assistant until the wedding at six. Then I'll meet you guys for the ceremony and we'll stay through the reception until the boys are finished."

"So, we're goin as couples attendin a friend's wedding?" asked Angela. "This couple know any black folks?"

"I don't know," Vince said. "I'll have Dave and Melissa get us information on them so we can keep our story straight on whose work friends we could be. Remember, we'll be at our own table, so no one will be able to ask us incriminating questions."

"If we're the only black couple there," Angela said with a wink at Sandy, "no one will ask us anything. But what about you two?"

"I'll just keep us busy being lovey-dovey," Venus said. "No one wants to interrupt a couple obviously in love and clinging to each other." She winked at Vince.

*Oh, boy. What have I gotten myself into now? Though clinging to her could be very enjoyable. Stop that.*

"Will there be dancing?" asked Venus

"Most weddings have dancing, don't they?" Vince asked with frown.

"Well I hope they take some old records off the shelf," Venus said.

Vince answered, "Bob Seger, 1979."

Venus sang, "I like that *Old Time Rock 'n' Roll*. That was the *Stranger In Town* album, Mr. Hardesty, 1978, not 79. The second most played song on a jukebox."

"What's the first?" asked Vince with a smirk.

"*Crazy*, Patsy Kline," Venus answered, "considering most jukes are in a bar."

"Who wrote it?" asked Vince

"A song writer?" Venus said sarcastically.

"Gotcha. Willie Nelson, 1961."

"Really?" asked Venus.

"Yep," Vince answered.

"Hate to interrupt this little trivia contest, but I noticed you ladies came in a cab. How are you gettin' home tonight?" Sandy asked.

"We thought there was a couple of gentlemen here who might give us girl a ride," Angela said with a wink. "Right Venus?"

"*Si*," Venus said with a wink back. "It's the least these two men could do for us after taking out a whole evening to plot and plan."

"Who's really plottin' and plannin' here?" asked Sandy.

"Really," Vince said with a wink at Venus.

"Has everybody got somethin' in their eye?" Sandy asked.

"I got my eye on you, big boy," Angela said. "So are you takin' me home, or what?"

"Sandy stood up and offered Angela his arm. "Right this way Ma'am. Your chariot awaits." Taking a small bow, he said good night to Venus and Vincent.

"*Ce la vie*, Venus and Mister Vee," Angela followed.

Standing and shaking hands, Vince and Venus wished them both a good night.

"Robbie Nevil, from the same titled album in 1986," Venus said before they sat down.

"You are good, Venus Sanchez," Vince said.

"So?" Venus said.

"So, what?" asked Vince.

"You know what, Mr. Hardesty, "Venus said. "I saw the look Sandy gave you when you were talking about the Port Huron Station Director. You left something out."

"Nothing is confirmed," Vince said looking down and shaking his head.

"Look, Vincent," Venus said as she lifted his chin and looked into his eyes. "There can be no holding back between us. Do you understand? If I'm to believe you, then I must trust you. To trust you means you must be honest with me."

*Oh man, how can I keep anything from those eyes?*

"All right," Vince said. "But you must promise me that you will neither tell anyone else or do anything about it until we agree on what to do. Understand?"

"Yes. We must agree. That means I can negotiate such agreements. *Si?*" Venus waited for his response.

After a long pause, Vince answered. "Agreed."

"Good. Now that we've settled that, what did you leave out?" Venus asked.

"Promise?" Vince asked.

"Promise," she answered.

"Frederick Williams lied to me about seeing Alberto after he left the bridge. The young Metro Guard officer said that Alberto came to the warehouse to do a final check of the inventory, but did not return the inventory clipboard to him. Instead, Williams returned it and said he brought it back as a favor to Alberto."

"In other words, Williams was the last person to see Alberto, and the last place he saw him was in the warehouse."

"Correct. I asked the guard what Williams was doing in the warehouse. He said Williams was picking up items he needed in court on Tuesday. Williams also said he returned to the Station headquarters afterward to do some paperwork. I had the Station receptionist look up the building entrance log and Williams did not return to the office."

"So, he lied about when he last saw Alberto and he lied about what he did afterwards," Venus said.

"Correct."

"Maybe Alberto caught Williams taking something he wasn't supposed to," Venus said looking up at the ceiling.

"Possible," Vince said. "Wouldn't Williams just lie about it and send Alberto on his way. He was his boss, after all."

"Then Alberto disappears," Venus said, clenching her hands into fists.

"Tomorrow I'll dig a little deeper and see if Williams was actually in court on Tuesday, and if so, what he needed out of the warehouse," Vince said.

"I think I don't like this Williams," Venus said.

"I don't either," Vince agreed.

"Was that so hard, Vincent?" asked Venus.

"No. Not as long as you let me handle this. Agreed?"

"For now," Venus said. "But you'll keep me informed, right?"

"I will. Now how about that ride home," asked Vince.

"Thank you. That would be nice. I hear you've got an ex-cop car. How enticing," Venus said.

"Oh, I think you'll like your ride home tonight, Venus," Vince said with a knowing smile.

When they walked up to the Mustang, Venus's eyes got wide. "Is this your ride?" she asked.

"'Hey baby, hop in the seat of my Ford.'" Vince said.

"Ted Nugent, first solo album of the *Motor City Madman*, 1975," Venus said.

"You are *good*," Vince said.

"True," Venus said as she got in the bucket seat. "Let's see if you're good enough to fly this thing."

~~~

After Vince put the Mustang through its paces, Venus demanded and got the opportunity to do the same. He dropped her off at her apartment in Mt. Clemens a few miles from Selfridge and gave Sandy a call.

"Got home early, hey Vince?"

"On my way. Got a question for you."

"Shoot."

"Don't take this personal. I need to know if Venus can take care of herself if things heat up? With Williams and Starke, it looks like they have."

"Take care of herself? You don't really know who you're dealing with, do you?"

"An Army and Coast Guard Heelo pilot."

"Yes, but more. Let me tell you what she said when I asked her the same question. She shared how she earned the Purple Heart.

"Purple Heart, huh?"

"Yep." Venus said, *Remember when the private female soldier was captured and then rescued during Operation Iraqi Freedom? That day she and her fellow prisoners were the lucky ones. Eleven soldiers died in an ambush that morning when their supply convoy took a wrong turn in An Nasiriyah, a city with a bridge across the Euphrates. Eighteen more Marines lost their lives that afternoon.*

*The marines came up the same road and found the remains of the supply convoy. They were surrounded and took on heavy fire, so they had to call in the Marine casualty evac: double blade Sea Knight choppers with Apache gunships to cover them. They didn't have enough room for all the injured, so they called in my Army rescue Black Hawk. The Apaches didn't know that, so they took off to defend the bridge.*

*I flew in and landed on the road next to a trench where the Marines were keeping the wounded. As they loaded up two stretchers, the Iraqis realized the gunships were gone and opened fire. The Marines returned fired, but as we slid the chopper door closed, an Iraqi ran out from beside a building and aimed an RPG right at us. I lifted off the road about five feet, turned toward the grenade launcher and slammed the cyclic forward with one hand and pulled out my 9mm with the other. He hesitated when he saw me heading straight for him, so I did a sharp ninety degree turn, unloaded my gun at him and then took the Hawk straight up and over the building. I took another ninety degree turn and caught a bullet in the shoulder as my ship got sprayed with an AK-47. They hit one engine, but I wrestled the smoking Hawk back to base while holding a wad of gauze against my bullet wound. So you think I can handle myself with Homeland?"*

"*I guess so*, I told her. She not only got the Purple Heart. She received the Army Air Medal for bravery in flight," Sandy added.

"Okay. I guess she can take care of herself," Vince said with a smile.

*Quite the woman!*

Blue Water Dead

131

## Part II  THE HOOK

*There are three things which are too wonderful for me, Four which I do not understand: The way of an eagle in the sky, The way of a serpent on a rock, The way of a ship on the sea, And the way of a man with a maid.* -- Proverbs 30:18-19

Chapter 14

Friday Morning

Vince made a call to his counselor for an appointment first thing Friday morning. He had tossed and turned most of the night; he hadn't felt this confused in a long time.

He cranked up the Impala and drove over to Woodward Ave and headed south toward Wayne State University. There, he picked up a couple of lattes at the University Bookstore coffee shop, ordering a double shot of espresso for himself. Caffeine worked for about six hours, but then he had to cut it off by four in the afternoon or he wouldn't sleep at night.

He had done tours of duty where he stayed awake for three days, but that was with the help of *Provigil,* or *Modafinil,* a medication assisting soldiers to remain alert for over seventy-two hours without side effects. Now, one sleepless night was creating some confusion and he couldn't let that go on. He didn't want to take any drugs for alertness anymore, and he hoped talking out whatever was jumbled up in his head would slow his thoughts down enough to relax.

He headed back north on Woodward and then east on Ferry Avenue, just past *The Inn on Ferry Street,* crossed John R and turned into the drive at *Faith House.* It was an ecumenical counseling and teaching center with a mission to unite peoples of all faiths and religions. It was started by a renegade Detroit Catholic Bishop, a Reformed Southfield Rabbi, a progressive Dearborn Muslim, a Presbyterian Detroit police chaplain and a Unity Church minister in Warren.

Most of the *Faith House* staff were professors at Wayne State University and the Detroit Medical Center and wanted to add spirituality to their intellectual and professional lives without religious competition.

He went in the main entrance off the back parking lot into a spacious waiting room, formerly the dining area of one of the nineteenth century *Dexter M. Ferry Seed Company* mansions. Mr. Ferry's seed company sought to encourage home gardening and was one of the first companies to package seeds and sell them in stores, guaranteeing fresh seeds and ones right for the vicinity. Now the ecumenical group was trying to plant seeds of another kind in the educational community.

It was too early for the receptionist, let alone any other clients, so he went straight to his counselor's office and knocked. He heard a quiet "come in" and opened the door. As always, he saw the welcoming smile of the Rev. Harriett Key, Ph.D. He already felt a little better.

He had been referred to *Faith House* by Sandy when he'd had trouble adjusting to civilian life, that is, life in a large city rather than a military base. He first went to see the Detroit police chaplain, a Presbyterian minister and trained therapist, but he had been called out on an officer killed in action. Harriett welcomed him to the House that day.

Harriett was a full blooded descendant of a North Carolina Cherokee tribe, Princeton educated and ordained in the then Southern Presbyterian Church, U.S.A. He connected with her tribal spiritual insight, reminding him of the desert Rabbi's admonishment that spirituality was not just an individualistic experience. She had been his counselor ever since.

He sat down in one of the most comfortable dark mocha leather Lay-Z-Boy Recliners ever made. He leaned back enough to get his feet up and still look into her caring eyes. She had said that he related well with her because she was a mother-figure to him, something he had missed growing up in a single father household.

His mother had died in childbirth in Gary, Indiana. His dad had moved them to Michigan to escape the memory of her death. Charles Hardesty was a History and Social Studies teacher in the local school, grades K-12, so he was always nearby. Growing up fifteen minutes east of Ludington in Scottville, Vince learned to love "the sea," as his dad called it: Lake Michigan.

When Harriett had revealed this mother-figure notion several sessions in, he said he didn't think so. It wasn't true because he had never had a mother, so how could he know what he'd missed? She said everyone is having a relationship with their mother and father, even if they're missing. We look for someone to replace them when they're missing and she currently filled that gap in his soul. He realized later that she was right. She had a comforting, *motherly* effect on him just by being in her presence.

"So, what's on your mind this morning, my dear Vincent?"

"I've got a situation with Homeland and it involves two young men, they're brothers, twins actually, that I feel particularly responsible for, especially since their mother died."

"Close to your heart, then, Vincent?"

"Yes, I suppose so."

"And?"

"I think they're possibly in some kind of danger." Vincent paused, as if to say that's what's bothering him.

"Well, we both know you're no stranger to danger."

"True. But this is different."

"Different how?"

Vince broke out in a sweat. The nerves were back.

Harriett paused, waiting for him to reply. After a full minute of silence, she asked again. "Different how, Vincent?"

"These boys are in danger and I feel like my intuitive abilities have been weakened." *Maybe I should have said they've been distracted.*

"I see."

"I have this fear that I won't be able to be there for them when they need me the most."

"That was very brave of you to say, Vincent. A decorated Special Forces warrior admitting he's vulnerable. That must feel humbling."

"I've felt fear before. It keeps you alert. It puts you on the edge. You might throw up, but you're ready to go."

"This is different how, Vincent?"

"That's just it. Before I would get more alert, relaxed and my intuitive abilities would kick in and I'd be in the zone. Everything outside of the mission would be blocked out. My focus would be on point. But, this time, that doesn't seem to be happening."

"You're in good health, in shape, thinking sharp?"

"Yes."

"So it's not physical or mental?"

"I guess not."

"Having any problem meditating, praying?"

"No."

"So, it's emotional, isn't it?"

"I guess so." *Crap. Do we have to go there?*

The deep emotional crevasse of missing a mother and then losing his wife was a scar he did not like to touch. It had been quiet for several years now, thanks to Harriet, and, as she said, her motherly ways.

"So, something or someone is intruding into your mind, your heart, and distracting you."

"I guess so."

"Who is she?"

"What do you mean?"

"You know what I mean."

"How do you know it's a she?"

"Come on, Vincent. I'm a professional, and, more importantly, I'm a woman. I've been a lover, a wife, and a mother of boys. Spit it out, Vince," she said, and waited.

"Yes, you're right. It is a woman."

"What's her name?"

"Her name is Venus."

"That's what I wanted to see. The look on your face change when you said her name."

"I haven't had feelings like this for many years."

"Not since meeting your wife in Kuwait?" asked Harriett.

"Uh, yes. I guess so."

After a pause. "So, what are you afraid of?"

"Afraid?"

"That's what you said when you came in."

"I don't know," Vince said. "Stirring up old grief?"

"No. I don't think so," Harriett answered. "I think that it's about this woman, Venus. You have an attraction to her and you think she will dull the memory of your wife. Are you afraid she will replace her and you'll lose Rachel forever? Are you afraid she will open you to love and dependence again, and if you do, you might lose her too and the terrible grief will be back?"

"So many questions, Doc. My answer to all of them is 'what are you talking about?'"

"Deep down, you know what I'm talking about, don't you Vince?"

"It's confusing."

"Exactly."

"Quit playing me, Doc. Exactly what?"

"You're in love."

"I hardly know the woman."

"Apparently, you know her well enough, or I should say, your body and soul know her well enough."

"Kind of personal, huh Doc?"

"It *is* very personal, and you better decide what you're going to do about it."

"Decide what?"

"Whether you're going to follow your body and soul, or you're going to say no thank you."

"I can just decide?"

"Yes, you can decide. To use a cliché, *love is always a decision*."

"How convenient."

"Follow your heart."

"Another cliché?"

"Your body and soul. The heart connects them and you've been disconnected a long time."

"He flipped down the foot rest and got up. "Gotta go."

"Come here, Vincent." She stood and extended her arms out to him.

He stepped into her embrace. "Thank you, Harriett."

"Go and keep in touch. You know how us mother-types hate to be ignored."

"Yes, *Mom*."

~~~

Vince hopped back in the Impala and turned on his phone. It immediately chirped. A call from Sandy. He pressed the return call button and after one ring Sandy answered.

"Vince. I found out somethin' on Starke and a high official in Homeland who might be behind all of this. My source tells me there's an operation of national security goin' down, but the details are zipped up. He saw Starke go into Homeland's conference room, but the Director's secretary, who always takes notes, was not invited. So this is bein' contained."

"Does someone in Homeland administration have ties to Starke in a previous life?" asked Vince.

"Workin' on it. See if your friend *Mike the Snipe* can find out anything. Most of Homeland's officials were appointed to their position through D.C. I'd rather not say any more on the phone."

"These phones are secure," Vince said.

"Right. I'll fill you in later, in person."

"Okay, Sandy."

Sandy gave Vince more to think about.

*At least that's a change from my other thoughts. Nothing like a developing mission to put me on point. Now I can block out all of the distractions, or as Harriett had called it, attraction. Great.*

~~~

Michio Matsumoto arrived at the George H.W. Bush Center for Central Intelligence, the CIA, in Langley, Virginia, at six a.m. to begin his twelve hour shift at the Mission Communications Center for Special Operations. He coordinated voice, optical, internet and satellite communications for the CIA SAD, Special Activities Department, operatives around the world. His colleagues nicknamed the Hawaiian born Japanese American *Mike the Snipe* because his name resembled the American name, and he had always gone undetected, until he was hired by the Agency.

He had successfully hacked into the CIA's HQ servers, set up audio and visual surveillance on Agency staff, and presented his PhD dissertation at MIT entitled "No Security in the Nation's Security." One of the Ph.D. review board members was on contract with the CIA and introduced him and his dissertation to the director. It was where Mike wanted to work anyway. He could snoop, or *snipe*, as he liked to call it, legally and with the best equipment in the world. The Agency was glad to have him.

When Mike saw that he was receiving a call from Vincent Hardesty from his secure cell phone, he always took it. It was the least he could do for the man who had given him commendations for his assistance during the Gulf War.

"Vin-cent, my man. How's the border baby-sitter?"

"Ha, ha. Good one, Mike. And how's the Agency's bad boy?"

"Oh, you know, *sniping*."

"I bet. What I'm calling about is I need a check on phone and internet communications between the Detroit Coast Guard Commander Clay Starke and the Detroit Homeland Security office."

"I've heard chatter about an operation to apprehend a Mid-Eastern terrorist cell in Dearborn, but I'm not on the support unit."

"I haven't heard anything about it, either" Vince said with concern.

"I haven't, officially. But you know, I always have ears on just about everything," Mike said with a chuckle.

"You're not sniping on your own agency again, are you Mike?"

"Who, me? No way!"

"Uh huh."

Mike continued. "It's a cell of three Arab brothers who recently moved to Dearborn via New Orleans and hurricane Katrina. They've been followed now for about a week and it sounds like an arrest will be made in the next couple of days, once they go on the move."

"Great. Can you get me some intel on Starke and Homeland in the midst of your agency sniping?" Vince asked.

"No prob, Bro."

"Good. Call me anytime. I have a couple of friends of mine who I think stepped in it."

"Hold on, hold on," Mike said. "Starke's name came up with this Arab cell. So, let me go back in and take another look."

"Call me back when you know more," Vince said.

"And call me if you find anything."

"What good would that do?" Vince asked. "You wouldn't be at the office."

"Like I said, no prob, Bro."

"Oh."

~~~

Al and Cane got up at sunup and snuck out of the house before Debra and Diane were awake. After catching breakfast at the local McDonalds, Al and Cane biked four miles north up Lakeshore drive to the Detroit Edison / Consumer Power Pump Storage Project. When they reached the five hundred foot high dyke surrounding the reservoir to their right, the shore line opened up on their left revealing the crystal blue waters of Lake Michigan dotted with tiny white caps as far as the eye could see.

They biked the two and half mile length of the reservoir and hiked up the stairs to the observation deck. They stood opened mouth when they reached the top. They had a bird's eye view of the expansive two and half mile long, one mile wide reservoir. Looking out toward the lake, they could see downtown Ludington and the beach with the Pier Head Lighthouse. Further north, they saw their intended destination: the sand dunes and beach along the shoreline of Ludington State Park.

They headed out riding east on the Pere Marquette Highway, then East Ludington Avenue down to the beach. They grabbed a sandwich and, of course, some ice cream, at the famous *House of Flavors*. While they were finishing their sundaes, Al got a call on his personal phone.

"Hello?"

"Al, Honey. This is Juanita at St. Vincent's. I was just calling to see how you and your brother are doing?

"You'll never guess where we are?"

Cane's eyes got big and he began shaking his head.

"Yes. I'll never guess," answered Juanita, "because I haven't seen you boys around here much this week. Where are you?"

"Right now we're sitting in the House of Flavors in Ludington."

Cane made a slashing motion across his throat to make Al cut the call.

"Oh, how nice. When did you and Cane go over to Lake Michigan. I love it over there."

"Vince sent us with a couple of his girlfriends." He decided not to say they were girlfriends to each other, a major bummer.

Cane started grabbing for the phone.

"Oh, Vincent has girlfriends?"

"No," he said to Cane. "I mean, yeah, I guess so. These two ladies are here to babysit us."

This got Juanita's attention. "Babysit? Why do you boys need watching? Are you two in trouble?"

"No, nothing like that, Ms. Juanita," Al said as he was waving his hand toward Cane signaling that he was about to hang up. "Vince just thought we needed to get away before the end of the warm weather. Right now we're going to bike up to the state park. So, gotta go."

Cane was now motioning for Al to zip his lip.

"Okay Al," Juanita said. "You be careful, and call me if you need me. Have a good time, and stay out of trouble, okay?"

"Yeah sure, we will. Bye now." Al clicked off.

Cane shook his head. "Dude, you weren't supposed to answer your phone."

"Hey, it was Ms. Juanita. You know I'm gonna answer a call from her."

"Really? Remember, we're trying to stay away from a couple of psychos. Turn that thing off right now."

"Cane, my brother, we're hundreds of miles away from those guys. So, quit worrying."

"Right. Let's go."

They picked up their backpacks, paid their bill and walked out into the bright noon day sun. Hopping on their bikes, they headed down to Lakeshore Drive against a brisk breeze coming off the lake. Turning north, they biked the six miles out to Ludington State Park. They stopped along the dunes where both locals and tourists were headed for the water on a beautiful Friday afternoon.

While Cane wasn't looking, Al turned his phone back on. He was expecting another important call.

## Chapter 15

Friday Noon

Angela answered the phone, "Commander Starke's office. How may I direct your call?"

"I need to talk with the commander right away. Interrupt him if you need to."

"May I ask who's calling?"

"Tell him Peters."

"Yes, Sir." Angela put him on hold and buzzed Starke.

"There's a Mr. Peters on the line, Sir. Yes, I know, but he says it's urgent. Yes, Sir, I'll put him through."

Angela transferred the call.

Since no one else was in the office, she went over to the commander's door and listened. When she heard him hang up and get out of his chair, she quickly walked over to the file cabinet, opened a drawer and acted like she was looking up a file. Starke came out of his office walking briskly to the door, telling her that he had to attend an urgent meeting over at Homeland. She answered with a "Yes Sir," and waited for him to leave.

When she heard his car leave the lot, she grabbed her purse, found the phone that Vince had given her and ran outside. She hit the speed dial number for him and he picked up on the second ring.

"Yes."

"This is Angela. Starke just got a call from a Mr. Peters. I heard him say something about Metro Guard and get somebody to Selfridge Air Base and something about Ludington. He ran out the door telling me that he had an urgent meeting at Homeland and left."

Vince told her thanks and hung up. He dialed Mike *the Snipe*.

"*Snipe* Enterprises, we listen so there's no dissin'."

"Call with Starke," Vince said.

"There was a call out of the Dearborn apartment to Starke. Then a call to Metro Guard. The last call was to a hanger at Selfridge. Apparently the Coast Guard's Aero 560 plane, a seven-seater, is being fueled up and a flight plan for Ludington is being requested with the tower."

"Thanks," Vince said. He dialed Sandy and filled him on Angela's message. Sandy said he would call over at Homeland and check on any urgent meetings.

Vince thought for a minute, paused, and then dialed Venus. He couldn't let his conflicting feelings with her interfere with what had to be done. She answered on the first ring.

"Hello Vincent."

"Hello Venus. Starke and at least one or two others are headed out to Selfridge to take a plane to Ludington. That's where I sent the twins. Somehow I think they found out where they're located. Can you meet me at City Airport in the next thirty minutes?"

"Yes, of course."

"Good. I've got a plane there: hangar fifty-seven off Conner. Bring some summer beach clothes."

Before Venus could answer, Vince had rung off. She ran to her bedroom, threw in some shorts, tops, underwear and put on *the* swimsuit: the cyan two piece tie-string nylon-spandex. *Oh yeah.*

She was glad she had several days off before working on Saturday. She wouldn't have to explain to anyone on the base where she was going, let alone that she was following a Coast Guard commander. And with Vincent Hardesty, one of the most attractive and intelligent eligible bachelors she had ever met. He was strong and sexy, as well as humble and thoughtful. His face lit up when he smiled, yet there was some deep sadness in his eyes. Maybe she could be the one to help him forget whatever caused his heartache.

When she pulled up to his hangar, Vince was pulling out the chocks from the wheels of his model 33 Beechcraft Bonanza. He motioned for her to move her Jeep past the double doors and come help him pull the plane out of the hangar.

"Need some help?" asked Venus.

"Grab the other side of this handle. We'll pull together," Vince said.

Venus got both hands next to his and she looked over into his eyes. *Green hazel.*

"Ready?" Vince asked.

"Yeah."

"Okay. One, two, three, *pull.*"

The plane hesitated for a second, then, started rolling out onto the drive. Once it was out in the sunlight, Vince told her to put her bag in the plane and then park her car in the nearby lot. He would disconnect the pull bar, start up the engine and taxi down to pick her up.

Venus parked, grabbed her carry-on bag and ran to the plane where Vince already had the engine warming up. She hopped in the passenger seat and put on her headphones. Vince was putting in his flight plan to Ludington. She looked over at Vince and her heart skipped a beat. As if reading her mind, he looked over at her and gave her an embarrassed smile.

"Ready to go?" he asked.

"Ready to go, Flyboy."

Vince called back to the tower and was given permission to taxi out to the southwest side of the runway for takeoff. Without thinking Venus was answering his pre-flight check list. When the tower gave them permission for takeoff, they looked at each other and smiled.

Pilots love the adrenalin rush of that moment running up the engines and then releasing the brakes to speed down the runway. In less than thirty seconds they were airborne and flying northeast over Grosse Pointe and Lake St. Clair. They climbed to ten thousand feet and turned west-north-west toward Lake Michigan. Once they leveled off, Vince filled Venus in on what was going on.

The plan was simple. Debra and Diane would drive from the lake to the residential street that ended at the airport fence and watch for Starke's airplane. They would call back with the vehicle he rented and then head back to the beach. They would locate the boys and find out what they had done that gave away their location. He and Venus would rent a car, preferably a convertible, change into some beach clothes and look like tourists. They would follow Starke and keep in contact with Debra and Diane. The goal was to get the boys back to his beach house and then out of the area. It sounded simple enough, but he knew there were always unpredictable elements, two of which were the twins themselves.

Vince reached altitude and had the speed up to maximum at a hundred and ninety miles per hour. They would land in Ludington in about an hour. He called the Mason County Airport and ordered a car. Then he realized he had an hour alone with Venus. He felt some perspiration form on his forehead. He looked over and saw that she was staring at him. He gave her a nervous little smile.

*Poor man,* thought Venus. *He's stuck in this plane with me and doesn't know what to say. So, I'll ask the questions. He can't go anywhere. Might as well get to the heart of the matter.* "Why did you call me to come along on this little trip?" She waited.

"Uh, well, Angela is working and we need her to keep an eye on Starke's office. Sandy's checking on Homeland to see if he can find anything about what's really going on. So, out of the group, that left you. And not to mention that you're a Coasty and you had the day off."

"Uh huh. So what does me being a Coasty have to do with this trip?"

"Well, the pursuers are Coast Guard and we're going to Lake Michigan which has a Coast Guard station. I might need somebody on the inside, you might say."

"What if the pursuers recognize me?"

"That's why the tourist and beach clothes. People don't recognize others they know if they're not in work clothes and don't expect to see them."

"That's it?"

"Pretty much."

"Pretty much? That means there's more?" *This is getting good now.*

"Maybe. Maybe not"

"I think maybe. You know why I say that?"

"No. Why?"

"Because you're sweating and you're hesitant. You're acting like a teenager on his first date."

"Oh. Well, I'm nervous about the twins and their predicament, which seems to be getting worse by the day."

"You seemed pretty calm and focused until we reached altitude and you realized you'd be in this plane with me for the next hour."

"Really?"

"Yeah, really. I know you've been a SEAL, Sandy gave me a quick sketch of your military career, however secret, and I know intercepting Starke and getting the twins out of harm's way is the most important thing to you right now. But, I think what makes you nervous is, well, *me*. Being alone with me. I'm not going to bite, Vincent." *At least not yet.*

Vince looked over at her and smiled. "Good to know."

"I make you nervous. I just haven't figured out why."

*Reading me like an open book. What can I say to that? Change the subject.* "Venus?"

She smiled and looked expectantly. "Yes?"

"Could you look out your window. We'll be flying south of Bishop Airport in Flint and then north of the Capitol Region airport in Lansing and we need to look out for other planes. You look out that way and I'll look out this way."

"Yes, Sir, Captain. Not looking at each other, Sir."

"Come on, I didn't mean it like that. I like looking at you, I mean..."

"Good to know, Sir," she said with a smile on her face. *I like that you like looking at me.* "Looking for planes north out my window."

They spent the next fifteen minutes looking for other aircraft as they flew by Flint and Lansing. With no planes spotted, Venus looked back at Vincent and was thinking what to say when his phone rang.

"Hi Debra," Vince answered.

"We're at the turn-around at the end of Johnson Road facing the airport runway. When should we expect the plane?" she asked.

"It's a Coast Guard Aero 560 seven-seater. It should be landing in the next ten minutes. We're about fifteen minutes behind them. Watch for what car they take and then head back to alert the twins."

"Will do."

Vince hung up and looked over at Venus. She had a tilt to her head. "Is there somebody else, Vincent? Debra. You could have just told me." She turned away and looked out the window.

"No, Venus. There's no one else. Debra is part of a body guard service that I use periodically."

"I bet you do. Body guard? Or is that Booty-call?"

"No, Venus. Debra has a partner and they're an item."

"Good to know."

"So, that was just an act to check out the competition?" Vince asked.

"Got to know the defense if you're going to have a good offense."

"You are slick."

"That's the nicest thing you've said to me today."

Vincent just shook his head. He pointed out the windshield. "You can see Lake Michigan from here. As beautiful a blue expanse of water you'll ever want to see. I think I'm homesick."

"You grew up in this area, right?"

"Yep. Scottville, home of the Clown Band."

"The what?"

"The Big Noise from Scottville. It's a great sounding marching band of locals dressed up in clown outfits."

"Okay. And why did you mention that of all things."

"It's the only thing we're famous for. It's a small town about seven miles east of Ludington."

"That explains a lot," Venus said.

"What?"

"Nothing"

Vince's phone rang. He answered. "Yeah. Got it. Thanks. See you at the beach."

"Debra again?" asked Venus

"Yes. Starke and three others landed and rented an eight passenger white Econoline van, no doubt making room for two more."

"How soon do we land?"

"Ten minutes out."

Vince prepared for landing, circling out over Lake Michigan to make a southerly approach to the Mason County Airport. Turning starboard, he saw his childhood landmarks: the Pump Storage reservoir, Pere Marquette Lake, downtown Ludington, and the dunes at the State Park.

"What a beautiful area," Venus said, seeing the entire Ludington area out her window as they were on approach to land. They touched down, taxied to the hangars and stopped in front of Vincent's hangar.

"Got a hangar here too, huh?" asked Venus.

"This is home."

They got out and secured the plane to the tarmac, not fooling with the hangar. Grabbing their bags, they headed to the car rental building where a new metallic red Mustang GT convertible with spoiler awaited them. Vince jogged into the rental office, picked up the keys and got back to the car as Venus finished putting their bags in the back seat. Vince put up the top as they drove out of the airport onto Ludington Avenue.

"Change into your tourist/beach clothes. We want to look like *fudgies* when we get to the beach."

"Look like what?"

"Fudgies. That's northern Michigan slang for tourist. You know. They always buy and eat fudge."

"Cute."

"Why don't you climb into the back seat and change."

"Now you tell me." As Venus struggled through the front bucket seats, she caught Vince checking her out. She smiled. "Don't look while I change." She broke into song. "*Keep your mind on your drivin, keep your hands on the wheel, keep your snoopy eyes on the road ahead.*"

"Paul Evans and the Curls, 1959," Vince said.

"Very good," Venus said, opening her bag. She looked up to the front, making sure Vince was looking forward and not in the rear view mirror. She scooted down in the narrow back seat and took off her top and kakis. She rustled through her bag and found a pair of short-shorts and put them on, glad she already had on her bikini.

"You all right back there?" asked Vince.

"Why, you interested?"

"Sorry." Vince shut up.

She found an open front white beach top, tied the top and bottom strings together and sat up. She looked out the window. "Where's the beach?"

"All dressed now? Climb back up front and I'll put the top down. We'll be at the beach shortly."

When Venus slipped up through the bucket seats and sat back down, Vince gulped and almost ran up on the curb.

"Hey watch it! Or was that what you were doing?"

"Sorry," Vince answered.

"What about you, Vince?"

"Got it on underneath. I'll change when we get to the beach."

"We'll see."

Chapter 16

Friday Afternoon

Al and Cane were lying on the beach in the sand dunes of the State Park with some of the local high school kids. After everyone was fried to a rare pink, they took a dip in the lake. Someone said they were hungry, so they decided to go into town for pizza. The twins said they had come out on bikes, so they couldn't go. The two girls they'd been hanging with said their car had a bicycle carrier and they could give them a ride. Al and Cane nodded together. They followed the girls, loaded up the bikes and hopped in the back seat of the girls' car.

Heading into town, they both stared out the window when they saw Debra and Diane going the other way in the Humvee.

The girl driver said, "Wow, look at that army Hummer with two girls."

Al and Cane looked at each other and laughed. They had eluded the lesbian babysitters.

"What's so funny?" asked one of the girls, offended. "Don't think girls can drive a Hummer?"

"No, not that," said Cane. "We met them the other day. They're girlfriends."

"So, you have girlfriends?"

"No," said Al. "They're *gurl-friends*, if you know what I mean?"

"Oh." She said. A smile came across her face as she looked in the rearview mirror. "And you two know, because you tried to pick them up, didn't you?" Both girls in the front seat started giggling.

The twins looked at each other and shook their heads. "If you only knew," they said in unison.

The girls' giggles turned into laughter.

Once on Main Street, they drove to a local pizza place with their friends pulling in behind them. They ordered to go, deciding to go to the downtown beach and eat by the water.

~~~

Debra pulled the Humvee back into a spot along the sand dunes where they had spotted the twins earlier. They climbed a tall dune where they could see most of the four miles of the park's beach. Two guys with red hair shouldn't be that hard to see. After scanning the beach with binoculars for several minutes, they realized the group and the twins had left, but they hadn't seen anyone on bikes heading back to town. Diane said she remembered seeing several cars with teenagers and one of them had a bike rack with two bikes. She called Vince.

`"We lost them, but we think they went back into town with a group of kids."

"Where did you see them last?" asked Vince.

"Out on the beach at the State Park," Diane answered.

"They're probably headed to *G-Park*."

"What's *Gee-Park*?

"*G-Park* is the nick name for the beach downtown. *Giraffe Park*, you know, lots of necking? Anyway, head back there and start your search at the bathrooms on the north end. You'll have a great view of the beach from there, and there's a water pump station that hides your view from the street. If you don't see them on the beach, they might be on the other side of the pump station."

"Okay, we're on the way. Have you seen the white van?"

"We found it going through a drive-thru at a burger place. We're at a party store picking up some sandwiches and drinks waiting for them to pass us so we can tail them. We'll keep you informed. Let me know if you spot the twins. Don't alert them just yet."

"Got it. Out."

As Vince hung up, Venus came out of the store carrying a couple of plastic bags. The wind caught her loosely laced up top and it flapped open revealing her midriff from her low riding shorts to the top of her bikini, what there was of it. He swallowed. *Dear God, I'm in trouble.*

Venus caught his look and smiled. "What you *lookin* at, *muchacho*? See something you like?"

"Yes, and get in. Diane called. The boys are missing at the dunes. We're heading downtown to the beach to look for them there."

Just then Starke's Econoline passed them headed toward the beach. Vince pealed out, pushing Venus back in her seat. She dropped the bags onto the floorboard and hurriedly put on her seat belt. She thought the surge was as much about his libido as about catching the van. It made for a lousy tail in any case.

Starke drove toward the lake on Main Street and stopped at the traffic light just past the county building. Two men got out of the van and split up. The light turned green, and the van pulled ahead and turned the corner at the next intersection. Vince and Venus saw Starke's crew looking through stores on either side of the street as they drove toward the lake.

"That'll keep them busy for a while," Vince said.

Debra and Diane turned into the park and stopped at the restrooms and concession stand.

Al and Cane were in the back seat of the car with the girls, slowing to find a parking place at the other end of the beach. "Let's eat at the picnic tables. Then, volleyball. You guys play?"

"Yeah, sure," answered Al. "Could we get out anytime soon? This pizza is hot."

"Oh, getting hot there, Mr. Major?" said the driver.

"Ha. He's hot all right," Cane said as he opened the box and got a piece of pepperoni with mushrooms and dug in.

"Hey, save some for the rest of us, *Dude*," the driver said.

They pulled into a spot across the drive from the nets where the rest of the group had already claimed a picnic table. Just as they got out of the car, Al's phone rang. He handed the pizza over to Cane, saying he had to take this. "It's the *Friend*."

"That you're '*girl-friend*?'" asked one of the girls, using her fingers as quotes.

Al got out of the car and answered, "Hello. Yes, this is Al Majors."

"Come on, girls," Cane said. "This pizza isn't getting any hotter, though you two are."

"Oh, pu-lease," said one of the girls. Cane and the girls met up with the others and sat at the picnic table.

Al's heart was beating fast. The call he'd been waiting for from Friend of the Court had finally come. "You can't give me the result over the phone, but you want me to appear in court?" He couldn't believe it. The one thing that he wanted to know was available, but they weren't allowed to actually say it. Medical confidentiality. "Yes, I can be there next week. Tuesday. Penobscot Building, the Friend of the Court. Got it. Yeah, bye."

Al looked out on the blue-silver waters of Lake Michigan. He knew that requesting his presence at a paternity hearing confirmed he was the father. The hearing would validate it for his ex and he would get visitation, no, *parenting time* with his little girl. He looked back at the beach. Instead of the girls in their bikinis, he saw a little two year old girl playing in the sand. His eyes welled up for a minute as he thought of the future with his daughter. His thoughts were interrupted when he heard his name.

"Al, Al!" yelled Cane. "Damnit, get off that phone, *Dawg*."

"I'm off. I'm off. It was FOC."

"Is that a *Dee-troit* way to say your hometown *screw*?" asked one of the girls.

"No," Cane answered. Looking back at Al he said, "You keep using that phone and we *will* be *FOCked.*"

The girls giggled.

As Vince turned onto Lakeshore Drive, his phone buzzed. "Talk." He looked over at Venus. "Yeah, I know. Thanks, Mike." He hung up. "Al used his personal phone again. He's here at the downtown beach."

Vince called Debra and Diane and told them about the call. He warned them that Starke would have gotten a call about their location as well.

Diane scanned the beach but couldn't see the twins. Debra motioned to her to get back in the Humvee. "Let's drive down to the other end." When they parked near the volleyball nets, they spotted Al sitting at some picnic tables.

The group of teens looked up as Debra and Diane got out of the Humvee and walked toward them. One of the girls sitting with the twins said, "Look boys, it's your *gurl-friends.*"

"Debra. Diane. What are you doin here?" Al asked, standing up.

"We gotta go. Grab your bikes."

"What's up?" Cane asked, seeing the serious look on her face.

"Need to go. Right now!" she commanded.

"I think you boys are in trouble," one of the girls said.

Debra and Diane quickly escorted the twins to their bikes.

"What gives?" Cane asked.

Diane answered, "The Metro Guard couple and a couple of their friends are here to catch you guys. Al, give me your phone."

"I told you, man," Cane said.

Al took out his phone and handed it to her. She grabbed it and took off running toward the lake.

"What the hell?" Al asked.

"Get on your bikes and head back to the house," Debra said. "We're going to send them in the other direction with another phone call. Get going."

"We're outa here!" they said in unison.

Vince drove into Stearns Park and saw his Humvee parked further down along the angled parking spots. He drove up and pulled into the space next to it. He pulled off his shirt, got out of the car, took off his shoes and pulled off his pants, leaving his swimming trunks.

He saw Diane running away from him going north along the beach at the water's edge. Debra was standing by a picnic table of teenagers watching her. Vince turned and saw the boys on bikes heading out of the park toward the marina. He turned back to Venus and told her to get her beach blanket and follow him. He walked toward Debra and motioned her over.

"What's up?" asked Vince.

"Diane has Al's phone and she's running it to the north end of the beach to make another call. I told the boys to get their bikes and head back to your place."

"Quick thinking. Take the Humvee and drive back north on Lakeshore, pass the entrance to the park and turn into the water pump station. Take the path down to the beach and pick up Debra after she makes the call, then drive north along the beach until you come to an open area about a mile down. The lawn there will take you to a side street back to Lakeshore. Head back to my place to catch Al and Cane."

Venus caught up with Vince as he finished talking with a muscular petite blonde. Debra ran to the Humvee, cranked it up and took off out of the park. "One of your girlfriends, *Gringo*?"

"Yes, *Señorita*. Debra, Diane's partner. Diane's running to the other end of the beach with Al's phone," Vince said as he pointed out a brunette running like an Olympian. "She's going to make another call near one of the houses up the shoreline. Deb will pick her up and meet us back at my place. We'll stay here, act like a couple at the beach, and watch for Starke and crew.

"*Act?*" Venus took the blanket and spread it out on the sand near the sidewalk. She took off her cover up and shorts, catching the eye of any man looking in her direction.

Vince froze and blew out a breath. *Keep your mind on the task at hand.* The blue-green stringy thing she had on sent his heart racing and he felt sweat beads form. *Maybe that's just from the heat. It was still summer, after all. Right.*

He sat down on the blanket next to Venus and looked out toward the lake. The water was the same color as the bikini she had on. *Dear God, it's an ambush.*

Venus gave Vince a once over and liked what she saw: a lean, toned body with broad shoulders and a swimmer's chest tapering down to a narrow waist. She began rubbing his back.

With Venus's touch, he snapped back to what he was there for and turned toward the park entrance. He spotted the white Econoline van creeping slowly up the park drive and pull into a parking spot where the Humvee had parked. He turned back to Venus, leaned in toward her, saw her breasts press against the skin tight bikini top, then quickly looked up to her face and gave her an embarrassed smile. Through his teeth he told her to smile at him and look to see what the van occupants were doing.

Venus put her arm around Vince's neck. "I like you, too. Nice abs, and, I might add, nice ass. Starke is answering his phone. He's looking through the windshield toward the beach, and now he's pointing north. The Metro woman is getting out and running that way."

The van backed up into the drive, causing a car to slam on its brakes and lay on the horn. The van peeled out toward the exit. Without stopping, it turned onto Lakeshore Drive and sped back toward the entrance.

"What you wanna do, Honey?" asked Venus with a seductive smile on her face.

"Find the twins."

Venus whispered, "That's not what a lover would say to a beautiful girl with barely anything on. Play the part, lover boy."

*Oh boy.* "Please," Vince said with a smile and then put his cheek next to hers and whispered. "We have to go now."

"Oh, honey. I love it when you talk like that." She looked over at another couple nearby and winked at them.

Vince stood and took one last look up the parking lot. The white van turned into the park entrance. "Starke's here." He saw him get out of the van and jog past the concession stand toward the beach. He leaned down and took Venus's hand. "Okay, babe. Let's go."

Venus picked up her clothes and shook the blanket, causing her body to sway back and forth. She saw Vince taking a quick look and smiled at him. "I'm ready."

They threw their stuff into the back seat and Vince peeled out onto Lakeshore Drive heading to the marina. When they got there, Al and Cane were nowhere to be seen.

"Where'd they go?" Venus asked.

Vince looked over and gave her a once over. "Uh, they're great cyclists. They probably hit thirty miles an hour getting out of town, so they might already be on the road to North Lakeshore."

Venus sand, "Well then, punch the ponies and let's go. And, keep your snoopy eyes on the road ahead."

~~~

Starke made it to the shoreline and looked north up the beach for Janet and the twins. He saw Janet wave back at him, shaking her head. His phone buzzed and he realized he'd missed a call.

Starke hit the return call button. "Yeah?"

"Answer your phone, man. Where are you?" Dick asked.

"At the beach, north past the park. We got another call in this direction."

"And you haven't seen them."

"Right. Why?" asked Starke

"I spotted two red heads on bikes booking it south, heading out of town."

"Can you catch them?" Starke asked.

Dick looked around and saw an ATV, All Terrain Vehicle, sitting in front of a store. "I can catch them. Found a four wheeler," he said as he ran down the block. He peeked in the store and saw no one looking, so he got on the seat and couldn't believe his luck, the key was in the ignition. He started the engine and roared south. A minute later he found himself in the dead end parking lot of the car ferries. He turned back around and headed down the first street going east. When he got past a Dow Chemical Plant, he caught a glimpse of the cyclists as they went south behind a hill on the old highway. He opened up the ATV and gave it as much gas as it would take.

When he got to the highway, he sped up the hill and around several curves hoping to catch a glimpse of them. He passed a couple of tourist driving slow in a Mustang and finally saw them as they were flying downhill toward Lake Michigan.

Vince let the ATV pass them. Venus saw the driver and yelled, "That's Daniels."

"Hold on," Vince yelled back. He floored it and the beach blanket flew out of the back seat. When they turned onto Lakeshore Drive, they saw the four wheeler catch up to the twins, pull around them and stop. Daniels took the twins' picture when they sped around him.

"Uh oh," said Venus. "He's calling in the troops."

"That's not all." Vince sped up to the ATV to catch him before he took off after the boys. Al and Cane were speeding up to get away from Daniels.

Vince got out his phone and called Debra. "The boys have been spotted on south Lakeshore Drive near the Pump Storage Project. Head back this way."

He hung up, passed the ATV just as it was going to take off, and like a tourist, braked as he pointed to the lake for his girlfriend to look. The ATV rear ended them and Daniels somersaulted over the handlebars and onto the trunk. Venus screamed on cue. Daniels fell backward to the road as Vince took off and sped up to the twins. He pulled up beside them and motioned them to pull over.

"Vince!" they both yelled in unison. "What the..."

"Drop the bikes and get in," he yelled.

"But Vince," Al said, trying to explain.

"Get in! Now!"

As Vince peeled out, he saw Daniels get back on the ATV in his rear view mirror. Vince put the Mustang into a sharp curve and Daniels was out of sight. After the curve straightened out, he stomped on the gas and hit a hundred for the next four miles.

He took his foot off the gas for a second to take the turn to his road and called Diane. "Take care of the ATV. He's on Lakeshore by the Pump Storage Project."

"We're almost there," she answered.

Vince punched a speed dial number on his phone and the gate to his house slid open. He hit the gas up the driveway and skidded into the garage, barely missing the rising garage door. Everyone climbed out and ran into the house.

Vince closed the door and looked over at Venus, still in her bikini, standing with her hands on her hips and her mouth open, out of breath.

"What?" he asked.

"That was some damn fine driving, Hardesty. Scared me shitless,"

"Thanks, I think."

"Yeah man. That was boss," Cane said.

"Hey guys, I'm starving," Al interjected. "All this excitement has made me hungry."

"Yeah. Me too," Cane said. "So, if you love birds can quit staring at each other, can we get something to eat?"

"Yeah, we almost had pizza at the beach, but then your *gurl-friends* made us take off," Al added.

"Hey!" Venus said exasperated. "We grab you from the jaws of defeat, and all you can think about is food?"

"Well, with you in that bikini, we could be thinking of something else," Al said with a stupid grin on his face.

Venus gave him a withering look. Cane grabbed Al and yanked him into the great room. Venus turned back to Vince. "And what are you looking at?"

"Mmm, you."

"Well, wipe that grin off your face, too. Men! I'm going back to the car and get my clothes.

Vince's phone rang. "Yeah. Okay. See you in a few."

"Who was that?" Venus asked.

"Deb and Diane. They ran the ATV off the road. Daniels will be walking until Starke picks him up. They're heading back here to hide the Humvee. We'll lay low until dark."

Chapter 17

Friday Evening

"So, how did they find us?" Cane asked.

"It was Al's phone," Vince said. "That's why you should have left it at home or kept it off. Those guys have electronic surveillance resources to track any call on any phone, well, except mine."

"Sorry Vince. I was expecting a call from FOC and I had to take it. It was about my little girl, man. It was about the DNA test."

"Did you make or answer any other calls today?"

"Just one, earlier. Juanita called me this morning before we biked out to the state park."

"That was the call," Vince said as he took out his phone and hit the speed dial. "No answer at the Center." He looked at his watch. "She's gone home already. It's Friday." Vince pushed a speed dial number.

"Sandy, can you have a couple of squad cars sent to Juanita Alvarez's house on Burt Road and McNichols?"

"Can do. What's up?"

"Juanita called the boys in Ludington. Al answered his personal phone and Starke traced the twins here. They got close to catching them. So, Starke probably had her call traced as well and might have her followed."

"Will do. I'll send a scout car over there right now. I'll let you know what the officers find. Hopefully her, and if they do, I'll have them take her to a friend's."

"Thanks," Vince said.

"Now they're after Juanita?" asked Cane. "Al, you're a dumbass. You should have..."

"Hold on," Vince interrupted. "We don't know that yet. Just covering all of the bases."

"Back to my question," Cane said.

"To answer your first question, it's the same guys who were after you in Detroit. It's why I had Debra and Diane bring you here in the first place, and keep you out of sight while we tried to figure out what was going on. Now we know they're hot to pick up you two."

"Because we got 'em on video?" asked Cane.

"Yes, and no. They took Cane's video from Millers, but there's nothing incriminating on that one. They're pretty sure you saw the actual drop, because they've got your wireless camera, but luckily, no video. Thanks to you guys, they've been compromised. And after today, we know they're desperate to catch you. So, now we have to get you guys out of here tonight. I'll have Debra and Diane drive you back to Detroit after dark. Venus and I will send Starke in another direction. So get cleaned up and start packing."

After everyone showered and put on dry clothes, they met downstairs in the kitchen. Debra and Diane had made sub sandwiches for everyone.

"We knew you guys have to be hungry since you didn't get to eat earlier, and not to mention the bike race out of town," Debra said.

"Thanks! At least somebody's thinking of us" Al said, winking at Cane.

Cane just shook his head.

Everybody took a sandwich to the dining room table and dug in. After a few minutes of quiet munching, Venus asked, "What's the plan?"

Vince answered. "Like I said, Debra and Diane will drive the boys back to Detroit and secure them at my house. You and I will create a diversion. They're still out there and they know a Mustang picked up the twins. We'll drive toward town while

Deb and Diane drive to Pentwater. When we've picked up their tail, Debra, I'll call you. Head south on 31, take the Stony Lake exit and go west through the National Forest."

"In other words," Diane said, "stay off the main road."

"Just a precaution," said Vince

"You got it," Debra answered.

"And guys, I mean it. Stay locked up until I get back. Starke's crew will be back in Detroit once they see the Mustang return to the airport."

"Yes, Faa-theer," the twins said in unison.

"As soon as you get done eating, hit the sack for a few hours. It'll be a late trip. Venus, we'll take the Mustang and drive into town for some ice cream, see if any of our friends follow. If they do, we'll drop the car and lose them. In the morning we'll head to the airport and take off before they know we're gone."

"How do we get to the airport?"

"Got a friend and a plan," Vince said with a smile. His phone rang.

"Yeah Sandy."

"The officers didn't find Juanita at home."

"Good or bad?" Vince asked.

"Not sure. Her car wasn't there, so that's good."

"And the bad?"

"The back door was pried open and some chairs were knocked over, like somebody was rushin through the house. The officers spoke with some of the neighbors and found out that Metro Guard had parked in the driveway for a few minutes and then left in a hurry."

"That can't be good," Vince replied.

"But, her next door neighbor said that Juanita usually doesn't come home on Fridays. She apparently meets friends for a fish dinner and then out to bingo for a late night and a sleepover."

"That *can* be good."

"Let's hope so," Sandy said, "but we should be prepared for the worst. I'll go to her house in the mornin' and see if she's back home. Does she have a cell phone?"

"No. Doesn't believe in them. Says she's got all the phone answering she needs at the Center."

"Good. At least Starke can't have her traced."

Vince filled Sandy in on everything that had happened. He asked Sandy if there were any urgent Homeland meetings earlier since that's where Starke had told Angela he went for the day.

"There was a special meeting called, but it's confidential and by invitation only," Sandy said.

"What about?" asked Vince.

"Security issues dealin' with the Federal Reserve."

"They're moving on Monday," Vince said.

"Exactly. High security, the highest."

"Well, apparently that didn't interest Starke," Vince responded.

"But it gives him a legitimate meeting to cover his day in Ludington."

"Right. Thanks Sandy. I'll see you back in town in the morning."

Everyone finished eating and headed to separate rooms, men on one side, women on the other. Vince went up to his office, turned on the computer and linked up with Mike in D.C. who was monitoring calls between Starke and his crew. Apparently Daniels and Roberts were searching up and down Lakeshore Drive for a Mustang.

Vince called his Korean neighbors, Dr. and Mrs. Lee, and asked if they would have their son, Jae-Sun, who Vince paid to check on the house whenever he wasn't here, answer the intercom to his gated drive. Vince had wired the speaker and camera to both his and their house.

Vince got a couple of hours sleep, and then checked in with his neighbor about any visitors. Only one, inquiring if someone lived nearby who owned a Mustang. Jae-Sun answered in Korean, then affected English, putting them off. Vince thanked the neighbor boy and told him there would be an extra fifty in his check next week.

After dark, with a quarter moon hanging high above Lake Michigan, Vince helped Debra and Diane load up their Jeep and got the boys settled in the back seat with some pillows and blankets.

He pulled out the Mustang, put the top down and waited for Venus. When she came out his mouth fell open and his palms went sweaty. Her black hair was loose and fell over her shoulders, swaying in the moon light. She had on a slinky silk top that outlined her curves and a long loose skirt with a slit up the side that opened with each stride. Obviously when not in danger, his libido was working just fine.

"What you smiling at *muchacho*?"

"There's a beautiful moon out."

"Yes there is. Anything else?" she asked with a smile.

*"You look wonderful tonight."*

"Clapton, 1979" she answered.

Vince looked back and saw both Debra and Diane smiling at him. *Everyone seems to know there's something between us.* He waved and drove the Mustang out first to test the road for the white van.

The gate opened and they drove to Lakeshore Drive toward Ludington. After one mile and two quick brakes for deer, Vince spotted a set of headlights. In a minute, the white van pulled up behind them. Vince punched the accelerator, made a curve and hit a hundred down a straightaway. He called Debra and told her they were good to go.

"So, what's the plan now?" Venus yelled over the wind rushing by.

"Taking you to the best ice cream store in Michigan, *The House of Flavors*."

"Woo-hoo, a real date."

"Yep. We'll order up some ice cream and see if our out of town guests pay us a visit."

"I hope they don't come inside and ruin my first date with you, Mr. Hardesty."

"They're looking for twin boys, not a dark haired beauty."

"Vincent! Are you getting sweet on me?"

He smiled at her as he slowed down at the Pump Storage Project. "Look at that," he said.

The quarter moon was dipping toward the horizon, creating a wavy line of moon light on the water below. Venus leaned over toward Vince to get a better look. She put her arm around his neck and laid her head on his shoulder. She sighed. "It's beautiful."

A warm tingly sensation went from Vince's shoulder to his toes.

"Hold on." He punched the accelerator and Venus slid back into her seat. Headlights from the van were closing in behind them again. Vince decided it was time to lose them. He kept the pedal down and took a turn with a slide, sending Venus back over to his side. She laid her head back on his shoulder.

"Woo hoo, courtesy curve," she said.

It was. He looked down past her hair to the front of her dress and saw her breasts highlighted in the blue light of the dash.

She looked up. "That's not the curve I was talking about. Keep your snoopy eyes on the road ahead."

Vince stopped at the flashing light on Pere Marquette Highway and watched the pair of headlights coming up behind them. Vince punched the accelerator again and turned onto the highway at seventy. He doused the lights and took a hard left and drove the back way into town.

~~~

Vince sat at the back wall so that Venus would be facing away from both entrances to the main dining room. He told Venus about the *House* specialty, the *Pig's Dinner*, and how there was no way she could eat the whole thing, so he offered to share.

Dick Daniels and Janet Schmidt walked through the main entrance looking for two male red heads. They looked down the restaurant and didn't recognize either Vince or Venus. They left.

A few minutes later, Jason Roberts came in a different door which entered midway into the main dining room. He scanned around the room and hesitated just for a second on Venus, her profile visible from his angle. He walked through the dining room and left by the main entrance.

"I think we have a problem," Vince said.

"What's that?"

"Roberts just spotted you."

"How?"

"He just walked in the side door to the dining room. And if anyone knows you and your looks, it would be another Guardy. Besides, you're hard to miss."

"I thought they're just looking for the twins."

"True, but they saw the couple in a Mustang, that is, you and me babe, their newest connection."

A cute waitress came to their table and smiled at Vincent. "Can I take your order?" "Might as well," Vince said, returning the smile. He felt a foot kick him in the shin.

"Oh, we'll have the specialty of the *House,* one *Pig's Dinner,* with two spoons, please."

After the waitress walked away, Vince held up his finger before Venus could say anything and made a quick phone call to a local friend.

Eating the towering seven scoops of ice cream with chocolate, strawberry and caramel toppings, along with fresh whipped cream and nuts, almost became a competition. After half of the challenge, they went slower and it became more like love making with *mmm's* and *aaahs*."

"I think we need a private booth," Vince said.

Venus agreed with a smile and a lick of her lips. He caught the innuendo and looked at her sensuous lips with chocolate dripping down her chin, then to her top as she leaned over the table. He looked up to her face and saw her wink. *This Pig's Dinner is turning me into a real pig. I'll have to compose myself before getting up from the table.*

Vince put down his spoon, sat back and wiped his face with the cloth napkin as if waving the white flag in surrender, both at the ice cream and Venus. She put down her spoon, looked into his eyes and said, "Was it as good for you as it was for me?" she asked.

"Ooh, yeaah," Vince said with the nod of his head.

Vince leaned toward Venus as she put her elbows on the table with her chin on her hands. With effort, he kept his eyes looking into her eyes. "We're not leaving the way we came. We're going out the back through the ice cream factory and ditching the Mustang."

"How are we getting back to your place?" she asked.

"You'll see."

During *Dinner*, Vince noticed that Daniels and Schmidt had taken a table at the other end of the restaurant and were eating sundaes. Good thinking on their part. He wondered if Starke and Roberts got take out.

Vince got up from the table and looked over at the ice cream counter. Three waitresses were smiling at him. *So much for being discreet.* He took Venus's hand, helped her up and led her to the register where the waitresses were suddenly busy with other things.

Vince smiled at the owner's wife who greeted him warmly at the cash register. Vince's dad and her parents had been good friends. He smiled back and greeted her in return, making a request to go through the warehouse and out the back. Evelyn told him that that was no problem

After paying, they were led through the warehouse, weaving around large vats and freezers to a metal door at the far end of the building. When Vince opened the door, his friend was waiting.

"Dude, longtime no see," Josh McMaster said, as he shook Vincent's hand. He looked at Venus and said, "Who's the lady?"

"Josh, this is Venus Sanchez of the United States Coast Guard."

"Pleased to meet you, Venus. Vince and me, we go way back. I'm Mr. All American's former high school wrestling teammate, hunting and fishing buddy."

"All American, huh?" Venus said.

"Yep. Wrestling champ. All State swimmer too. He didn't tell you?" He looked back at Vincent. "We've got *Kodachrome*."

"You mean, all the crap you learned in high school?" Venus quipped. "Paul Simon, 1973."

Vincent just shook his head.

"Yep. But he saw the writing on the wall. So, even though he was all set for the Olympics in college, he did his country proud and joined the Navy."

"Really!" Venus said as she looked back at Vince.

Vincent just hung and shook his head. "Thanks, buddy."

"Don't mention it. Coming up for deer season?" Josh asked.

"You bet. Bringing some of the brothers," Vince answered with a smile.

"Great. Always like a shootout with the *S.aF.eR. Brothers*."

Venus cocked her head in curiosity.

Vince looked at Venus. "Special Forces Reserve," he said as explanation.

Vince looked back at Josh. "Love to chat, but right now we need to scoot." He handed the Mustang keys to Josh. "This is for you. You and your lovely wife, Dawn, have some fun. It's rented for a week."

"Cool. As our Paul Simon says, it's *Late in the Evening*," handing Vince two helmets.

"*One-Trick Pony*, 1980, and we're going to blow the room away," answered Vince.

"Are you serious?" Venus exclaimed.

"Right this way," Josh said as he led them down the street to a neighborhood park. There sat an all-black Honda CBR 600 crotch rocket.

"Hop on my pony," Vince said as he handed her a helmet.

"In this skirt?"

"Just hike it up and tie it around your waist. It'll blow up in the wind anyway."

"Lucky you'll be looking the other way. You get on first."

"Not so lucky," he said as he straddled the bike and started it up. Venus motioned to his friend to look away as she pulled up her skirt and got on. The jump seat caused her to lean forward onto Vince's back.

*Maybe lucky after all,* thought Vince. He cranked up the engine and took off like a rocket. They flew down the back streets of Ludington and headed out of town. Venus screamed in Vince's ear as they went airborne over the hills to Lakeshore Drive. Vince only slowed down enough to get out his phone and hit the speed dial number for his driveway gate. He took the drive all the way to the back and parked the bike under the deck. Venus jumped off, pulled down her skirt and pushed off the helmet, shaking out her long black hair.

"Oh. My. God!" Venus said laughing, taking in gulps of air. "That was wild!"

Vince met Venus's smile with a big grin as he took off his helmet. Her chest was heaving up and down in a very appealing way. With his best flight attendant voice, he said, "We hoped you enjoyed your flight. Please ride with us again, and exit this way."

Venus marched up to him as instructed and put her arms around his neck and planted a big wet kiss on his responsive mouth. They held each other tightly and kissed longingly. When they finally broke apart, Venus asked, "Should we take this inside?"

"No, not yet," Vince said. "Let's go up on the deck and enjoy the moon setting over the lake."

"You *bastardo romántico.*"

Vince took her hand and led her up the stairs and pulled out two armless lounge chairs. He set them side by side facing the lake. Once seated and quiet, they could hear the waves lapping at the shore line. Venus took Vince's hand and held it in her lap. When he looked at her, he saw tears well up in her eyes, and then one rolled down her cheek.

"What is it Venus?"

"It is so beautiful, and so peaceful," she said as she looked over at Vince. "And I'm sitting with a beautiful and caring man. I feel at one with God's creation. It reminds me of something from my childhood."

"What's that?"

"My dad took me fishing on the Detroit River or on Lake Erie every Friday after school, rain or shine. He had to work Saturday and Sunday as a guard at the Ambassador Bridge, so he'd park and wait at my school at the corner of Vernor and Junction in Southwest Detroit. I'd be the first out the door. We'd fish all night. The sounds of the water and the feel of the air were just like tonight."

"You really miss your dad, don't you?"

"Very much. When I started dating, he'd take my current boyfriend with us. He said that any man, young or old, who couldn't catch his own dinner wasn't a keeper and I should throw him back. Besides his test for manhood, he gave me a desire for the water."

"Do I pass muster?" Vince asked.

"Yes you do."

"Well, just like your dad, my dad took me out on this lake, fishing for steelhead. We would go out through the Ludington harbor, lower our downriggers and head out a couple of miles. We would always have one or two after several hours. Nothing like fresh Salmon grilled to perfection. But, then he died when I was in college."

"Is that why you didn't make it to the Olympics?"

"I was too young for '84. He died in '87. I returned home to care for him during his last six months. I was his only family. A friend of his who visited was a Navy Officer, and the rest is history."

They both sat silent, thinking of their past.

Vince looked over at Venus and saw the tears in her eyes and his eyes welled up as well. It reminded him of another night. It was in the desert of Kuwait as a full moon set on a horizon of sand. Venus squeezed his hand. She reached over and tenderly touched his cheek. She tentatively turned her head toward him and he kissed her lightly on the lips, a tender and long kiss. She moved from her lounge chair to his and kissed him in return. They held each other as they watched the moon descend into the lake.

Venus tilted her head up to kiss again. Vince moved toward her, taking her lips more hungrily this time. Their tongues met.

She crossed her leg over his and felt a bulge in his pants rub on her thigh. She felt a vibration and lifted her head.

"What's that?" Venus asked.

Vince pushed up and reached into his front pocket and pulled out his phone. He cleared his voice and said, "Uh, hello?"

"Am I interruptin' anything?" Sandy asked.

"Hi Sandy. No, just laying out on the deck." He looked over at Venus and she gave him a wink.

"You're lyin', not layin'. Anyway, did you get the boys in the clear?" asked Sandy.

"Uh, yeah. Debra and Diane are driving them back as we speak."

"Venus with you?"

"Yes."

"When you headin' back?"

"We'll fly out in the morning."

"Good. I've been watchin' Juanita's house in case she had a change of plans and came home before mornin'. Let's get together for lunch. It sounds like this whole thing has gone to another level."

"You're right. Will do, Sandy. Have a good night," Vince said, hoping he didn't sound too rushed.

"No, Vince. You have a good night, lyin', uh layin', on the deck." Sandy rang off.

"Sandy says *Hello*. He's staked out Juanita's house 'till she hopefully gets back in the morning."

Venus said, "You know, at first I thought there was something else vibrating in your pants."

"Oh, there is something else vibrating in my pants, but I don't think I'm quite ready for that," he said, sweating.

"I understand. I know you have a deep sadness in your heart and I don't want to do anything that you might regret," she replied.

*She can read my heart as well as my mind.* "I don't regret sitting here with you," he said. *I could sit here for a very long time.*

"You want to tell me about it?" she asked.

Vince took a deep breath, let it out slowly and sat quiet for a moment.

"I was stationed in Kuwait after Desert Storm. I was training their Special Forces. I met a Sheik and his family and I fell in love with his daughter. We were married for three years. We were going to have a baby. She was three months along, but..." He paused.

Venus took his hand and squeezed it. "But?"

"She was killed by a stray bullet when a Republican Guard Commander returned for a revenge attack." Tears welled up in Vince's eyes, and then rolled down his cheeks. "She and the baby were killed."

Venus said nothing. She held his hand and waited.

Vince looked into her eyes and saw tears well up. *I can't tell her the rest, not now.*

"I stayed another year training soldiers and grieving in the desert. I returned to the States, trained SEALs and went on missions for the next seven years. My father-in-law set me up in an oil import business and had his sons manage it until I moved to Detroit. The company is housed in my home."

Venus wiped the tears from her cheeks.

"Thank you," Vince said.

"For what?" asked Venus.

"For not saying anything that most people say when they hear about Rachel."

Venus squeezed his hand again and nodded.

"I like you very much, Venus. I like being with you. I have feelings for you that I haven't had in many years."

"Not since your wife some ten years ago?" Venus asked.

"That's right. I want to see you on a personal basis, but..." He paused.

"And I want to see you, too. But there's no hurry. Take your time, Vincent."

"Thank you."

"Speaking of taking time, I have to be at work at eight in the morning, and I know we have to get up at five. So I need to get to sleep, and so do you, *mi amore*."

"Good thinking, I think."

"So good night, Vincent Hardesty. And thank you for a first date, or should I say a first day?"

"It was a wonderful day, and night. So, good night."

Chapter 18


Saturday Morning

Vince woke up and turned off the alarm five minutes before five. He heard noises downstairs, so he got up, dressed, opened the bedroom door and caught the smell of coffee brewing and bacon frying.

He called good morning as he trotted down the stairs and found Venus dressed in khakis and in the kitchen scrambling eggs and making biscuits with every cupboard opened.

"I hope you found everything you needed," he said, extending his arms and motioning to the cluttered counters. He moved closer to her. "Mmmm, you smell wonderful."

"Good morning *mi amor.* You just smell the bacon."

"True, but I also smell the scent of beautiful flowers," Vince said.

"Thank you," Venus said. "And yes, I eventually found everything I needed. Please sit down and I will serve you breakfast."

"Yes, Ma'am."

"Hope you're hungry. It looks like I made enough for three people."

"I'm starving," he said.

Vince's phone rang. He listened for a minute, said thanks and hung up. "Debra said they deposited the twins safely at my house and that she and Diane will stay there until we get back."

Venus handed him a plate overflowing with eggs and bacon and biscuits. She sat down and gave him a big smile. Neither one said another word until they had devoured the food.

*She's thinking this would be a great way to start every morning. Is that what I want?*

Venus looked up at Vince all business. "What time do we leave?"

"Thirty minutes," he said, noting her serious demeanor. He started to feel confused and a little guilty about last night. "The sun rises at six fifty-five and I want us in the air by six hundred hours."

Venus nodded. "Good. I'll be ready."

"Can we talk about last ni..."

Venus cut him off with a swipe of her fork across her mouth. "Shush! Finish your breakfast."

Vince ate a few more bites. "But, I just wanted to say..."

She cut him off again with another swipe. "What you say today means nothing, *muchacho*, but what you *do* from here on means everything. *Comprende*?"

"Yes, Ma'am."

Vince looked back at his empty plate, unable to look at her piercing brown eyes. She got up from the table and put her dishes in the sink. He got up and did the same. "Don't worry about cleaning up. I have a housekeeper that comes in everyday when someone's here," he said.

"Nice," Venus said. "I'll get my bag... Oh, wait. We're taking the motorcycle, right?"

"Yep. I have a backpack you can use."

Vince went to a walk-in closet just off the kitchen, pulled out the pack and threw it at her. Venus caught it with one hand.

"Nice catch," he said.

"Yes I am," she said with a smile.

*Oh Boy, are you ever.*

Vince picked up the two helmets. "With the tinted face shields down, our faces will be hidden. They have night vision capability, so we'll be able to see with no problem. I'd rather not have Starke and crew on our tail to the airport. At this point they don't know that the twins are gone and they don't know where we disappeared to with my friend taking them on a wild goose chase with the Mustang. Hopefully we'll fly out of here before they know we're gone."

"Okay. I'll go pack my things."

Vince locked up and turned on the security system. Venus came back downstairs with the pack strapped to her back, pressing the material of her top tightly against the outline of her bra. A flash back of last night raced through his thoughts and a wave of desire rushed through him. He handed her a helmet and put his on so she wouldn't see his face flush.

Outside, Vince started up the bike with a loud whine. Venus put on her helmet and hopped on the rear seat. She leaned forward into Vince's broad back and put her arms around his waist, holding tight as he took off down the drive. She felt light headed as they sped through the gate and onto the road.

She hoped this wasn't the last time she held him in her arms. She knew he needed to sort things out before getting more serious. She said a short prayer for him to make the right choice, that is, her choice. She felt like a contestant on *The Bachelor*. The difference was that she wasn't up against seven other women competitors, she was only up against one: his beautiful dead wife.

They took the road to Lakeshore Drive and headed south through Pentwater to old US-31. He took it at sixty miles per hour and ten minutes later they were at the airport. He drove through the entrance and pulled up to his hangar, the plane secured inside with the sliding door locked just as he had requested. Before pushing it open, he looked back up the drive to see if anyone had followed them. No one. He scanned the airport to see if the Coast Guard Aero was tied down anywhere. The plane was gone. After his Ludington friend took Starke and his crew on a wild goose chase that no Econoline van could catch, they must have given up and flown out last night.

*Why would they give up so easily?*

They pulled out the plane and stored the motorcycle in the hangar. Vince fired up the 33 Beechcraft and went through the pre-flight check list as he taxied to the north end of the runway. He called the tower, asked about Starke's flight and listened for a minute. After given the okay, he told Venus that Starke had taken off at midnight. He revved up the seven cylinders and took off, a glimmer of pre-dawn light beginning to grow on the eastern horizon.

Once in the air, Venus announced she was taking a nap. She would need to check in at Selfridge at eight a.m. She figured with a little over an hour flight time and thirty minutes on I-94 from City Airport, she would make it on time.

Vince landed the pane at seven-ten a.m. and taxied up to Venus's Jeep. "I think I know why Starke took off last night."

"Because he knows that I know the twins," said Venus

"And that means..."

"They'll be following me. Well, he'll know where I'll be today."

"Watch your back," Vince warned.

"I thought that was your job," Venus said with a smile.

As Venus got out of the plane and gave him a peck on the cheek, she asked, "We're still on for tonight, right?"

"Yes, Ma'am."

"Don't worry, I can take care of myself," Venus said, and then walked to her Jeep.

*Yes, I'm watching your back side, quite literally.*

Vince taxied to the hangar, shut down the engine and called Sandy.

"I'm back. Let's meet for some breakfast at the I-Hop on Jefferson."

"Everybody alright?"

"Yep. The boys are back at my place, Venus is off to Selfridge, and I need to get to the gym by ten.

~~~

Venus drove through the Selfridge main gate off Hall Road and Jefferson, took a right on North Perimeter Drive and turned in at the Air Station Detroit. She checked in with the dispatcher and took a seat in the lounge area. She dosed off for a few minutes until she heard her name announced over the intercom speaker to pick up the phone for a call from the commander.

"Hello, this is Warrant Officer Sanchez."

"Good morning, Venus. This is Commander Starke at headquarters."

She swallowed and licked her lips. "Good morning, sir."

"I know you just had a day off and you're back on for today until three, right?"

"Yes Sir."

"As you know, it's going to be a busy day and a busy weekend. So, I'd like you to come in on Sunday as back up."

Venus swallowed again and cleared her voice, "Yes sir."

"That's all, Sanchez."

"Yes sir." Venus hung up and let out a sigh of relief. She swiped the back of her hand across her forehead and found it damp. She headed for the bathroom and splashed cold water on her face, washed her hands and dried off with several paper towels. She thought of calling Vince, but decided she would stick to her ultimatum of not calling him until he made the next move.

She pulled out her phone and gave Angela a call. "Angela, call me back when you get a chance."

"Yes Ma'am. Thank you."

Angela hit the intercom and told Starke she was going on break. She walked outside by the river and called Venus. "I'm back."

"I just got a call from Commander Starke. He changed my schedule and put me on backup for Sunday. Is anything special going on?"

"Well, as you know, today is that end of summer *Jobbie Nooner* at Gull Island on Lake St. Clair. Maybe he thinks there'll be a lot of drunkin, hung over boaters Sunday mornin. Other than that, no."

Venus sighed. "The Michigan Mardi Gras, and in boats. What a great combination."

"Get some beads while you're out there, Venus. Flash 'em from the chopper. That'll be some *things* for them to remember."

"I'll have my diver do that. He's got some pretty good pecs," Venus said.

"Nice. By the way, Starke has had quite a busy morning on the phone. First a long call with some folks at Metro Guard, a lengthy call from Roberts, then an involved and sometimes heated conversation from somebody who did not identify himself at the Federal Building."

"How'd you know it was a Fed?"

"The number on the caller I.D. It's one of the few calls that the person's name doesn't show up, but I've gotten so many from over there, I recognize the number."

"You say it was a heated conversation?"

Just then, Starke came outside and waved Angela back into the office.

"Gotta go. The boss is wavin me in.

"Thanks Angela. Call me after work."

"Okay. Goodbye."

Angela walked back in the office to see what Starke wanted.

He said, "I'll be out of the office this morning with another meeting over at the McNamara Building. Just take my calls and I'll return them when I get back this afternoon."

"Yes sir."

Starke walked out of the office to his car and drove out of the parking lot, Angela went back outside and called Venus back.

"He left for a meeting at the downtown federal building, and just after being there almost all day yesterday," Angela said.

"He wasn't at the Feds yesterday," Venus said. "He and his crew were in Ludington chasing down Al and Cane."

"What? You kiddin me? Starke sure wants those boys, doesn't he? But, hey, wait a minute. How do you know that?"

"Because I was there with Vincent ."

"You were with the Mr. Vincent Hardbody? Well now, I have to hear more 'bout that, Mz. Vee."

"I can't talk now. I'm heading to today's briefing,"

"What time you get off today?" asked Angela

"Three. Then have to get ready for our wedding date tonight."

"So, let's go together," said Angela.

"I don't know. Vince and I both think that Starke will have me followed, probably by Roberts. I don't want to put you in the middle of this right now."

"You're kiddin. I'm already smack dab in the middle of this here *cray-zeeness*," Angela said. "Besides, I'm goin to be at the wedding anyway, but with a police detective, yes sir!"

"Okay, okay," Venus agreed. "Let's not meet at either of our houses. Somewhere neutral."

"Oh, oh! I know where," Angela said excitedly. "Let's meet at Victoria's Secret at Somerset. You go in the south entrance and I'll go in the north entrance and I'll meet you in the changin room. Roberts or none of those guys will follow us in there. Besides, you might need somethin new to wear for Vincent."

"I'm almost at the briefing, Angela."

"Okay Venus," said Angela. "See you in the lingerie department."

"Good bye Angela." Venus hung up with a giggle.

~~~

Even though it was lunch time, Vince and Sandy both ordered the breakfast special with a stack of pancakes at the IHOP. Sandy told Vince that he'd met Juanita as she drove in her driveway this morning. She said she thought something was going on with the twins and that's why she called them. She's now safe and sound and back to her friend's house for the weekend.

Vince filled Sandy in on everything that had taken place in the last twenty-four hours. Almost everything. Talking it out had made him realize how crazy the whole situation had become.

"If yesterday taught us anything, it's that Starke's undercover operation is off protocol," Vince said. "They want to question the twins about the drop on Lake Erie, and we now know that they're tracking the boys' phones. When Al answered Juanita's call, Starke and his crew flew to Ludington to pick them up."

"Why did Al have his personal phone? You told him not to?."

"Al was expecting a call from Friend of the Court about his paternity. Juanita called, he took it. The court called, he took that one too."

"Man, that's too bad. Okay, you're right. It's more than some normal operation. And because it involves the twins and anybody near 'em, you seem more worked up than usual. Maybe a little too passionate for good thinkin'. So, take a deep breath, slow down and let's make a plan."

Vince nodded. *Sandy's right. I'm too 'passionate,' as he calls it. Between the twins, Juanita and my feelings for Venus, good or bad, I'm not thinking clearly. Too many emotions and hormones running in my blood. The boys have become like sons to me, Juanita is like an aunt, and Venus's like a girlfri… a good friend. Harriett would be proud.*

"We have proof that Starke is trying to kidnap them, maybe harm them, for some cover up, and I promised myself that I would never lose young men close to me again."

"That's what I'm talkin' about," Sandy said.

After the waitress brought their food and refilled their coffee, Vince asked Sandy if he'd found anything at Homeland.

"Lots of meetings lately," said Sandy. "Somethin's goin' down, but no one knows except for the brass. For all we know, they're followin' another tip on Jimmy Hoffa. My friend at McNamara can only tell me that Homeland, the FBI, the Secret Service, and the local Metro Guard are all involved. If the twins saw somethin' related, they'd have been picked up and questioned by one of those agencies, not Starke and his crew. Unless the feds don't want to be seen takin' in a couple of twenty year-olds. That would definitely bring a lot of unwanted attention."

"True, but why all the cloak and dagger?" Vince asked. "Hell, it's domestic. Why doesn't the FBI have one of their own pick them up? Nothing would be out of the ordinary about that. They could even use the local sheriff with the paternity case to pick up Al and take Cane along as a witness."

"Well, Vince, remember, you're the one hidin' 'em, and you're the one whiskin' 'em out to Ludington and back. So far, they just can't catch 'em."

"Right. And that's the way it's got to be, though I hate to think that instead of keeping the twins safe, I'm actually putting them at risk."

Sandy saw that Vince was working it through. It was true. Vince was the reason Starke or the police couldn't pick them up, and he wasn't so sure that it was a bad idea to keep the boys out of all of this. There was something off about all of it. As if reading his mind, Vince looked up at him.

"The drop. A Coast Guard skiff making a drop of what, we don't know, at a public beach, handed off to two Metro Guards playing as a couple in a romantic tryst," Vince said. "My gut says we're doing the right thing."

"I'll keep diggin'," said Sandy.

"We're still on for tonight," Vince said. "The boys will be back at work for a wedding with Miller at The Royal Park Hotel in Rochester. You, me, Angela, and Venus will be there as guests. We'll keep an eye on the twins. If the Feds want to pick them up, then so be it. At least we'll know it's legit."

"Puttin' the twins out there as bait and switch, huh, Vincent?"

"I guess so. At least we'll be around."

"Right," said Sandy. "By the way, you took Venus along with you. Why?"

"Better a couple than a guy casing out some young boys. Besides, Venus *is* distracting."

"That she is. So how was it, bein' a couple and all?"

Vince felt a bead of sweat form on his upper lip. "We were a good disguise."

"At least you were tryin'."

"Trying to what?"

"Disguise you two," Sandy said with a smile.

"It's not what you think," Vince said.

"Me thinks you're thinkin' too much."

"Well, I think I gotta go. Keep digging."

~~~

Matek Hakam pulled the used Dodge Caravan into the parking lot of the American Islamic Center on Ford Road. The familiar domed building with its book end towers was a comfort to him and his brothers. And right now, Matek thought they needed some comfort and counsel.

Musa had spoken with the *Iman* of the Center and requested an audience with him and his brothers. Matek had concurred. Malik thought it was ridiculous, but he was along for the ride. At least they now had a vehicle.

The *Iman* welcomed them with the traditional greeting, "*Asalaamu Alaykum,*" and had them sit down in his office. After introductions the *Iman* said "What can I do for you, my brothers."

Musa looked to Matek to speak first, since he was the oldest.

"We were moved here from New Orleans. We were rescued by the Coast Guard only ten days ago, and one of the local officers set us up in an apartment here in Dearborn earlier this week. Today, he gave us a used van and an opportunity for work with a cell phone distributor. Our younger brother thinks this is all a great opportunity, but Musa, our middle brother who talked to you on the phone, is very nervous about all of it, especially today."

"What about today?" the *Iman* asked.

"We are to deliver two crates of cell phones to the west side of Michigan. Ludington is the name of the city."

Musa interrupted. "The destination was changed just this morning. Earlier in the week it was to be Mackinac Island. Now it's Ludington."

"I see. What do you think about it, Matek."

"I'm torn between my two brothers. I think it could be a good opportunity for us to establish ourselves as good, faithful workers, but I share some of Musa's concerns. It has all happened so fast, and the sudden change in delivery is a concern."

"Too soon," interrupted Musa. "Forgive me, *Iman*. If I may speak?"

The *Iman* looked at Matek, and Matek nodded. "Please, continue."

"It is too good. We've only just recuperated in the last couple of days. Suddenly, the officer shows up and says he has a job for us. *You can't live on charity forever,* he says, like we would do that. We were hard workers in New Orleans. He gives us a van and entrusts us with a thousand cell phones and expects us to deliver them to a wholesaler in this city called Ludington. I think it's too much, too fast."

"Thank you," said the *Iman*. He looked back to Matek.

Matek looked at Musa. "My brother is always skeptical. Maybe Allah has blessed us for all the hardship we've endured." He looked back at the cleric. "*Iman*, we have lost everything. But thanks to the generosity of the Coast Guard, who saved us from the roof top of our apartment, we at least have a dry place to live, and now an opportunity to pay for what we have."

The *Iman* looked at Malik and nodded, offering him to speak.

"I say we must take whatever we can get. If we refuse now, it will show the officer and the community that we are lazy."

"He just wants to make money so he can spend it on loose women," Musa interrupted.

"Musa. stop it," Matek said.

The *Iman* lifted his hand. "My brothers, let us pause and take a moment of silence." Musa sighed. Malik shook his head in disgust. Matek bowed his head in prayer.

After a long minute of silence, the *Iman* spoke to Matek. "It is your decision as the eldest brother. I believe you should take the opportunity given you, since it was given by a member of the Coast Guard. I believe they can be trusted. They saved your life. But, I also believe you should proceed with caution. Sometimes gifts that are too good to be true are just that. I will inquire about this officer with my contacts in the police department. If you will give me your number, I will call you with whatever I find."

"Thank you, *Iman*. I believe your counsel is good and inspired by Allah."

Musa now bowed his head as Malik raised his.

The three brothers said their goodbyes and left the *Iman* as he blessed them from the doorway of the Center.

~~~

Bob Salem convinced his wife, Marsha, to join him for a warm and sunny day on Lake St. Clair. She was reluctant because this wasn't just any day on the northeast side of the lake. It was the second Saturday in September, the day of the *Jobbie Nooner II*.

The *Jobbie Nooner* is a wild boat party that's held on the northeast side of Lake St. Clair twice every summer. History has it that it originated with a small group of automotive designers, *Jobbies*, who wanted to take a co-worker out for his birthday. They decided to blow off work at lunchtime one Friday, i.e. *pull a Nooner*, get together on their boats and have a good time. It started two decades ago with four boats and seventeen friends. Now it's the two biggest parties of the summer: *Nooner I,* the third Friday in June, and *Nooner II,* the second Saturday in September, with several thousand boats and eight thousand people attending. It has been nicknamed the *Mardi Gras of the Midwest*. Not exactly a quiet time on the lake with your husband.

Bob put his *Boating Outlet's* newest boat in at the Captain Cove's Marina on Jefferson, just north of Selfridge. They headed southeast across the lake to Gull Island where the St. Clair River spills into Lake St. Clair, the epicenter of the *Nooner*. Thirty minutes later they could see multiple rows of sport boats and cruisers rafted together in concentric circles around the north side of the small island. Bob was showing off his new 2006 Bayliner 265 Cruiser. He thought the boat would get a few looks from *Nooners*, that is, when they weren't looking at women dropping their tops for beads.

After handing out brochures for his *Boating Outlet* on the outer ring, he trolled east to the other side of Gull Island and passed out more. When Marsha had had enough, she said, "Can we get out of the middle of this nude drunken boat party?"

"Oh alright," Bob said and pulled around to the south side of the island where the sight-seers were more scattered. When they reached the South Channel of the river, a freighter pushed through the St. Clair Cutoff, the main channel cut through a small island to form a straight-a-way into the lake.

Marsha took the binoculars from Bob. "You don't need these any more. I think you've seen enough of the bead wearing flasher babes." She scanned the freighter as it turned port side and headed directly south toward the Detroit River. Looking from the super structure aft to the narrow stern, she saw a flash of sunlight just to the side of the five story tall ship. She focused on the light reflecting off what looked to be a small silver boat bobbing in the water.

Marsha handed the binoculars to Bob. "Take a look at the water along the ship. Tell me what you see."

Bob slowed the boat until it idled. He took the binoculars and scanned the water beside the ship. "Oh, I see it. Looks like a shallow fishing boat. Must have been hit by the freighter in the main channel."

"Oh my God, Bob! Quick, call the Coast Guard."

Bob turned on his ship to shore VHF radio and called on the emergency channel. "This is kilo, delta, eight, victor, frank, whiskey. Bob Salem, Bayliner Cruiser. I'm at the South Channel of the St. Clair River near Gull Island. I've spotted a shallow fishing boat in the main channel. It might have been hit by a freighter."

"Roger," returned the Coast Guard dispatch.

"Bob, Bob. Look!" cried Marsha. "There's a body floating next to the boat."

"Mayday! Mayday! Coast Guard. We spotted a body in the water."

"Sending a rescue helicopter to your location. I'll patch you through."

"Roger," answered Bob. He turned his boat starboard and slowly headed toward the fishing boat now bobbing in the wake of the freighter.

Venus and her crew of co-pilot, flight mechanic and swimmer were dispatched to the St. Clair River, South Channel Cut. She thought it was probably some drunk who floated away from the *Jobbie Nooner*.

Venus flew at max speed of one hundred forty knots, one hundred sixty miles per hour, always assuming a live rescue. They reached the south side of Gull Island in five minutes and then hovered.

"This is Guardian Two, HH-65 Hee-lo, Coast Guard pilot Venus Sanchez. Over."

"Bob Salem here. My wife is waving a red and white striped beach towel over her head. Over."

Venus's co-pilot spotted the red and white blanket and said that the boat was located at their two o'clock. Venus slowly descended to see the woman waving the towel and her husband pointing to a small aluminum boat drifting in the channel.

"Swimmer ready?" Venus called over the headphones.

"Ready. Hundred feet starboard," he answered.

Venus moved the cyclic slightly to the right until the swimmer called "Bingo!" He jumped into the water, cleared his mask and swam to the small boat. Three minutes later he radioed PIW, *Person In the Water*. He cut the body from the boat and pulled it a short distance away.

Venus's mechanic lowered the basket into the water. The swimmer floated the body into the basket and gave a thumbs-up. The line was hoisted up and the basket pulled into the open door.

"Got a *BWD*," the mechanic announced.

Venus looked back and saw something that took her breath away. It was the insignia on the sleeve: *U.S. Customs and Border Protection.*

"Take the controls," she ordered the co-pilot.

She quickly slid out of her seat and moved to face the body. The name plate on the uniform shirt read *A. Martinez.*

*Oh God, no.*

*Alberto. Blue Water Dead.*

## Part III  THE SWITCH

*When you love a man, he becomes more than a body. His physical limbs expand, and the outline recedes, vanishes. He is rich and sweet and right. He is part of the world, the atmosphere, the blue sky and the blue water.* -- Gwendolyn Elizabeth Brooks

Chapter 19

Saturday Afternoon

When Vince finished his martial arts workout at St. Vincent's gym, he told the young fathers to hit the showers. Al and Cane were on lock down in his garage apartment.

He had always trained young men, many who needed a father-figure in their lives, but he had done most of it at the Naval Special Warfare Center (NSWC), in Coronado, California, and in Kuwait. He trained them to become efficient killers on the battle field.

It wasn't much different for most of Detroit's young fathers. They were living in a third world country called *The Hood,* and saw death and violence on a regular basis. It was why he gave free weekly classes in *Krav-Maga,* a hand to hand grappling and striking method developed in Israel. It was a combinations of eastern martial arts, western boxing and Olympic wrestling. It was used by Special Forces stationed around the world and it could be used on the mean streets of the '*D.*' It built self-confidence, self-discipline and self-defense in young men where it seemed everyone had a gun. Too often those guns were maiming or killing children, and young fathers wanted nothing to do with that.

His phone rang. "Vincent here."

"Oh, Vincent," Venus whispered. She was crying.

His heart skipped a beat. "What is it, Venus?"

"We found Alberto's body," she said sobbing.

"Where?"

"He was lashed to a fishing boat. Hit and dragged by a grain freighter in the St. Clair River."

"How do you know?" Vince asked.

Venus composed herself. "I flew out on a rescue call near Gull Island, thinking it was just some drunk boater from the *Nooner*. But Vincent, it was Alberto, and he was BWD."

"BW what?" Vince asked.

"BWD. Blue Water Dead. It's what Coasties in the great lakes call drowning victims. He'd been in the water several days. It was awful."

"How did you know it was Alberto?"

"He had on his Border Patrol uniform. His name plate. Oh my God, Vince. He was murdered......"

"Murdered? How do you know?" Vince asked.

"The sheriff and coroner are saying it looks like an accident, a fisherman drowning. But I *know* that's not true, Vincent," Venus said with conviction.

"How's that?"

"Alberto never fished a day in his life. Let me explain. He and my dad were best friends. They helped each other build their homes, they were Godparents to each other's children, and they bowled and played sports together. But, every time my dad invited him to go fishing with us on the river, he always refused. My dad said Alberto hated rivers and lakes because he had seen his father drown when he was only ten. His father was bringing his brother's family across the border on the Rio Grande River."

"I'm so sorry, Venus," Vince said, a pressure building in his chest.

"You know what this means, Vincent. That station supervisor has something to do with this. You said that he signed Alberto out on his last day?"

"Yes. That's right."

"He's hiding something," Venus said starting to cry again.

"I'm so sorry, Venus. I promised to get to the bottom of this, and I keep my promises. We'll figure this out."

"Thank you, Vincent. Uh, I've gotta go now. Just got another rescue call, at least I hope this one's a rescue. Oh, and Vincent. Angela and I will be going together. We'll meet you and Sandy there."

"Okay. See you then."

As Vincent hung up, Sandy called. "There's been quite a few meetings going on at Homeland. Whatever's goin down involves local, state, and federal agencies, as well as Coast Guard."

"What about?" Vince asked.

"Need to know," Sandy said. "Even my DHS contacts haven't been told what it is. Better call *the Snipe*."

"Will do. Thanks, Sandy."

"See you tonight."

"Oh, Sandy. Venus called. She pulled her friend's dad, Alberto Martinez, out of Lake St. Clair."

"Drowned?"

"Yep. The coroner is calling it a fisherman boating accident, but Venus doesn't think so."

"Why's that?"

"Venus said that Alberto hated the water. Never fished a day in his life."

"Sonofabitch."

"I'm calling the second shift supervisor to see if he can find out what Williams was doing in the warehouse when he signed out Alberto."

"What do you want me to do?" asked Sandy.

"Escort Dave Miller and his wife to the Royal Park Hotel. I suspect he'll be followed."

"Will do. Later."

~~~

Starke had everyone together at the apartment and he wasn't pleased. They had missed the twins in Ludington, but at least they now had a connection to them that he knew. He thought it ironic that the person that would help them apprehend the twins was also in the Coast Guard: Venus Sanchez.

Who was the mystery man? A boyfriend? They looked like they were tourists out for a drive, but then *accidentally* knocked Daniels off the ATV. To top it off, he'd gotten a call from the Air Station that Sanchez's helicopter had pulled a body out of Lake St. Clair. She identified the body as the missing CPB officer from the Blue Water Bridge. The simple mis-direct plan was getting too complicated. They had to act fast. He told Williams to head out immediately.

It looked like some group that included Venus Sanchez was onto them. The plan had gone too far now to blow it. But then he thought of a way to turn it around. He ran his idea by the Fed. He said whatever you've got to do, do it.

He reviewed with the crew where they stood, told them the plan and checked that everybody had what they needed. Peters had the pictures. Dick and Janet were to follow Sanchez. Roberts had loaded the package in the van and the Arabs had left for their new destination. The vehicles were ready. They only needed forty-eight hours. In the meantime, he called the Fed to put an FBI tail on Miller. They would find the twins, and maybe the mystery man too.

~~~

Venus parked her Jeep Sahara and watched the Escalade in her rear view mirror that had been following her since leaving work. The big black SUV was not hard to spot, especially when they slowed down when you slowed down, stopped when you stopped, sped up when you sped up. She drove around the mall twice to be sure they were following *her*. Yep. She wiped her palms on some Kleenex.

She got out of the Jeep in a grey-black stretch mini skirt with a white scooped silk blouse complete with four inch black stilettos. Her exit from any vehicle, let alone an all-sport Jeep, in such an outfit usually turned a few heads. But, this was the Somerset Collection, Michigan's premier shopping and dining destination. A girl couldn't just walk in here with sweats. That's why she loved coming here. She could dress up, feel sexy, and blend right in, even getting out of a Jeep with mud on it.

She looked at the reflection inside her oversized sunglasses. The couple getting out of the Cadillac SUV were trying not to look conspicuous. To the trained eye, they were anything but. They dressed like they were at the Gibralter Flea Market.

Once in the door, she hurried toward Victoria Secret. She picked up some push-up bras from the front rack and headed toward the dressing room. She whispered Angela's name.

"I'm in here, Venus," Angela said as she opened the very last door.

Venus shut the door and put her index finger up to her lips. She mouthed for Angela to not say her name. Angela took the bras hanging from Venus's upright finger.

In her most exaggerated urban Detroit accent, Angela started talking as if to a *sista*. "Why, what ya got here, gurl? Geme dat hooker bra. Oooweee. You gonna ge'dat boyee now. Put dat on and push dem boobies up for all to see."

Venus actually blushed at Angela's acting.

"You should be blushin, girlfriend. Who you got in mind for these?"

Venus slipped off her top and undid the clasp on her miniskirt, motioning for Angela to call an attendant.

Angela cracked the door. "Excuse me. Could ya'll come in here a second? *Uh-huh*, that means you white girl."

The embarrassed attendant quickly walked to the dressing room to not attract attention. Angela grabbed her and pulled her inside. "Lookie here, honey. What kind of size is this for this buxom woman," she said, pointing to her large bust. "Give me some re-*spect.*" While pointing to Venus, Angela started singing like Aretha Franklin, *"R-E-S-P-E-C-T."*

Angela continued singing while Venus came up to the attendant and whispered in her ear that she needed a pair of sweats and a sweat shirt. She explained that there was a stalker in the mall and she needed to lose him. The attendant put her hand up to her mouth and said the obligatory "Oh. My. God." Angela was just finishing up with her complaint when the attendant ran out into the showroom.

"Get me some big pink bras, honey," Angela said after her.

The attendant picked up some large size passion pink bras and a set of plain grey pajamas, the closest to sweats that Victoria stocked. While she was gone Venus called Vince on the secure cell phone.

"Vince, this is Venus. Hi. Look, I'm being followed by that Metro Guard couple and I need to lose them. I'm at Victoria's Secret at the Somerset Mall. Yeah, I wish you were here, too. Look, could you send your girlfriends over? They've got a Jeep Wrangler, right? I need to make a switch and one of them could put on my outfit and distract the tail. Very funny. Thanks. Bye."

The attendant returned with the clothes.

"Thanks, Dearie." The attendant walked away and Angela gave the pajamas to Venus as she hung up the phone. "Girlfriends, huh? You mean Mr. Hardbody has other girlfriends? And that's plural?"

"I'll explain when we get out of here. Act like you're trying on bras. Sing or something."

"Right. Cause Black women sing while they tryin on bras. Okay, sometimes I do if I'm thinkin about the man I'm goin to catch with this," Angela said as she held up the largest and brightest hot pink bra she had ever seen. "Damn. This is a beacon for a see-in impaired brother. I could hook Stevie

Wonder with this." She said with a laugh, and then started singing, "Isn't me lovely?"

"*Song in the key of Life,* 1976," Venus said.

"What year is this, smarty pants," Angela said as she switched to *Swing Low, Sweet Chariot,* leaning over to pull the straps up and over her shoulders.

"You sing religious songs while putting *that* on?" whispered Venus.

"Honey, when I got this on, the man will get religion. I'm gonna be that *brick, uh, house* that Lionel Richie sings about. The brother seeing this will be calling out *Lord have mercy.*"

Sporting her new pink bra, Angela opened the door and called for the attendant. The young woman ran over to the changing room and closed the door, worried her other customers would see. Venus asked her if there was a back way out. The attendant said she could use the employee's entrance. To stall for more time, Angela asked the attendant for lingerie this time. "I'm kinda getting into this now. Hope those girlfriends take their time."

The attendant brought the lingerie, and Angela switched to Motown singers, first with Marvin Gay's *Sexual Healing.*

"Marvin Gay, 1982, *Columbia Records,*" Venus said. "And with what you have on, there will definitely be some healing going on, like a man going from limp-ing to stand-ing *up,* if you know what I mean."

"Amen, Sister. I *know* what you mean."

The attendant brought two girls to the changing room. Debra and Diane closed the door behind them. Debra was in a tailored pants suit while Diane was in grey sweats.

"So, these Hardesty's girlfriends?" Angela asked with some contempt in her voice.

"We're girlfriends," said Debra, kissing Diane.

"Oh! I see. Um, sorry *ladies.*" Angela looked over to Angela and whispered, "Why didn't you tell me they were *lesbians*?"

"I thought meeting them in person and seeing for yourself would be better," said Venus. "Now let's exchange clothes and get out of here."

With a smile on her face, Debra said Diane would look best in the mini-skirt.

After the exchange, Angela and the girls went to the cash register to check out. Angela paid for a hot pink bra and a black lacey number, talking and singing loudly the whole way: "I'm doin' my dance; get me some love, *Get Down Tonight.*"

"K.C. and the Sunshine Band, 1975," Debra said.

"You too? Whatever," Angela said shaking her head.

Venus slipped out the back way in the grey pajamas. She headed toward her Jeep and saw the girls' matching Jeep parked next to hers. As she started up and took off, she didn't see the couple.

Debra and Diane walked out with Angela as she continued commentary on her new underwear and the effect it would have on her imaginary boyfriend. When they reached the main entrance, Angela walked out the north door and the girls sauntered out the south. As they left, Angela turned around and saw a couple following the girls. The deception worked.

On the way to the Royal Park, Venus called Vince to let him know she had evaded the tail for now. She planned on meeting Angela at the hotel.

"Do you need to change?" Vince asked.

"Yes, I do. I've got my formal wear in the back seat."

"I've reserved a room under Hardesty with four keys. They have your first name."

"Oh. Will we be staying the night?" Venus asked.

"No. It's just a staging room."

"Oh, okay. Well, thanks, Vincent. I'll see you in the *staging room.*"

"And, Venus?"

"Yes.

"Did you make any purchases at Victoria Secret?"

"No. Why, you interested?"

"No. Uh, I mean, I'll see you later."

"Want me to model something sexy in the *staging room*? Angela bought some hot stuff." *As Angela would say, 'You could always show off for Mr. Hardbody.'*

"Uh, bye, now."

"Goodbye, Vincent."

~~~

Matek Hakam was driving slower now that they had turned off US 31 at the second Pentwater exit and were heading north on Lake Shore Drive. The hand drawn map that the officer had given them was very clear: Another five miles and they would reach their destination. Musa was comparing the officer's map with a Michigan road map and wondering out loud why the Pentwater wholesale warehouse was not in the city of Pentwater.

Malik stirred in the back seat, sat up and said, "Are we there yet?"

"Always the little brother," Musa said. Matek laughed.

Malik saw three young women in bikinis walking along the road. "I hope we're there yet."

"Another five miles," Musa said. "But I think we should go back to the main road and drive into Pentwater. This seems to be leaving the business area, not getting closer."

Turning around to see the bikinis, Malik's view was obstructed by the two crates of TracFones. "Yeah, let's go back," he said.

"We will follow the officer's instructions. The large warehouse is near an electric plant. He said we couldn't miss it."

"I don't like it," Musa said.

A couple of miles later, Malik started to see the brilliant blue water of Lake Michigan through an opening in the white pines. "Look to your left. There must be a very large beach over there."

Matek and Musa turned to see, but the trees obstructed their view.

A few miles later, the trees parted on the right. Musa looked up from the maps. "There it is." The Mound of the Pump Storage reservoir loomed before them. "We should soon cross a bridge and see the entrance to the parking lot."

Multiple power lines on tall metal towers lined the road. As they drove up to the bridge, the line converged and dropped below the road on the left where the expansiveness of the Great Lake shown like liquid silver in the sun. A foreboding came over all three as they slowed down to see a grid of metal structures overlooking an inlet of water below them.

"Look!" yelled Malik pointing out to the lake. "There are two Coast Guard boats near the shore line."

"Up, ahead," Musa yelled. There were two blue uniformed officers on an overhead walkway. When they saw the van, one pulled a walkie-talkie off his belt and radioed.

"We should turn around and go back, Matek," Musa said.

"Okay, okay. I will."

Matek saw the parking area and turned in. When he rounded the entrance, he was facing two army transport trucks and soldiers surrounding the perimeter. Suddenly a helicopter flew up and over the reservoir and landed behind them.

A screech pierced their ears and a soldier barked from a megaphone. "Out of the van! Get out of the van, now!"

The three brothers complied.

"Hands up!" the soldier barked. "Take them!" A dozen soldiers ran forward and slammed them on the ground and cuffed them.

"You are under arrest for the intent to commit an act of terrorism on U.S. soil with a weapon of mass destruction. Read them their rights."

Chapter 20

Saturday Evening

A Metro Car arrived at the front gate and the boys whooped and hollered. They hopped in, switched on the stereo and cranked up Eminem's hit song, *Lose Yourself,* until the windows started vibrating. Vince hoped they wouldn't *lose themselves* anytime today.

Vince's secure cell phone rang. When he saw it was Mike *the Snipe*, he turned down the music and took the call.

"Vince, I've been coordinating a take down near Ludington. The Feds and the Coast Guard, including your Commander Starke, are apprehending an Arab terrorist cell that intel said were attempting to blow up the Pump Storage Plant in Ludington using C-4 and TracFones as detonators. If memory serves, you were just there yesterday, right? Coincidence?

He didn't answer. "Thanks Mike." He turned the music back up so the twins wouldn't ask him about the call.

When they arrived at the Royal Park Hotel, Vince had the driver take them to the basement delivery entrance. They took the back elevators to the fourth floor. Vince rang the doorbell of the Presidential suite he'd reserved and Venus welcomed them, admiring Vince's handsome form in a stylish black suit. She had on a stunning burgundy mini dress with a low cut top. She followed them into the sitting room and saw all three staring at her, their eyes riveted on everything south of her neck.

"Boys!" They looked up at once. She shook her head. "Men!"

Vince saw a slight smile on her lips. "You love it."

The doorbell sounded and Vince answered the door. Sandy walked in with Angela hand in hand. "Look who I found in the library downstairs."

"*Vaca santa*," Venus said as she saw the red sequined dress with a split up the thigh and lace of a bright pink push up bra showing at the top edge of the low cut bodice.

"And look at your *hot stuff*, Ms. *Tamale*," Angela answered.

"Gonna get some *Hot Stuff*," Venus announced. "Donna Summer, *Bad Girls*, 1979. And we're going to be a couple of bad girls tonight, aren't we Angela?"

"Oh, yes you are," Vince said. "Now, if I could interrupt this mutual admiration moment, we need to update tonight's plan."

"First thing," Sandy said, "David and Melissa Miller are at the entrance 'round back unloadin' equipment. I counted four FBI agents tryin' to look like guests, and probably a couple more in cars parked in the garage. So, before the twins get to work, we need to pay our *fibbies* a visit."

"How'd they trace us here?" Vince asked.

"David and Melissa were followed by two dark blue Fords," Sandy said.

"Really? The FBI?" Venus asked.

"Yes," Sandy continued. "My friend at McNamara said that an arrest was goin' down on the west side of the State. FBI and ICE agents were picked up by a couple of military helicopters this afternoon."

Vince interrupted. "Got a call from Mike *the Snipe* a few minutes ago. A terrorist cell was apprehended at the Pump Storage Plant near Ludington. C-4 and TracFones were confiscated." He gave Venus a knowing look.

"Al and Cane are being set up," Venus said.

"Are you *shittin'* me?" Al asked.

"No. Venus is right," Vince said.

"What are we going to do?" Cane asked.

"In a few minutes, your job. But, right now, I want you both in the bedroom and lock the door."

"Ah shit," Al said.

"Ah, shut up," Cane replied.

After the boys left the room, Vince said, "Sandy and I will now have our little chat with our fed friends. You ladies take the front elevators and have a drink in the bar. We'll call you when the coast is clear. Afterward, we'll be attending the wedding and reception as planned. When the twins are done working, Venus and I will take them to my house in the limo. I'll have Debra and Diane pick up your Jeep and take it to their house. Sandy? You and Angela can have this room for the night."

Sandy smiled. "Well, I don't want to..."

Angela interrupted. "Thank you, Mr. Vincent. We would be more than happy to make use of this be-yue-tiful suite tonight." She winked. "And into the mornin.'"

Sandy cleared his throat and said, "Uh, yes *Sir.*"

"Okay, great," Vince said. "Ladies, after you."

"But, how are you going to get the FBI to back off?"

"I've got connections, Ms. Sanchez," Vince answered. "We'll give you a call when our task is done. So, if you please."

"Yes, *Sir,*" Venus and Angela said together, imitating Sandy. Vince rolled his eyes.

When Vince and Sandy stepped out of the back elevator on the ground floor, they saw two men in blue suits down the hall talking with Dave Miller. Vince walked up to them and asked to see their badges. They asked, "And who are you?" and "You're interfering with a Federal investigation."

Vince pulled out his Department of Homeland Security credentials and Sandy flipped out his Homeland/DPD badge. The agents stopped talking. Vince asked them to join him and Sandy upstairs. They escorted the two suits to the top floor and invited them to the Presidential suite.

Vince shut the door. "Why are you following two young men who happen to be friends of mine?"

"We apologize, Sir. We were ordered to keep tabs on the Major twins due to an investigation and apprehension of a terrorist cell that took place about an hour ago."

"I'm aware of it," Vince said.

"We weren't told the connection, excuse me, a possible connection to these two young men."

"Who's involved in the investigation?" Vince asked.

"FBI, ICE, Secret Service and the Coast Guard."

"Why the Coast Guard?" Sandy asked.

"The terrorist suspects were found with bomb-related electronics that were possibly smuggled through Canada into Michigan a week ago."

Sandy asked, "What were the supposed bomb-related electronics?"

"TracFones. Untraceable cheap phones that can be used as detonators."

Vince looked at Sandy and back to the agents. "How many phones?"

"One thousand."

"What was the target?" Sandy asked.

"Pump Storage Project on Lake Michigan. Plant a series of small bombs to create both an earth quake and tidal wave to destroy the Pump Storage reservoir, thereby causing a drop-surge in the electric grid, causing a cascading blackout across the Midwest to the East Coast like a couple of years ago."

Vince looked at Sandy, then back to the agents to ask the question they wanted the answer to the most.

"And the connection to the boys?" Sandy asked.

"They were seen receiving two crates of TracFones from a boat off Lake Erie. Apparently there are pictures of the Major twins both at the Lake Erie Metro Park where the drop was made, and in Ludington, casing the Pump Storage Project a couple of days ago. That is exactly where the three Arabs suspects were arrested."

"Why would two young men who are supposedly part of a terrorist plot be here at the Royal Park Hotel?" Vince asked.

"Dave Miller said they were to arrive here and work their normal schedule," the agent said.

Sandy looked at Vince. It was time to tell them what they knew.

Vince said, "We have evidence that the Major twins did not receive a drop of phones at the Lake Erie Metro Park. Rather, they accidentally shot video of the actual recipients and we have the clip stored in a safe location.

"We will need that video."

"The Agency will get it later," Vince said. "I will personally turn over the evidence to your Director on Monday morning. For now, you will cease and desist from apprehending or following the Major twins."

"We can't do that unless ordered by our Director, Sir"

"I will have a call put into your boss. You should get the call in a few minutes."

Vince slipped out of the room into the hallway and called the Director of National Security, assistant to the President, and explained the situation. The Chief said to keep him appraised and that he would call the FBI Director in D.C. Five minutes later, the agents received the call.

"Sorry for the inconvenience Mr. Hardesty, Sir, Officer Sandelen. Our Director said you are now responsible for the twins and expects the evidence and the eyewitnesses to be in his office Monday morning."

"Consider it done," Vince said. "Now, if you'll call off your men in and around the building, officer Sandelen will escort you back to your car. Good night." Vince stood up and motioned them to the door.

They stood up in unison. "Good night, Sir."

After the agents were escorted out with Sandy, Vince called downstairs and told Venus and Angela they'd be down in a minute. Once Sandy gave the *all clear*, he would bring Al and Cane down to meet with the Millers. He looked out the window and down onto the glass roof of the Conservatory where the bride and groom and their families were posing for pre-wedding photos.

Vince called the boys out of the bedroom and told them they were in the clear for now. He called Miller next and told him that the twins would be down in a minute. Vince escorted them down the hall to the front elevators. He told them that he would have to keep close tabs on them until he turned in evidence on Monday. He knew Starke and crew were still out there and wanted the incriminating video more than ever. The FBI call-off wasn't going to stop them from framing the twins.

Sandy met Venus and Angela in the bar. Angela told Venus and Sandy that she had found the shift log for Roberts on the evening of September 5th. She had brought a copy to show them, but Sandy told her to wait and show him and Vincent at the same time.

When Vince arrived, Angela said, "I checked on the daily log for the skiff that made the drop at the Lake Erie Park. Roberts, against regulations, was alone in the boat that evenin. The entry prior to that was reconnaissance on the Detroit River. Before that, it was reconnaissance on the St. Clair River and Lake St. Clair. "

"So, that means he was in the Port Huron area that afternoon," Venus said.

"Yes. The entry states: *acquisition of electronic equipment at the Port Huron Station.*"

"That means Roberts picked up the equipment in Port Huron, and handed it off at the Lake Erie Park to the Metro Guard couple," Venus added.

"TracFones," interjected Vince. "We were told by the FBI agents that the electronic equipment was TracFones. As you know, they've been used in Iraq to detonate car bombs. A thousand of them were confiscated today from the three Arabs who were supposedly attempting to blow up the Pump Storage Plant and take down the electric grid."

"That's not all," Sandy said. "The Feds said that the boys received the phones at the Lake Erie Park and that they're suspects, co-conspirators in the plot."

"That's crazy," Venus said. "We know who really picked them up. And we now know who sent it to them via Robert's skiff: Williams, the CBP Station Supervisor. Alberto must have caught him taking them out of the warehouse on his last day. Williams killed him and tried to make it look like an accident."

"So does that mean Starke and Williams and Roberts and that Metro Guard couple are the real co-conspirators?" asked Angela.

"And found three Arabs to do the dirty work and take the fall," Sandy added.

"And they've tried to frame the twins along with them," Vince said.

"Ho-lee *shit*. I bet that sonofabitch Starke is behind this whole thing," Angela said, looking at everyone for confirmation.

Venus nodded her head. "And Williams is one of his unseen partners."

"I was told Starke was there in Ludington on a Coast Guard cutter when they arrested the Arabs at the Pump Storage Plant," Vince said.

"Makin' sure they arrested them as prime suspects," Sandy added.

"So, what are we going to do about all of this?" asked Venus.

"For now, nothing," Vince said. "We have the evidence that clears the twins and implicates Roberts, and possibly Williams. So far, Starke is clean, unless we can connect him to the Arabs. I promised the FBI agents and their Director that I would be delivering the evidence to his office on Monday morning."

"Wait a minute," Angela said. "Roberts rescued some Arab brothers in N'Orlens. Starke personally sponsored them and moved them to Dearborn. He had Roberts and a roommate livin below them. I've seen the invoices."

"Sounds like a set up. Can you make copies of those on Monday?" asked Sandy.

"Damn skippy. I'll incriminate the bastard," Angela said.

"For now, we'll have to keep on doin' what we would normally be doin'," Sandy said.

Vince said, "We can't give away our intel and evidence 'til we can prove it."

"Which means I have to go to work tomorrow, just like Starke ordered," Venus said.

"That's right," Vince said.

"*Hijo de puto!*"

"Well, we know how this is goin to end. Sooo, we might as well enjoy our evenin'," Sandy said.

Angela smiled back at him. "*Yes Surrr.*"

They left the bar and walked out to the patio overlooking a creek. "Remember," Vince said. "We are friends of the groom attending his wedding ceremony and having a good time at the reception while we watch the twins."

"I'm ready for that," Venus said. "I'd like to forget about what we've learned today, at least for the evening."

"I'm with you," Vince said.

"Yes, you are, Mr. Hardesty," Venus said.

"After you," Sandy said, taking Angela's hand

Vince led Venus outside and down the steps to the picturesque stream where the twins were videoing the bride and groom by the water as the photographer took pictures. They were getting zoom shots from the water and through the trees of the couple, relying on Miller to edit it into a seamless wedding production.

Vince held Venus's hand. He was sure they looked like a normal couple waiting for a ceremony. *If you can call a dark haired beauty in a mini dress normal.*

"What you thinking about, Vincent?"

"Who's coming for the twins next."

"Is that all, Mr. Hardesty?" Venus squeezed his hand. He looked into her eyes and had to answer truthfully.

"No, that's not all. I was thinking how great you looked in that dress." *Lord, have mercy.*

"I bet you were thinking about how great I looked in Victoria's Secret."

"To quote a comic, I don't think Victoria's got many secrets left."

"Oh. I have more secrets than she does," she said, wiggling her eyebrows up and down.

"Is that right?"

"*Si, mi amore.* How about you. I think you have some secrets too."

"Are we speaking of the same kind of secrets?" Vince asked.

"You tell me," Venus answered.

Vince didn't want to get into his secret life right now, though he would have to eventually. When the time was right. Right now, it was more about love and sex, the universal themes of a wedding.

"*Amor -vence.*"

"What's that? My new name?"

"*Si, a mi,*" Venus answered as she reached up and pressed her lips to his. He returned the kiss and then remembered they were in public. He quickly looked around and found the boys with their cameras pointed toward them. Al gave him the *O.K.* sign. *Great.*

Chapter 21

Saturday Night

The sun was setting as the guests were arriving for the candlelight ceremony. Vince and Venus met Sandy and Angela in the glass *Conservatory*. Small white lights twinkled on the branches of small trees just outside the windows. Vince and Sandy shook hands and Venus and Angela kissed like good friends meeting again. They sat down in the back row near a string quartet. Soon, all the guests were seated and the minister walked to the front to begin the ceremony.

The strings began *Canon in D* as four couples, two flower girls and a ring bearer processed down the aisle. Everyone stood at the minister's invitation, and the bride was escorted by her father. Vince glanced at Venus and noticed tears in her eyes. He instinctively put his arm around her waist and she held it against her. No doubt she was thinking of her future wedding day and the reality that her father would not be there to escort her down the aisle.

As the bride passed, they looked up the aisle and saw the groom looking at his soon-to-be wife with tears in his eyes. Vince felt tears well up in his eyes as a pang of grief filled his heart, remembering his wedding day with Rachel in a palm circled garden on the Kuwait shore line of the Persian Gulf. He looked at Venus.

*This beautiful woman I'm holding today might become my wife.*

Venus turned toward him and wiped the tears from his cheeks, so he returned the favor. They held each other's hands through the rest of the service.

Following the ceremony, the four of them went for cocktails and Hors d'œuvres, staying together so no one would ask them if they were with the bride or the groom. Vince had called in Debra and Diane for backup. They were posing as Hotel staff, taking down the ceremony chairs in the Conservatory for the bridal party and family pictures.

Later, Vince and Sandy eventually excused themselves to the men's room. Afterward, they met Deb and Diane in the library and Vince gave them the keys to Venus's Jeep and told them to be on the look-out for a tail. He had called off the FBI, but that didn't mean Starke wouldn't have someone following them. They said not to worry.

Vince was sure that Starke couldn't get a fix on him. He was no longer in any data base in the world. Only his boss and the President, and his Kuwait relatives, knew his true identity and whereabouts. He would continue to be the mystery man, but that would not be true for Venus, and now Sandy and Angela. Maybe he had just put them in jeopardy.

Venus said she could take care of herself. Sandy said he was untouchable as an officer and liaison with Homeland. When he mentioned it to Angela, she said "that dumbass Starke could *kiss my ass for all I care.*"

Vince and Sandy returned to their table and the women went to the ladies room.

"I've got a room and a man friend for the night," Angela said, as she trussed up her top. "What you gonna do, *Mz. Vee?*"

Venus refreshed her lipstick. "Vince said he was taking me to his house."

"Oh, goin to *get down* in the *Motown?*"

"To tell you the truth, I don't really know. Might just be shown to my room and told to go to sleep. He's so preoccupied with everything going on with the boys, and..."

"And?" Angela asked.

"*And*, I'll see what I can do." *Or, should I say, see what he will do.*

When they returned to their table, Vince reminded them that they needed to keep looking like couples. The ladies got into it. Vince didn't think it was much of an act on their part. Sandy winked at him, knowing what was going on between him and Venus. Vince thought he saw the same wink between Angela and Venus.

*Co-conspirators of another kind.*

The DJ started some R&B songs, so Angela started singing to Sandy. *"Mr. Big Stuff, who do you think you are? Mr. Big Stuff, you ever gonna get my love?"*

Venus jumped in, "Oh yeah, ooh."

"Jean Knight, 1971, Stax Records," Vince said.

Angela came back with her own lyrics. "'When I try to keep you happy, I will try to keep you satisfied.'" Angela's hand went under the table and Sandy's eyes got wide."

Vince cleared his throat and said, "Get a room."

"Uh, we have one, remember? Thanks to you," answered Sandy.

"You're welcome," Vince said. He looked over at Venus, but she was looking away.

The DJ announced the entrance of the wedding party. The trumpets to the *Rocky* theme started and everyone stood and applauded. Finally, the happy couple was introduced, the cake was cut and dinner commenced. Vince saw Debra and Diane pouring water for guests and Al and Cane were getting every conceivable video shot possible.

After the couple's first dance and the father-daughter, mother-son dance, the DJ started the dance music with "Celebration." Venus called it: "Kool and the Gang, 1980's." Everyone got up and danced.

Next was the distinctive beat of *the* 'Detroit Hustle,' *My Eyes Don't Cry No More*. Vince leaned toward Venus and said, "Stevie Wonder, *Characters*, 1987"

Venus fell right into step with the dancers. She had to help Vince get in sync, but once he did, he realized that like the lyrics, his heart didn't ache anymore since Venus walked through his door.

A few numbers later, Vince helped the twins pack up their gear. *Luckily, we don't have to stay for the whole thing. Can't dance worth a dime.*

Once the video equipment was loaded up in Miller's van, Vince called up the limo and sent the twins to the hotel basement.

Vince and Venus escorted Sandy and Angela up to the suite to say goodnight. After a hand shake and kisses, Vince grabbed Venus' hand and led her back out into the hallway, telling Sandy and Angela to enjoy the room.

Angela came to the doorway as he and Venus walked to the elevator and said, "*Pink* would be opening in the room tonight."

Venus told Vince about the Victoria Secret passion pink push up bra. She said Sandy was about to be in the *pink* shortly. A bead of sweat broke out on Vince's forehead. They held hands and laughed as they got on the elevator. Once the door closed he leaned toward her. She raised her face. They kissed. She brought his hand up to her breast and he kissed her more passionately. Luckily, no one else got on the elevator as they rode it down five floors to the basement. The elevator dinged, she straightened up her top and they walked out into the basement of the hotel with smiles on their faces.

"Where are we going, *Señor*?" she asked.

"My place." The Metro Car pulled up and the driver got out and opened the back door.

"Taking me for a ride, Mr. Hardesty?"

"Hop in."

The door on the other side opened and Al and Cane jumped in.

*So much for a racy ride home.*

~~~

Vince instructed the driver to pull around to the back of the mansion and park next to the garage. He asked Venus to go into the house as he escorted the twins upstairs to the apartment. He told them that he had called off the FBI, but that Starke and crew were still trying to apprehend and question them. He had no intention of that happening. They were to stay in the apartment or the house at all times. If they got up late, he would be going to Unity House in the morning for services, so they were to stay put until he returned. He wished them a good night, closed the door, went back down to the garage and turned on the motion detectors.

Vince walked in the kitchen and was greeted by Greta with a jump and paws on his chest, then a few wet kisses. He asked her where Venus had gone to, but she ignored the question, wanting all of his attention.

He looked all through the first floor, but there was no sign of Venus. He went to the stairs and caught a whiff of her perfume. He took two steps at a time, reached the landing and heard her call his name. She was sitting on the couch in his private office and sitting room.

"The twins are safe and secure in the apartment."

"Good," she said.

"Now, I'm worried about you. I feel like you'll be walking right into the lion's den when you go to work in the morning."

"The Lions are not so good this year, *mi amore.*"

"You know what I mean."

"What *do* you mean?" Venus asked.

He sat on the couch next to her and turned to face her. He looked into her eyes and swallowed. "I mean, I care about *you*. I don't want to put you in any kind of danger. Sending you to Starke at Selfridge, I think it puts you right in the middle..."

"Look, Vincent," Venus interrupted. "I voluntarily went with you to Ludington yesterday. After finding Alberto's body today, I am in the middle of this and that's where I want to be. I want to find Williams and make sure he pays for the murder of my friend's father and prove that he's a part of whatever Starke is up to. I don't want to be anywhere but in the middle of this, whatever *it* is. *Comprende*?"

"Okay. As long as you let me know the minute something's off at Selfridge. I think Starke is now a desperate man; desperate enough to try something stupid, and, yes, dangerous."

"I can take care of myself, Vincent. But, I would like to go back to what you first said. You know, caring for me."

Vince put his arm around her and drew her close and touched his lips to hers. He kissed more passionately as she parted her lips and found his tongue with hers. They slid down on the couch until they were lying together with their legs entwined.

Venus whispered, "Oh, Vincent, I am scared. I want to stay here in your strong arms. I want to be protected."

"And I want to hold you and protect you, for better or worse."

"In sickness and health?" Venus asked.

"You look pretty healthy to me," he said.

She rubbed her thigh on the bulge in his pants. "You feel pretty healthy yourself, *mi amore*."

Vince pressed himself against her and kissed her again. She opened her thighs and her mini skirt slid up to her waist.

Vince pulled away.

"Vincent, please."

"Let's go someplace more comfortable," he said.

"Yes, lets."

He took her hand and led her down the hallway.

"You can sleep in one of the extra bedrooms," he said.

"Oh?"

He turned a corner, opened a door and switched on candle shaped sconces. The room had a queen size canopy bed draped with sheer white curtains. The walls displayed classic paintings of gardens and flowers, and the painting next to the bathroom door depicted a young woman entering a garden pool discarding a long white robe. Across from the bed was a large flat screen TV. When he picked up the remote and turned it on, the room was filled with the sights and sounds of blue-green ocean waves washing over a sandy white beach with palm trees swaying in the breeze.

"I thought you'd like something more feminine, and I know you love the water," said Vince

"It's like a small paradise," Venus said as she walked around the room, taking in its beauty. She looked at him from across the bed. "Thank you."

Vince walked further in the room and closed the door behind him. Venus gave a small gasp. She moved away from the bed and stood still, waiting for him to come to her. He stood in front of her, putting his hands on either side of her face and lifted her mouth to his. He kissed her softly and sensually. She responded in kind. When he released her, she let out a deep sigh. "Oh Vincent."

"Like I said, I thought you'd like something more feminine." He waved his hand across the bed.

"*I'd like* something more *masculino*," Venus said, putting her hands on her hips and giving him a stern look. "So, you just waltz me in here and think I'm going to sleep? Is that with or without you?"

"No. I didn't mean that," he said shaking his head. "Look . . ."

"No, you look."

She reached her arms around her back and unzipped her dress. She slid the straps off and let it slide to the floor. Underneath, she had on a black lace corset that hugged her hips and just covered her uplifted breasts. He took a slow look up to her top when she barked out "Hey."

She had a hand back on a hip. "Up here," she said, pointing two fingers to her eyes. "I thought *you'd* like something more *femenina*." Her lips produced a pout as her hips swayed from side to side. His eyes followed her movements as if being hypnotized.

Venus sang, "I'll dance for you..." She paused.

"Jessica Simpson, *Forbidden Fruit* from *In This Skin*," Vince said hoarsely.

"Uh, huh," Venus said, then, continued, "You like, huh, *muchacho*?"

"I like," he answered with a whisper.

"What was that? I didn't hear you."

"I said 'I like,'" he answered.

"Then, shut up and sit down!" She said as she pushed him backward until he went down on a soft chaise lounge in the corner of the room. She started swaying her hips more provocatively, gyrating as she turned slowly around. When her back was turned toward him, she put her arms up in the air and waved them back and forth in a hula style befitting the sandy ocean scene on the TV screen. She lowered her hands to the back of her corset and unzipped it. She pulled down the top and looked over her shoulder to see if he was enjoying the show. He had a smile on his face.

She covered her breasts and turned around. He looked up from her hips to her hands pressed against her breasts, then looked up and saw her lips form a seductive smile. He tried to say something, but he couldn't form the words. She put her hands down and her breasts bounced free.

"*Rendición, mi amor.*"

She put her hands on the sides of the chaise and leaned over, pressing her breasts to his chest and her open lips on his, slipping her tongue in his mouth. He reciprocated until she pulled away. They came up for air as if they had taken a long dive into deep water.

*I'm out of the kiddy pool and into the deep water now,* Vince thought.

She unbuttoned his shirt and pulled it over his head. His firm, toned chest rose and fell with anticipation. She loosened his belt and unclasped his pants. Vince lifted himself up long enough for her to pull them down. She leaned completely over and took off his shoes and pulled the pants all the way off. All he had left were his jockeys.

She crawled back up the chaise lounge and knelt over him on all fours. *"Ay, mi amor, eres muy guapo."*

He tried to respond, but she put her hand over his mouth. "It's my turn to make the next move. Action speaks louder than words."

Vince pulled her down and kissed her hard. He grabbed her under the arms and moved her up so he could press his mouth to her breasts. She threw her head back and moaned. He leaned forward, picked her up and switched positions.

Vince took off his shorts and then began to excuse himself. "Hold that thought. I'll be right back," he said.

"Trying to protect me, *mi amore*?" Venus asked

"Yes. Protection," he answered

"Got that covered," she said.

Vince lowered himself and knelt before her. He pulled her legs toward him, leaned forward and she guided him inside her. Their mouths met with a wet and sloppy kiss as her body adjusted to his. Soon they were both moving in unison, slowly and lovingly at first, then with passionate abandon. Because it had been so long, Vince came quickly, but kept thrusting. A minute later she let out a whimper with quick short gasps.

They lay silent for several minutes, holding each other, kissing and cuddling one another. He started to say something, but Venus pressed her fingers to his lips, shaking her head. She pushed him up and off her. He thought she was getting up to go to the bathroom. Instead, she took his hand and led him to the bed. She pushed aside the sheer curtain, pulled back the covers and shoved him on his back. She knelt in front of him, took him in her hands and began massaging him back to life. In a few minutes he was more than ready.

She straddled him, he slipped inside her, and she started a slow seductive lap dance. She picked up speed and grabbed his hands and pressed them against her breasts, her hips thrusting forward. She moaned with each deep thrust until she arched her back in release. After several shudders, she fell forward onto his chest.

Vince rubbed her back with gentle strokes until she recovered. He grabbed her bottom and slowly started thrusting upwards. She soon moved with him and squealed with pleasure as he increased the pace. When he could hold back no longer, he yelled with the sharp pain and pleasure of his orgasm. She responded with a scream of her own.

They lay together sweating and panting. He started to speak, but she just kissed him long and soft, saying they needed no words right now. She moved off him and they lay together side by side, wrapped in each other's arms and legs. She stroked his face until he fell fast asleep.

Vince woke up ten minutes later in Venus's bedroom to the sound of splashing water filling the tub. He decided to give her some privacy, so he grabbed his clothes and went back to his bedroom and took a hot shower. He toweled off, fell into bed and went sound to sleep.

After a long hot bubble bath, Venus put on a long white terry cloth robe and walked down the hall to Vince's bedroom. When she cracked the door, a sliver of light ran across the room to his bed. Lying on the floor next to the bed, Greta lifted her head and gave Venus a quick look and laid her head back down. Vince was sound asleep.

Venus went to his side, saw his face relaxed with the hint of a smile on his lips. She kissed him on the cheek, turned and left the room, closing the door quietly.

~~~

*I heard the sound of the door open, soft footsteps and then felt a light kiss on my cheek. I opened my eyes. A woman wearing the Hijaab, a head to toe floor robe, stepped back from the bed. She untied the robe and let it slide to the floor. Underneath she was wearing a red baby doll. I sat up. It wasn't Venus.*

*This was a younger woman, a beautiful mid-eastern woman wearing lingerie under her robes. I remember when my wife and her friends would often wear expensive gowns or lingerie under their Hijaab, keeping the Islamic law as respectful religious women while wearing the latest European fashion. Like vixens in sheep's clothing.*

*She sat on the bed. She placed her hand on my chest and pushed me back until I was flat on the bed and lay down beside me. She discarded the head dress and veil and looked into my eyes. It was Rachel.*

*I tried to speak, "Rachel. I've..."*

*She stopped me, putting her hand to my lips. She smiled. She didn't really speak, but she was telling me we only had a little time together.*

*It reminded me of when we would walk together without a word out into the desert and watch the sunset. Once the heat of the day had cooled, she would disrobe to show her latest lingerie. We would spread a blanket, cover ourselves and make love under the stars. We would then lie together until the moon rose and the bright silver light on the sand and the cold of the desert would chase us back to the compound.*

*She was telling me I needed to trust my instincts, my body, my soul. The twins would be okay, but the woman I lay with would do something that I wouldn't understand. I should remember the moonlight on the desert and the moonlight on the lake. She smiled again, caressed the side of my face and put her arms around me. Love, faith, hope, grace. Grace will heal me.*

*She kissed me lightly on the lips, raised her hand to my face, spread her fingers and lightly closed my eyes.*

Chapter 22

Sunday Morning

Vince woke up early, completely rested, even refreshed. He looked up from his bed and saw the picture of him and Rachel on their wedding day. It looked as though she was smiling at him.

In the shower he remembered the dream. Was it just a dream, or had she really been there? He thought about what Rachel said. For now, it was enough to *know* that the twins will be safe. Her mention of moonlight seemed to say she approved of Venus.

By the time he toweled off, he knew what he would do for the boys. He shaved and checked himself in the mirror. He had a smile on his face.

*I like how I feel this morning. No confusion. The mind is clear and alert. Venus should move in, have her own bedroom, or stay in my room. That would be nice.*

He took the stairs to the kitchen humming *Sexual Healing*. As Venus would say before he could, "Marvin Gaye, the *Midnight Love* album, 1982." And it had been a midnight love.

He was greeted by Maria cooking breakfast. "We have a guest in the house," he said, giving Maria a hug. She looked up and a smile came across her face. "Is about time you got some, uh, I mean, got a girlfriend, *Señor.*"

"How did you know it was a woman, Maria?"

"That grin on your face and twinkle in your eye is hard to miss, *Señor* Vincent."

"Her name is Venus."

"Ah, the goddess of love. You have been loved. *Si?* And for my people, it is short for Venusuela, meaning *by the water,* like Venice.'"

"She and her late father loved the water. They fished together when she was young." Vince said

"That is good. Means she has no issues with men," Maria said. "And you are *Sincere*," she continued.

"Meaning?" Vince asked.

"To conquer," Maria said with a sly grin.

"More like conquering love," said Venus as she entered the kitchen in one of his white cotton robes.

A tingling sensation ran up Vince's spine and he felt his face flush. She was sexy even in an over-sized robe. He walked up to her, took her hand and gave her a once over. He began to imagine removing said robe and pressing himself up against her with only what was underneath.

Venus interrupted his day dream. "Stop that."

"Stop what?" he asked.

"Taking my robe off, silly."

"With all respect. I was just admiring how well you looked in my robe."

"Uh huh," she said as she stepped toward Maria and shook her hand. "*Buenos dias, Maria. Soy Venus.*"

"*Señor* Vincent told me your name," Maria said as she glanced at him.

"He only told you the name my father gave me from his mother. My father called me by my first name, Grace, short for *Graciella.*"

"Oh, and I can see you have given my Vincent grace, and love," Maria said with a tear rolling down her cheek. She went to Venus and hugged her.

"My full name in Mexico is *Graciella Venusuela Sanchez Rivera.*"

"Excuse me?" Vince said.

"It means her mother's maiden name is last, and that her family lived on the riverbank," Maria explained.

Venus smiled at Vincent. "Probably why I like rivers and lakes so much."

"She does look great in a bikini," Vince said.

Maria and Venus ignored him and got into a Spanish bonding rag that he found too fast and feminine for his interpretive taste. Vince grabbed some coffee and filled a plate with Maria's famous burrito omelet. By the time he finished, the two women were hugging and smiling again with conspirator eyes looking at him.

*Grace. I'm surrounded, outnumbered: A substitute mom and a potential wife?* Looking at Greta sitting at Maria's foot, she seemed to be smiling up at them. *And a German bitch.*

*Slow down, pardner. Let's keep it at girlfriend for now.*

After breakfast, Venus said she needed something to wear and a ride to her apartment. Vince produced a pair of his sweats and promised to keep her gown and unmentionables in safe keeping.

"A *Metro Car* will be here in five minutes. Just enough time to have a little talk," Vince said as he took her into his arms.

"Is this where you caution me about Starke and his cohorts again?" she asked.

"Yes. You have my secure cell phone. Punch send and it will ring my phone. I'll hear whatever's going on."

"Yes, Sir. Sir? Do I have permission to call you if there is no problem?" She smiled and gave him a kiss.

"Yes, of course. But, listen. Starke is now desperate to find the twins and he lost them once. He'll do everything he can not to miss them again. I'm sure he's heard from his Fed contact that the FBI's been called off by the D.C. Director. So, he will try to get them on his own. Right now, you're the only one he knows that helped them get away."

Venus stepped back. "Listen, Mr. Vincent Hardesty, Warrant Officer Venus Sanchez backs down from no man or assignment. I know I'm bait, but I know how to make the switch.

If he shows, I'll click on your phone and you'll have recorded documentation of his inquires. You can record these calls, right?"

"Yes. I will have Mike record all calls."

"Who's Mike?"

"Friend in D.C., actually at Langley."

"Oooh, *Friends in Low Places,*" she said.

"*Garth Brooks, 1990,*" Vince replied.

"Know a little country, cowboy?"

"Yes Ma'am."

Just then the *Metro Car* pulled into the driveway.

"Here's your coach, my lady."

She put her arms around him and kissed him.

"And you have my glass slipper, among other *things.*

"If the shoe fits, I'll pick you up tonight."

~~~

Vince let the boys sleep in, figuring they wouldn't want up until noon anyway. His plan was to take them out on Lake St. Clair in the early afternoon for some Muskie fishing off his boat.

He drove his Impala down Woodward to the Ecumenical Center on Ferry Street. His counselor, Harriett, invited him to join her and about thirty others for prayer, meditation, and a talk from one of the members. It was similar to a Quaker meeting, but with all types of religions represented: Jewish, Christian, Muslim and Unitarian. Naturally, the orthodox of any of those faiths would not want to attend.

The minister stated that the topic today was *The Universal Religious Experience of Spiritual Messages and Messengers.* As he started his message, Vince thought of last night's dream. Maybe Rachel was as real as she seemed and not just a dream. A *messenger.* Then he remembered his experience with the

Rabbi. He met him in the desert of Kuwait after Rachel had been killed.

The Republican Guard had sent in an assassination squad to kill the Kuwaiti Emir Sheikh. Vincent had been training the elite troops to be the country's Special Forces. He and his wife Rachel were vacationing with family at their Persian Gulf beach compound at *Qasr As Sayliyah* when the attack occurred. The newly trained Special Forces thwarted the attack, but Rachel was struck by a stray bullet, and along with the baby she was carrying, died the next day.

He didn't leave the compound for over a year, except for walks along the Gulf, and then into the desert. There he met a Bedouin Rabbi who taught as he would walk along the desert paths. He would teach in his tent from scrolls that appeared to be old and worn. The Rabbi often told stories about the biblical Joshua and David, who, he said, were warriors like him.

The Rabbi listened to his grief, all of his regrets and guilt. When they met for the last time, the Rabbi's final message to him was that it was providential that they had met, and that he should "follow the spirit," pointing at his heart.

*Providence: the hospital that led me to St. Vincent's, and then to the twins, and now here. Providence? Or my choice?* The Rabbi said, "Why does it have to be one or the other? In the Person, in the One, the contradictions of human thought are complimentary. As the scribe Isaiah wrote, *'My thoughts are not your thoughts, neither are your ways my ways.'*"

*Then why did Rachel have to die?*

"Your questions are not my questions. *Time and chance happen to all,*" the Rabbi had said, quoting Solomon's *Book of Vanity.*

Returning to the compound, he turned around to take one last look at the Rabbi's tents, but like the chaplain's messenger, they had disappeared. He thought then it was the result of sand whipped up from the desert floor that had blocked his view. Now, he wasn't so sure.

The chaplain finished his message saying: *"When our modern culture gave up the spiritual and the Spirit to explain mystery, it adopted either, scientific mysticism, irrational conspiracies or pharisaic and millennial fundamentalism to explain events. Every culture and every faith yearns to explain the unseen. Every culture and every faith looks to a higher power who is Person. And that Person sends a personal message or messenger."*

As the meeting went on, Vince realized something inside him had changed. He believed that his oath to never marry again following Rachel's death was simply a part of his grief, and the fear that he might forget her if he did. Just like his meetings with the Rabbi and his marriage to Rachel, everything on earth was temporal, even promises to dead spouses.

It was time to move on. It was time to finally give himself to a new committed relationship. Grace had come to him. Now it was his choice.

His mind drifted to Venus. He had made his choice, but he had a bad feeling about her today.

Vince hung out for a while after the meeting, drinking coffee and eating pastries, as was the custom of most faith gatherings. A few of the group invited him out for lunch at the IHOP when the *Iman* from the Islamic Center in Dearborn approached him.

"I spoke with the chaplain a minute ago and he directed me to you," the *Iman* said, and led Vince to an empty office.

"How can I help?" Vincent asked.

"Three Lebanese brothers were arrested yesterday evening on the west side of the state. They are being charged with an act of terrorism because they were in possession of TracFones."

"Yes, I am aware of the arrest."

"I am sure they are innocent. They were allowed only one phone call and they called me. You see, they visited me yesterday morning concerned about the generosity of a Coast Guard officer who gave them a used van and the TracFones to deliver to, first Mackinac, then changed to the city where they were arrested. I am concerned for their safety."

Vince paused. "I share your concern, *Iman*. I know something of this incident and I will do everything in my power to see that the truth is revealed."

"Thank you," the *Iman* said. "May Allah bless your endeavors."

"Thank you, and God bless you too."

Vincent's cell phone buzzed. He took it out and stared at the message. Someone had penetrated the house perimeter.

"I must go now, *Iman*. Thank you for sharing with me."

As he left the center, he declined the invitation to lunch and headed home. He sped down Woodward with his grill and rear window police lights flashing.

Chapter 23

Sunday Noon

Vince turned off Woodward one block past Boston Boulevard and turned off his flashers. He drove past the back of his property and saw an Escalade with a Metro Guard plate at the back gate. *Maybe security had intercepted the intruders.*

As he passed the open gate, it looked like the locks had been cut off. He turned the corner and went around to the front driveway, expecting a second Metro Guard car. No one. *Where are they?*

He took his phone and punched in the front gate code and drove down the drive and pulled up behind the mansion expecting to see the guards on the grounds. There were none.

He unlocked the house and was greeted by Greta, pacing and whining. "What's the matter girl?" She growled and barked. Someone had been on the property.

Maria came through the kitchen door. "Some Metro Guards knocked on the door. They asked if I was alright. Said someone came onto the property and that they would check the grounds for intruders."

"Who were the officers?" Vincent asked.

"A couple. Daniels was his name. I didn't check the lady."

*The Metro Guard couple. Security called off?*

"Okay. Good job. I'll go out and talk with them. Come on Greta."

He walked out of the house to the garage, Greta following. He yelled Al and Cane's names as he ran up the stairs. No answer.

When he reached the kitchen, he saw Al unconscious on the floor and Cane tied to a chair. The next thing he knew he was on the floor, waking up and staring at the ceiling. A Metro Guard uniform came into view. *Daniels.*

"Want another shot?"

Vince felt a burning sensation on his chest. He looked down and found a thin wire stuck in his shirt leading back to Daniels. *Taser.*

"What do you want?" Vince croaked.

Another uniform came into view. A woman. *Schmidt.*

"You know what we want, Mr. Hardesty. Your girlfriend ratted you out. She's back in the fold."

"What makes you think I'm going to give you what you want?"

Janet Schmidt answered by pulling out her taser gun and shooting Cane. He convulsed in his chair and passed out. "Too bad. He was the nice one. Already got the long-haired, big mouth," she said pointing at Al on the floor. "But I can up the power and do some permanent damage. That is, after he wakes up. I want him to feel it, the son of a bitch."

"Okay. Okay. I'll get the video file," Vince said as he sat up and then struggled to his feet.

"Giving up that easy?" Schmidt asked. "And you're *Special Forces* Reserve? Come on. I want to zap big mouth again."

Vince pulled the wire out of his chest. "We have to go into the house. I recommend you hide the gun. My housekeeper will call the police if she suspects anything."

"Fine," Daniels said. "I'll have the walky-talky on, so Janet knows what's going on the whole time."

Schmidt interrupted. "One false move and long hair gets another shot of my love. Screw his brain cells a little. Fuck him up good. So go ahead, *punk*, make my..."

"Got it," Vince said. "Let's go."

Vince went back down the stairs and to the house with Daniels following. He opened the back door and commanded Greta to back off and sit. She did reluctantly with a low growl.

He told Maria that the Metro Guard officer was going with him to his office to check out the alarm system. Once upstairs, Vince went to the back wall, took out some books and spun the combination to a small safe. He handed Daniels a flash drive.

"Is this the only copy?"

"This is the only copy," Vince answered.

"It better be. Let's go," Daniels said, waving the stun gun toward the door.

"Got what you want. Leave."

"Only with you and your side kicks."

From the walky-talky, Vince heard Schmidt say, "The twins are coming with us. Go peacefully, and they don't get zapped again."

Vince led the way back out of the house. As he passed the kitchen, he raised his palm, telling Greta to stay, but then gave her a signal behind his leg. He told Maria to let the dog out after he and the Metro Guards left. He and the guard would be going through the neighborhood to find whoever breached the perimeter.

The couple led Vince and the twins to the Escalade, took their IDs, phones and keys and put them in the back seat. They drove around the corner and down Hamilton to the Lodge. Vince asked for the back windows to be rolled down to give Al and Cane some air. Daniels complied.

Schmidt radioed Starke. "We've got the video file, the Majors and Hardesty. Where you want them?"

"Dearborn's swarming with media. Take them to the Station on Mt. Elliott off Jefferson. Call up a couple of Metros to guard them. Got a couple of old holding cells in the basement. That'll keep them 'til Monday."

"Roger that. Out."

Vince leaned up to the back of the front seat. "Let the twins go. You've got what you came for: evidence of your complicity with Roberts in framing the Arabs for a fake plot."

"Oh, honey. You don't know the half of it. You're boys here are going to prison, and maybe you along with them. You'll be..." Suddenly she stopped talking. She saw a look in Vince's eyes that was dark and cold. The eyes of a killer. She quickly turned around.

A mile behind and out of sight, a German Shepherd was running down Hamilton toward the Lodge.

The Escalade pulled up to the Coast Guard Station side entrance and Vince and the twins were hustled out of the car and through a door held by seaman Roberts. Once inside, they were led through a hallway to a set of stairs that led down to the hundred year old building's basement holding cells. All three were put into one cell with two bunks.

"Conspiracy is one thing," Vince said. "To leave us for dead is another."

"A guard will bring you supper later," Roberts said. "Commander Starke will come for the twins on Tuesday for arraignment."

"What about me?" Vince asked.

The steel bar door slammed shut and the key lock turned in answer to his question.

After Roberts ran back upstairs, Al whispered, "What are we going to do now?"

Cane answered. "We're stuck here, brother. We're not going anywhere, anytime soon."

"Hit the bunks, boys," Vince answered, and then whispered: "*Help is on the way.*"

Al took the top and Cane took the bottom bed and quickly fell asleep, exhausted from the effects of scrambled nerves and shaking muscles produced by the taser. Vince sat quietly on the concrete floor facing the bars and thought about Venus.

*Could she really be one of them, inserting herself in our group after she saw the video? Schmidt said 'Back in the fold.' The operation was to set up Arabs to take the fall for a terrorist plot, but why? Make Starke and crew heroes? Give them promotions in DHS? Get Metro Guard an expanded contract?*

*The twins were just unlucky enough to see a part of that operation at the Metropark. Starke needed to know what they saw and wanted any video they might have made of the drop. Then, he couldn't find them, or so it seemed. Did they plant Venus to be their eyes and ears on the inside? Maybe they've been followed from the very beginning, making sure the twins didn't interfere. She knew I was hiding them, but didn't know where once I sent them out of town. It was sheer luck, bad luck, that they caught Al's phone call, and even worse luck that I invited Venus along to Ludington. Was she their insurance if Starke missed them?*

*When I called off the Feds, she pursued me to stay close, real close, and I fell for her. Like a puppy dog, she led me around on a leash of lust. But something doesn't sit right.*

He lowered his head to meditate. An hour passed and he woke with a start. Had the dream come back? *Rachel.* Then, he heard what had startled him: a dog bark.

*Greta. Good girl!*

Vince gave a shrill long, then short whistle. He heard one bark in response. She would come in when someone opened the door. God help them if they tried to stop her.

*Which came first? Sandy called Venus, right? But, did it make any difference? Even if Sandy had called Venus for assistance, she could have reported to Starke and then made sure she was included in the group. Infiltrating the enemy camp is always the best strategy. She was one great actress. Or for real.*

Vince heard one of the guards upstairs ask the other one, "Is this your dog out here by the door?

"Nope. Not mine. Don't have a dog."

"It's a good looking shepherd. It's sitting by the door like it's waiting for someone."

"Shoo it away."

As the guard opened the door to kick Greta out of the way, she leapt past him, her paws scrambling down the hall. Vince whistled when he heard her reach the top of the stairs and she bounded down steps and jumped the other guard near the cell.

"Keys!" Vince commanded.

Greta growled menacingly, her teeth bared as she grabbed the key ring. The guard tried once to push her away, but quickly found his arm bitten, bleeding and immovable. She pulled the keys to Vince from the guard's belt. The other guard ran down the stairs and began hitting Greta with a night stick.

"Big mistake," Vince said as Greta grabbed the stick with her teeth and pushed the guard on his back, pressing it to his throat.

"Hold," Vince ordered. He unlocked the door, ushered out the twins and wrestled the guards into the cell and locked it. "Supper will be served in an hour."

Vince led the twins upstairs, found their personal items and phones, and called Sandy. "Need you to pick me and the twins up at the Coast Guard Station off Jefferson. We were tasered, taken from my house and locked up."

"What the hell?" Sandy replied.

"Venus gave us up," Vince said matter-of-factly, and then went silent and waited.

Sandy paused and then said, "No way, man. She was never one of *them.* Besides, Angela's been tryin' to reach her all afternoon. They always check in with each other and she's got nothin'."

"Okay. On your way over here, call the Air Station and ask for Lieutenant Sanchez and see what they say."

"You got it," Sandy answered. "Hey, wait a minute. How'd you get out of jail?"

"Veteran police officer tracked us and subdued two Metro Guards," Vince answered with pride.

"Greta?"

"The one and only. Now, make that call."

A few minutes later Sandy called back. "The officer in charge said that Venus is on lock down. She was questioned this mornin' by the commander. She will be extradited on Tuesday. She must have been pressured, Vince, or worse, to give up you and the twins," Sandy said.

"Good to know," Vince said.

"Don't think for a minute that Venus had anything to do with Starke," Sandy said with some irritation in his voice, Angela saying "No *way*" in the background.

"Did you contact her in the beginning or did she somehow put herself in your path?" Vince asked.

"I initiated the contact. She's my friend, remember? And it was Angela that let us know 'bout all the activity goin' on with Starke. Venus never came up."

"They're friends," Vince said.

"Wait, *Man*. Why all this doubt? Whose lies you been listenin' to?"

*'Back in the fold.' The Metro Guard woman. Liar, liar. Now I'm on fire.*

"You're right, Sandy. Just needed to hear your reaction. I think the taser scrambled some brain cells for a minute."

"Well, unscramble them. The facts are that she's locked up and involuntarily given up people she loves."

*Love. What did Rachel say? 'The woman will do something I won't understand.'*

"How soon will you be here?" Vince asked.

"I'm turning onto I-75. Give me fifteen."

"Turn on your lights and make it ten."

When Sandy and Angela pulled up, Vince, the twins and Greta got in the back seat. As Sandy took off, Angela turned around in the front seat. "They've done somethin' to Venus, Vince. She is as honest as this summer day is hot. And now I'm hot about that Starke. Son-bitch, sneakin' around, sellin' lies right under my nose. *Shit*!"

"I believe you, Angela," Vince said. "Sorry I doubted for a second. Sandy? Take us back to my place. I'm taking Al and Cane to the boat house on Lake St. Clair. I need to pick up my car and some things."

"That's MacRay Marina, right? Next to Selfridge?"

"Right."

"Vince, please don't do anythin' stupid," pleaded Angela.

"Wouldn't think of it."

## Chapter 24

Sunday Evening

Vince's arsenal was unknown and underground, in the mansion's basement behind a false stone wall at the back of an extensive wine cellar. It was steel lined, well lit, locked with an encrypted electronic combination and a battery backup.

He spun the combination, pulled opened the door and the overhead lights came on, revealing shelves with every weapon he had used over the years. He opened a steel cabinet at the end of the vault and took out his Tactical .50 Caliber LRSR: Long Range Sniper Rifle. Knowing it was going to be the longest shot of his life, for good luck, he put on what the sniper community called a *Hog's Tooth*. It was the bullet in the chamber from the first enemy sniper he killed in Iraq. It had a hole drilled in it with a leather strap running through it. It meant you had control of the round that the enemy meant for you. The medal christened him a *Hunter Gun*.

*Get them first before they get you. Did it for Sandy. Worked it out for the twins. Missed it for Venus. Won't miss again.*

If Venus was actually locked up in a holding cell in the Coast Guard Air Station at Selfridge, the holding cell was secured with electric locks. Knock out the power and the prisoner goes free. Vince would have to take out the transformer, and the .50 caliber would do nicely. The backup diesel generator that was installed after the northeastern blackout a few years earlier could be disabled when he got there. Sunset would be twenty-hundred hours. The second shift would be taking lunch and relaxing. By ten they would be tired and probably watching T.V.

*Get some rest Warrant Officer Sanchez. If you're really locked up, the cavalry is on its way.*

Vince stored the sniper rifle in the trunk of the Impala, backed out of the garage, and had the twins get in the back seat with their backpacks. Greta was riding shotgun.

It was a slow go on the Lodge with the first Lions vs. Packers game getting out at Ford Field, but once they got past downtown on I-94, it was smooth sailing to his boathouse.

Vince locked the twins in the apartment to play video games with Greta on guard duty. He took a pair of high powered binoculars and climbed to the roof. He sighted-in the Air Station and found an electric pole with the transformer behind it. He would have a straight shot to take out the power on the west side of Selfridge.

He went back down to the apartment and called up Mike *the Snipe.*

"What's up Bro?" answered Mike.

"Got a problem."

"Why else would you call me on a beautiful Sunday evening?"

"There's a Guardy locked up in the Air Station at Selfridge. I'm going in after dark. I need you to call up a pair of National Guard Warthogs for a night run."

"Oh, I thought it would be something little, you know, like an invasion of Canada. You just want me to send two fighter jets on a mission to where, nowhere? That'll be four thousand dollars plus pilot over-time."

"Put it on my tab. I'll pay for it personally," Vince replied.

"Oh, it's personal, is it? It's not that female heelo pilot you've been flying?" asked Mike.

"How do you know it's a woman?"

"Can't hide the shite from *the Snipe.*"

"Great. Send them off at twenty-two hundred hours."

"And to where, oh commandant?"

"Two Fly-bys of Selfridge, turning over the lake."

"Shootin for distractions, eh my friend?" Mike asked.

*More like the other way around.*

"There might be more requests in the next couple of days," Vince answered.

"I'll be sitting right here by the phone holding my breath."

"Thanks."

*Starke wouldn't physically harm Venus to get information, would he? No, he needed her for harboring the twins as fugitives. Any sign of coercion would cause suspicion on his part, and so far, he'd been able to stay out of the limelight on his own undercover operation. For her to give up their location that quickly, Venus had probably been drugged. Starke was a desperate man.*

~~~

It was a clear night. Perfect for an A-10 Thunderbolt show. Vince put on his desert fatigues with black night gear underneath, adjustable infrared goggles and grabbed his 50 cal. sniper rifle. He climbed to the roof and sighted in the transformer: twenty-five hundred yards, about one and half miles. Lucky for him, at this distance, the transformer was bigger than a man, his normal target. He shifted the scope to the right and saw the spotlighted Coast Guard Base American flag flapping in a southwest breeze. He made a final slight adjustment for the wind and waited for the jets to taxi to the end of the runway.

Detroit twenty-two hundred hours, Zulu two hundred on the dot, the first A-10 Thunderbolt Warthog took off with a loud blast from its twin GE jet engines. It screamed straight up and over Lake St. Clair, reverberating through the metal roof Vince was laying on. He would have to hit the transformer with the first shot before the second A-10 took off.

He scoped in the transformer. As the second jet wound up its engines for takeoff, he squeezed off a round. With the distinctive blast of a fifty caliber shot sounding like the crack of lightening, a blue fireball erupted on the electric pole near the Air Station as the second Thunderbolt lifted off the tarmac. Vince ran down from the roof while the Warthog accelerated over him and out to Lake St. Clair. Together in formation, the fighter jets started their turn around back to the air base for the first fly-by.

He stashed the rifle in the trunk, fired up the Impala and took off to Selfridge's south gate, better known to the locals as the *Golf Gate*. It faced the base's eighteen-hole golf course.

He drove up to the gate and flashed his Homeland Badge at the night guard. "Transformer blew. Just checking it out," Vince said to the guard.

"Yes, Sir," the guard said as he stiffened to attention and saluted.

The Thunderbolts were flying back toward the air base as Vince took the South Perimeter Road to the Station. He began singing; well, more like growling to a CD he was playing of an AC/DC riff: *Awaaa-aaaa-waaa-aaaaaa, THUNDER!*

Vince parked in the Air Station parking lot just west of the building and stripped off his army camo down to his black tights. Several Coasties were standing outside, but they were looking up at the fireball shooting out of the destroyed transformer, then toward the air base as the Thunderbolts headed straight toward them. With everyone distracted, Vince jumped out of the car and ran up to the thirty-five foot long back-up generator. He picked the lock and opened the panel door.

The jets flew directly overhead, pushed the throttle and darted straight up. The sound blast of the afterburners was deafening as Vince pulled the electronic module control unit. The 1100 kilowatt Detroit diesel died and all the lights went out. "You've been – *Thunderstruck!*"

As the jets turned sideways and headed back out over Lake St. Clair, Vince flipped down his night vision goggles and ran to the other side of the building. He pushed through double doors and found the lobby empty. He ran through the building to the back of the station where lock up was located. He threw open the disengaged doors and found Venus lying on a cot in the second cell. She was covering her ears from the transformer explosion and the Thunderbolts fly-by. He knelt down next to her and yelled her name. She looked up at him and screamed. He had forgotten to take off his night vision goggles.

He quickly flipped the goggles up, turned on his Mag-lite and pointed it up so she could see his face. She flung her arms around him and began sobbing incoherently, rambling something in Spanish. He turned off the Mag-lite and told her to take off her top. She shook her head no. He explained that he needed to stuff it with some towels and put it under the blankets to make it look like she was still asleep. She nodded and complied.

Vince picked her up, carried her out of the cell and then closed the steel door so it would look like it was still locked. He carried her out through the front door as the Warthogs made a Michigan U-turn over Lake St. Clair. When they came screaming back at tree top level, Vince ran Venus to the car, laid her down in the back seat and covered her up with an army blanket. He took off the night vision goggles and looked around to see if anyone had seen them, but everyone was transfixed by the unusual air show. He jumped into the car, put his army fatigues back on and drove off.

Back on Perimeter Road, he flipped on the Impala's headlights. He heard Venus sobbing something in Spanish. He told her she needed to keep quiet and cover up with the blanket. When he pulled up to the south gate, the guard waved at him, but then signaled for him to stop. *Great*.

When Vince pulled up to the booth, the guard stuck his head in the car window. "If you don't mind my asking, Sir. What the hell is going on out there?"

"Transformer blew out at the Coast Guard Air Station," Vince answered.

"No, Sir," he said as he pointed upward. "I mean the Warthogs."

"Just a couple of fly-bys. I guess to see if they are emergency ready."

"Never seen anything like it," the guard said as he took a cursory look in the car. He saw the green army blanket covering the back seat. He looked back to Vincent and paused.

Vince could tell he was thinking about asking the question, so he gave the guard his *don't even think about it* look.

"Okay, Sir. Thank you Sir. Have a good night."

"You too, officer." Vince drove through the gate and toward the marina as the Thunderbolts made their landing.

He parked the car in the boathouse garage. When he turned off the engine, he heard Venus sobbing again in the back seat.

"I'm sorry Vince. I'm so sorry."

Vince picked her up and carried her from the car to the boathouse, holding her to his chest, kissing her cheek, telling her everything was all right and that the twins were safe. He took her to his bedroom, laid her down on the bed, propped up her head and got her a cold glass of water. Tears were still spilling down her cheeks. He kissed them away and handed her a tissue box. She took some and blew her nose.

He sat down next to her and put his arm around her. "Did they hurt you in any way?"

"No," she said. "Just my pride and my loyalty."

"Did they drug you?"

"The MP's held me and Starke had a short black man stick a needle in my arm. After that I became groggy."

"They threaten you?"

She started crying again. He lifted her into his arms and held her.

253

"They said that I would be court marshaled and prosecuted for assisting suspects in a terrorist plot if I didn't cooperate in locating them. I told them everything. Vince, I couldn't stop talking."

*Just like now. Sodium Pentothal.*

"You have to save the boys, Vincent. They're in danger."

"They're here. I have the twins."

"Thank God," she said with a sigh. "They just kept going at me, Vince. They gave me the shot and started an hour later. They didn't let up until I told them where to find the boys." She started crying again. "They said I would be on trial for treason, I would lose my commission, ruin my name, my father's name and would spend the rest of my life in a federal prison. They wore me down, Vince. My only hope was that they would find you along with the boys and you could stop them."

"They drugged you, Venus. You couldn't help but tell them anything they asked."

"Is that why I couldn't stop talking?"

"Yes. But I have an important question for you?"

"I guess you can ask me anything. *Si*?"

"Did they ask you about recovering Alberto's body yesterday?"

"Yes. I told them that I recognized him and that it looked to me like he was murdered by Williams."

*Another reason for Starke to be so desperate to locate the video, the twins, Venus and me.*

"Good. Okay. Everything's okay, Venus. Take some deep breaths. That's it. Lie down. Be still. Everything will be all right." He kissed her softly on the lips and stroked her hair.

Venus lay quietly with her eyes closed for a few minutes, then looked up at Vincent.

"Anything else you want to ask me, Vincent?" she asked with a small smile. "I guess I can't help but tell you anything you want to know."

"Not really. You've been open and honest with me from day one." He returned the smile.

"Did you doubt me when they came for the twins?"

"For a minute, but I got over it."

"Oh, no. I was so worried you'd think I betrayed you. I would never do it willingly. I love you too much. I want to..."

"It's all right. Ssshh. It's all right. Go to sleep. The drug will wear off by morning. I'm sorry I got
you in the middle of all of this."

She pulled away and gave him a look. "I volunteered, and don't you forget it."

"Ah, the fighter's back."

She started to slap him, but he caught her wrist. He pulled her to him and kissed her. Her tight lips relaxed and she threw her arms around him again. When they finished, she spoke with a whisper.

"After they got all they wanted, I was afraid you'd think I had turned on you and the boys, that I was in it with Starke to set you up. Please tell me you don't think that."

"A little Angel told me you hadn't."

Venus let go and sat up on the bed. "Angela. I need to call her. She's probably worried sick that I didn't call her today."

"Yes she is. She'll be glad to hear from you. That's how we knew you were locked up." He gave her his phone and she called Angela.

Vince went to the kitchen, brewed some tea and opened a well-stocked chest freezer, pulling out some steaks for the grill. Venus walked into the kitchen wearing his bathrobe and gave him the phone and said she had to have a shower. He asked if she was hungry and wanted to eat before sleep. She said yes, she did. He told her that a steak and potato would be ready in twenty minutes. She protested, saying that she needed longer to wash out the sweat and stink of the past fourteen hours. He told her she needed to sleep because they had a long day ahead of them. She agreed and headed to the shower.

After she got dressed with a T-shirt of Vince's, Venus ate her steak and potato slathered with butter and sour cream. She said they gave her nothing to eat, just water.

"Who questioned you?" Vince asked.

"It was Starke and Roberts, with two MP's guarding, and a short black guy who gave me the truth drug. When I told them that the twins were in the garage apartment at your house, Starke made a phone call. Sometime later, I don't know how long, Starke got a return call that made him happy and left immediately. The MP's locked me up and left, telling the clerk and flight crew that I was a flight risk and I was to remain there until morning. The FBI would pick me up in the morning."

"Did anyone question you after that?" he asked.

"No. Before Starke left, he said the twins were apprehended and they would be charged with assisting the terrorists and that you and I would be arraigned on aiding and abetting."

"Anything else?"

She thought for a minute. "He said they had a video of the boys with the two pallets of TracFones. He said they had an eyewitness and pictures that put you and me in Ludington with the twins. So, apparently they think they have a case. But through it all, I knew you had the real video and that you could clear all of us once you got free. By the way, how did you get free?"

"My partner: Greta. She followed us and distracted the guards."

At the sound of her name, the Shepherd walked into the room and up to Venus. "Good girl," Venus said, scratching Greta's ears.

Looking back to Vince, she asked, "You do have the video, right?"

"The Metro Guard couple has it, but we have another one, the original."

"Where?" Venus asked.

"Where you saw it. Sandy's laptop."

"Right."

"Did they ask about anything else?"

Venus thought for a minute. "Yes. A couple of questions about finding Alberto's body. He said it was ruled a boating accident. That got me mad and I blurted out that I knew Williams had killed him and covered it up, and that he sent the TracFones downriver with Roberts to the Metro Guards. He said I had no proof. He then had the black guy give me another shot. The MP's dragged me to the cell and I blacked out."

"No wonder they wanted all of us in custody."

"Well, what are we going to do about it now that we're out?" Venus asked.

"First thing, I'm calling the boss."

"You have a boss? Homeland?"

"No. Somebody higher," he said. "And he'll still be up." Vince took his phone and dialed the number only a few had at their disposal. Someone answered.

"Saint Vincent," he said. Then silence. Venus frowned. He looked down at the floor. "Yes, good evening, Mr. President. I have a situation, Sir. It needs your attention." He looked back at Venus and her eyes were as wide as saucers.

"Have you been briefed on the arrest of suspected terrorists in Michigan, sir?" Vince asked, looking back at the floor. "I have more information that might clear up a few things."

The President put him on conference call.

"Is that *The* President?" Venus mouthed.

Vince nodded. When they came back on, Vince explained the situation and his concerns about the undercover operation. The president said he would call the FBI Director and tell them that the twins were in custody in a new location and that an operative would be coming in to bring them new evidence. The President hung up with a thank you. Vince completed the conversation with his Assistant, filling in the details. When the conversation ended, he looked back at Venus.

"Oh. My. God. *The* President of *The* United States?" she asked again.

"One and the same. Along with my former boss, the Director of National Intelligence."

"Who are you, really?" she asked, reaching up and stroking his cheek.

Vince hesitated, wondering for a minute if what he was about to say might change their relationship. "I'm a reserve member of the CIA's Freelance Unit, and I'm now the undercover backup to Homeland Security, the Detroit Canadian border."

Venus just looked at him. Then she relaxed. "Who else knows?"

"Just Sandy, and Debra and Diane," he answered. "And, now you."

"And now me." She paused. "And if I tell anyone, you'll shoot me."

"Well, no," Vince said. "But I might have to change your name and put you in the witness protection program."

"Oh, really!"

"Well, I already have you in protective custody." He took her into his arms.

"Meaning, you're not going to let Starke or the FBI take me away or ruin my career?"

"That is correct, Warrant Officer Sanchez."

She looked into his eyes. "So, you're not really going to change my name or my commission, right?" she asked.

"No. Uh, not yet anyway."

"Thank you." Then she backed up and looked at him. "What do you mean, 'not yet?'"

"Meaning I'm going to have to work on giving you a new commission, a new rank, and maybe a new name." *Did I just say that out loud? I do want to protect you, love you, and yes, change your last name.*

"I like my name," she said.

"Never mind. I don't have time to explain right now."

"So what do we do now?" she asked.

"You get some sleep. I'll call Sandy and have him bring his laptop and meet me downtown. We'll find out what Starke and crew are telling the F.B.I. before we hand over the video file."

"What about me?" Venus asked with an edge to her voice. "You can't just leave me out of this now. I want to be in on it when you reveal the truth."

"Kick ass, take names?"

Her lips tightened into a thin line. "If need be."

"I like your attitude. And you're pretty sexy when you're mad. How did Sandy say it? *'One Hot Tamale?'*"

"Enough with the Mexican epithets. What can I do?" she asked.

"You'll stay here and guard the boys until we know the charges have been dropped. In the morning, I'll head back to my house on Boston to change clothes and get ready to visit the FBI. When Sandy calls, I'll call you with what to do next."

"Yes, Sir."

"Now get some sleep, Officer," Vince said in his most commanding voice. "And be awake and ready in the morning. Tomorrow is going to be a busy day."

"Yes, *Surrr!*"

## Part IV  THE CUT

*"Unlike people who cross our southern border to gain a better life, people cross our northern border to harm our way of life."* -- Michigan Immigration and Customs Enforcement (I.C.E.) Officer

Chapter 25

Monday Morning

Vince cleaned his long rifle and stored it in the Impala. He unlocked his boathouse gun safe and grabbed his M-16, the AR-15 Colt semi-automatic. He took it to his bedroom and gave it to Venus.

"Just in case," he said. "I don't expect any trouble, but..."

"Be prepared," Venus interrupted.

"Exactly."

Venus checked to see there was a cartridge in the chamber. She pulled the magazine and saw that it was full, giving her multiple rounds that could be shot in three round bursts.

"Wow. I'm playing with the big boys now," she said.

"The big girls too. I've called Debra and Diane. They'll be here any minute," Vince said.

"I'll be fine with this M-16," she said, grabbing his hand, "and you."

"I might need you to join me later. I want someone with the twins at all times until I give the all clear."

"Got it," she said.

"I'll call you after my meeting with the Director." He leaned down and kissed her.

"You think you can convince him we're innocent?" Venus asked.

"Between the video file and my credentials, yeah, I think so."

"Ooh. Secret Agent Man. "

"Johnny Rivers, 1966," Vince answered.

She took both of his hands. "And you're my *Dangerous Man* and I pray to God you're right," she said with tears welling up in her eyes.

Vince leaned in and kissed her again.

~~~

As Vince drove out of the marina and turned on North River Road by Selfridge, he could see the Detroit Edison truck's yellow flashing lights at work replacing the transformer. Any evidence of it being knocked out with a .50 caliber round had disintegrated in the fireball. Not to mention, that didn't happen very often.

He drove down I-94 west with his flashers on, but Monday morning traffic into Detroit was slowing down in all lanes. He jumped off at the Mt. Elliott exit and skirted the General Motors Hamtramck Plant until he was on East Grand Boulevard. He turned onto Woodward and then on Boston. There was a white Detroit PD Crown Vic sitting in front of his house. *Better than Metro Guard any day.*

Maria met him at the back door. "Iss everything all right, *Señor* Vincent? Iss Venus O-kay?"

"Yes, Maria. Everything will be all right, and Venus and the twins are at my boathouse safe and sound."

"Thank God."

"Amen, sister. Has anyone else been snooping around?"

"Not since Sandy has had his police cruiser out in front and in back."

"Good. I'm meeting with the Feds at nine. I'll hit the shower and change clothes. Could you iron a white shirt for me?"

"Yess, *Señor* Vincent. You hungry?"

"No. Ate at the boathouse. But, thanks."

After the shower and a shave, he changed into what he liked to call his *Secret-Serviceman* look: black suit, white shirt with black tie, Kevlar vest, earpiece, sunglasses, Department of Homeland Security I.D. and a bulge in the side of the jacket: standard issue Sig Sauer 357 caliber pistol.

He went to his office, put in a memory stick in his pocket to copy the video file from Sandy's laptop. He took another memory stick, surrounded it in bubble wrap and placed it between two pieces of foam in his black brief case. He added one other item, clicked it shut and attached a pair of handcuffs to the handle.

~~~

Knowing the Lodge would be backed up with the morning rush, he took Woodward toward downtown. By the time he got to Church Row near King Street, traffic began to slow. It gave him time to think.

*Starke and Roberts put the Arab brothers in a Dearborn apartment, set them up with the TracFones and sent them to Ludington. He called in the Feds and helped apprehend them with the TracFones, the lynchpin to the entire operation. Starke had to have the twins, then he and Venus, implicated. The Border Patrol Officer was killed by Williams when he was caught stealing the TracFones. And it was all done to make Starke and his crew out as heroes?*

*Missing something here. A set-up, a cover-up and a murder just for fame? No. For fortune? Maybe.*

When he finally made it to West Grand Boulevard, Woodward was backed up bumper to bumper and going nowhere. He switched on the AM news channel *with traffic on the eights* to find out what was going on. The report was that all traffic on several streets was being stopped for fifteen minutes or more for an undisclosed convoy with a police escort.

First he heard them. Then he looked up to see what he thought to be media choppers. Instead, they were Coast Guard and FBI. He turned on his police scanner to hear any chatter about the convoy. Four semi trucks were moving up Cass

Avenue and turning onto Warren heading northeast across Woodward. *No wonder the backup.*

He called Sandy. "Is what I think going on, going on?"

"There's a Convoy of Metro Guard semi trucks movin' the Federal Reserve Bank to its new location on Warren and Forest. I found out just this mornin'. This was top secret, only on a need-to-know basis. I guess they didn't want the mob or the gangs to know that money was on the move this mornin'."

"That explains why I'm stuck on Woodward at the Boulevard," Vince said. "I'm headed to the McNamara building to meet with the FBI Director. Meet me in the lobby."

"Will do," answered Sandy.

Vince checked through security flashing his Homeland Security badge in his Secret Service outfit. He checked in the Sig Sauer, but it was returned to him due to his credentials. His black attaché case was examined, but it only contained one bubble wrapped package and a Snickers bar, his little joke. It got a smile from the female security guard who searched it. He gave her his thousand watt smile in return and winked. She let him pass without questions. Sandy was waiting for him just on the other side of the check point.

While they took the elevator to the twenty-sixth floor, Vince copied the video file from Sandy's laptop onto the memory stick in his pocket. The elevator opened in the lobby of the Federal Bureau of Investigation and they were met by a pleasant but all business like receptionist. They flashed their credentials and asked for the Director. She got on the phone and immediately waved them through.

Vince walked briskly across the office, extended his hand and shook it firmly. "Good morning, Director."

"Good to meet you, Mr. Vincent. You must have some influential friends in Washington. Takes some pull to have *The* Director call and tell me to meet you. Must be that Regent International Petroleum money that persuades certain politicians to call in favors. Yes, I looked you up. Former Navy SEAL, now The Reserve, sometimes on special assignment. Well, I love a patriot who knows how the government works. Good to know we have such an experienced veteran of your caliber in our neighborhood."

*You mean you don't appreciate having someone who doesn't have to report to you lurking around your jurisdiction, influencing your agency. Everyone hates the FBI's interference, now you know what it's like and hate it too.*

"Thank you, sir." Vince said with a polite smile. "Good to meet you too. This is detective Patrick Sandelen, a good friend and liaison to Homeland Security for the Detroit Police Department."

"How do you do?"

"Good. Thank you, sir."

"It's been a little crazy down here, gentlemen, as you might imagine," continued the Director. "Please take a seat."

The Director's office faced south with a glass wall window overlooking the Detroit River and the Ambassador Bridge. The morning sun had turned the normally murky Detroit River bright blue.

"We're here sir about the arrests made over the weekend of several terrorist suspects," Vince said.

"Yes. Quite a coup. We've had surveillance on three Lebanese brothers in Dearborn for some time."

"Did that surveillance involve Coast Guard Lieutenant Commander Clay Starke, Sir?"

"In part. One of his officers has a house in Dearborn and Starke arranged moving the Arabs into the upper flat so we could keep an eye on them. In fact, it was Starke who tipped us off about these guys. He found them when they were rescued in New Orleans after Katrina. They were very excited about moving into the Detroit area and they were interested in acquiring and selling cell phones. Starke had a tech expert he knew move in with Roberts and install video and listening devices to see if the cell phone angle became anything more than retail. In the past week, we knew it was more than just sales."

"So, Starke has recordings of these men plotting an act of terrorism?" asked Vince.

"Well, not exactly. It was witnessed by Roberts and a tech guy named Peters. They didn't have the recording on when the men incriminated themselves."

"Is Starke and his crew here for debriefing?" asked Sandy.

"No. They haven't been here all morning. We did the initial interviews yesterday. He and Roberts were assigned to part of the security detail on the river for the Federal Reserve this morning. In fact, I'm surprised you weren't notified and on call, having the moniker 'Federal Reserve' and all. Get it?" The Director chuckled at his little joke.

Vince was not amused. "It wasn't border patrol. I'm dealing with other matters, Sir. The boss thought you and the other agencies had it under control. I'm just back-up, remember?"

"Sure. Anyway, what did you want to talk about?" the Director asked.

"Just wondering how the terrorist investigation was coming along; interviews and the collection of evidence?" Vincent asked.

"We've got all we need. The TracFones are in hand and the eye witnesses will testify. We will continue interviews tomorrow, this time with the prosecutor and court ordered defense lawyers. Naturally, the Arabs are yelling they have no idea what we're talking about. They were just being tourists on their way to sell the phones to a wholesale company that supplies stores in Pentwater, Ludington, Manistee and most of the north-west side of the state. Likely story."

"I heard agents were following two young American brothers who were thought to be accomplices. Is that true?" Vince asked.

"Yes, we were, until Washington called it off. My agents said someone flashing a DHS badge with your description called it in."

"I happen to know the twins personally," Vince said.

"Quite a coincidence," the Director added.

"Quite." *You're not getting any more than that.*

There was a long pause. Vince waited.

The Director cleared his throat. "Well, D.C. has told me to stand down on whoever provided the cell phones for now."

*A round-about way of saying he was ordered to clear the twins. That means Starke used the Metro Guards for his own purposes.*

"So, Starke isn't here today for a debriefing?" Vince asked.

"That's right. Like I said, he's part of the Reserve Bank move to their new location over on Warren and Dequindre."

Sandy and Vince exchanged a glance.

"Let's see," the Director continued. "He was in charge of a couple of troop transport trucks from the National Guard. They were stationed at the river front along with one Coast Guard helicopter. Why do you ask?"

"Just checking. You know, on the border, Sir. One of my assignments."

"Of course. Anything else?"

*The Director is telling us the interview is over.*

"No sir. Thank you for your time," Vince said.

"One more thing," the Director said and paused

*Here comes the question I always get when I pull strings.*

"Yes?"

"What if I need you? A man with your experience and, uh, *persuasion*, could come in handy now and then."

Vince gave him his stock answer. "Have your people call my people." He smiled.

"Very funny," said the Director with a false chuckle.

*It's no joke.*

~~~

Vince and Sandy took the elevator in silence. Once they were a block away from the McNamara Building, Sandy said, "He doesn't really know who you are, does he?"

"And that's the way it has to stay. I think I know why Starke was having all of those extra meetings: the move of the Federal Reserve Bank."

"What's that got to do with the twins, and Venus, and you?" Sandy asked.

"CCD: *Conceal, Contain, Deceive.*"

"You're talking in code, now."

*The Federal Reserve Bank, whose mission is 'to maintain the stability of the U.S. financial system and provide services and security to depositories.' And the Detroit Branch holding multiple billions in cash.*

"I'll explain more, later," Vince said. He took out his phone and called Debra.

"Do you have your Homeland credentials?"

"Yes," she answered.

"Good. Take Venus and the twins to the Coast Guard Air Base at Selfridge. Hide them in the backseat. Park near Venus' Dolphin. Tell her she's going to fly it out without logging in. You and Diane go into the station office and occupy whoever's there with a story about orders from Coast Guard HQ in Maryland. I'll call and arrange the order. Have Venus bring the M-16. Call me back when you get there."

"Sandy, go to the new Federal Reserve building on Warren. Call me when you get there."

"Can you tell me what's goin' on?"

"Once I have evidence," Vince answered.

After Sandy left, Vince called his boss. He filled him in and had him call in Venus's flight plan through the Maryland Coast Guard Director. "We need to find out He where the semi-trucks were are going after unloading.

He got back to his car and headed to the Juvenile Court on Forest that is across the street from the new Federal Reserve. He'd been there several times with young fathers and had seen the construction of the new state of the art bank building.

He followed the route the Metro Guard semi-trucks had taken since it was the most direct route from the former location of the bank on Fort to the new one on Warren. He drove over the Chrysler Freeway and turned on Russell to Forest next to the new bank building, but it was now a dead end. He turned around and took Russell to Canfield that crossed Dequindre. All of the police and federal agencies in the high security contingent were no longer visible. Apparently the cash laden trucks were unloaded and gone

Vince was following Dequindre south until it turned into Mack Avenue west when Sandy called.

"I talked with one of the guards at the gate. The trucks headed back to the Metro Guard warehouse at Mack and St. Aubin. They were to be inspected one last time at the Metro Guard garage. The last one left an hour ago."

"Thanks Sandy. Hang loose. I'll call you back."

Vince turned around and drove east on Mack. A few blocks past Dequindre at St. Aubin he found the Metro Guard building. He drove up to the fenced and barbed wire parking lot gate. He flashed his badge and asked the guard if the trucks for the Fed Reserve move had arrived. The guard said that they hadn't arrived yet due to some hold up at the bank. *Could that be literally true?*

He called Sandy back and confirmed that the trucks had left the Reserve over an hour ago. He turned around on Mack and went slowly back to the intersection of Mack and Dequindre. He saw two wide black tread marks that looked like a truck had zig-zagged from Dequindre onto a dirt-packed railroad bed that ran parallel to the street. He turned and drove down the abandoned rail path a few yards, stopped and got out for a better look. He found multiple fresh tire tracks in the abandoned railroad bed. *The Dequindre Cut.*

Vince followed the track bed under Mack Avenue, then several blocks past a school parking lot and under another bridge. The rail path continued south past the next street bridge where he saw the back of a semi inside an abandoned factory. He stopped the car, got out and pulled out the Beretta.

He walked carefully up to the semi and jerked open the doors to the trailer. Empty. He went around to the front of the truck and saw the back of the other three trucks with their doors flung open. Again, nothing.

He went back to the first truck where the sun light would allow him to see further inside. He hoisted himself up on the truck bed and walked halfway down the trailer. He found a light collapsible metal frame with large pieces of a light weight tarp hanging from one side. It looked to be a light weight Mylar material. It had some kind of image on one side.

He pulled it out to see what resembled the back wall of the truck. *What the hell?*

Stepping further into the truck, he could see anchors for the tarp about four to five feet from the back of the wall. Enough distance for a pallet, and enough room across for two or three.

*Metro Guard was used to load trucks at the old Federal Reserve building yesterday. Apparently they erected false walls in all of the trailers, hiding the length of what looks like one standard pallet. The truck width looked wider than normal. Two or three pallets could easily fit across the width of each truck. Three pallets, four trucks. Twelve pallets of Federal Reserve cash. A Dequindre Cut indeed.*

He searched the other three trucks with his Maglite and saw the same collapsible frame and Mylar tarp in the trailers. He went back to his car and called Sandy. He remembered the FBI Director saying that Starke was in charge of two National Guard transport trucks.

*Two trucks could carry tons of cargo, easily accommodating four pallets each. Take another one to handle twelve. Hundreds of millions, maybe a billion.*

Vince called Sandy. "I found the semi-trucks. They weren't at Metro Guard. They were abandoned down the old railroad bed that runs parallel to Dequindre."

"*The Cut?*" Sandy asked.

"Yep. It looks like they skimmed off a number of cash pallets. I need you to drive over here, call it in to the FBI Director and wait for the agents. We'll let them have the win, or the loss, whichever way you look at it."

"You *shittin'* me, Man? This is all about a bank heist?" Sandy asked.

"Not any bank," Vince said. "The Federal Reserve."

Sandy sighed. "Goddamn! Word gets out, this could send the banks and the markets into a dive. The country's financial security is on the line."

"And that line leads straight to Starke," Vince said. "No wonder the big terrorist media hype. It distracted everyone."

"Even you."

"Even me."

"Vince, no time for reflectin'. It's time to get checkin'. Back to the detective's first rule."

"Follow the money."

"You got it."

~~~

Vince drove toward the river on the rail path, watching for any sign of the tracks from the military transport trucks. He saw wide black tread marks turning off the Cut onto the first opportunity to be on pavement one block south of the Jefferson Street Bridge. They had turned east on Woodbridge, then a block away, north on St. Aubin Street to East Jefferson Avenue. He had a good idea where they were headed.

He called Debra just as they were pulling into the Coast Guard Air Station. "Proceed as planned. Send the twins with Venus. After they're away, watch for two or three National Guard Transports pulling into the base."

He hung up and called Venus's phone and told her what he'd found. There was a pause on the other end, and then in a whisper she said, "*FUBAR.*"

*Oh, you are so right, my dear Venus. You are so right.*

"Debra's going into the Station to confirm your flight. Take the Dolphin and pick me up on the riverfront just west of the large white tent at Chene Park. We have some thieves to catch."

"Fuckin right we do," Venus said. "What about the twins?" she asked.

"Bring 'em with you. I'm not letting them out of our sight," Vince said. "Do you have a vest?"

"Got one in the chopper. Remember? We're the shallow water Navy that can arrest. How about you?"

"Got mine on. Remember? I was at the Fed building."

"Right. *Federales* with guns. Always dangerous. By the way, where we headed?" Venus asked

"I'll tell you when you get here."

Chapter 26


Monday Noon


The fire-engine red Coast Guard helicopter landed on an abandoned lot just west of Chene Park on the Detroit River. Its twin Arriel turbo shaft engines created quite a stir on the riverfront, attracting residents as well as boaters. Vince grabbed his back-up bag from the trunk, ducked down and led Greta into the helicopter, telling her to sit in between the twins in the back seats. He got in the navigator's seat across from Venus, buckled in, and put on the headphones.

"Where to?" she asked over the headphones.

"North, back toward Selfridge," Vince answered.

"I just came from there," she complained. "Not in any hurry to get back. Wanna find me some *Gringos*."

"Did you see any army transport trucks heading east on your way in?" Vince asked.

"No," she replied.

"Then, to Port Huron."

"Yes, Sir."

Venus lifted off at an angle that would make a fighter pilot proud, pushing Vince down in the harness. She turned the Dolphin one hundred eighty degrees while ascending, giving the passengers a feeling of vertigo. Venus appeared unfazed. The twins whooped out loud.

Once leveled out, the twins got on the headphones. "Vince, are we in the clear?" asked Cane.

"Yes, you're both in the clear. All this has nothing to do with you and the video. You two just ended up in the wrong place at the wrong time. But, as far as I'm concerned, the right place at the right time. You caught the Metro Guard couple and Roberts transporting the TracFones, the ones Starke used to set up the

Arabs: the detonator of choice in Iraqi car bombs. And after 9/11, all Arabs became the *terrorist de jour*."

Venus added, "Same Arabs arrested for attempting to blow up the Pump Storage reservoir in Ludington. Starke wanted it to look like they were attempting to bring down the electric grid."

"It was just the CCD for their real operation," Vince said.

"CCD?" Al asked.

"That's military for *Concealment, Containment, Deception*," answered Vince. "They were concealing and then deceiving everyone from their real operation, a Federal Reserve Bank robbery. They stole eight to twelve pallets of cold hard cash worth up to a billion dollars during the move from the old Fed Reserve Bank to the new more secure Bank."

"Wow!" said Al.

"Yeah, wow," said Cane. "So, we're off the hook?

"Yes, you're off the hook."

"And we're off to catch them?" Al asked.

"That's what Venus and I are off to do. You're here to just keep from being picked up again."

"Cool," they said in unison.

"This chopper is bitchin," said Cane.

"Watch what you call the pilot," said Venus.

"No, I meant..."

"I know what you meant," replied Venus. "And in a sense she is a bitch. It's a she, and she does search and rescue, just like a mother."

"She is one awesome motha," said Al.

"I call her *"She-wolf*," Venus said.

"*She-wolf*?" Vince asked.

"Yep. Guardies call this latest version *Tupperwolf*, adapting the name of the helicopter from the TV show, *Airwolf*. I watch all the re-runs," she said with a smile.

"*Tupper-wolf?*" Vince asked.

"Most of the structure, including rotor head, rotor blades and fuselage, consists of corrosion-resistant composite materials, hence *Tupperwear.*"

"And you're a bi...woman pilot flying the ..." Vince said. Venus interrupted, "Yeah. Now there is a bitch flyin this one. It's *She-wolf*, got that? And this bitch is out to get those badass Coasties."

Both boys broke up laughing.

Vince didn't laugh. He hoped he could bring Starke and crew in alive, not dead or alive.

Venus called in her new flight plan to the Air Base, pushing the Dolphin up to a hundred knots, one hundred twenty miles an hour, cruising at tree top level, the air field approach altitude of five hundred feet. She zeroed in on I-94 and in a few minutes she was doing a fly-by of Selfridge.

"No transport trucks," she said.

"Port Huron," Vince said. "I don't think they'll be flying out anywhere close to the scene of the crime. Starke would know that if there was any chance of being discovered, they would need to high tail it to another state or out of the country."

"More like out of the country." Venus said. She throttled up to one hundred fifty knots. At that speed, they were tilted forward in their seats, giving them a good view of the highway.

It had been over three hours since the heist, but Vince was betting that it took at least an hour or more to unload the four trucks, sending the last transport out a little over an hour ago. Since they were going twice as fast, he hoped they would spot the last transport about the time they reached the outskirts of Port Huron.

As they approached the south side of the city, Venus pulled back on the cyclic and everyone kept their eyes peeled on the exits off the interstate. They could see where I-94 and I-69 merged and Vince could only hope they would see something before they ended up in town. Just then, Cane yelled in their earphones. "What's that?"

Off to the right side of the helicopter, Vince could see the top of a troop transport heading up and out of sight on Gratiot Avenue, business I-94. He signaled Venus to take a turn toward the St. Clair River. The Dolphin jerked and dove sideways, throwing everyone into their harness. They were just above trees heading toward the river when Cane said, "Lost it."

Venus slowed down to almost a hover. The transport was nowhere to be seen. She continued forward until they were flying along the river following Military Street until they were over downtown. They had lost the transport.

"Damn it," Venus yelled into the headphones.

"Any ideas?" Vince asked.

Venus shook her head no, too angry to talk. She flew further north and then over the Blue Water Bridge, the glistening waters of Lake Huron filling the windshield. She dipped to port, took a one eighty Michigan turn and dropped to land on a grassy lot just inside the Port Huron Coast Guard Station.

Venus turned off the engines, unfastened her harness, jumped out of the pilot's seat and started running to the largest of the red brick buildings that made up the station. Vince unhooked his harness, grabbed his bag with his fatigues and boots, leapt out and ran after her.

"Hold up," he yelled, grabbing her arm. She slung her arm out of his grip, shoved him backward and continued running. He took one more lunge for her and tackled her just before the parking lot. She tried to jump up and start swinging, but he buried his head into her mid-section and held her down.

"Let me go, goddamnit. I've got to catch that son of a bitch," she screamed. She continued to struggle, but finally gave up when she realized he wasn't letting go.

"Hold on. Hold on," Vince said. "We've got to think about this. We've got to think like Starke and figure out where they're going. Calling out the Calvary would just tip them off and drive them underground."

"Let me go, damn it," Venus yelled. The anger she had been holding for the past forty-eight hours boiled over.

"No, Venus. No."

"Okay, okay. But you still have to let me go."

"No, not yet."

"I've got to go to the bathroom," she said.

"Oh, okay. Sorry. I'll get the boys and we'll all go."

Venus got up and walked across the parking lot to the office entrance. Vince looked back and saw the boys standing by the helicopter staring at them. He waved them over and whistled for Greta.

Vince changed into his Navy issue camo, came out of the bathroom and heard Venus still in the women's room kicking a trash can and yelling something in Spanish. He wasn't sure he wanted a translation. The station clerk just sat at his counter busy with paperwork pretending not to hear. When Venus came out, she grabbed Vince's hand and led him out the door. The station clerk looked relieved.

Venus led him to a picnic table, sat down across from him and looked him in the eye. "What now, Mr. Top Secret?"

Vince sat silently looking into her eyes. Venus stared back, looking right through him, tapping her finger nails on the wooden table.

"Well?" she asked.

"Well," Vince paused. "Where would you go with transport trucks filled with pallets worth hundreds of millions?" he asked.

"Oh, make me figure it out," she said testily.

"Just thinking out loud, okay?"

"Well, I wouldn't go across the Blue Water Bridge. Too many inspectors," she answered.

"What if you had military papers. Would they allow you to cross without inspection?" Vince asked.

Venus shook her head. "No. You forget. My dad was border patrol. He was suspicious of everyone. And more than that, the Michigan Militia has transport trucks too."

"Good point. Okay, no bridge. Is there an airport nearby?"

"The St. Clair County International," Venus said,

"I called the boss. All Michigan airports will be on alert, and I think Starke would anticipate that. Are there any closed airports that could handle a cargo plane big enough to carry two loaded transport trucks?" Vince asked.

Venus thought for a minute. She looked across the river into Canada. "Sarnia!"

"Does it have an airport?"

"Yes," she said with a tone that hinted Vince's stupidity.

"How big is it?" he asked.

"The main runway would be long enough for a transport. Most only need a little over three thousand feet to get off the ground, and once it takes off, it can go over twenty-five hundred miles at over three hundred knots."

"They could be in the Caymans in four hours," Vince said.

Venus suddenly stood and pounded the table. "Then, we've got to find them today, damn it!"

"Okay, we will. We will," Vince said. "Could you please sit down and calm down. Think with me."

"Okay already."

"Let's assume they're flying out of Sarnia in some kind of transport. How are they going to get there without using the bridge?"

"Let's go back inside and ask whoever's on duty," Venus answered. She was already up and jogging back inside before Vince could stand up.

By the time Vince walked in, the duty captain was looking up at the ceiling. His name tag said Thomas E. Michaels. "They could take a boat. They could hide the money in cars and go across the bridge."

Venus just shook her head no to each of the man's suggestions.

"They could take a train." Michaels asked.

Venus's head stopped and she looked over at Vince.

"Train?" they asked in unison.

"Sure," he said. "There's a train tunnel that runs from Port Huron to Sarnia, Canada, under the river. It's part of the Border Patrol's responsibilities."

*Drive them underground*, Vince thought.

"Border Patrol?" asked Venus.

"Michaels?" Vince asked. "Can I call you Tom?"

Michaels nodded. "Sure."

"I'm Vincent Hardesty with Homeland, and this is Warrant Officer Venus Sanchez, the Coast Guard Pilot."

"Nice to meet you. Are you two married?" he asked.

"No!" they said in unison.

"Oh," Michaels said.

"Okay, Tom. I have an important question. The person in charge of the train tunnel to Canada, would that be Supervisor Frederick Williams?" Vince asked.

"Well, yes. Do you know him?" Tom asked.

"We've met," Vince said. He looked over at Venus. Her face was flushed and her eyes were like daggers. He put up his palms and shook his head to stop her from exploding. She mumbled something in Spanish. *I've got to learn to translate better.*

"Where does the tunnel start?" Vince asked.

"Just east of the Amtrak Station on the south side of town," Tom answered.

Venus grabbed Vince's hand and started for the door. "Let's go."

"Hold on, hold on. We're not flying there or anywhere." Vince said. "The Dolphin can be heard a mile away. They'll scatter like river rats."

"She-wolf," she said as she stopped in her tracks. "Shee-it! You're right."

"You can use my car," Tom offered.

"We'll take it," Vince said.

Tom threw him the keys. "It's the refurbished chartreuse 57 Chevy hardtop."

Vince stared at him, knowing how poorly classic cars could run. "Will it get us there?" he asked.

"It's got a rebuilt three fifty ramjet engine with headers. It'll probably get you there with a ticket," Tom answered with a grin.

Vince smiled. They won't think it's us in that."

This time he grabbed Venus's hand and they were out the door. He told the twins to stay at the station, handing them a twenty dollar bill. "We'll be back in thirty minutes. Go inside and get some snacks out of the canteen."

"Cool," they said in unison.

Vince opened the long driver's side door, pushed forward the seat and whistled for Greta to get into the back. He and Venus jumped in and slammed their doors shut. He started the engine and it roared to life. The sport mufflers would not be inconspicuous.

They drove south on Military and made their way to 16th Street where the Amtrak Station was located. As they crossed the tracks and just before turning right into the station's parking lot, they could see the St. Clair Train Tunnel. Vince parked, got out his twin monocular, one for daylight and one infrared, and looked up the tracks.

The rails on the other side of the Amtrak train led right into a new tunnel running under the St. Clair River into Sarnia. Looking just to the right, he could see another tunnel that looked abandoned and over grown, just like the rail path on the Dequindre Cut. Why not? If a plan worked once, it would work twice. He zoomed in, but could see nothing inside the tunnel. A perfect place to literally go underground, he thought. Turning on the infrared, sure enough, he could pick out several heat shadows.

Vince told Venus what he saw. "Due to high security, wouldn't the US and Canada seal the old tunnel?" asked Venus.

"It didn't look like the entrance was filled," Vince answered. "Maybe they left just enough room to park two transport trucks. Makes sense. If you're smart enough to haul off pallets of money from the Federal Reserve Bank, you'd make damn sure you had room to hide it for a day. Just long enough to possibly use the active tunnel to get into Canada and to the airport. Which brings up a new question."

"How are they getting the transports and the money out of Canada?"

"This is Williams' territory. This would be his assignment. We need to find out more about what he did with his time."

"We could have Angela look into it. Remember, she was in intelligence."

"No, wait. I've got a better idea," Vince said, reaching for his billfold. He took out a small slip of paper and read the number. He pulled out his phone and dialed.

"Hi Pat, this is Mr. Hardesty. Yes, good to hear your voice too. Yes, I'm in town. I would love to come up and see the view. Great. How about in a half hour. Great. I'll see you then."

"See the view?" asked Venus with a raised eye brow.

"How'd you like to meet my Port of Entry girlfriend?"

"Just like a sailor, one in every port," Venus said, punching him in the arm.

"Hey, careful. I'm sensitive."

"I'll make you *sensitive, Gringo. You got some splaining to do!"*

"This is the receptionist in Williams' office. She's the one that gave me the schedule that incriminated him in Alberto's murder. I had to turn on the charm and she reciprocated. She gave me her number and invited me to see her whenever I was back in town. She wants to show me the view from her high rise apartment."

"I just bet she does," Venus said.

~~~

Vince rang the doorbell at the seventh floor apartment of Pat Posey. Venus stood to the side so she wouldn't be seen and ruin the *rendezvous*. They heard the lock turn and the door opened.

"Hello, Reggie," Pat Posey said with a big smile.

Vince hesitated, the site of the young woman momentarily distracting him. Venus pushed him through the door and followed, closing the door behind them.

"Who are *you*?" Pat asked.

"I'm the *real* girlfriend, *Chucha*!"

"What'd she call me?"

"I don't think you want to know," Vince said. "This is Warrant Officer Venus Sanchez. We're actually here to ask you some questions about your boss, Frederick Williams. Sorry for the deception. Could you take a seat, please?"

"Sonofabitch, and you too, bitch."

"*Puta perra!*"

Vince raised his hands. "We need you to sit down, Pat."

"It's Ms. Posey to you," she said as she stomped over to the couch and fell into the cushions.

Venus looked at Vince. "Kinda touchy, huh?"

"I think she just got the biggest turn-off of her life," Vince said.

"I can start fires," Venus said winking at Vince," and I can put 'em out."

"Ask your questions and then get out."

"Pat..."

She gave Vince an evil eye.

"Uh, Ms. Posey. We're in a crisis here of the highest order. We need your help. We need to know about all of the activities of Station Commander Williams."

"Is he in any danger?" she asked.

With a groan, Venus said, "Oh, he's in danger, alright."

"He's in a lot of trouble," Vince continued.

"What's he done now?" Pat asked.

"Conspiracy to cover up a threat to national security," Vince said.

"And the murder of Alberto Martinez," Venus added.

"Oh my God. I knew he was slimy, possibly smuggling shit for who knows who. But conspiracy, murder?"

"Back to my question, what were some of his extracurricular activities?"

"Well, he loved to fish and party on his boat. He cycled, both bike and motor bike."

"Is he a pilot?" asked Venus.

"Oh, yeah. He liked to fly the big planes."

"How's that?" asked Vince.

"He's been training in one of those old Vietnam era transport planes. He even buzzed the station once showing off. He called all of us out of the office to see him fly over."

"Where did he get the plane?"

"At first, out of Selfridge. But lately, he said he was heading up north, Oscola, or something like that."

"There's the decommissioned Wurtsmith Air Force Base in Oscoda," Venus said. "Used to fly B-52's during the Cold War. Plenty of runway for a Hercules. Let's go."

"Okay. Thanks, Ms. Posey. You've been a big help."

"Just wasn't the kind of help I was hoping to give," she responded.

"That's enough, *Miss Pussy*," Venus said. "Time to go, Vince."

"Right," he said. As they walked out the door, he pulled out his phone and made a call. They needed backup.

Chapter 27

Monday Afternoon

"They sealed the core of the old railroad tunnel. They filled it with the rock and dirt they bore out of the new tunnel," explained Tom, the Station Clerk.

"It didn't look like the entrance was completely filled," Vince said.

"Williams did contract repairs on the tunnel for, as he said, 'tougher security,'" Tom added. "Maybe in the process he made room for future use."

"You're right," Vince said. "All you need is just enough room to park two transport trucks, and then use the active tunnel to get into Canada. Which brings us to the next question."

"Two questions," answered Venus.

"Okay, two questions," Vince said.

"First," Venus interjected, "and I think we just found out. How do they get out of Sarnia?"

"Right. And second?" Vince asked.

"Who's the inside man at the Federal Reserve?"

"Right. They had to have someone on the inside to change the number of pallets so the total shipment would be the same as at loading. I'll have *the Snipe* look into the personnel files at the Detroit Branch."

"The who?" Tom asked

"Mike the *Snipe*. Friend of mine who works at Langley. Handles all the communications for special ops. We've done a lot of operations together. He checked out your Wurtsmith Air Force Base in Oscoda. Seems that a certain CPB Supervisor from Port Huron leases a decommissioned Hercules from time to time."

"That son of a bitch!" Venus said. "Vincent, I want that guy so bad."

"We will, Venus. We will. My guess is that he's made all the arrangements to get them and the money out of Sarnia. He's got all the contacts, both this side and the other side of the border."

Outside a truck horn sounded twice.

"My ride is here," Vince said.

They walked outside to find the twins admiring a shiny new black double cab Dodge RAM truck. Vince walked up to the Enterprise Rental Agency rep and said, imitating the T.V. commercial, "That thang gotta *Hemee*?"

"Right," the driver said.

"Sweeet," Vince answered. "Okay, sorry. Couldn't help myself." Vince signed the paperwork and took the keys to the RAM pickup truck.

"What's this?" Venus asked.

"Needed the biggest truck available. I'll follow Starke's transports through the tunnel to Sarnia. We'll arrest them there."

"You, and who else?"

"My boss, the Director, said we're on our own. The President got on the line and said no one needs to know that the Federal Reserve was compromised, given the state of the economy, and the economy of this state. We can call in any help we need as long as it's not official. And that means we're sworn to secrecy, including the Coast Guard Station clerk."

"Well shit! I'm probably going to get shot for sure," Venus said.

"Not if I can help it," Vince said.

"*FUBAR*, Vince."

"You're right. It's going to be *FUBAR*.

"So, you think it's all 'fucked up...'"

Vince interrupted, "'beyond all recognition.' Yes, it will be. It's the moniker for my friends. Reserves, like myself, *Freelance Unit -- Brothers in Arms Reserve*. The boss said I could call in any help we needed, so I've called a *brother* who's undercover in Dearborn monitoring the upcoming Iraqi election. and he'll bring a friend."

"I hope they can get here by tonight," Venus said, "or this will be *FUBAR*."

"They'll be here in time."

"What about Williams?" Venus asked.

Vince answered as he climbed into the truck passenger seat. "Hang loose till I get back. Debra and Diane should be here anytime now."

*We'll see about that*, Venus thought.

~~~

Vince opened the cab door and ducked under the steering wheel to pull the fuses for the head lights, tail lights, dash lights and the overhead cab lights. He needed a total black out to pull off following Starke's transports through the St. Clair Tunnel at night. As he was getting out from under the dash, he heard the sound of a helicopter. He looked up in time to see the Coast Guard Dolphin flying south. *Damnit! She's going for Starke.*

He put the truck in gear and peeled out of the car rental parking lot, driving back to the Coast Guard station to confirm it was Venus. When he pulled into the station, he saw the Dolphin gone and the twins running up to the truck.

"She just flew out of here," Cane said.

"It was awesome, Vince," Al added. "She was mad as hell."

A black GMC Yukon pulled up. Debra and Diane got out. "Was that chopper Venus?" Debra asked.

"Fraid so," Vince answered. "Grab the gear and hop in. Al and Cane, stay here with Greta."

"Greta. Guard!"

Greta answered with one bark.

Vince called his friend in Dearborn.

~~~

Venus flew under the radar at tree top level, reached the Amtrak Station and took a hard left up the tracks following a Canadian Rail train to the entrance of the active tunnel. She lowered the Dolphin to six feet off the ground and followed the last car to the tunnel entrance. She pulled right and then up to buzz the old tunnel. As she elevated, someone ran out into the sunlight shading their eyes and took a wild shot at her. She flew up and over the tunnel and headed toward the St. Clair River. She laughed out loud.

*Stirred up Starke's hornet's nest. That should get 'em moving.* She yelled, "Call up Williams to fly his sorry butt down here."

She flew the Dolphin low over the St. Clair River and out to Lake Huron, leaving a ten foot high wake and upsetting boaters in her path. She radioed the Sarnia airport and requested permission to land. They answered that a *Border Tours* sight-seeing helicopter was just taking off, and that she could approach south-south east from the lake. She turned around, flew to the Canadian shoreline and up the main runway. She taxied up to a group of hangars and slowly maneuvered around to the opposite side, looking for a place to land.

She spotted the open doors of an empty hangar for private jets. To the surprise of a line of tourists waiting for the tour helicopter to return, she flew right into the hangar and landed. She cut the engines, unfastened her harness, jumped out and ran to the tall hangar door controls. She punched a large red button and a loud horn blared on and off as the tall folded doors began to close.

*Come on down, Mr. Williams. I'm behind door number one.*

~~~

Jimmy *James Homer* Moorehouse, CIA Freelance Unit operator investigating U.S. / Canadian border weaknesses, received the call on his secure cell phone. He turned off the tourist helicopter cabin microphone and patched the call through to his headphones. "Moore."

"Homer. This is Bashnir Al-Rashid. *FUBAR.*"

"Bashem! I'm working right now."

"CovOp 9.1.1. Meet me at Selfridge, ASAP.

"I've got a crew of tourists on board flying up the St. Clair River. I need to return them to Sarnia."

"You shittin me?" Bashnir said. "That's our destination, but we need a Herc. So, drop the bodies and pick me up at the Dearborn Fairlane Town Center Mall parking lot at Southfield and Michigan Ave."

"Who's call?"

"Hardesty."

"*Commander Hardass*?"

"One and the same."

"On my way."

Moorehouse pulled the choke and the helicopter backfired. He wiggled the cyclic to create turbulence and said, "Ladies and gentlemen, we are experiencing mechanical difficulties. We will be making an emergency landing." He heard a scream from the back. "Please remain calm. We'll be safe. We're setting down at the Windsor airport. *Border Tours* will arrange your ride back to Sarnia."

~~~

Vince called Mike the Snipe. "Hey, you know that crack you made about how a small invasion of Canada would be no problem?"

"You're kidding, right?"

"Nope. We've followed Starke and crew to Port Huron. They were planning to cross the border at night, but we think a bird roused them from their nest."

"Run for the border? What is this, Taco Bell?" Mike asked.

"They're using the St. Clair River Train Tunnel. So, I need the Canadian National Rail schedule."

"Hold on."

Vince could hear lightning fast taps on a computer keyboard.

"There will be a double stack freight train from Chicago to Toronto crossing the Port Huron – Sarnia corridor in the next hour."

"Okay, thanks, Mike. I've called *FUBAR*. You'll handle our radios, right?"

"I'm on the job," Mike answered. "And *for your ears only*. Hate to have the Canadian government listening in on an international invasion of their sovereignty, eh?"

"Thanks. I'll keep an open phone from here on in."

"By the way. There's one other thing you need to know, Vince."

"Yeah, what's that?"

"There's a freight train from Toronto heading west scheduled to pass through your tunnel about fifteen minutes later."

"Good to know, Mike. Thanks."

"And Vince?"

"What?"

"Look out for that light at the end of the tunnel."

"Ha, ha."

~~~

Vince turned onto Griswold to approach the Amtrak station from the north. A Canadian Rail double stack container train heading east blocked the street. It would hide them from the view of the old tunnel as it passed. While they waited, Diane unloaded the gear Vince requested from the back seat and passed it up front.

When the train passed and the crossing arms lifted, Vince pulled slowly forward across the tracks. He could see two transports coming out of the old tunnel. It looked like they would have to drive about five hundred feet down the rail path before they could make a U-turn over to the active tunnel tracks. He pulled into the Amtrak station parking lot and waited. He asked Debra for his monocular. He zoomed in and watched as the trucks disappeared into the tunnel.

"Show time." Vince pulled out of the Amtrak parking lot, crossed the street and drove onto the rock bed of the tracks. He wanted to stay just out of sight of Starke's side view mirrors. He didn't have to worry about Starke hearing the Dodge RAM engine with both the screech of the train wheels on the tracks and the noise of the transport's diesel engines in the tunnel.

As he drove into the tunnel, daylight turned to darkness. Debra handed Vince a helmet with night vision goggles. The tail lights of the last transport provided enough ambient light for Vince to see the tracks glow green ahead of them. When they reached the lowest point in the tunnel under the St. Clair River, Vince remembered Tom Michaels saying, "At half way, you'll be fifty-five feet below grade: thirty feet under water and twenty feet under clay, rock and concrete." *Not something I want to think about right now.*

Suddenly, Vince saw the brake lights of the transports heading up the slope of the tunnel into Canada. He stopped dead on the tracks. The train must have slowed down slightly as it moved up from the bottom of the river, putting them in view of Starke's mirrors. He didn't want the glow of the brake lights to illuminate the chrome on the Ram's front bumper and give them away. Surprise was their only chance of ending this without bloodshed.

Five long minutes later, the brake lights and heat trail disappeared and the tunnel became eerily quiet. All they could hear now was their truck's Hemi engine. Slowly, Vince moved up the tunnel toward the Canadian exit, making sure Starke hadn't spotted them and stopped. A train horn sounded in the distance. After a second time, Debra said, "It's headed toward us."

*How much time later did the Snipe say the U.S. bound train was due through the tunnel? Fifteen minutes?* He glanced at his phosphorus watch dial. "Right on time."

Vince stepped on the gas, spewing rock and splinters off the back wheels, barreling up the tracks to get out of the tunnel. As he reached the exit, the bright swirling headlight of the train suddenly blinded him through his night vision goggles. He quickly flipped up the goggles and floored it.

Debra ripped off her goggles and screamed "Clear!" as the truck flew out of the tunnel. Vince frantically turned the steering wheel and the truck's right side lifted off the ground. The back left tire dug into the loose rock, the truck righted itself and bounced off the tracks, swerving away from the oncoming train. Diane screamed as the train's cow catcher clipped the rear bumper and shoved them off the elevated track bed, sending them down an embankment.

Still blind, Vince slammed on the brakes as he heard the train pass behind them. He gulped for air, realizing he had held his breath for the final minutes as the train bore down on them. He looked over at Debra. She had her head back, breathing in gasps. Her feet were pressed to the floor board and both hands were white knuckled to the side grip.

As his breathing slowed, he heard Diane from the backseat say, "I'm still alive. We're still alive."

"Yes, we are," Vince answered. "Just trains passing in the daylight."

"Very *effin* funny," Diane said. "You really know how to give a girl a good ride."

Debra looked over at Vince, winked and mouthed the word *close*.

Vince hung his head and nodded. He put the truck in gear, spun the rear tires and pulled out of the rail bed trench to a dirt road running parallel to the tracks.

"Two *deuces* at twelve o'clock," Debra said, pointing to the transport trucks crossing a street bridge above them.

"We need a way out of the yard," Vince said.

Debra looked to the right and saw a trucking company that fronted a city street. She pointed right and said, "Through the shrubs."

He turned right and saw a section of the fence that had been run through by trucks. He drove through it and took a left toward the street with the bridge. He turned north and soon saw a sign directing them to the 402 East for the airport. He figured the transports were a couple miles ahead of them by now.

Vince radioed Venus, believing she'd have her headset on. "*Deuces* on the move."

Silence.

He tried her on his phone. No answer.

His phone rang. "C-130 wheels up," Bashnir called.

"High tail it over here. Approach Hadfield south south-east from Lake Huron."

"See you in ten."

Vince pulled up to the Airport Road intersection. Debra took a look through the binoculars and reported, "Double *deuce* in view."

The transport trucks turned on Airport Road, drove past the main terminal and turned toward the main runway in front of the hangars. Vince proceeded up Airport Road and turned left around the north side of the hangars opposite the runways.

*Where is Venus?*

~~~

Frederick Williams had just finished lunch at the Oscoda's Office Lounge when Starke called him in a panic. *His chopper bitch escaped, stole a Dolphin and buzzed the tunnel. I'll take care of what he wouldn't do.*

He sped to the Oscoda Wurtsmith Airport and screeched to a stop at the Yankee Air Force Museum hangars. As nonchalantly as possible, he told the clerk he wanted to take the Hercules for a ride this afternoon rather than later as scheduled. The clerk said he was the regular and the only one on the calendar for the whole week. So, no problem.

The clerk opened the hangar doors as Williams quickly went through his check list and started the four Allison turbines. He called in his flight plan as he taxied to the end of the runway, rolling through the turn and taking off as he received permission from the tower. A few minutes later he was flying south over the blue water of Lake Huron. He landed at the Sarnia airport thirty minutes later.

Once his wheels were on the ground, he spotted Starke's two transport trucks. He taxied right on the short runway and then toward the hangars, where he turned again toward the main runway and stopped just past the trucks and just short of the tarmac. He kept the turboprops running at idle and hit the switch to lower the aft cargo ramp.

~~~

296

Vince had stopped the Ram west of the hangars, grabbing his M-4 Carbine, handing Debra his M-16 with Diane bringing her own Colt AR-15. Vince had them attach silencers. They had jumped out of the truck, eased the doors shut and trotted over to the west side of the hangars

When Vince heard the four turboprop engines taxi up to the side of the hangars, he looked around to see the hundred foot long plane turn back toward the runway and stop. The cargo ramp began lowering from the top of the horizontal stabilizer with Starke and crew standing together watching the dark mouth of the cargo hold open as if to swallow them.

Vince and Debra took the opportunity to run to a baggage trailer sitting out front of the first hangar, leaving Diane to cover their rear. They climbed in one of the covered compartments and peered through a slit in the tarp.

Roberts and Daniels had pulled the transports up past the main hangar and turned around, backing up until the trucks were flush with the plane's extended ramp. Standing behind the trucks next to the plane's ramp, they heard Starke yell over the noise of the turboprops: "Ladies and gentlemen, our ride to freedom has arrived." Everyone cheered. "Let's get to work," Starke yelled. "This money's not ours till we load it up and fly it out of here."

"Turning over Port Huron for approach," Vince heard in his phone earpiece. He looked out toward the lake and saw the National Guard Hercules lining up with the runway.

"Roger," Vince answered. "C-130 on the ground and preparing to load up."

~~~

Starke's phone buzzed in his shirt pocket. He pulled it out, put it to his ear and stuck his finger in his other ear. "Yeah?"

"I'm hearing encrypted calls near your location," Paul Peters said, monitoring radio traffic from his room in the apartment. "Were you followed?""

"Haven't seen anyone. Sanchez could be around. We saw her chopper earlier, but it's nowhere to be found now."

"What about her boyfriend?"

"Saw no one. Heard no one," Starke answered.

"Well, I think you better have a look around, cowboy, cause somebody's got high tech chatter nearby," Peters said. "I don't want my moolah sittin around anywhere but in my new Cayman account."

"We'll have a look," Starke replied. As he hung up, he saw a National Guard Hercules coming in for a landing.

"What the fuck?"

Stephen M. Goodrum

## Part V  THE CATCH

*My dove in the clefts of the rock, in the hiding places on the mountainside, show me your face, let me hear your voice; for your voice is sweet, and your face is lovely. Catch for us the foxes, the little foxes that ruin the vineyards, our vineyards that are in bloom.* -- Song of Songs 2:14-15

# Chapter 28

Monday Afternoon

When Venus saw everyone turn to look down the runway and watch the Hercules land, she ran out from the hangar and across the tarmac to the nose of Williams' C-130. From there she knew he wouldn't be able to look down and see her. *When Starke and crew begin loading the pallets into the hold, I'll slip around to the other side of the plane and go through the pilot door. Then you'll be mine.*

"On the ground. Target straight ahead," Venus heard Bashnir say over her earpiece.

"C.C.D. Take a right at the short runway and wait at the turn to the hangars," Vince answered. "Gotta have the green in the belly of the beast before we can take 'em."

Venus knew that the theft was still on U.S. government property as long as the money was in the National Guard transports. They didn't want Starke spinning some story about being authorized to transport money to be destroyed. Once all of the pallets were in the plane's cargo bay, Starke and crew would be witnessed felons and federal fugitives. *Come on!*

She looked around the side of the plane and saw a baggage tug drive out toward Bashnir's Hercules. *Vince.*

She saw Starke watch the National Guard Hercules stop on the short runway and a baggage tug pull up to the back and wait for the ramp to lower. He looked back toward Roberts and the Metro Guard couple and yelled, "Load up, now!"

Venus waited for them to start loading. Hugging the plane's skin, she slid around the side of the plane and unlatched the pilot's side door. She climbed up the stairs to the flight deck and sat down in the co-pilot's seat. *Your ass-sistant awaits.*

She could hear Daniels, Schmidt and Williams barking at each other, loading the pallets up the ramp with two pallet jacks. Starke was yelling for them to hurry like a nervous coach straining for a touchdown in the final seconds of the big game.

*Who's missing?*

"Someone's listening," she heard Mike the Snipe call Vincent. "They can't make out what's being said, but they know you're there."

"Roger," Vince answered as he stood with Bashnir and Moorehouse watching Roberts drive the first transport away and Starke back up the second one to the ramp. "Half down. Half to go. We go when the last pallet's in the hold."

Starke got out of the transport, answered his phone and looked toward the Hercules.

"Uh-oh," Vince said. "Debra, Diane. Get ready to take the plane. I'll create a diversion."

Vince jogged down the ramp and hopped back in the driver's seat of the tug. He started it up and told Debra in the back to hang on. He drove quickly back toward the hangars and parked facing Starke's transports. Starke looked straight at him as Daniels and Williams pulled the last pallet up the cargo ramp.

"Go!" Vince ordered.

Flash-bang/tear gas canisters shot out from the National Guard Hercules into the C-130's cargo hold and went off as the last pallet was being secured. The Metro Guard couple doubled over, holding one arm over their eyes and a hand over an ear, staggering out onto the loading ramp, unable to see or hear. They fell from the ramp into the bed of the last transport truck.

Venus jumped as the canisters exploded ten feet away in the hold. She covered her mouth and nose with the sleeve of her flight suit and ran to shut the flight deck door when Williams crashed through, knocking her down.

"Get the bitch!" Williams yelled to the man running in behind him. In a daze, Venus saw that it was Roberts. He grabbed her by the collar and dragged her up off the floor. He then shoved her down the flight deck stairs to the side door.

As Bashnir and Moorehouse rushed the back of William's C-130, Vince saw Jason Roberts come out from around the right side of the plane brandishing a sawed off rifle with one hand, and holding a woman around the neck with the other.

*Venus.*

"Hold!" Vince yelled as he saw Robert's gun come up.

"Back off or she dies," Roberts yelled over the noise of the plane's engines, pushing Venus forward, holding her flight suit with his fist and pointing the barrel of his gun at her head.

Vince motioned Debra to stay down and out of Robert's view. "You're surrounded," yelled Vince. "Drop the gun and let her go."

"Anyone moves, she's dead."

"Got the shot if he turns back, Vince," Debra whispered into his earpiece.

Vince looked to his left and spotted a fuel truck with *A-1 Jet Grade* stenciled on the side sitting just off the short runway. "Get ready," he answered.

Vince slowly grabbed his M-4, sighted in the front left tire of the fuel truck and pulled the trigger. The gun made a soft *pffft* sound, but the front tire blew out with a bang like a rifle.

Roberts swung his rifle away from Venus's head and took a wild shot at the tanker cab. The bullet missed the cab and pierced the front edge of the tank. A blinding yellow ball of fire erupted with an ear splitting explosion.

When Roberts turned and fired at the fuel truck, Debra fired and took the back of Robert's head off in a spray of blood and brains. Vince dove out of the tug, hit the ground and covered his head. After the explosion, he looked up to see a column of black smoke billowing from the remains of the tanker.

"Venus, are you alright?" Diane yelled as she ran up the side of the hangar, waving her rifle back and forth in case of any more gunfire. She found her lying on top of Roberts's body. "Venus?"

"Yes. I'm okay. I'm okay. Could you help me up?"

Diane grabbed her hand and pulled her up. "How the hell did he get you by the plane?"

Venus turned toward the C-130. "Williams..."

Sirens of fire trucks and emergency vehicles drowned out her words as they sped from the other side of the hangars to the burning fuel truck. With everyone looking the other way, the C-130's Allison turbo-props roared to life. Everyone turned back and quickly shielded their eyes as dirt and grit flew off the tarmac. The plane lumbered forward to the main runway and made a sharp left turn for takeoff.

"Williams is going for it," Vince yelled. He knew there was no way they could stop the forty-five tons of metal slowly accelerating down the runway, so he commanded everyone to hold fire. He wanted Williams captured alive. He knew Venus wanted him to stand trial for the murder.

*Where is Venus?*

Venus had grabbed Diane and ran back to the hangar where she parked the Dolphin. Diane hit the door button and climbed in the co-pilot's seat as Venus started up the Arriel turboshaft engines.

"Venus! Venus? We're letting the C-130 go," Vince said, hoping for an answer.

"Not if I can help it," she answered. She looked over to Diane. "You okay with this?"

"Let's go for it, Babe," Diane said. "This beats guarding rich bitches any day."

"*She-Wolf* making a Michigan U-turn," Venus announced as she skidded the Dolphin out of the hangar, lifting ten feet off the ground and making a one-eighty to head toward the lake.

Moving parallel with the runway, she pushed the Arriel twin engines up to a speed of one hundred and fifty knots, one hundred and seventy mph.

Frederick Williams lowered the flaps, pulled the throttle levers back and thirty seconds later the Hercules lifted off the ground. The plane shuddered for a second as the extended ramp scraped the tarmac. He realized he'd forgotten to close the aft cargo ramp, so he pulled back harder on the throttles and the tail finally cleared the ground.

Gaining altitude, he felt the front end tilt upward more than usual as the weight of the pallets in the cargo hold shifted backwards. "Damn it. You didn't secure all the pallets," he yelled.

He reached for the lever to pull up the ramp and seal the cargo hold when he saw a flash of sunlight off the glass bubble of a Coast Guard helicopter. *Where the hell did that come from?*

"Catch me if you can, bitch!"

The Vietnam vintage C-130 labored to gain altitude at one hundred thirty knots. Venus pushed the dolphin to the maximum speed of one hundred seventy-five and reached the plane as it flew past the shoreline and out over Lake Huron. As the cargo plane reached her altitude and speed, Venus pulled over and above the plane's one hundred and thirty-two foot wing span.

"This is surreal," Diane said, feeling like she was in some special effects action movie.

"Oh, this is for *fucking* real," Venus said as she mirrored the plane's lift and speed.

"Venus," she heard Vince yell in her headset. "What the hell?"

"Just going piggy back on Williams' ass," she said.

"Stop now!" Vince ordered.

"No way. I've got 'em right where I want 'em."

She dropped down and hit the Hercules right wing, trying to sit the skids on it and bring the plane down for a water landing. "Take that you motherfucker," she yelled.

She felt a sudden dip as the vintage C-130's right wing cracked.

Venus quickly pulled up on the cyclic and flew off the wing. She circled around to look back toward the Hercules to see what had happened. Her mouth dropped open as Diane gasped. They couldn't believe what they were seeing.

The plane's right wing titled down at an odd angle, a fire licking out between its two engines. The plane rolled starboard and lifted upward as the eight pallets of money shifted and then slid backwards on the cargo floor rollers toward the extended ramp. All four engines stalled and died.

One pallet broke free of its straps, bounced down the ramp and fell into the lake. The loss of weight caused the front of the plane to return to horizontal and Williams somehow righted the plane as it glided down toward the water. He pushed the ignition to restart the engines, but the spark in the turboprops ignited the fuel spilling on the wing and the entire right side of the plane blew away in a thundering fireball.

The plane plowed into the water at one hundred and fifty knots, lifting the tail up in the air and causing it to do a cartwheel through the waves. The windshield disintegrated in the collision and water rushed into the compartment. Williams was crushed in his seat as it was pushed into the flight deck wall. The Hercules sank in a matter of minutes, extinguishing the fire with a geyser of steam shooting up in the air.

"Venus, Venus Are you all right?" Vince yelled into his phone, her screams transmitting into his earpiece as the plane exploded.

Between gulps of air, she called, "Yes. *She-wolf* stable."

"Williams?" Vince asked.

"Blue. Water. Dead." she answered.

~~~

T-Bone Wheeler and Hector Smith from Northport had been Walleye fishing in the deepest waters of Lake Huron since sunup. The water was still warm from the summer heat, so they moved to deeper, cooler waters where they had a better chance of finding the best catch. They'd caught three twenty-five pound olive-gold Walleye on the American side, and then cruised past the shipping lane toward Canada at about noon to catch more. There would be no Michigan DNR patrols in these waters, so they figured they could go beyond the daily bag limit. They caught a few more, but their luck had changed and they'd caught nothing for a couple of hours.

"I think it's time to call it quits, Hec," T-Bone said. "Let's haul in our lines and head home for a fresh fish dinner."

"How 'bout 'nother beer and a half hour?" Hector asked. "We might as well kill tha case 'fore we head back."

"You sure know how to twist a man's arm," T-Bone said. They both laughed.

They were drifting a few miles off the north shoreline of Sarnia when the quiet still waters were disturbed by the sound of four turboprops flying in low. When it flew over them, the plane splashed water inside the boat, nearly capsizing them.

"Shit!" T-Bone said, wiping water spray out of his eyes. "Hec, you all right?"

"Yep. I'm okay. Let's stop and check the boat. Ain't no fish comin near us now."

"I'll drink to dat," Hector said, holding on to the railing and swigging the last of his beer.

They checked their catch and their poles before casting their lines back in the water one more time. Thirty minutes later they heard the rumble of the turbo-prop engines again.

"What the hell?" T-Bone said, looking up as the C-130 roared over them.

"It's that damn Herc," Hector yelled. The two men watched as the plane slowly rose over the lake.

"What's that?" T-Bone yelled back, spotting something riding on the plane's wing.

Hector didn't answer. What they saw next left them speechless. It would be something they would never forget, and could never tell another soul as long as they lived.

The giant plane suddenly dipped to the right, then lurched upward on fire as a large container slid and bounced out of the cargo hold and down the ramp. Then everything went quiet. They thought they heard the rhythmic wump-wump of a helicopter, but they were transfixed at the sight of the plane falling out of the sky and then exploding in a shower of fireworks. Steam shot up out of the water as the plane crashed and slid into the lake. A few seconds later, a huge wave lifted the boat up almost out of the water, and then dropped them back down with a splash.

"Goddam!" T-Bone screamed.

Hector yelled in a high voice, "Oh my Gawd! It's all blowed up."

"Let's get the fuck outta here," T-Bone yelled.

"But, it's all blowed up!" Hector repeated.

"Yeah, yeah. Come on, Hec. Get us outta here."

"Oh, hell yeah," he answered. He started the engine and began to pull away.

"Wait, wait. Stop, Hec. Stop!" T-Bone yelled, looking down in the water. "Hold on a minute here, hold on."

"What now?" Hector yelled back, impatient to get off the lake.

"Get your net, man. Hurry, get your net," T-Bone said as he waved his hand in the direction of the water.

Hector killed the engine and went to see what T-Bone was yelling about. He was leaning over the back of the boat, dipping his fish net into the water and hauling in what looked like bundles of green paper.

T-Bone looked up with a wide grin. "I think our luck just changed, Hec. Yes, sir. Our luck has finally changed."

## Chapter 29

Monday Evening

Venus landed on the Sarnia Airport tarmac near the two transports and shut down the twin Arriel engines. She jumped down from the pilot's seat and ran straight to Vincent. Without a word, she threw her arms around him and pressed herself into his chest.

He held her close and reciprocated the embrace. When she let go, he looked Venus in the eye and said, "Thank God you're still alive. When I heard that crash in the water I thought maybe I'd lost you."

She answered in tears. "You're not going to lose me, big boy. But I got that murdering son of a bitch." She hugged him again and they held each other, rocking back and forth for several minutes.

Vince broke away. "By the way," Vince said, "that's the most amazing bit of flying I've ever seen."

Venus smiled and wiped the tears from her cheeks. "Routine for *She-Bitch*," she said.

"Cool under pressure too," he said.

"It's my temperament."

"Good, cause we're not quite done yet. Our special guest is now singing like a bird," Vince said, pointing toward the transports.

"Commander Clay Starke, I presume?" Venus asked.

"Correct. I'll have Sandy pick him up at Selfridge and take him into custody. My operator friends, *Bashem* and *Homer*, have him cuffed and talking."

"*Bashem*?" Venus asked.

At the sound of his name, a short mid-eastern looking man approached.

"Yeah. This is my good friend..."

"Bashnir Al-Rashid," he interrupted, taking her hand and kissing it. "So happy to meet you, and, I might add, it looks like you two make a great team. As I saw a minute ago, you two have apparently gotten to *know* each other quite well."

Embarrassed, Vince stated, "This is Warrant Officer G. Venus Sanchez, U.S. Coast Guard."

Venus hugged Bashnir. "A friend of Vince's is a friend of mine. Thanks for your assist. And you can call me Venus."

Now Bashnir was blushing. "You're welcome, Warrant Officer Sanchez, uh Venus".

"Hate to break up this little meet and greet, but we've got to high tail it out of here. *Bashem*, you'll drive one transport with Starke secured in the back along with Robert's body. Debra will drive the other one with Schmidt and Daniels to Selfridge. Diane will lead you through the tunnel in the Dodge. She, uh, knows the way." He winked at her. "I'll call Mike the *Snipe* for the Canadian Rail schedule so you don't get railroaded getting out of the country. Detective Sandy Sandelen, Detroit Police and Homeland Security, will take our guests into custody."

"Oh, that reminds me," Venus interrupted. "I need to call Angela and let her know how it all turned out. She'll be happy to know her boss won't be in today, or any day."

"Starke's talking, hoping for a deal," Bashnir said.

"What's he got to deal?" Venus asked.

"Two things. One, he said the National Guard trucks are expected back at Selfridge with crates of evidence from the Blue Water Bridge Port of Entry. He and Roberts were driving them back tonight."

"That's not much. And, second?" Venus asked.

"The second question you had earlier today."

"You mean, 'Who's the inside man at the Reserve?'"

"Right," Vince answered. "He says it was one of the deputy directors of security named Robert Fowler. He was the one who supervised the Federal Reserve Bank move from Fort Street to the new location on Warren. Along with Williams, he lined up the trucks for the move from a Mafia connected trucking company and the drivers and their *Capo* were paid off with three pallets. Fowler flew to the Caymans after the trucks were unloaded and the money accounted for, incorrectly as we now know. He's expecting the Herc piloted by Williams to land at the airport at sunrise with the Metro Guard couple along to unload the money. Starke's willing to call him at midnight and tell him they are on their way as planned. He just called a tech guy named Peters that the money is in hand."

"So, what are we going to do about that?" Venus asked.

"How about *we* take a trip to the Islands?" Vince said.

"What?" she asked.

Vince waved Moorehouse over to meet Venus. *James* will take us," he said, "a romantic get-away on a National Guard Hercules."

"Nice to meet you Venus. *James,* as in *take-us-home, James,* at your service."

"Oooh. Combining an arrest with a rest and romance. You really know how to show a Warrant Officer a good time." Venus said with a smile. "And nice to meet you, *James.*"

"You have no idea," Vince said

~~~

Mike *the Snipe* got on the headset with Vince and confirmed his log of the incidents that had taken place.

"So *Bashem* and *Crashem* are back together again?"

"Hey, in all my years on special ops, I only lost one Lear and one Black Hawk," Vince said with a chuckle.

"And now we can add a Herc to the tote board. Not to mention multiple pallets of U.S. *Gubment* money?"

"Yeah, whatever. I'm..."

"I'm proposing to the illustrious rat pack known as *FUBAR* that your moniker become *Crashem-Cashem Cowboy,*" Mike interrupted.

"Ha, ha."

"Like the song you played on the Cole when it sailed out of Yemen and you and Bashem had caught the Al-Queda leaders?"

"Kid Rock, *American Bad Ass,*1998," Vince said.

"Yeah, that's right. And you're the All American *Hardass,*" Mike said.

"Speaking of which," Vince said. "We're taking back the transports, detainees and one body to Selfridge. The cash, C-130 and the pilot's body, one Port Huron CBP Station Supervisor Frederick Williams, will have to be fished out by the Coast Guard. Starke is spilling his guts, probably thinking if he can't have the cash, no one else can. He says the inside man at the Federal Reserve Bank is Deputy Director of Security, Robert Fowler. We need an Agency directive for his capture. Please check to see if he flew out earlier today for a *vacate-sion* to the Cayman Islands."

"Will do," Mike said. "Always fun to reel in a Fed with his hand in the cookie jar, isn't it? Only, this time it's illegally."

"Yeah. According to Starke, Fowler's expecting the plane to land at the Grand Cayman airport in the morning. I'm having Moorehouse fly us in the National Guard Herc later tonight and we'll switch the bait for a catch."

"What do you mean, *we* white man? Planning to snatch a little *beach* time afterwards with, how does she say, the *She-bitch*?" Mike asked.

"Uh, right *Snipe*. Will you just set up the flight plan?"

"Yes, *Kimosabe*. And FYI, I looked up your Fed, Robert Fowler, while you were avoiding my question. Apparently he was a candidate but passed over for Branch Manager in 2002 when the new Reserve Detroit Branch building was announced.

Me thinks the Fowler felt he was *fowled-over* by a higher-up, if you know what I mean, and decided to, as they say, *cash out*."

"Uh, huh. Good to know," Vince answered. "And, Mike? How do you find this stuff so fast?"

"*Google*, cowboy. Ever heard of the *intra*-net?"

"Funny."

"One other thing," Mike said. "The Canadian government has issued a press release stating that, and I quote, 'the Canadian and U.S. National Guard held a joint military training exercise at the Port Huron / Sarnia border, simulating a breach in Homeland Security. The exercise was successful. It was completed at Sarnia's Hadfield International Airport with a controlled explosion.'"

"That should cover our tails," Vince said. "Did you Google that too?"

"Sometimes the *A-gency* is good for something, *Kimosabe*."

"Good to know," Vince said.

"Speaking of tail, I know you're hoping to catch a little in the Caymans, right? God and all of us know you need some," Mike said.

"Yes, I mean no," Vince said embarrassed. "We're just hoping to catch the Fed," Vince countered.

"Whatever you can catch, *Cowboy*."

Chapter 30

Tuesday Morning

Vince woke up to the sun coming over the horizon as the Hercules flew over the Gulf Coast of Alabama. Exhaustion and the drone and vibration of the four turboprops had put him and Venus asleep soon after takeoff. He asked Homer how they were doing.

Moorehouse answered, "Fine, considering I drank two large cold *Selfridge Sludge* coffees during the night, and now *we headin to tha Islands, Mon.*"

Vince nudged Venus awake a half hour later as they flew just west of Cuba and east of Cancun. "Good morning sunshine."

"Good more-aaah-ning," she said with a yawn. "I slept like the dead."

"After yesterday, thankfully, you're not." Vince stroked her cheek and gave her a kiss.

They watched the sunlight spread over the ocean as Moorehouse turned the plane eastward, heading to the north side of Grand Cayman Island. The blue-green waters of the Caribbean glittered with silver caps under the morning sun.

Venus assisted as co-pilot as Moorehouse ran through the landing checklist flying the plane around the island to land westward over the North Sound at Owen Roberts International Airport. Vince watched with a smile on his face.

*Oh, just to sit on the beach with our tired feet in the lapping waves of the ocean. And maybe not just our feet, but the rest of us as well.*

Living up to his reputation, *James* brought the Herc *home* as if it was as small as Vince's Model 33 Bonanza and as smooth as a Boeing 737.

"Dee plane, Boss. Dee plane," James announced. "And tank you for flyin with *Homair Air-lines*. Please take your carry-ons and assault rifles wit you. En-joy your stay on da Fantasy Island."

"You're good," Vince said. "But the flight suit isn't very flowery, fella."

"Well, tank-you bery bery much," Moorehouse replied. "Lucky you both got a change of clothes for this party." Then in a high voice, "Please, *Dee-plane, Boss. Dee-plane.*"

The plane was directed to the east side of the runway to a jet airline hangar with fifty foot high double doors. When Moorehouse pulled the plane up to a stop, the hangar doors slowly opened and four white Ford Transits pulled out and drove around to the back of the plane.

"Show time," Vince said. "Hold off on lowering the ramp until our Fed Reserve man shows himself."

They didn't have to wait long. Two white Hummers drove out of the hangar, each with a man standing up out of the sun roof brandishing AK-47s.

"SNAFU!" Venus said, "Situation normal, all fucked up."

"Amen to that, Sister," Vince said.

A third white Hummer pulled up in front of the plane. A man stood up through the open top waving both arms at them. He gave a thumbs-up, then pointed to the back of the plane and gave a thumbs-down, signaling the pilot to lower the ramp.

"He's obviously very excited," Venus said.

"Who wouldn't be," Vince said. "He's expecting eight pallets of shrink wrapped bills worth one hundred million dollars."

"I'm so sorry, Mr. Fowler," Venus said formally. "Your check did not clear. Security will escort you out at this time."

Vince had Moorehouse open his window and signal the Hummer to pull around to the back of the plane. He looked over at Venus. "You ready to get down?"

"Ready to party," she answered.

They climbed down from the flight deck and walked to the back of the cargo hold. Vince lowered a tarp over the doorway where the ramp was hinged to the floor.

"What's the plan?" Venus asked. "We look surrounded."

"We get him up the cargo ramp and on this side of the tarp. Then we have a nice little chat."

"A little chat?"

"Yeah, you know. *'How you doin?'*"

"I think he'll be asking most of the questions."

"That's the plan. He won't be able to see the interior of the cargo compartment until he's around the tarp and in the dark. While his eyes adjust, we'll have a few seconds of *shock and 'Oh Shit!'* to disarm and subdue."

Vince called Moorehouse on his headset. "We're ready. Keep the turboprops running. The noise and debris will keep the Hummers at bay."

The Cargo ramp hydraulics kicked in and a glimmer of daylight appeared around the frame of the opening. Vince grabbed his Carbine and handed Venus the M-16, both set on short bursts with flash and noise suppressors attached.

"Great. What about the two AKs?" Venus asked.

"One step at a time, girlfriend. One step at a time," he answered.

The whine of the hydraulic motors lowering the ramp filled the empty cargo hold as Vince and Venus stood hidden from view on either side of the doorway. Their Fed-man would have to walk by them as he went around the tarp and into the hold.

The whine of the hydraulics stopped as the ramp hit the ground. They heard the acceleration of an engine and the tires of the Hummer pull up the ramp and screech to a halt. The man jumped down from the Hummer and walked around the tarp. Vince recognized Fowler from the picture Mike sent him over his phone.

"Hey, anybody home?" Fowler yelled. He stood still, waiting for a response and for his eyes to adjust to the relative darkness of the plane's interior. "Starke, you back here?"

The answer came in the press of a cold muzzle at the back of his head, then a woman appeared pointing an M-16 at his chest.

Vince kicked Fowler behind the knees and put him down on the floor and cuffed his wrists behind him with zip ties. He duct-taped his mouth shut, shoved him into a troop seat and harnessed him to the wall.

Vince looked over at Venus. "Hold him."

He looked back at Fowler. "She's got an itchy finger, Fowler. So, don't try anything like your buddy Williams. He's at the bottom of the lake as we speak."

Vince went back to the tarp where the Hummer was idling on the ramp just on the other side. He crawled under the tarp and came up to the driver's side pointing the Carbine through the open window.

"Everybody out!"

The driver opened the door to step out when the man with the AK-47 brought up his gun and aimed to fire. Vince put him down with a burst of bullets. The AK flew out the man's hand and his head dissolved in a spray of blood all over the back seat. The driver lunged around Vince to escape, but Vince karate kicked him behind the knee and he fell head first to the ground.

"Don't move or you're dead like your gunner."

Vince raised the butt of the gun and hit him on the head. "That'll keep you for now."

Vince called Moorehouse. "Raise the ramp, rev up the props and head into the hangar."

As the ramp hydraulics engaged and the plane's wheels began moving forward, the men outside in the Hummers realized something was off and began firing into the cargo hold. Before Venus could get down, she was hit. Vince returned fire and took out the gunner. He dragged her out of the line of fire, spraying both vehicles with short bursts. The AK's returned fire, but Vince had gotten Venus behind the ramp door frame. He knelt down, checked her pulse, still strong, and made sure she was still breathing. He ripped open her top hoping to find her Kevlar vest. He did. He unfastened her Kevlar to find a bruised indentation in her chest just above her left bra cup. She stirred and then groaned in pain.

Bullets were flying into the hold and then against the outside of the ramp as the plane rumbled forward. After what seemed like forever, the ramp finally raised high enough to offer protection from the gunmen. Vince carried Venus through the cargo hold to the cockpit and strapped her into the navigator's seat. The nose of the plane was now flush to the back of the hangar.

"Keep the props engaged," Vince told Moorehouse.

"Roger, Commander."

Vince went back down the flight deck to the pilot's door when he heard the screeching of tires and then a crash behind them. He looked back into the cargo area and saw that the Hummer had slid down the ramp as it was raised and slammed into the bulkhead.

*That was close. Another minute and we might have been a grill ornament.*

Venus woke up with the crash. She unbuckled herself and put her Kevlar vest back on. "Get a sneak peek at my underwear, big boy?" she asked.

"Black lace. Like it," he answered. "Are you up for more action?"

Venus nodded. "Soon as I catch my breath."

Vince looked through the pilot's side view mirror and saw that the turboprops were holding back the Hummers. He took Venus's hand and led her down the flight deck stairs to the side door. "Stay here and cover me."

"I got your back-side, *Hardass*."

"Nice," Vince answered and called for Moorehouse to turn off the engines and open the crew's side door. It unlatched and Vince ran to the side of the hangar. He saw that the gunners were still inside the Hummers, avoiding the wind and dirt thrown up by the Herc's turboprops. He sprayed the vehicles' grills and front tires with two sweeps of the M-4.

When he saw the barrels of the AK's come back up through the sun roofs, he shot away the gun of the Hummer nearest him. By the time he looked over to the other one, the gunner was slumped forward with a red dot in the middle of his head. Venus screamed.

Vince looked back and saw Venus on her hands and knees coughing. He ran over to her looking for blood, but couldn't fine any.

"Son. Of. A. Bitch. That hurt," she yelled, and then mumbled something in Spanish.

"You all right?" asked Vince.

Venus looked up at him. "The recoil of the M-16 hit me where the bullet caught the Kevlar."

"Ouch," Vince said. He grabbed her under the arms and lifted her up, holding her close to keep her from falling over. They heard sirens pull up to the doors of the hangar and watched the local police run in and ordered them to drop their guns and put their hands up.

"Don't think so," Vince yelled. "Guns are on the ground. She's wounded."

Moorehouse walked out of the Pilot's side door with his hands up. "These are the guys you came here to save, officers," he told the police. "They're just here for a romantic get-away, right Vince?"

The lead officer came forward and asked for their IDs. Vince held Venus with one arm and pulled out his Homeland Security ID with the other. The officer clicked on his lapel walkie-talkie and called for his captain. Four other officers were checking out the Hummers and arresting the drivers when a man in a light tan suit walked up and offered his hand in greeting.

"I'm Captain Demont Mbalou, at your service Commander Hardesty."

Vince shook his hand, continuing to hold Venus up with the other. "How did you find out we were here, and in trouble, Captain?" Vince asked.

"Our Premier received a call this morning from your President. He said we should watch for your plane and any vehicles that come to meet it. We intercepted several white Ford Transits trying to escape when we heard gunfire erupt. We then proceeded cautiously, not wanting to interfere in an international incident."

"Probably leaving us to fight our own battles," Vince said, "not wanting any of the island residents to get caught in the crossfire."

"I am at your service, Commander," Captain Mbalou said as he clicked his heels.

"We have a Federal agent tied up in the cargo hold who we believe is the ring leader of this international incident. Could you hold him for us until we have the necessary repairs made on our plane?"

"Most certainly," the Captain replied. He called two officers over and instructed them to bring out the suspect. The Captain wished them a good day.

Vince turned his attention back to Venus. "You really going to be all right?" he asked. "We need to get you to a doctor."

"You're the only doctor I need," she whispered. "And a bag of ice for this bruised rib."

"Yes, Ma'am. Doctor Hardesty on call."

They saw Captain Mbalou lead the officers escorting Fowler out of the plane to a police van.

"Look", Vince said. "He's pickin up the prisoner, and puttin 'em in a van."

"But , *all She Wants to do is Dance*. Don Henley, 1984," she answered.

"You're good, even when injured."

A white Lincoln pulled up in front of the hangar. The driver got out and opened the door for them.

"What's this?" Venus asked.

"Your coach, my lady." Vince carefully walked Venus to the car, helped her inside, got in and sat next to her. The driver shut the door.

"Where we going?" Venus asked.

"To enjoy the island, my dear. Remember, this is a romantic get-away."

"Well, it's had a hell of a start."

~~~

Vince called the White House and filled in the Assistant to the President for National Security on the arrest of the former Deputy Director of Security of the Federal Reserve, Robert Fowler. A jet would be sent to pick him up.

"You know, Vince, all we have on Fowler right now is stealing a mothballed Hercules 130 from a northern Michigan deactivated Air Force Base. We can hold him on that, but not for long. So, I hope you have evidence that proves his complicity in the Reserve heist."

"We'll have it, Sir," Vince said. "I believe he lead this whole bait and switch, with a mock terrorist plot and changing the pallet numbers to take a multi-million dollar cut from the Reserve's move yesterday morning."

"Good," answered the Assistant. "For now, we'll have him join his partners at the Federal Prison in Milan, Michigan. A Coast Guard Cutter is at the Hercules crash site. The money in the hold will be enough proof to convict Fowler, Starke and the Metro Guard couple."

"All of it should be there," Vince said. "Hopefully none of it got burned in the fire."

"It was all slated for destruction anyway, Vince. That's why they took those pallets. Untraceable."

"What about my operators?" Vince asked.

"I have no idea what you're talking about," the Assistant answered. "Our story is that the Federal Reserve completed a successful move from the old building to its state-of-the-art facility that surpasses the new standards for post 9 / 11 security protocol."

"Mission accomplished," Vince responded.

"Exactly. So, what are your plans, Vince?"

"Time for a little *R and R*, Sir," Vince said.

"Along with Warrant Officer Venus Sanchez?" he asked.

"I believe she has earned some, Sir."

"I concur, Commander. We have authorized such for both of you. And Vince?"

"Yes, Sir."

"The President says to take good care of her. He's booked you a couple of rooms at the Ritz on Seven Mile Beach for the rest of the week."

"Tell the President thank you, Sir. And I will, Sir, take good care of her."

*Great, the Director of National Security and the President of the United States are encouraging my love life.*

Vince thought the President believed he and Venus *might* need two separate rooms, respecting his lack of dating over his extended time of grieving for Rachel. Instead, Vince gave both rooms to *James* Moorehouse along with a week's supply of Caribbean flowery shirts. Vince included an unlimited tab and a note that read: "En-joy da Island, Mon. Look like you be-long. Invite some friends."

Vince booked a private villa at Mahogany Point on the north side of the island away from the tourist hotels. They checked in and had lunch delivered. They took turns eating and soaking in the full body seven headed shower. When Vince came out of the shower, he found Venus passed out on the king size bed in the master suite. He fell in beside her and they slept until evening

Chapter 31


Tuesday Night


The setting sun was streaming in the draped western glass wall when Vince woke up. He propped himself up on one elbow and saw the vivid blue and turquoise waters of the Caribbean outside the door wall. A gentle flower scented breeze was blowing through the door screens on the side wall, ruffling the long white curtains.

Vince looked down to see Venus asleep on her back, the covers down to her waist, her breasts gently rising and falling with each breath. He looked at the darkening black and blue bruise above her left breast where the Kevlar had saved her life but cracked a rib. He lowered his head to kiss it gently when she stirred and opened one eye.

"What are you up to, *mi amore*?" Venus asked. She looked over to the door "Is that the sun coming up?"

"It's the sun setting," Vince answered. "And it's setting beautifully on you."

She looked at her bruise and said, "Not so beautiful."

"You want Vince to kiss your boo-boo and make it better?"

"Yes, please," she answered.

He lowered himself to kiss the bruised spot, but she guided his lips to her nipple and said, "I'd rather have Vince kiss my boob-boobs and make me better all over."

"Your male nurse is in the house," he said as he gently kissed her. She moaned and moved closer until their bodies were entwined. With slow and gentle rhythm, they made love. Something about nearly dying made their love making deeper and more fulfilling.

~~~

Vince and Venus sat and had drinks on the patio facing the ocean until a white Transit van pulled up in the driveway. Venus went for her gun.

"It's okay. It's not Fowler and his friends," Vince said as he took the gun from her.

When she saw two women get out, open the back doors and bring in a set of women's clothes, she giggled with glee and said, "Okay. Now I believe you."

There were also a few outfits for Vince. He went for the white linen pants and a flowered island shirt. While Venus was having fun trying on clothes, shoes and accessories, Vince left, telling her he would be back in an hour and she should be ready to go out for dinner and dancing.

The Lincoln Town Car pulled up and Vince had the driver take him to the shopping district with a recommendation for what he was looking for. Along the way, he called the concierge to make a reservation for them at the Royal Palms. He wanted to make their first formal date to be unforgettable.

Shopping done, Vince had the driver return to the private villa to pick up Venus. She walked out dressed in a multi-colored Caribbean halter maxi dress that clung to her hips and legs with any passing breeze.

Vince stepped out of the limo and she twirled around like a runway model. Her hair was loose around her shoulders and tied back with a matching print ribbon that fell down her bare back, the dress scooped below her waist. He waved off the driver who was coming around to shut their door, ushered her into the car and sat by her speechless.

She gave him a kiss on the cheek. "Finally taking me out on a real date, Mr. Hardesty?"

He nodded, still unable to talk after noticing that the long dress was slit up the side, showing off most of her thigh. "Up here, bad boy," she said taking her index finger and raising his chin. He finally got out a whisper. "Wow."

"I thought you'd like it. And thank you for the new clothes. When I got done choosing this one, the ladies said I was supposed to keep all of them."

Clearing his throat, he finally found his voice. "You're welcome."

"How'd you do that, as well as the villa?" she asked.

"Well, our thieves are not the only ones with a Cayman bank account." In a business like voice he continued. "Regent International Petroleum requires an American as well as an international bank to do business."

"Uh huh. And who knows about that little bank account?" Venus asked, tickling his chin.

"People who only 'need to know,' and now you know," Vince said with a smile.

She smiled back. "Why do I need to know?"

"I'll explain later," he said. He kissed her on the lips, his hand finding her thigh.

"Down boy. I don't want to mess with the dress."

"If you insist."

They arrived at the Palms and were ushered to their reserved table nearest the beach at the Reef Grill. They ordered drinks and assorted appetizers and enjoyed the lights along the beach. Venus ordered the Sea Bass with honey soy marinade and red Thai curry. That brought a smile to his face because it confirmed Sandy's description of her as *one hot tamale.*

"What are you smiling about?" she asked.

"Uh, just how *hot* you look tonight," he said.

"I'm breaking out in a sweat from this food," she said.

Vince had ordered the grilled Tuna with sticky rice and pickled cucumber. They ate ravenously, either because of not eating whole meals for the last several days, or because they were worn out from love making.

After dinner, Vince took Venus's hand and guided her toward the beach. They passed a bonfire with people dancing to a live band and couples here and there making out near the water. He found a secluded spot and stopped. He looked out to the ocean and she joined him in seeing what had to be millions of stars. It reminded him of the night sky he saw so many times in the desert of Kuwait.

He turned to her and looked into her eyes as tears welled up in his own. He knew he needed to say what he needed to say before he lost it.

"What is it, Vincent? Are you all right?" Venus asked.

"Yes. I've never been better. I haven't felt this way in many years. I'm falling in love with you and I want to give you something as a token of my feelings." He reached into his jacket pocket and pulled out an oblong black velvet box. He opened it and a string of pearls lit up reflecting the moon light.

"Vincent!"

"Please, let me..."

He looked up to see tears rolling down her cheeks.

"But Vincent..."

"Please Venus, I ..."

She took the pearls out of the box and held them in her hand. "Would you do the honors?" she asked as she turned around.

"Yes," he answered, taking the string of pearls, unclasping them, and placing them delicately around her neck. When he re-clasped them on her neck, they slid in place just above her breasts.

Venus looked down at the pearls glowing on her chest and said, "They're beautiful, as beautiful as the stars in the sky."

"I love you, Graciella Venus Sanchez."

"And I love you, Reginald Vincent Hardesty. You are the best part of my world: all the blue sky and all the blue water."

Chapter 32


One Week Later


Vincent and Venus, Sandy and Angela, and Al and Cane all met together at the triangle-shaped American Coney Island on Michigan Avenue where Lafayette and Griswold meet near Campus Martius Park. The Detroit restaurant icon is conveniently situated two blocks from the U.S. District Court, the McNamara Federal Building, the Metro Guard headquarters, the Penobscot Building, and the original site of the Federal Reserve Bank.

The group was, to use a military term, triangulated within walking distance of all of the crime scenes. Well, except for Al who fathered a daughter in the back seat of a Chevy in some other undisclosed Detroit location. There is no crime in that, just court hearings, sometimes a DNA test, and child support payments.

Vince ordered the breakfast plate for everyone, promising they would be back for the world famous Coney Islands for lunch. Venus and Angela were busy talking a mile a minute about their new love relationships.

"I'm so in love, Angela. And I think he likes me a lot too."

"Ya think?"

Vince and Sandy were discussing the evidence in the Federal case against Robert Fowler, the former Federal Reserve Bank Security Deputy Director, and Lt. Commander Clay Starke and the Metro Guard couple. Sandy found an Eastern Market food supply truck with four pallets of money and arrested the *partnership* drivers of the Metro Guard semis. The Hercules transport plane had been salvaged out of Lake Huron in a hundred feet of water. It was missing one pallet of money, later found in fifty-five feet of water. Somehow it was missing six million dollars and change.

"What'ya figure?" asked Sandy. "Think some fisherman caught the big one?"

"If they did, they aren't telling anyone," Vince answered. "Probably in the Caymans themselves."

"Probably. Speakin' of big catch, I think Venus has caught *you*, Brother, hook, line, and sinker."

"Yep. She reeled me in, thanks to you, Mr. Sandman. She says it's like a dream and I've gotten over my nightmare."

"Good for you."

~~~

They entered the Theodore Levin Courthouse on West Lafayette for the ten a.m. hearing. Venus and Angela glared at Clay Starke as he hobbled in from the front of the court room, forced to walk in small steps with his ankles shackled. Venus testified to being incarcerated by Starke on false charges of conspiracy, and testified about her knowledge of the Blue Water Port of Entry Shift Supervisor, Alberto Martinez, who was killed because he discovered Border Patrol Supervisor, Frederick Williams, confiscating two crates containing one thousand TracFones from the Port of Entry warehouse.

Angela testified that the TracFones were ordered to be picked up and dropped off at the Lake Erie Metro Park by Coast Guard officer Jason Roberts. She provided the official log of the skiff commander, as well as a log of intercepted phone calls between Starke, Roberts and the other bank heist members.

Al and Cane testified that they had been followed, harassed, and kidnapped because they had been witnesses to the phone drop by a Coast Guard skiff at the Lake Erie Metro Park. Vince submitted their video file, confirming for the court that they had nothing to do with the staged conspiracy. The video was shown on a projection screen and the boat, the two cases of phones and the faces of Coast Guard officer Roberts and the Metro Guards, Daniels and Schmidt, were clearly visible.

The video file, the testimony of the twins, Angela and Venus, as well as a notarized letter from the Islamic Center *Iman*, was sufficient evidence to clear the twins and the three Lebanese brothers who had been charged with an attempted terrorist attack on American soil. The local prosecutors had dropped all charges since the evidence against them had been manufactured by Starke. It was determined that they had been moved here and set up as a bait and switch by Starke and Fowler to divert the FBI's attention away from the Federal Reserve Bank robbery. They were only guilty of being in possession of one thousand stolen TracFones.

Sandy corroborated the bank robbery, recalling how he discovered the abandoned Metro Guard semis and their contents. He was not asked to identify who tipped him off to their location. There would be no mention of the amount of stolen hundreds of millions from the Detroit Branch of the Chicago Federal Reserve in the official record. He gave his official report on the arrest of the *partnership* semi drivers and their boss, the *Nuovo Capo*.

With no further questions, the witnesses were released and Vince led them back to the Coney Island for lunch. Everyone felt relieved except Al. His paternity case was next at Friend of the Court. Vince assured him that since the DNA test proved he was the father, he would be allowed to parent his daughter for the rest of his life.

They celebrated the completion of their mission to free the twins, convict Starke, Fowler and the Metro Guard couple with the largest stuffed Coney dogs in the U.S.A.

"Now, this is what I call an old fashioned Dee-troit celebration," Venus said.

"Amen to that," Angela said.

"A-men," the men chimed in.

~~~

Next stop, the Penobscot building, where they were greeted by two new Metro Guards. Al smiled as they walked down the stairs to the basement for frisking, feeling much different than the first time. They went up to the sixth floor crammed together in the small elevator.

The Bailiff called, "Butterfield versus Majors for Referee Manville."

Al looked over at Vince and Vince nodded. "We're all with you, Al," Vince said. "I'll be in the back row if they need to ask me any questions."

Everyone walked into the small court room and noticed that the mother of Al's baby was not present.

"The Family Court of Referee D. Manville is now in session." A graying man with a goatee in a black robe walked in and sat down behind a tall mahogany desk. The court recorder was seated and the Bailiff called for Lisa Butterfield and Alpha Majors.

Al stood up and went forward. He was motioned to the judge's right as the Bailiff called out Lisa's name. When no one stepped forward, Manville looked around the court room. When he saw Vince in the back, the judge nodded in recognition. They had met here before with other fathers and were both members of the Michigan Fatherhood Coalition.

"Lisa Butterfield?" Manville called.

There was a commotion at the door to the courtroom when an older woman walked in. "She's right here, Sir. We had to take her little girl to the restroom for a diaper change."

The young mother sauntered through the door with the little girl crying in her arms. "I'm here, your honor. Those damn guards wouldn't let me take her to potty downstairs. They made me come up here and take her to that disgusting bathroom you have up here."

"Daddy. Daddy," the little girl cried, reaching out toward Al as her mother handed her to the grandmother.

"It's all right, Emma. It's all right baby," Al said.

"Please come forward, Miss Butterfield. We will start the proceedings," Manville said as he motioned her to his left.

"Butterfield versus Majors for equal legal and physical custody," called out the Bailiff.

"She's my baby," said Lisa. She pointed at Al. "This is not his child. Hell, he couldn't even get it up." A few chuckles rippled through the gallery.

"That's enough, Miss Butterfield," Manville said. "Bailiff, could you present the evidential findings, please."

"Yes your honor. The DNA test shows a ninety-five percent match that Alpha Canis Majors is the biological father of Emma Butterfield."

"This court hereby recognizes the legal paternity of Alpha Majors for his daughter Emma Butterfield," Manville said.

"That can't be true, your honor," Lisa protested, shaking her head. "It's just not true."

"Yes, Miss Butterfield, it is true. It's scientific evidence allowed by every court in the United States of America. Not to mention your little girl's beautiful red hair." Manville smiled as he said this. "See anyone standing before me that *has* red hair?" he asked. Everyone in the room looked over at Al.

"I rest my case. Now for the matter of equal physical custody."

"Your honor, you must be kidding," Lisa's mother interjected. "This boy can't take care of a three year old. He doesn't have a crib or a high chair or a room for my granddaughter. He doesn't know how to mother a child..."

Manville interrupted before she could go on. "Not completely true, Mrs. Butterfield. Bailiff, please read the items recently purchased by Mr. Majors."

"Yes, your honor. Youth bed, chest of drawers, high chair, numerous toys, pull ups, potty chair, stroller, car seat, and several gallons of paint in a shade of pink."

"Thank you, Bailiff. I might add that you are right, Mrs. Butterfield. He cannot mother his child. He's the father. He will parent his child as a man. It is my firm belief that all children need both a mother and a father, as well as grandparents and extended family and friends of the family." Manville paused and looked back at Vince when he said this. "And for this reason, I am awarding Mr. Alpha Canis Majors equal physical custody of Emma Butterfield."

"But your honor," cried Lisa Butterfield.

"No but's about it, young woman. You have kept this child from her father for the last six months. That will not continue. In fact, Miss Butterfield... are you listening to me young lady?"

She nodded.

"Good. If I hear one word that you have not allowed Mr. Majors, Emma's father, to have equal parenting time with his daughter, I will put you in jail. Do you understand?"

"Yes, sir," Lisa answered.

"And do you understand, Mrs. Butterfield?"

"Yes your honor."

"Good. Now for you Mr. Majors."

"Yes, your honor."

"You will begin paying child support through Friend of the Court in the amount of four hundred dollars per month. Twenty-five percent of this amount will be paid to the State of Michigan for the child's support for the past two years. The remainder will be paid to the child's mother, Lisa Butterfield, through the Court."

"But that's less than I'm getting now, Sir," Lisa said with her hands raised in disbelief.

"You're the one that put this through the court, Miss Butterfield. Remember, you will only have Emma half the time now. Mr. Majors will be purchasing food and necessities besides what he pays the court."

"Lisa, hush," her mother said.

"Now, Mr. Majors. Will you be able to handle all of this financially?"

"Yes, your honor. I now have a full time job with Miller's studio in Southfield."

"Good. And do you have family and friends to assist you in caring for your daughter?"

"Yes, your honor. They are here with me in the court room."

"Could those of you who are family and friends of Mr. Majors please stand."

Cane, then Vince, Venus, Sandy and Angela all stood up in the back row.

"I see you have Mr. Hardesty from St. Vincent's here with you. Is he here as a Young Fatherhood counselor?"

"Yes, and no, your honor?" answered Al.

"How's that, Mr. Majors?" asked the judge.

"He's my friend too."

"Good. Bailiff, could you have the couple sign the appropriate paperwork. Mr. Major's time with his daughter will begin today. This session is adjourned.

When everyone stood, Emma could hold back no longer. "Daddy, Daddy!"

Al went to her, took her in his arms and hugged her. She put her little arms around his neck and held on like she wouldn't let go. Everyone could see tears in Al's eyes as he kissed his daughter on the cheek. "It's okay, baby girl. It's all going to be okay. Daddy loves you."

Looking over at Venus, Vince saw tears rolling down her cheeks. He felt something wet in his eyes as well. They held each other arm in arm watching Al hold and comfort his daughter.

Chapter 33

One Month Later

The Federal Correctional Institution (FCI) in Milan, Michigan is located forty-five miles south of downtown Detroit. It is a low security facility housing male inmates with a detention center for pretrial and holdover male inmates from the Eastern Michigan Judicial District.

The Detention Center Administrator welcomed the well-tailored Federal official and escorted him to a secure, private visitation room. This was not an ordinary visit during normal visiting hours. The official's request had been made through a clerk from the Federal Court of Appeals in Washington, D.C.

The visitor was offered refreshments as well as any assistance that might be needed in his visit with the well-known pretrial detainee. Lt. Commander Clay Starke was ushered into the room several minutes later. The official stood and offered his hand.

"Commander Starke?"

"Yes. Sir. Good to meet you, Sir."

"Have a seat, Commander," the official said as the guard shut the door. He looked through the reinforced glass of the small window in the visitation room to be sure the guard had left. "We now have total privacy, Clay."

"Good. What are you doing to get me outta here?" Starke asked.

"I've submitted a letter to the Chief Judge of the Federal Court of Appeals. I've outlined the lack of tangible evidence linking you to the Federal Reserve robbery. Of our team, only Williams was implicated with possession of the money, and he's dead. Only Roberts was recorded in possession of the TracFones, and he's dead. Only the Metro Guard couple, Daniels and Schmidt, were recorded receiving the TracFones and securing the pallets of money in the cargo plane. They won't be getting out anytime soon. Fowler was charged with attempted murder in the act of holding up a National Guard plane, and he won't be getting out, period. Our *partnership* with the *Nuvo Capo* is contained by his family. He's here at Milan for drug smuggling and money laundering. That leaves just you and Peters."

"And you," Starke said.

"And no one but you two know that. Peters can't be implicated for anything because there's no evidence that he was even near the money or had possession of the phones. Not to mention, he's disappeared.

"You, on the other hand, gave the orders for Roberts to pick up the phones, but there's no offense in coordinating the pickup of confiscated electronics to implicate possible terrorists. You were seen at the Sarnia Airport with the National Guard transports, but they were assigned to you. There's no evidence that you touched the money and there is no evidence that you were doing anything but having it transported through Canada to Washington for destruction.

"You assisted in the capture of the Metro Guard couple and, thanks to you, the Federal Reserve Bank officer. You directed the agency to the *Capo* and his drivers who provided the trucks for the money transfer. These facts and the belief that you stopped a terrorist attack on American soil has prompted a Federal appeals judge to review your case."

"What about the sonofabitch who fucked us over?" Starke asked.

"One Reginald Vincent Hardesty. Former SEAL. He's just a local rich guy with connections. Don't worry about him, or his girlfriend. I'll take care of all the loose ends."

"Good." Starke gave out a long sigh. "So when do I get outta here?"

"By Thanksgiving."

"Thanks," Starke said.

They shook hands and parted.

The officer left by the front gate. Starke was cuffed and escorted out of the room and taken to a hallway leading back to his solitary cell. The guard left him alone for a minute while he went to get the cell key. Without warning, Starke's head was snapped back and his throat sliced from ear to ear. The last thing he heard was a whisper: "Your boss says our *partner-ship* is terminated."

## About the Author

Stephen M. Goodrum is an ordained minister and a licensed social worker. He has worked for an outreach program in Detroit for the past eighteen years. He lives with his wife, Donna, and their dog and cat in Holly, Michigan. He has two married sons and two grandchildren.

He is the author of *The Perfect Wedding Day... Disaster.*

Contact him on his website:
www.authorstephenmgoodrum.com,
on Facebook/authorstephenmgoodrum,
and on Twitter @StephenMGoodrum

## Acknowledgements
Thanks to all of the staff and tutors at *The Education Experience*, St. Vincent and Sarah Fisher Center, for their reading and comments on the final editions of BWD. Thanks to members of the *Michigan Fatherhood Coalition*.

Thanks to family and friends: David Goodrum and his wife, Melissa Carter Goodrum, Tom Goodrum and his wife, Evelyn Benoit, Janet Goodrum Greer and her husband, Richard Greer, Marsha Lesher Wolfe and her husband, Bob Wolfe, Pat Lesher Hadden.

I especially want to thank my two sons, Michael and Joshua Goodrum, their wives, Deborah and Dawn, and my *first reader*, my wife, Donna, for reading and re-reading and editing the many versions of this *before dawn* writing adventure.

**Cover Design** by Joshua Goodrum

**Author's Note**
In the fall of 2005, the Detroit Branch of the Federal Reserve Bank moved from its old location in the city's business district on Fort Street to its new, state of the art location on Warren and Dequindre without incident.

Three Palestinian American brothers were arrested after authorities found one thousand TracFones in their van. The FBI said they found no information to indicate they had a direct connection to any known terrorist group and later released them. The brothers said that they had bought the phones in bulk for resale. Relatives believed the brothers were targeted because of their Arab descent.

www.ingramcontent.com/pod-product-compliance
Lightning Source LLC
Chambersburg PA
CBHW061925170626
46813CB00006B/2310